KU-711-476

THE DANGER WITHIN

Books by Hilary Bonner include

The David Vogel mysteries

DEADLY DANCE *
WHEEL OF FIRE *
DREAMS OF FEAR *

Other titles

THE CRUELLEST GAME
FRIENDS TO DIE FOR
DEATH COMES FIRST
CRY DARKNESS *

* *available from Severn House*

THE DANGER WITHIN

Hilary Bonner

First world edition published in Great Britain and the USA in 2021
by Severn House, an imprint of Canongate Books Ltd,
14 High Street, Edinburgh EH1 1TE.

Trade paperback edition first published in Great Britain and the USA in 2022
by Severn House, an imprint of Canongate Books Ltd.

severnhouse.com

British Library Cataloguing-in-Publication Data
A CIP catalogue record for this title is available from the British Library.

ISBN-13: 978-0-7278-5041-6 (cased)
ISBN-13: 978-1-4483-0582-7 (trade paper)
ISBN-13: 978-1-4483-0581-0 (e-book)

All Severn House titles are printed on acid-free paper.

Typeset by Palimpsest Book Product
Falkirk, Stirlingshire, Scotland.
Printed and bound in Great Britain b
TJ Books, Padstow, Cornwall.

In memory of:

Chris Barrett. 1944–2020

Heather Chasen. 1927–2020

Hazel Gunnell. 1926–2021

Alan St Clair. 1948–2021

ONE

North Devon, 2021

The man was clearly dead. He lay sprawled across the kitchen floor, face down, arms stretched out to each side, legs slightly apart, almost as he were trying to do the breast stroke through the partially congealed pool of dark blood which surrounded him.

DCI David Vogel, already appointed senior investigating officer and the first detective at the scene, could see no obvious signs of injury to the dead man's back, so it seemed reasonable to assume that his attacker had struck from the front and, judging from the amount of blood, that he had been stabbed to death. Almost certainly a number of times. It was possible that he could have been shot, but there was no sign of any exit wounds, and gun crime remained rare in the UK.

In spite of more than twenty years as a police officer and having frequently been faced with extreme violence and its inevitable consequences, Vogel had never got used to it. Particularly when that violence resulted in the most extreme of consequences. All too often the sight of a dead body left him desperately fighting against nausea and even faintness. On this occasion, although his stomach had lurched involuntarily as soon as he saw the blood surrounding the corpse, Vogel had so far been spared a more extreme reaction because neither the victim's face nor his wounds were visible.

A woman, her face, clothes and hands heavily bloodstained, was sitting on the floor in a corner of the room, alongside the fridge. Her knees were drawn up almost to her chin, held there by trembling arms. She stared straight ahead in such a way that Vogel was unsure whether or not she was actually aware of his presence. Or, indeed, aware of anything. And she was silent. Totally silent. In fact, apart from the shocking brutality of the scene which had greeted him upon his arrival, silence was what

Vogel was most conscious of. All he could hear was the gentle hum of the fridge.

The house had been cordoned off. The crime scene investigators were already in attendance but had yet to start work. They had provided Vogel with mask, over-shoes, latex gloves, and a set of white polyethylene coveralls which he had pulled on over his own clothes before entering the house. He was still wearing his favourite, honourably ancient, brown corduroy jacket underneath. And he so wished he had taken it off before donning the coveralls. It had been a warm July day and, although now mid-evening, the kitchen was hot and stuffy. He had started to sweat and his skin felt itchy, particularly around his neck beneath his collar which seemed uncomfortably tight within the constraints of the hooded suit. He also wished he had removed his tie. He wondered why he never thought of such things. Vogel wasn't good at considering his own physical comfort at the best of times. When heading a murder investigation, he could think of nothing except the case in hand. Even his wife and daughter, both of whom he adored, were rarely in his thoughts.

The only other officers present were the first responders, two uniforms who had been dispatched to the property, which was located on an exclusive estate just off the Appledore road on the outskirts of Northam, in response to a 999 call.

They were silent too, awaiting further instructions from the SIO.

The crime scene guys were also waiting silently.

The fridge, one of the American sort, made a sudden loud rumbling sound like a minor avalanche. It was, of course, manufacturing ice, a large quantity of which had presumably dropped into its internal container.

Vogel was momentarily startled. A mild nervous spasm ran through his body. He hoped it hadn't shown.

The woman sitting alongside the fridge did not react at all. Why should she? Vogel assumed that she must be Mrs Gillian Quinn, who had dialled 999 to report the death of her husband, Thomas Quinn.

This was her kitchen, and her fridge.

She shouldn't really be in the room with her husband's dead body, the room where the attack had presumably occurred. But he supposed nobody had dared move her, in the state she was clearly in, without medical professionals being in attendance. And the presence of the SIO.

Somewhat to his relief, he glimpsed through the kitchen window the arrival of a paramedic team in full PPE, which, ever since the outbreak of the pandemic that had overwhelmed an amazed world the previous year, they would have been wearing on any call-out, whether or not attending the scene of a serious crime.

The paramedics weren't going to be much use to the dead man, thought Vogel, but there was little doubt that the woman needed their help.

He stepped forward and introduced himself to Gillian Quinn, very gently, trying to make contact.

There was still no response. Blank eyes stared at him. Unseeingly, he suspected.

'Mrs Quinn,' he continued, his voice still soft. 'We need to move you from here, get you checked over, cleaned up, and then we'll have a chat later. We want to help you . . .'

The woman still failed to respond.

One of the uniforms, PC Phil Lake, who Vogel remembered from a previous case in the area, stepped towards him. He was a big man with the build of a rugby forward and a gentle, slightly diffident, air about him,

'She's not said a word since Docherty and I arrived, boss,' he said. 'The door was open when we got here. So, we just walked in . . . Well, we didn't know it was anything like this. Not at all, I mean . . .'

'Of course not. That's perfectly all right, constable. Where was Mrs Quinn when you two arrived?'

'Exactly where she is now, boss,' replied Morag Docherty.

Vogel had met Docherty, who was about half Lake's size but had a considerable presence about her, on the same previous case, and remembered being impressed by her then. The Docherty-Lake team were still working together, it seemed. He wondered if Docherty remained very much the leader. He suspected she did, and that the arrangement probably suited both of them.

'We found her just sitting there,' Docherty continued. 'She hasn't moved. We tried to speak to her at first, but she didn't respond at all. So we thought it best to leave her alone until you got here.'

'Quite right, Docherty,' said Vogel.

She and Lake were still in their uniforms. As first responders they'd not had the opportunity to suit up.

'You two should move outside now,' he instructed. 'We need to avoid unnecessary contamination of the scene. And I want you on sentry duty. Nobody who isn't directly involved with this case comes in here unless I say so.'

As Docherty and Lake left, the paramedics entered. Vogel quickly introduced himself.

'Obviously you guys must do what you have to do, but I want you to liaise with CSI,' he instructed. 'We need the integrity of your patient protected as much as is possible for forensics . . .'

A welcome interruption caused Vogel to pause in mid-sentence. Detective Sergeant Dawn Saslow had arrived, bringing with her an element of the banter which made life a little more bearable for all front-line workers. Even at a time like this.

'How did you get here without me, then, boss, did you hitch?' she asked.

Vogel, a former Met officer whose beat, albeit as a very senior detective, now covered largely a semi-rural area, had never learned to drive, which was a constant source of mild amusement to his colleagues. When it didn't inconvenience them, of course.

The DCI had been at Barnstaple nick when the 999 call had been passed on. Saslow had been off-duty.

'You know that twelve-year-old probationer with too much hair who seems to have taken a bit of a shine to you?' murmured Vogel.

'You surely don't mean Constable Wickes?' countered Saslow.

'I certainly do. Well, it seems he prefers me to you after all. He gave me a lift.'

Saslow grinned. The grimness of the moment had been just very slightly alleviated. Vogel managed almost a smile back. It continued to surprise him how much more comfortable he felt with Dawn around. Particularly if there was any sort of tricky situation involving women.

In such circumstances Saslow was his obvious first choice, but he preferred to have any female officer in attendance. He knew that was an old-fashioned sort of view, and would probably be regarded as a kind of inverted sexism. He couldn't help how he felt. How he was. He believed absolutely that Dawn was far better equipped to deal with a severely traumatized woman than he was. And he was also self-aware enough to realize that his gender might be only a part of the reason for that.

Vogel was not a man who found other people's emotions easy to deal with at the best of times. When the other person was a traumatized wreck following the violent death of her husband, and in addition was almost certainly going to be the primary suspect in his death, Vogel's instinct was to pull back in favour of others whom he considered to be better qualified.

The paramedics, a tall woman and a much shorter man, carried on into the kitchen. Vogel and Saslow, wearing coveralls clearly at least two sizes too big for her, followed.

Saslow's quick eyes took in the scene before her at once. A small, feisty, athletic and very modern young woman, she was the antithesis of Vogel in almost every way. Nobody could ever accuse Vogel of being modern, except in his IT ability perhaps. He was tall and studious looking, with a manner often rather more reminiscent of a clergyman than a policeman, and he towered above Saslow in spite of his very slight stoop. They were still regarded by some fellow officers as something of an odd couple, but the pair had made a good team from the start.

Saslow was masked, of course. However, the DCI knew, that even without a mask, if the sight of the dead man on the floor was causing Dawn Saslow any distress, it would not show in her face. She wouldn't allow it.

He gestured for her to step back again into the hallway.

'The woman in there is in total shock,' he explained, now absolutely serious. 'I'm going to need your help with her, maybe not this evening, but at some stage. As you know we are working on the assumption that she is Mrs Gillian Quinn and that the dead man is her husband Thomas. Have you managed to find out anything about the family?'

'Yes, boss. Thomas Quinn, forty-three years old, a successful businessman and a former town councillor. Something of a pillar of the local community, it seems . . .'

Oh, he just would be, wouldn't he, thought Vogel.

The DCI felt his heart sinking. There was something about pillars of the community which always seemed to make any sort of police investigation more difficult. Particularly a murder investigation. People's standing in any community, regional or national, made no difference at all to David Vogel when he was conducting an investigation. But he had come to learn that was not necessarily always so with those he had to deal with in the pursuit of any such inquiry.

'He's had a finger in a lot of pies over the years, seems to have made his money originally out of the tourist industry, a theme park just outside the town, holiday chalets, a hotel, that sort of thing,' Saslow continued. 'Recently he's moved with the times. Has an internet trading and delivery company, buying and selling internationally. Not sure of the details, but the word is that business boomed during lockdown, and he made a lot of money.'

'All right for some,' muttered Vogel.

Although he realized it was illogical, he had an aversion towards anyone whose finances had ballooned thanks to the pandemic which had destroyed so many lives.

'What about the wife?' he continued.

'Gillian Quinn, known to almost everyone as Gill, is a primary school teacher,' said Saslow. 'She reported her husband's death without explanation when she called emergency services. The operator pushed her, and asked if she thought her husband had died of natural causes, but apparently Mrs Quinn just replied . . .'

Saslow consulted her notebook.

'"You'd better send somebody quickly." Then she hung up, and didn't answer call-backs. The operator said she sounded totally calm, though.'

'Really,' Vogel remarked. 'Well, she certainly isn't calm now, that's for sure. It's like her brain and her body have very nearly ceased to function.'

He glanced back into the kitchen. The paramedics had succeeded in coaxing Gill Quinn to her feet with barely any fuss at all, which Vogel reckoned was a considerable tribute to their skill and professionalism. He and Saslow stood to one side as they led Gill into the hall. He was mildly surprised the woman could walk. But she seemed able to do so well enough, whilst still in an apparently trance-like condition.

Vogel asked the paramedics what their plan was.

'We'll have to take her straight to the NDDH,' replied the tall woman. 'No choice. She's in extreme shock.'

That was the North Devon District Hospital at Barnstaple. Vogel didn't argue. It was, in any case, quite clear that Gill Quinn was in no condition to be interviewed. He merely pointed out that he would need to send an officer with Gill, which the paramedics accepted without comment.

At least the CSIs could now begin their examination of the rest of the kitchen. But they would have to wait until the arrival of the district Home Office pathologist – who was based in Exeter, an hour-and-a-half drive's away – before touching the body.

Mrs Quinn looked neither to the left or right as she stumbled her way out of the house, supported on either side by a paramedic, eyes staring straight ahead. There was a wildness in them which Vogel, following closely, found most disturbing.

Shock came in all shapes and sizes, he knew well enough, and often displayed itself in all of those affected by violent crime, not just the victims and perpetrators, but also witnesses.

Nonetheless, every shred of evidence, albeit mostly circumstantial, that had so far been gleaned, pointed directly towards Gill Quinn. The DCI lived and worked by the mantra of opportunity, motive, and intent. It had served him well over the years. It seemed clear that Mrs Quinn would have had opportunity. He did not know yet whether she'd also had motive and intent, but if she had the former, he'd doubtless find out soon enough. The latter sometimes took a little longer to reveal itself.

The paramedics began to help the traumatized woman into the waiting ambulance.

Vogel looked around for the two officers he had posted on sentry duty, protecting the crime scene. Morag Docherty was standing just outside the front door.

'PC Docherty, get in that ambulance,' he commanded. 'I want you to stick to Gill Quinn like glue, and you're to bring her to me for questioning as soon as the medics allow. Have you got that?'

TWO

London, 1997

Lilian St John climbed awkwardly into the waiting taxi, half tripping over the crutches which were supposed to support her. The driver turned in his seat and glanced at her enquiringly. She realized she still had no clear idea where she was going.

She held on tightly to the plastic bag which contained the bloodstained clothes she had been wearing the night it happened, and the few possessions they had collected for her from the place that had once been her home. Allegedly her home.

These included her mobile phone and her credit cards. At least she still had those.

'Take me to the Dorchester,' she instructed the driver rather grandly. Or it could have been grand, she thought, if she didn't look so awful. Her face still bore the scars and bruises of the beating she had received. She had earlier spilled her final cup of hospital tea down the front of her white cotton shirt, crumpled from being stuffed into the locker by her bed, and totally inadequate for the unseasonably cool late-spring afternoon. And her once stylish navy-blue trousers had been slit up the seam of one leg to accommodate the lump of already grubby plaster encasing her left ankle.

She shivered. Nobody had thought to bring her a coat.

The Dorchester doorman, tall, elegant and presumably warm, in his grey topper and frock coat, helped her out of the taxi. Managing to look only slightly askance, he carried her bright-blue hospital-issue plastic bag into reception as she hobbled behind him.

The receptionist, a pinstriped young woman with spectacles and a nose which turned conveniently upwards at the end, attended to two other customers before Lilian, at least one of whom, Lilian was quite sure, had arrived at the desk after her. She did not have the strength to protest.

Eventually the pinstriped young woman turned to her. The eyes behind the spectacles which took in Lilian's battered appearance, her unsuitable stained clothes, and the plastic bag, were both suspicious and disapproving.

'I would like to book a room for tonight,' said Lilian, rather more loudly than she had intended.

Pinstripe consulted the computer in front of her in silence.

'I'm afraid all we have available is a junior suite,' she said eventually. Then, with a considerable degree of smugness, as if knowing full well that would be the end of the matter, she added, 'And it's seven hundred and fifty pounds a night.'

'I'll take it,' said Lilian producing her platinum American Express card. The expression on Pinstripe's face altered very slightly.

Just a few moments later the smug look was back.

'I'm afraid your card has been declined, madam,' she said, in a tone of voice which indicated that this was only what she had expected.

Lilian felt her blood chill.

'There must be some mistake,' she began.

Pinstripe, with an almost audible sigh, tried the card again.

'No mistake, madam,' she said.

Lilian stared at her for just a few seconds. Then, afraid she was about to burst into tears, hurried from the Dorchester foyer as quickly as her crutches would allow.

Outside she stumbled across to the little wall which separated the grand old hotel from Park Lane proper and sat down wearily. She checked through the contents of her plastic bag. She had asked for her handbag to be collected, but, instead, whoever had gone to the flat had merely emptied into that hospital issue bag all that they could find of her life which might be considered an essential.

She realized that her fingers, still sore from being bent backwards during her attempts to defend herself, were trembling. Eventually underneath a small tangle of underwear, she found the envelope she was looking for. It contained just over a hundred pounds in cash. There was also a five-pound note and some coins in the back pocket of her trousers. About £110 in all. That certainly wouldn't pay for a decent London hotel room.

The doorman was staring at her. Eventually he walked across.

'Can I help you, madam?' he asked. 'Would you like a taxi?'

Lilian knew that he just wanted her off the premises. Her head ached. The cold was biting into her. Her injured ankle was throbbing. She couldn't walk anywhere. She didn't feel that she had anyone to turn to. So she really had no choice, did she?

She would have to return to the scene of the crime until she sorted herself out. To the Mayfair apartment where she had suffered so much abuse.

Her husband, Kurt St John, a UK-based South African, had, however, returned to his native land. Or so she'd been told. And he wouldn't risk returning to the UK with the police looking for him, she was pretty sure of that. If indeed they really were looking for him.

She did not have her keys to the flat. She assumed they were still in the handbag she had wanted brought to her in hospital. But at this time of day she expected Ben, the head porter, to be on duty at Penbourne Villas. He would let her in, as he presumably had whoever the hospital had sent to collect her belongings, armed with the note of authorization she had written. Even if Kurt had changed the locks – which she felt was unlikely as he would surely not want to discourage her from returning to the one place where he could so easily find her – Ben would still let her in.

She allowed the doorman to summon her a cab and climbed in without tipping him. He did not look as if he expected a tip from her.

At the Villas she stood for a moment looking up at the towering old mansion block, which dominated one corner of Berkeley Square. She remembered the high hopes she had held when Kurt first invited her there, and the terrible despair she'd ultimately been reduced to within its red-brick Edwardian walls.

There was a porter on duty, as she had expected. But she did not recognize him. He stared at her crutches as she blundered through the revolving doors. The plastic bag somehow got caught up in the mechanism. She was momentarily stuck. The porter rose to his feet from behind his desk and took a few steps towards her. He was very tall, very thin, and moved like an athlete. She thought he looked like an American basketball player, although he was probably of Caribbean descent.

'Do you need any assistance, ma'am?'

'Thank you. Yes. Oh, and I don't seem to have my keys . . .'

'No problem, ma'am.'

He was swiftly at her side. Smiling, he manipulated the doors with ease, took the plastic bag from her, and escorted her to the lift, pushing the button for the fifth floor.

Then he used his master key to unlock flat fifty-six.

'Is there anything more I can do for you, ma'am?' he asked.

'No. Thank you very much.'

She tipped him five pounds. A habit she had got into with the porters. One she would not be able to continue.

It was only as he walked away that the obvious thought struck her. How had he known who she was and which flat she lived in? She was sure she had never seen the man before. Yet it had been almost as if he had been expecting her.

Although the apartment was warm, heated even when unoccupied by Penbourne Villas' efficient communal heating system, Lilian realized she was still shivering.

She walked across the sitting room to the safe built into the far wall and tapped in the combination Kurt had made her memorize. It did not work. She tried again. It still did not work. If the various pieces of expensive jewellery, he had given her remained inside it seemed she had no way of getting at them. She did not even have her engagement ring, a substantial diamond, or her Cartier watch. She was sure she'd been wearing both the night it happened, but the hospital was adamant that she had not been. Either someone had stolen them, or Kurt had removed them before the paramedics took her away. She favoured the latter.

She wandered fitfully around the rest of the apartment. Everything was in order and immaculately tidy. She opened the door to Kurt's wardrobe. Jackets and trousers neatly hung, shoes on racks, sweaters and shirts folded on shelves. There did not seem to be any significant amount of clothing missing. But then, he kept a complete wardrobe in at least two homes.

She opened her own wardrobe doors. At a glance her clothes – almost all of them chosen either by him or by her with him in mind – seemed to be all there. Kurt St John had not just married her, he had completely taken over her life. And she had let him. In fact, hard as it was for her to accept, she had, in the beginning, wanted him to do just that.

The declined Amex card, and two others in her sad plastic bag, had been linked to shared accounts. She had no bank account of her own. Indeed, she'd felt for some time, long before the events that had landed her in hospital, that she no longer had anything that was entirely hers. Except her rabbits, Loppy and Lena, the two no longer fluffy bunnies – she never referred to them as toys – that had been her solace in times of strife since childhood, but had ceased to live on her bed from the moment Kurt came into her life. She took them from their box in the bottom of the wardrobe, stroked their balding heads, and held them close. Their glass eyes glinted. If they could have spoken she reckoned they would have said, 'Told you so!'

She had a bath, climbing in with difficulty and dangling her plaster-cast leg over the edge. The warm water felt good, but the bath would have helped much more if she had not been so aware that she was using toiletries he had also used.

THREE

Vogel watched as Morag Docherty hopped nimbly into the ambulance. As the doors closed he caught a final glimpse of Gill Quinn, lying on a stretcher. He could not see her face, but he doubted it would give much away.

Soon, possibly later that night, if not the next day, he would be formally interviewing Gill. His feelings, as ever, were mixed. He didn't know what had happened inside 11 St Anne's Avenue, of course, but if he had to hazard a guess at this stage, it would be that the death of Thomas Quinn was yet another domestic tragedy, born primarily of a deeply tormented marriage, one of a long list of such personal tragedies that he had encountered in his career.

The ambulance pulled away, coasting down the short driveway to the main drag, its siren breaking the silence which had previously, and somewhat eerily, engulfed number eleven.

Vogel glanced back at the house. It was a place that smacked of money; Vogel suspected his mother would have called it 'new money', a large and well-kept property, probably just pre-war, with one or two features, like a porticoed entrance and diamond-mullioned windows, which were probably supposed to add grandeur, although Vogel thought they were out of place and a tad vulgar.

Aware of another vehicle approaching, he turned to see a black Mini Cooper with tinted windows roar up the driveway and into the parking place the ambulance had just vacated. A blast of heavy metal momentarily filled the cooling evening air as the driver's door swung open.

Out stepped a young woman, also cloaked in black. A black leather jacket with shiny epaulettes, black leggings, and black Doc Martens. Her hair was a tawny mane. Her lips a blaze of orange. Her spectacles orange-framed and vaguely tinted.

Vogel was momentarily perplexed. Perhaps this was a Quinn family member or friend, who may or may not yet know of the fate which had befallen Thomas Quinn. But PC Lake, who he knew to be on sentry duty down at the gate, had apparently allowed the driver of the Mini to proceed right up to the crime scene unhindered. Perhaps she was a member of the local team who Vogel had yet to meet. One of the emerging breed of sassy young detectives of varying gender that every force in the country seemed to be bringing on.

The young woman carelessly slammed the car door shut behind her and, carrying a large black doctor's bag, strode towards Vogel, every movement fluid and radiating confidence.

It dawned on him then. This must be the new pathologist.

Ever since moving west from his native London, Vogel had worked only with Dr Karen Crow, one of the most experienced Home Office pathologists in the country. Indeed, many years previously, she had been the first woman in the UK to be appointed to the job. Karen Crow smoked a lot – which Vogel hated – swore a lot, and had talked down to him most of the time. But he had grown used to her, and respected her as a leader in her field who was only very rarely wrong about anything.

He knew, however, that Karen Crow – unmarried, not overly attractive, rarely inclined to attempt to charm, predictably assumed by most of her colleagues to be gay – had recently taken early retirement and gone to live in Brazil with a man. Her younger and allegedly very handsome South American lover. A football coach.

This had, of course, become the stuff of much joyful gossip in police and medical circles throughout Devon and Somerset, which, Vogel had to admit, he had enjoyed as much as anyone.

However, as he watched the redoubtable Dr Crow's successor approach, Vogel feared he may yet regret her departure even more than he had thought he might.

'DCI Vogel? queried the young woman, flashing an easy smile.

Vogel nodded. He had been aware that a successor to Dr Crow had been appointed. And he'd known it was another woman. But that was all he'd known. He waited.

'Daisy Dobbs, pathology,' she announced unceremoniously, thrusting an outstretched hand in Vogel's direction.

Vogel did not take it. After such a long period of Covid restrictions he still wasn't entirely comfortable shaking hands. In explanation he gestured towards his own gloved hands.

'Pleased to meet you, Dr Dobbs,' he murmured.

'It's Professor, only call me Daisy, for God's sake,' she replied.

Vogel found himself blinking rapidly behind his thick rimmed spectacles, a mannerism quite beyond his control inclined to overcome him whenever events took a turn with which he was in some way uncomfortable. He silently cursed himself. This was his crime scene. He had already been appointed senior investigating officer. He was in charge. He had nothing to feel uncomfortable about. But he did feel uncomfortable. And it was just so annoying.

Daisy Dobbs looked about fifteen to him. How on earth could she be a professor? Which kindergarten had she qualified at? He realized he really shouldn't think like this, but the truth was that Vogel was somewhat afraid of youth. He knew he wasn't sexist or racist, and he tried very hard not to be classist, not to fall into the trap of so many otherwise highly laudable police officers who were inclined to slot criminal behaviour into the various boxes of British class society.

However, the older he got and the greater seniority he achieved, the less he seemed able to stop himself being ageist. Or perhaps it was youthist?

He just did not see how the teenager standing before him, looking more like a rock singer or a reality show contestant than a professor of medicine, could possibly have the knowledge and ability to even approach the achievements of her predecessor.

He waited while she swiftly kitted up in PPE, then followed her into the house. He hadn't really taken much notice of the interior before. The kitchen was slick and ultra-modern. Everything seemed to be white or stainless steel, including the floor tiles, against which the deep red of the dead man's blood stood out with a disturbing intensity. Vogel shivered slightly.

A bottle of whisky and just one glass, half filled, stood on the kitchen table. So only one person had been drinking. Vogel wondered if that was significant.

Daisy Dobbs immediately crouched by the body and made what appeared to be a preliminary examination of the dead man in the position in which he had been found.

Then she asked a CSI to help her turn him over.

It was immediately clear that Vogel's initial assumption that Thomas Quinn had been stabbed to death was almost certainly correct. And the murder weapon's points of entry were fairly clear, even though the victim remained fully clothed, in jeans and a shirt which looked as if it had once been a crisp pale blue. There appeared to be a number of stab wounds, indicated by damage to the clothing and a deeper blood stainage, all in the area of the dead man's chest. Except one. Thomas Quinn had also been stabbed in the middle of his throat.

Vogel found that especially disturbing. In his long and varied experience he had never before seen such a thing. He thought that it must take a particular kind of human being, or maybe just someone in a particularly extreme emotional state, to be able to stab another human being directly in the throat. Presumably whilst facing him.

Thomas Quinn's face was set in a silent scream. The lips pulled back over the teeth in a ghastly grin. The eyes wide open.

It was altogether a sight almost bound to trigger in Vogel the involuntary reaction he had so far managed to keep at bay on this occasion.

He felt the familiar rise of bile within his digestive system. He had as yet avoided throughout his career actually being sick over a crime scene. But more than once he had been obliged to move swiftly away as a matter of urgency in order to find somewhere he could empty the contents of his stomach without damaging the investigation he was working on.

Nausea when faced with the consequences of violence continued to plague him. Nowadays he could usually control it. But not always. He was determined that he would do so this time, and averted his gaze from the corpse on the floor to glance at Saslow.

She was standing alongside the crouching pathologist, bending over the body. As close as any detective should get, even with a suit on. Dawn did not share Vogel's physical sensitivities in such matters, that was for sure.

But then, the young DS was a tough cookie who, in her short career, had already survived a degree of physical and psychological pressure far beyond the call of duty.

Daisy Dobbs continued to examine the corpse, and had opened the dead man's shirt revealing the expected patchwork of deep stab wounds. She worked in silence. Vogel was grateful for that. If he did not have to enter into conversation then he could concentrate all his efforts on controlling his wayward digestive system.

After a few minutes the pathologist stood up and turned to face Vogel.

'Well, not much doubt about this one,' she remarked. 'Death by multiple stab wounds, almost certainly. I've counted eleven, all in the torso and throat. Almost certainly inflicted by a long straight knife.'

She paused, looking around.

'I don't see any sign of a murder weapon nearby,' she said. 'Have you found anything?'

'Not yet,' said Vogel.

He immediately considered a common scenario, particularly in the case of a murder that might be regarded as a domestic.

'Could it be a standard carving knife?' he asked.

'Quite possibly,' Daisy replied. 'Look, I'll conduct a full examination when we get him back to the morgue, and I should be able to give you a more accurate assessment of the kind of knife that was used. But I don't think you're going to need or get a great deal more help from me on this one. The cause of death could not be much clearer, and the victim certainly didn't inflict those wounds on himself.'

Vogel nodded. Daisy Dobbs had been swift, sharp and sensible. And no doubt accurate in her assessment. But she was right, pathology was unlikely to prove to be of much assistance in this case. He would like to see how the young doctor coped with a more challenging, and less obvious, set of circumstances.

'Time of death?' he queried.

'Well, rigor mortis has set in but is far from complete,' Daisy replied. 'So he definitely died today, probably this afternoon, and I would guess from the degree of rigor that it is highly unlikely that death occurred less than four hours or so ago.'

'Can you be any more precise than that?' asked Vogel.

'I may be able to after I've got him back to the morgue,' said Daisy. 'We'll do a rectal temperature check and so on. I'll let you know.'

The pathologist's answer was only what Vogel had expected. He would have to wait. Meanwhile he considered the significance of the information she had already given. He knew that Gill Quinn's emergency call had been logged at six forty-one p.m. He glanced at his watch. Precisely two hours and two minutes earlier.

So if Mrs Quinn had killed her husband, then presumably she had remained with his dead body during the period after his death, before making the 999 call reporting it. That would have been at least two hours, if Daisy Dodd's initial time of death assessment was correct, which might appear at first sight to be somewhat strange behaviour. But on the other hand, perhaps the woman had been debating whether to report the crime or not, or whether perhaps to flee the scene. She may also have been attempting to conceal evidence which might incriminate her. However, if that were the case, she certainly hadn't made a very good job of it.

Or perhaps she had been reduced to such a state of shock by the enormity of what she had done that she had been rendered incapable of doing anything to help herself. Or of contacting anyone who might help her.

Gill Quinn had seemed to be in that sort of state to Vogel, for sure, when he'd first encountered her squatting on the kitchen floor. But there seemed little doubt that she had eventually made the 999 call, and he would expect voice-match software to confirm that. And, there was no sign of the murder weapon so far. So perhaps she had contrived to hide that.

There was a wooden block on the worktop which contained a number of knives, three of which were not in their slots. Vogel glanced towards the dishwasher. He had seen that trick before.

He asked a CSI to open it, which the man did, slowly and with care, but eventually pulling the door wide open. The contents were clearly clean. And there were at least two large knives visible.

'Any idea when the machine may have been last used?' Vogel asked.

'Well, it isn't warm, so not within the last couple of hours,' the CSI replied. 'But probably today judging from the amount of water about. Can't go beyond that.'

Vogel thanked him, and considered asking for an electrical engineer to be called in just in case it was possible to get a more accurate estimate, but he wasn't optimistic.

If one of the knives inside the dishwasher was the murder weapon and it had gone through a complete cleaning cycle, then there would be little or no chance of obtaining any forensic evidence from it. But would Gill Quinn really have had the presence of mind to do that?

Vogel reflected briefly on the possibility that a third party had murdered Thomas Quinn. If so, had Gill Quinn been present, and was she therefore aware of who had committed the terrible crime, or even complicit with them, or had she merely arrived home to find the corpse? So far, Vogel and his team knew nothing of the woman's movements that day. But they would find out, that was for sure.

Daisy Dobbs packed up her bag and left. Her job completed for the moment. The CSIs continued their work, painstakingly combing every inch of the property, particularly in the vicinity of the dead man, and bagging up all possible evidence. Everything would be loaded into their vehicles and taken away for further examination. A mobile phone had been found in the dead man's pocket, presumably his. Mrs Quinn had not had a phone on her person, and so far no other mobile phone had been found on the premises. The search for any further mobiles would continue. They were invariably a vital part of any investigation.

A CSI walked past the open kitchen door carrying a laptop and an iPad. In the world of modern forensic investigation, IT evidence invariably proved to be every bit as important as a post-mortem and other medical examinations.

Vogel had seen enough. He couldn't wait to interview Gill Quinn. But he hoped to have considerably more information about her, and her recent movements, before doing so. The wider investigation was already beginning, including door-to-door enquiries. Relatives, friends and colleagues were being contacted.

'C'mon, Saslow,' began Vogel. 'Let's get back to the incident room and see what else we've got—'

He was interrupted by an excited looking Phil Lake.

'Boss, I've just been talking to one of the neighbours, Mavis Tanner. Lives opposite. She came by to see what was going on. I stopped her coming up to the house, obviously, but, well, I know we'll be knocking on doors soon, only I thought it wouldn't hurt to have a chat . . .'

Lake stopped abruptly. A thought seemed to occur to him. Vogel was already aware that Lake lacked the self-assurance of his partner, PC Docherty. He was, however, a solid and intelligent young officer.

'Hope that's all right, boss?'

'Get on with it, Lake,' muttered Vogel impatiently.

'Yes, boss. Seems Mrs Tanner was walking her dog past the Quinn house this afternoon. She says a window was open at the front, and she heard what she described as a "bit of a rumpus".'

"Did she know what time it was?'

'About three or four,' replied PC Docherty.

That fitted almost exactly with the probable time of death, and could be a vital piece of evidence, thought Vogel.

'Was she any more clear about what she actually heard?' asked Vogel.

'A little, boss.'

PC Lake consulted his notebook.

'She heard what she described as "a bang, then a scraping noise, like something being dropped and maybe a piece of furniture being moved. And raised voices".'

'Raised voices? Male or female?'

'Both, she thought, but she wasn't sure. And she couldn't

actually hear what they were saying, even though she paused to listen for a few seconds – bit shamefaced she was about that, boss. Then it all went quiet, she said, so she just walked on home.'

'She wasn't overly disturbed by what she'd heard, then?'

'Not at all, boss.'

'Presumably there were no screams, or anything like that.'

'Not that Mrs Tanner was aware of, I don't think. She said it had sounded to her like a perfectly normal argument between a married couple.'

PC Lake consulted his notes again.

'This is what she told me. "It was nothing untoward. Well, I didn't think so at the time. Just a bit of a rumpus. It happens in even the happiest marriages, and if I'd thought for a minute there was any violence going on I'd have called the police".'

'So, she was reasonably sure the voices she heard were those of Thomas and Gill Quinn, was she?'

'I asked her that, boss. She admitted that she couldn't be sure, and not even entirely sure that it was a man and a woman, but she asked who else it was likely to be? And she pointed out that it was a Saturday afternoon, and so quite likely that the Quinns would be at home together.'

Which was probably a fair enough assumption, thought Vogel. It seemed, rather sadly, as he'd suspected, that this case was not going to take long to solve.

FOUR

Early the following morning, after a fitful night's sleep, Lilian decided to dress and hobble to the nearby twenty-four-hour store. She was desperate for a cup of tea, and there was no milk in the fridge.

He stepped in front of her just before she reached the lift. A big man with an incongruously small head. She turned towards the stairs. Even though she had no idea how she could manage them. Another man stood looking at her impassively. Broad-shouldered and hairy. Except for the top of his head which was bald, pink and shiny. His arms hung loosely at his side, like a boxer. Both men were clichés of their kind.

'We have a message from Mr St John,' said the one with the small head.

She nodded. Afraid and weary at the same time.

'He says we're to look out for you. Stick around, make sure you're OK.'

Lilian knew full well what that meant. Kurt had sent two of his goons to watch her. To make sure that he would always know where she was and what she was doing.

She said nothing.

'So,' Small Head continued, glancing pointedly at her crutches, 'is there anything we can do to help?'

Lilian managed to find some spirit. 'Yes, you can ask Mr St John to restore my credit cards and my access to our joint account.'

Small Head shrugged. 'Mr St John says, withdraw the charges and everything can go back to normal.'

'You mean he can use me as a punch bag again?'

Small Head was impassive. 'He's your husband.'

'Not for much longer.'

'That ain't what he says.'

'Please get out of my way?' she instructed, not very optimistically. 'I need to go to the shop.'

Rather to her surprise the man moved.

'Got enough to pay, have you?' he asked.

Lilian ignored him.

Small Head pushed the lift button for her and leaned his huge bulk against the door to ensure it stayed open as she shuffled awkwardly in.

'Allow me,' he said, stretching his lips into what presumably passed for a smile. It still looked like a leer.

He did not attempt to follow her in. Downstairs in the foyer there was no sign of the basketball player. In one way this was a relief. But it did mean she had to struggle with those stupid revolving doors on her own.

She needed to cross the lower side of Berkeley Square to get to the shop, which was tucked away up a little alleyway off Fitzmaurice Place. It was less than two hundred yards away. Nonetheless, getting there was a considerable challenge.

A vehicle, a big black SUV, slowed alongside her. The tinted window slid down revealing a male head, orange hair cropped close over bony features, pale eyes staring levelly at her.

The head spoke softly. 'Can I give you a lift?'

She heard herself reply politely, almost as if everything were normal.

'No, thank you.'

But, instinctively, she backed away from the street side of the pavement. Orange hair stared for several long seconds more, then the SUV, a Range Rover she now registered, pulled smoothly away. She continued her short journey shakily, hurrying as best she could.

The lift offer could, of course, have been just the kindness of a stranger. But she didn't think so for one moment.

When she emerged from the shop onto Fitzmaurice Place again she glanced up and down the street. The same black Range Rover was illegally parked on the corner of Berkeley Square. She had to pass it in order to get back to the flat. She was soon aware of the engine starting and the purr of the big motor crawling along behind her. It took a great effort of will not to look around.

She had bought more than she had intended to, filling two plastic carrier bags not just with food – she supposed she'd have to eat at some stage – but with other necessities. There hadn't even been any toilet paper in the flat. She held one bag on each side while at the same time manipulating her crutches. The bags swung awkwardly every time she took a step.

The thought occurred to her obscurely that if orange hair pulled alongside her and offered her a lift again she might well accept the invitation. After all, it would probably make no difference. Kurt's goons were all over her like crows pecking at a carcass.

In the foyer of Penbourne Villas, the basketball player was now at his desk. This at least meant that he once again sprang to his feet, helped her through those blessed doors, took the carrier bags from her and offered to carry them upstairs.

She agreed with alacrity.

The basketball player was the very picture of consideration. She decided to take the initiative.

'What's your name?' she asked.

'Warren, ma'am,' he replied, smiling the warmest and widest of smiles.

'And where's Ben?'

'I understand he resigned, ma'am.'

'So, you're the new head porter?'

'Yes I am, ma'am.'

The man was infuriatingly polite. Probably quite unfairly, Lilian wanted to slap him.

She remembered with fondness the way Ben had been far from obsequious, a small, chirpy, jockey-like man, always ready with a wry remark or a spot of banter. And she remembered how he'd looked at her on those occasions when even heavy make-up and dark glasses could do little to conceal the beating she'd received at her husband's hands the night before.

'Do you know what happened to Ben?' she asked.

'No idea, ma'am. I was just told there was a vacancy for the job here, and applied. That's all.'

The phraseology struck Lilian as being not quite right. *I was just told there was a vacancy for the job . . .*

'Who told you?' she enquired sharply.

Warren was no longer smiling his big warm smile. 'Uh, I don't really know, ma'am.'

'What do you mean, you don't know?'

'I . . . it was just the Job Centre, ma'am. I mean I don't know who exactly, you don't, do you . . .'

Warren's voice tailed away. His body language screamed out his unease. He probably wasn't such a bad bloke. Just another piece of flotsam struggling to keep afloat in murky, wreckage-strewn waters.

'I see,' she said as they stepped from the lift onto the fifth floor. 'So, as head porter can you please tell me what you were doing this morning allowing strangers to wander around the place accosting residents?'

'I don't know what you mean, ma'am. I didn't see any strangers come in. No visitors at all. Not today. Not yet.'

'What about two extremely large men who look exactly like the thugs they undoubtedly are?'

Warren shook his head. His expression was one of exquisite puzzlement. But she reckoned he was definitely squirming.

She swiftly took in the empty corridor ahead. Not a goon in sight. Of course there wouldn't be, would there? Not while she was in the company of the erstwhile porter. She heard a dull clunk, the sound of a door closing. But she had no idea which apartment the sound had come from. Indeed everything seemed as normal on the fifth floor. She had nothing more to say to Warren. She watched in stony silence as he dropped her carrier bags in the hall of number fifty-six and beat a swift retreat. This time she didn't even consider tipping him.

She slumped into the nearest chair. Any remaining hope that she might have been clinging to had been emptied from her.

FIVE

The setting up of the incident room at Bideford nick was already well under way by the time Vogel and Saslow arrived there just before nine thirty p.m. But then, the head of Devon and Cornwall Police's Major Crimes Team, Superintendent Nobby Clarke, had issued her instructions. And she was a woman who expected her every directive to be carried out both with alacrity and total efficiency.

The place and a number of the people were familiar to Vogel. He and Saslow had been seconded to North Devon a couple of years previously to investigate a suspicious death which had carried with it considerable local significance.

Now, and somewhat unexpectedly considering some of the events which had accompanied that investigation, he was permanently attached to the region's MCT and was in the process of looking for a home in North Devon for himself and his family. Hopefully on the coast, with which, also rather unexpectedly, he had fallen a little in love. Although he hadn't quite admitted it yet, not even to himself.

Vogel was London born and bred, and had spent the bulk of his career as a Met detective, based in the heart of the city. He remained unsure of exactly how he had come to be relocating for good, or certainly the foreseeable future, to a largely rural and curiously remote part of the world, only linked to the rest of the UK by a thoroughly ghastly road and an equally ghastly and inadequate rail service. But that's what he was doing. And he suspected the fresh sea air must be addling his brain, because he was more than a little looking forward to being settled there with his wife, his daughter and a beach-mad dog.

Vogel remembered Bideford nick well, a forbidding red-brick building, built on high ground opposite and above the River Torridge. He also remembered its access road, a disconcertingly steep ramp leading up from the riverside road, and its limited parking facilities. Vogel didn't much like motor cars or anything about them. Indeed, his ideal method of transportation would be to be beamed from one place to another, as in the American space fiction series *Star Trek*, his childhood favourite TV show.

The police station had been closed to the public for years, but local CID and Uniform still operated on a day-to-day basis behind its closed doors.

In many ways the old nick was ill-suited to house an operation the scale of which was now being launched within its towering walls. Major Crimes Team officers were busy slotting themselves in amongst the resident force members, and extra officers from other stations in the region were currently being assigned, in order to form a suitably sized team for a murder investigation.

Vogel's personal opinion might be that this particular investigation would not last long, but no force would launch an inquiry into a violent death based on that assumption. And he understood well enough Nobby Clarke's reasons for choosing Bideford police station as the inquiry's HQ. The only real alternative in the area would have been the Devon and Cornwall's major regional station in Barnstaple. And Nobby, like so many senior detectives, Vogel included, preferred, in the case of murder investigations in particular, to set up a separate Major Incident Room away from base and close to the location of the crime. The Bideford station was very nearly on the spot. Just ten minutes or so from St Anne's Avenue.

Vogel spotted DI Janet Peters, whom he knew Clarke had appointed deputy SIO and office manager, hurrying by, clipboard in one hand, phone in the other. Janet had played the same role in his previous North Devon murder investigation.

She looked slightly less dishevelled than he remembered. Her previously rather wild, dark-blonde hair was shorter than before, and shaped into a neat bob.

He had at first been a tad disappointed with her during their previous encounter, comparing her unfavourably, and probably unfairly, with the woman DI who had been his deputy on major inquiries throughout his time at MIT Bristol. But Janet Peters had grown on him. She had proven to be considerably better organized than she sometimes appeared, and both diligent and loyal, qualities Vogel always admired.

She did not notice him until he called out to her.

'Oh hi, boss, Saslow,' she said. 'Sorry. My mind's in a million places . . .'

'I'm sure it is,' Vogel replied. 'Everything seems to be coming together pretty well though?'

'Hopefully, boss. The boys and girls being sent up from Plymouth haven't arrived yet, mind. And I'm not entirely sure where I'm going to put them.'

DI Peters' easy smile somewhat belied her words, which might otherwise have indicated a degree of stress and anxiety. Vogel thought she had a pretty fair idea exactly what she was going to do with the Plymouth contingent. She seemed more relaxed under pressure than he remembered. Which was a good sign.

'You're in the same place as before,' she told Vogel. 'Not very big, but at least you get some privacy. I'll take you along there, then give you an update, if that suits.'

Vogel nodded his thanks.

With Saslow following closely, he and Peters had just reached his temporary office when a young man approached who Vogel also recognized from his previous Bideford-based investigation. The DC's appearance was quite memorable. He had very black hair and a long, thin, overly pale face well-suited to his more or less permanent worried expression. Vogel couldn't remember his name though. But he was saved from any potential embarrassment.

'Ricky Perkins, sir,' said the young man smartly. 'Good to be working with you again.'

Vogel nodded curtly. He was not, by nature, discourteous, but he had little time for niceties when embarking upon a murder investigation. Perkins did not seem to expect any further response.

'Thought you should know straight away, boss, and you, ma'am, just had a call from Morag Docherty at the hospital, apparently they're keeping Gill Quinn in overnight. She still hasn't spoken, or not to Morag, anyway.'

Vogel nodded. That was more or less what he had expected. But he had yet to receive an official report of the examination she would have received upon arrival at the NDDH.

'Did Docherty know if they'd found any sign of physical injury?'

'Yes, boss, she said to tell you they discovered signs of old bruising around her rib area, but Gill apparently said she'd hit the steering wheel doing an emergency stop. Nothing else, boss.'

Vogel was mildly surprised that Gill had volunteered any information at all, and hoped it augured well for his own interview at a later stage.

He thanked Perkins, who hurried back into the heart of the incident room.

Vogel turned to his deputy SIO. 'OK, DI Peters, we need a complete picture of this family as a matter of urgency,' he began. 'How are we getting on so far?'

'I'm not sure how much you know, boss . . .'

Vogel gave Peters a brief summary of the information Saslow had supplied earlier. Mostly concerning the professional lives of the Quinns.

'Gill Quinn is deputy headmistress actually, of Elm Tree Primary School, just along the road from here,' the DI pointed out.

Vogel was a little surprised. When Saslow had told him back at the scene that Gill was a teacher, he hadn't given it much thought. But now he had learned that she was a deputy head. It was difficult for him to imagine the woman he had earlier encountered holding down a position of any sort of responsibility. He had to remind himself that Gill Quinn, whether or not guilty of murder, had certainly been in a state of extreme shock.

'Gill and Thomas came to Bideford twenty years or so ago with their young son,' Peters continued. 'We've done all the usual checks, of course. Neither of them is known to us. Nothing to report beyond a couple of speeding tickets. It seems that Thomas had done pretty well for himself, as you know. They moved to

St Anne's Avenue nine years ago. Posh sort of place, as you'd have seen, boss. One of the best residential roads in the area. There doesn't seem to be any other family. Well, not local, that is. Not sure at all about Thomas, but it seems Gill has a sister, and her father is still alive. We're trying to trace them.'

'What about the son? He'd be in his twenties, wouldn't he? Didn't see any sign of him last night. Do we know whether or not he still lives at home?'

'He's twenty-three, boss,' responded DI Peters. 'Gregory Quinn, known as Greg. Seems he moved out some years ago, but he still lives locally. Educated at West Buckland School, one of the best public schools around here. Might have been expected to go to college or do something professional, I suppose. But he didn't. He works for Durrants, the builders.'

So in spite of his expensive education the young man hadn't followed his parents down an academic or professional route, Vogel pondered, wondering whether or not that was significant.

'Have we managed to get hold of Gregory?'

'We're still trying to contact him. We have a number for a mobile, but it seems to be switched off. We also have an address for him. He's not there, though.'

'What about Thomas' work colleagues?'

'There's a business partner, Jason Patel. An accountant by trade. Used to have a practice at the top of the High Street until he teamed up with Quinn a couple of years ago. More money, I should think. We'll be sending a team round to see him, and also the headmaster of Elm Tree, Gill's school.'

'And the door-to-door enquiries. Anything from that?'

'Not really, boss. No suggestion of any other disturbances, nothing about any trouble at home at all. Early days, of course, but the neighbours we've talked to so far seem by and large to have a good opinion of both. Expressed surprise that anything like this could happen, and so on. The only one who had anything constructive to say was the woman who lives opposite, Mavis Tanner, who reported some kind of row. But you know about that, don't you, boss.'

'Yes. She's the nearest thing we have to a lead at the moment. I may go round and see her myself tomorrow. What about reports of any comings and goings at the Quinn house yesterday?'

'Nothing at all, boss. But like most of the properties on that side of St Anne's Avenue, the Quinn house has a back entrance onto an alleyway which leads to a little park. There's garages and car parking there too. Seems the residents are inclined much of the time to use that route to access their properties, and it's all very secluded and private. Not overlooked at all.'

'Yet they have those impressive driveways and parking areas at the front,' interjected Saslow. 'Why don't they use those?'

'I think they're for show, Dawn. The residents of St Anne's Avenue certainly wouldn't want vehicles permanently parked outside the front of their houses. Any callers, apart probably from family and perhaps close friends, would more than likely use the front. But we have no reports yet of any callers today.'

'So, however much Mrs and Mrs Quinn may have been in and out of their house today, it's quite likely nobody would have seen them?' continued Saslow.

'That's right enough.'

'And no CCTV at the back, I don't suppose?' queried Vogel.

'None at all, boss. None along the road at the front either. Although a few of the houses have their own systems.'

'But not number eleven?' guessed Vogel, primarily because DI Peters had not already mentioned the possibility of any CCTV coverage.

'Indeed not, boss.'

Vogel was thoughtful. He was still fairly convinced that Gill Quinn, for whatever reasons, had murdered her husband, but he would have liked at least some evidence that wasn't circumstantial. At the moment their best hope of a quick conclusion seemed to be a confession, and he had no idea whether or not that was likely to be forthcoming.

His pondering was interrupted by the return of Perkins, looking as worried as ever.

'Excuse me, boss,' he said. 'Could I have a word with DI Peters?'

Vogel nodded, still wrapped up in his own thoughts.

'The extra desks have arrived, ma'am, where do you want us to put them?'

'I'll be with you in a minute, Ricky,' said Peters. 'Anything else, boss?'

'No,' said Vogel. 'Just keep me informed of all developments. Instruct the team too. Whatever time of the night anything significant comes in, I want to be notified at once.'

'Of course,' said DI Peters.

Vogel turned to Saslow.

'Well, nothing yet to indicate anything other than the obvious. And it doesn't look like we're going to get a chance to interview Gill Quinn until tomorrow morning at the earliest. So I suggest we spend an hour or two studying all the info that's been collated so far, and then pick up a takeaway and head back to our digs.'

Saslow said nothing, but looked distinctly cheered. Vogel knew she found the kind of hours he took for granted pretty hard sometimes. She was a woman who liked her sleep.

As they drove back to Barnstaple, Daisy Dobbs called from the morgue.

'I'm prepared to give you a tighter estimate of time of death, David,' she said, having clearly decided they should both be on Christian name terms. 'We've done all the possible tests now, and I reckon Thomas Quinn died between about three and five, probably nearer to three, only that's a bit of a guess.'

So all they needed to do now, Vogel considered, was to ascertain that Gill Quinn had been at her home within that time span and the case would be more or less completed.

SIX

It was a while before Lilian felt able to do anything to help herself. Eventually she called DS Pamela Mitchell, the detective who had visited her in hospital, the one with whom she had finally logged her formal complaint against Kurt, and the only police officer she'd had any dealings with who had shown her any real understanding. She told Mitchell about her finances being cut off and the visit from the goons.

The DS was as sympathetic as previously. There was however little more she could do, she said.

'Has your husband actually threatened you since the incident?' she asked, glossing over the matter of the truncated credit cards with merely a vague reference to financial affairs between married couples being a matter for the civil courts.

Lilian sighed inwardly. He hadn't threatened her, of course. Well, not in the way DS Mitchell meant, anyway. She ended the call.

The only direct approaches from Kurt during the last three weeks had been a succession of messages expressing undying love. It was impossible to explain to anyone, and certainly not a police officer, even a sympathetic one, just how threatening Lilian found those messages.

She had never before felt quite so desolate. Nor so alone. She had no family left worth mentioning. Few friends either. Not that she was in touch with, anyway. He had seen to that. Or to be fair, him and her pride. Her damned stupid pride.

She hadn't told anybody what was happening in her marriage. Not even Kate, her oldest and most dependable friend. Kate still called occasionally. And Lilian continued to lie to her.

Kate had left two messages on her mobile while Lilian was fighting for her life in her hospital bed.

When well enough to reply Lilian had called back and told her that she and Kurt had been travelling together in a remote part of Africa where her phone hadn't worked. Kate wanted to arrange lunch or a shopping expedition. Lilian had made excuses, as she had done so often before when in no fit state to meet anyone.

In the mirror on the far wall she caught a glimpse of a woman who was not only broken and bruised, but almost anorexic looking, with arms like sticks. The sleek, shoulder-length, reddish-blonde hair she had always considered one of her best points, freshly washed but unkempt, framed a painfully thin pale face, and haunted hazel eyes that seemed sunken in her flesh. Her abundance of freckles, which she now hated more than ever because Kurt had told her they were what had first attracted him to her, stood out starkly. She looked away quickly.

She hobbled into the kitchen and made tea and toast, which

she forced herself to eat. From the kitchen window she could see right across Berkeley Square, a small green oasis in the heart of the West End. A beautiful morning was beginning, in sharp contrast to the grey chill of the previous day. Sunlight laced through the plane trees, almost in full leaf. Already, though it was not long after nine, the life of the small park was in full swing. A boy and a girl sat wrapped around each other on the grass beneath a cherry tree in full blossom. A black Labrador cocked its leg dangerously close to them. They remained oblivious. Two children were running circles around each other, engrossed in some incomprehensibly wonderful game. This was such a familiar scene.

But the black Range Rover still lurked, parked illegally again almost directly opposite the entrance to Penbourne Villas. Of course, if she ever attempted to park there she'd have a ticket slapped on her windscreen almost instantly. But these guys . . . these guys were different. Those they couldn't bribe they would bully, she supposed. Pretty much like Kurt.

A man stepped out of the passenger side, leaned against the side of the car and lit a cigarette. He seemed familiar, but she couldn't quite see his face at first. Then he looked up. And she had a clear view of him.

She gasped, and stepped back into the room. It had seemed as if he was staring straight at her. She had recognized him at once. It was, without doubt, Kurt's brother William. He was a little shorter that Kurt and more thick set, with a distinctive shock of prematurely white hair. The family good looks had passed him by. He was heavy featured and had suffered a badly broken nose at some stage in his life, which did not help. She had, in some ways, always found him even more intimidating than Kurt. Kurt was the acceptable face of the St John business activities. Except, perhaps, in his dealings with her. William, who rarely left South Africa, ran the more nefarious side, of which she knew little, but had become increasingly aware of since her marriage. Cautiously she moved forward and peeped out of the window for a second look. The man was no longer leaning against the Range Rover, which remained parked in the same place. But it had been William, she was sure of it. And that meant even bigger trouble for her.

She at once called DS Mitchell again.

'Kurt's brother is here,' she began. 'William controls what the family call "security". He's usually in Johannesburg. I dread to think what it might mean for him to have come over here and be watching me. He's nothing but a thug, like the others. Only more powerful. They're sitting outside in their vehicle. Right beneath the flat. Can't you at least send somebody to make them go away?

'They're not breaking the law,' said the detective sergeant.

'Well, they are actually. They're illegally parked.'

DS Mitchell chuckled.

'All right, I'll speak to Uniform,' she said. 'I just wish I could do more, Lilian. As you know, we are seeking to arrest your husband on suspicion of causing grievous bodily harm. But until we can get to question Kurt, there's very little we can do.'

'And Kurt is safely in South Africa and will probably remain there until he and his lawyers have found a way of wriggling out of any charge at all. Which he will, by the way.'

'I don't see how.'

'You don't know him.'

'Look Lilian, we are in touch with the South African authorities over this, I'm sure it's just a matter of time . . .'

'You don't understand, Pam, do you? You really don't understand. Time is a luxury I do not have.'

She ended the call then. It was hopeless. She felt as if she were going around in circles, just like those children outside in the square. Only this was no game. The law, she was well aware, was at best cumbersome. From the moment a police investigation began, right through to the conclusion of a trial in a court of law. Even if eventually it lumbered its way to a fair result, it rarely did so at speed. And that alone could have disastrous consequences for Lilian.

She wondered how long she had. What would Kurt and William do next? They weren't the kind of men who did nothing. Just as she had told Pamela Mitchell, Kurt would have his lawyers on the case. If anyone could manipulate the law, it would be Kurt. And if anyone could strike even more fear in her heart than him, it was his brother.

She had told herself she was probably not in direct physical danger from Kurt. Not the way she had been. And, in any case, his attacks had always been provoked by aspects of his character which she sincerely hoped were no longer relevant in her life.

But the family goons had already been sent around to frighten her. They were not just outside in the street, but able to lurk in the corridors of Penbourne Villas, it seemed. And William St John, a man she believed capable of almost anything, and who she suspected rarely bothered even to pretend that he was operating inside the law, was with them.

She was trapped. Escape seemed impossible.

SEVEN

Vogel was woken by the shrill tone of his mobile at what seemed like the middle of the night. He checked the time as he answered it. It was actually five forty-five a.m. And the caller was Morag Docherty.

'It's Gill Quinn,' said the PC breathlessly. 'She's trying to discharge herself from hospital, I don't know what to do . . .'

'Stall,' replied Vogel, struggling to shake himself from a heavy sleep and make his brain work. 'There'll be paperwork. Do what you can to slow everything up . . .'

A thought occurred to him.

'Presumably she hasn't got any clothes?'

'No, boss. She's wearing a hospital gown. Her clothes have gone to Forensics. Anyway, they're covered in blood.'

'OK, tell her you're going to organize some fresh clothes for her. Then take your time.'

'Right, boss.'

'Saslow and I will be with you soonest. Just don't let her leave.'

'I'll try not to, boss.'

'Don't just try, Docherty. Make sure you succeed. Use your initiative.'

'Yes, boss.'

Vogel was temporarily staying at an Airbnb within walking distance of Barnstaple police station. As a city boy he had never felt the need to learn to drive, and had, until now, in spite of a certain pressure from his superiors in Bristol, continued to avoid doing so. But the move to North Devon was beginning to make it unavoidable. Even for Vogel. He liked to be as independent as possible, and without a motor car in that part of the world he was more reliant on others than he had ever been. He had signed up for driving lessons, but not even Saslow knew about that, and he hadn't actually started his course yet. So he suspected it would be some time before he was no longer reliant on her for transport.

He called Saslow, who had, rather to Vogel's surprise, welcomed the opportunity of moving to North Devon with him. She had, of course, been offered permanent promotion, from detective constable to sergeant, but Vogel also suspected that she had grasped the opportunity to escape from an unhappy love affair. Not that he knew for sure. Saslow always preferred to keep her private life just that.

The DS had already secured a short-hold tenancy on a terraced cottage on the outskirts of the town. Her phone rang several times, then switched to messages. He dialled again. She picked up on the second ring. In spite of sounding completely dopey, she was with him in twenty minutes. It took them only ten minutes more to reach the NDDH.

Morag Docherty greeted them at the entrance to the ward in which Gill Quinn had been persuaded to remain.

The DCI noticed that Morag was carrying a pair of trainers, which she put behind her back as they approached Mrs Quinn, who was sitting bolt upright on the edge of the bed nearest the door, feet on the floor, hands clasped in her lap. She showed no reaction at all as the three police officers entered, instead staring straight ahead just as she had done the last time Vogel saw her, at her home following her husband's murder.

She was wearing blue tracksuit bottoms and a brown top with orange flashes. Not only did they fail to go together as any kind of outfit, but neither did they fit. The top was too small, and the bottoms were too big.

These were presumably the clothes the hospital and Docherty had found for her.

'Hello again, Mrs Quinn,' said Vogel gently. 'I'm DCI Vogel. Do you remember me?'

Nothing.

'Are you feeling any better?'

Nothing.

'We really need to talk to you about what happened at your house yesterday,' he continued in the same tone of voice. 'Do you think you may be well enough to help me with that?'

Suddenly Gill Quinn looked directly at him.

'I need shoes,' she said. 'I want to go home.'

Her voice was toneless, staccato.

Vogel glanced down at the woman's bare feet. So, he thought, that was why Morag Docherty was carrying a pair of trainers behind her back. She certainly had used her initiative.

'I am afraid your home is a crime scene at the moment,' said Vogel. 'It is likely to be some days before you can return there.'

'I want to go home,' Gill Quinn repeated, still staring directly at Vogel, but with that same blank expressionless look in her eyes.

'Do you remember what happened at your house, what happened to your husband?' Vogel persisted.

Did the eyelids flicker? The DCI wasn't sure. But Gill made no attempt to answer his questions.

'You can't make me stay here,' she said.

'No, we can't,' Vogel agreed. 'But we can ask you to come to the station with us. We really do need to talk to you as a matter of urgency.'

'I want to go home,' said the woman for the third time.

'Mrs Quinn, that will not be possible . . .'

'Are you arresting me?' Gillian Quinn asked suddenly and quite sharply.

Perhaps she was coming back to life, thought Vogel. Or had her behaviour so far been an act? He hadn't thought so, but he had in the past experienced instances of some pretty impressive acting performances from suspects.

'No, I'm not arresting you,' he replied quietly. 'I am asking you to cooperate with us. We need to ascertain exactly how your husband died. And we do need to conduct a formal interview with you.'

'So, then can I go home?'

'I have explained.' Vogel paused. 'Do you mind if I call you Gill?' he asked.

Using Christian names is not uncommon practice in modern policing. All part of the process of building a relationship with a suspect. And most police officers would probably not even bother to ask. But Vogel was a naturally courteous man. Particularly when dealing with a woman who, whatever she may have done, was clearly vulnerable and in distress.

However, when there was no response, Vogel proceeded as if there had been.

'Your home is a crime scene, Gill. Is there anyone you can stay with? Your son perhaps—'

'No, not him,' Gill Quinn interrupted swiftly. 'He'll be angry . . .'

Vogel was taken by surprise. 'Why will he be angry?' he asked.

'He will be, that's all.'

'Have you tried to call him? Maybe to ask him to come and pick you up. Have you been in touch with him at all?'

Gill Quinn shook her head. 'I don't have my phone. I don't know where it is.'

'We have his number, would you like us to try to call him now.'

It was just before six thirty a.m. Gregory Quinn had not been answering his phone or responding to messages all night. It was probably unlikely that he would do so at this time of the morning. But Vogel wanted to show willing.

Gill shook her head again. 'I don't want him to know,' she said bluntly.

'You can't keep this from your son, Gill. Or indeed anyone else. You do understand that your husband is dead, don't you? That he has been murdered.'

The eyes went blank again.

'I don't know,' she said. 'I don't know anything.'

EIGHT

Lilian took to her bed for the best part of three days and three nights. She did not have the will to do anything else. She lost track of time. She had no wish to think about her past, and she could contemplate no future. Even sleep, frequently interrupted by nightmares, brought little respite. She rose from the bed only for calls of nature and, just occasionally, to nibble at some of the dwindling supplies she had bought on her visit to the twenty-four-hour shop. It appeared that she still had some survival instincts in place, in spite of having, perhaps almost wistfully, contemplated her available supplies of painkiller and other pills.

The doorbell rang several times. She ignored it. She had switched off her mobile, but the house phone rang regularly in the sitting room. She ignored that too. When she heard it, she could not think of anyone she wanted to see or speak to, and it could be Kurt calling.

Eventually, and somewhat to her surprise, Lilian finally felt a tweak of curiosity. She had disconnected the phone by the bed. She uncurled herself from the foetal position, sat up, swung her legs over the side, reconnected the phone, and dialled 1571, the answerphone service.

Seventeen missed calls and five messages were listed. Each one was from Kurt. Brief and apparently warm, but to her, absolutely chilling.

'Hello darling, welcome home.'

'Hello darling, so glad you're home. Can't wait to speak to you.'

'Sweetheart. I know you're there. Please pick up the phone. I miss you.'

'Hello sweetie. We need to talk.'

And finally and most chillingly: 'Hi darling. Sorry we can't speak. But I just wanted you to know I can't wait to see you.'

Lilian unplugged the phone again and checked her mobile. There was a long list of similar messages from Kurt sent whilst she had been in hospital, and her one reply, posted as soon as her phone was returned to her, telling Kurt that he should stay away from her, and that there was a warrant out for his arrest. Surprisingly perhaps, there appeared to be no more recent messages and no missed calls from Kurt or anyone else. She looked again, hastily pushing the phone's controls. There was no mistake. Her mobile had been cut off. The bill, of course, was paid by direct debit from her joint account with Kurt. Lilian felt numb.

She stood up. Kurt was all around her still. His power, if not his presence, was everywhere.

She had to leave this flat. That was for certain. A thought occurred to her. She hurried to the little desk in the sitting room. Her car key was still in the place she always kept it. That was a start. But would her car still be in the car park below the building? She should at least check that out. The lift went straight down to the car park.

She made her way to the door. Outside, placed in a neat line by the doorway, were three enormous bouquets of flowers, one looking quite fresh and the others in different stages of decay. They were, of course, from Kurt. The messages echoed those left on the answering service.

Lilian leaned out and picked up the flowers in one enormous armful. She stepped back into the flat pushing the door shut with her hip, then hobbled into the kitchen where she fed the flowers into the rubbish shoot, breaking and crushing the blooms in an almost savage frenzy.

NINE

Docherty and Saslow helped Gill Quinn put on the trainers the PC had been concealing. They appeared to fit rather better than the tracksuit. At least she'd be able to walk, thought Vogel. Assuming she was willing to do so.

Docherty looked all in. Unsurprisingly. She had taken Vogel's instruction to stick close to Gill Quinn quite literally, and stayed at the hospital all night. Vogel continued to be impressed by Morag Docherty.

For whatever reason, maybe because she had realized there was little alternative, Gillian Quinn appeared to have decided to cooperate. On the surface, at any rate. Certainly she seemed calm enough, outwardly at least, in stark contrast to how she had been the previous evening.

She allowed herself to be escorted out of the hospital without any further incident. And once she was safely installed in Saslow's car, illegally parked outside, Vogel felt able to release Docherty.

'Go home, get some rest, I'll square it with your sergeant,' he told her.

During the short drive to Barnstaple police station, Gill did not speak at all. Which suited Vogel. He preferred there to be no further conversation between them until he could begin a formal videoed interview.

It was vital to provide no opportunity for any evidence she might give to be declared invalid at a later date.

She was offered a solicitor upon arrival at the station. She declined.

'Why would I need a solicitor?' she asked.

Vogel studied her carefully. He didn't know what to make of that. Was she being disingenuous? She was a professional woman. She was not stupid. Perhaps she still wasn't in a fit condition to be interviewed. He dismissed that thought. He had an opportunity to interview his number one suspect without the presence of a solicitor. He was a decent man and a principled police officer, but he wasn't a saint.

Gill was therefore taken straight to an interview room where she was duly cautioned. Vogel had designated himself to lead the interview, aided by DS Saslow.

He began by asking Gill about her whereabouts on the previous day, particularly during the afternoon at around the time her husband was believed to have been killed.

'I don't remember,' she said.

'Well, did you go out at all, or were you at home all day?'

'I think I went out.'

'Where did you go?'

'I don't remember.'

Vogel consoled himself that at least the woman was speaking now. She was saying something. Even if it wasn't anything constructive. He persisted.

'Do you know what time you went out yesterday?'

'No.'

'Were you at home during the afternoon yesterday, before your husband died?'

'I'm not sure.'

Vogel paused and glanced towards Saslow, his look inviting the DS to join in. He certainly wasn't having any success. He wasn't sure if Gill Quinn was being deliberately obstructive, or if she was genuinely still in deep shock.

'Gill, we want to help you,' Saslow interjected. 'Really we do. But you do understand that we need to know everything that happened yesterday, don't you?'

Gill Quinn nodded slightly.

'We need you to answer for the record,' said Saslow.

'I understand,' said Gill Quinn.

'So, I will ask you again,' Saslow continued. 'Were you at home yesterday before, say, five p.m.?'

'I don't remember.'

'We know that you were at your home at six forty-one p.m. yesterday evening when you reported your husband's death. Can you remember if there was anyone else in your house with you at any stage, apart from you and your husband?'

'I don't know,' said Gill again.

Saslow continued with the gentle approach.

'If there was anyone else present at any time, or if you could remember when you were away from your house, and where you went, that would be very valuable information. Then we could work towards finding you somewhere to stay, and getting you the help you clearly need.'

Gill Quinn folded her arms tightly around her upper body and looked down at the table. She did not respond.

Vogel had had enough. He was beginning to distrust this woman, and it was time to do something about it. He was not necessarily a fan of the old good cop, bad cop routine. For a start he'd always regarded it as too darned obvious. But it had its uses on occasion. And this, he felt, might be one of those occasions.

'If you do not reply, then I can only assume that you were alone with your husband,' he said curtly. 'I need a full explanation from you concerning whatever may have happened in your home to lead to your husband's death. Do you understand me? And I need it now.'

Gill Quinn looked up. Her eyes were blank again. It really was impossible to work out what was going on behind them. She did not speak.

'You know how your husband died, don't you?' Vogel continued. 'I need you to tell me what happened, do you understand? Please answer me.'

Yet again there was no response. Vogel wasn't sure what further approach to take. The woman could well still be genuinely confused and in shock. But this was a murder investigation. He decided to proceed on the basis that one way to deal with shock was to meet it with further shock. At least that way he might get some sort of a response.

He raised his voice considerably, which was unusual for Vogel.

'You must know that your husband was stabbed violently, several times. You do know that, don't you?' he began. 'Eleven times actually. He suffered cataclysmic knife wounds to his belly, upper torso, and to his throat. A blade entered the base of his throat just below the larynx and slashed open the jugular. He would have bled to death from that wound alone. There was no need for any further wounds to be inflicted. But his attacker was clearly in a frenzy, out of control . . .'

Gill Quinn shut her eyes, blocked her ears, then lowered her head almost onto the table.

'I need you to listen to me, Gill,' continued Vogel. 'And I need you to cooperate with me, for your own good.'

Gill remained silent, sitting quite still, her head still bowed.

'If you do not answer my questions I can only assume that you have reasons for not wishing to do so,' continued the DCI sternly. 'And I suspect those reasons might incriminate you. We are getting close to my being left with no alternative but to arrest you on suspicion of the murder of your husband.'

Gill raised her head, unblocked her ears and opened her eyes. From the expression on her face, Vogel suspected that she had heard him well enough, in spite of the blocked ears.

'Shall we try again?' asked Vogel. 'Starting right at the beginning. Let's go through your movements yesterday. You said that you think that you went out, but that you could not remember where you went. Can you remember when you left the house?'

Again Gill remained silent.

'Are you sure you did leave the house?'

Nothing.

Vogel repeated some more of his earlier questions. These were also answered only with silence, and indeed no visible response at all.

Vogel was frustrated. His earlier shock approach had met with at least some response, if not that which he had hoped for. He decided to really go for it. This interview had ground to a halt. It seemed he had little to lose.

'Gill, did you kill your husband?' he asked abruptly. 'Did you attack him with a knife and inflict multiple stab wounds? Did you continue to stab him repeatedly until you were sure that he was dead? Did you kill Thomas, Gill?'

For a few seconds the woman remained silent and failed to respond in any way. Her facial expression did not change.

Then suddenly she opened her mouth. It was almost as if her jaw dropped without her control.

And she began to scream at the top of her voice.

TEN

It was just after two thirty in the morning when Lilian made her move. She had once read that we are all at our lowest ebb at around that time. She hoped that was true of those who were watching her.

Curiously perhaps, Lilian had felt much calmer once she'd so violently disposed of Kurt's flowers. Maybe it was because she had vented some of her inner fury.

She'd also realized that her ankle was throbbing less. All that bed-rest had probably helped her injuries, if nothing else. She took one of Kurt's collection of ornate walking sticks from the stand in the hall and experimented with putting more weight on her plaster-cast leg.

She'd decided there could be no trial run, no rehearsal. If her car wasn't in the car park then that would be the end of her immediate plan of escape. But she couldn't risk destroying any element of surprise.

She hoisted a rucksack, packed with as many of her things as she could carry, over her shoulders. It left her arms free, and she still needed at least the support of a walking stick.

Even without crutches her progress seemed to her to be both clumsy and excessively noisy. She clumped her way across the polished floor towards the front door. In the hallway she hesitated. The little Hockney she'd always admired, with its trademark swimming pool, adorned the far wall above the consul table in solitary splendour. What would it be worth? Fifty thousand pounds? One hundred thousand pounds? More? Lilian wasn't sure, but whatever the figure was, Kurt St John owed her one heck of a lot more.

Impulsively she took the Hockney off the wall and tucked it into the front pocket of her rucksack, wrapping a sweater around it to keep it safe.

She opened the door as quietly as possible and made her way to the lift, grateful that the communal areas of Penbourne Villas were thickly carpeted. There was no sign of the goons. Or of William. She pushed the button for the basement car park. It was brightly lit down there as usual. She could see at once that her car was still parked in the place where she'd left it.

She was relieved and mildly surprised. Had Kurt overlooked the car? She doubted that. Or did he just trust his brother and the goons – not to mention the basketball player who she was quite sure was on the St John payroll – to keep her under surveillance.

It made no difference. The customized top-of-the range BMW, white with red leather upholstery, represented the only hope of escape that she could think of. Kurt had presented it to her soon after their wedding, gift-wrapped and encircled with an enormous golden ribbon tied in a bow. At the time she had thought it incredibly romantic. Now the mere sight of the car sickened her. The BMW was a talisman of all that had happened. Top of the list of expensive gifts her husband had used to try to buy her body and soul, and perhaps to salve his own conscience. If he had one.

She bleeped the key. The car blinked its lights at her. She climbed in and turned on the ignition, grateful both that the vehicle was an automatic and that it was her left ankle which had been broken. She switched on and glanced at the petrol gauge. Almost half a tank. Enough fuel to take her a fair distance away. Could have been better, but it also could have been worse.

Once at the top of the ramp, she put her foot down, shooting along Berkeley Street and swinging an illegal right onto Piccadilly. She smacked the car round Hyde Park Corner, roaring up Park Lane, round Marble Arch and along the Edgware Road. Even in central London there was not much traffic at that hour in the morning. Traffic lights and road junctions she more or less ignored, keeping an eye out for traffic police, who seemed in any case to have been more or less taken over by CCTV cameras nowadays. And she really didn't care a jot about those.

She was vaguely aware once or twice of lights in her rear mirror, perhaps a suspiciously steady distance behind, and of at least one vehicle following her through at least one set of red lights. But she had a plan to shake off anyone who might be tailing her.

Once she hit the M1 Lilian let rip. She pushed the car as fast as it would go, exceeding a hundred and twenty miles per hour at one point. At the first turning after the M25 she swung abruptly off the motorway, then round the roundabout and on to the bridge over the M1 where she slowed almost to a stop. There seemed to be nothing following her. At a more restrained speed she pulled back onto the London-bound stretch then turned right onto the M25 and ultimately the M4.

Lilian was heading west. She was going to Bristol. Apart from her long-gone little flat in Chiswick, Bristol, where she'd been brought up by her single-parent mother, was the only place she'd ever thought of as home.

Lilian's mother had died the year before she met Kurt, one of the many reasons, perhaps, why Lilian had been so catastrophically eager to create a family for herself. But Bristol remained her first thought as a place of refuge.

There was certainly nowhere else.

ELEVEN

Vogel didn't move. In fact, he froze. It was obviously not the first time he had been confronted by a hysterical witness or suspect. But he never got any better at dealing with it. He was, of course, not much good at dealing with any overt displays of emotion.

Also, he suspected that on this occasion Gill Quinn's outburst of hysteria had been at least partially his fault.

Saslow, conversely, had always seemed to be good at that sort of thing. Thank God, thought Vogel.

The DS moved fast, propelling herself up out of her chair and around the table which separated the two officers from their suspect. Then she just wrapped her arms right around Gill, rather startling Vogel. Rightly or wrongly, social distancing rules had ended in the UK, and masks were no longer required by law in England, but the pandemic was far from over worldwide.

'It's all right,' she said. 'You're still in shock. You'll feel better soon. Things will be clearer . . .'

PC Jack Porter, the uniformed constable on sentry duty at the door, stepped forward, looking as if he was ready to help. Vogel stood up, stepped sideways, and moved slightly closer to the two women. But he had no intention of touching Gill Quinn.

Saslow continued to speak softly. Eventually, and it felt like a very long 'eventually' to Vogel, Gill stopped screaming. Then she buried her head in Saslow's shoulder and began to sob. Her shoulders heaved. She seemed to be gasping for breath.

Vogel turned to PC Porter.

'We'd better get a doctor in here,' he said. 'Soonest.'

The PC turned and headed back to the door. As he opened it, DC Perkins entered, then stopped abruptly, as if mesmerized by the sobbing woman before him.

'What is it, Perkins?' Vogel snapped, displaying none of his usual patience.

'C-could I have a word with you outside, boss?' the young DC asked, stumbling slightly over his words.

Vogel followed him into the corridor.

'We've made contact with Gregory Quinn, the son, boss, and . . .' Perkins began, then he paused, clearly agitated, and also distracted by the sounds of sobbing which could still be heard clearly through the closed door.

'C'mon, lad, spit it out,' instructed Vogel.

'Sorry, boss. Well, when told of his father's death, he seemed more concerned about his mother apparently. We had to tell him where she was, and he's on his way here. He's been informed that we couldn't even guarantee he could see his mother. But he was quite determined. Apparently he spent the night in Torrington with a mate. They went out drinking and he had a skinful. That's what he says, anyway. Don't think he'll be long. Sorry, boss . . .'

'Don't be sorry, Perkins. He may be just what we need . . .'

'Really, boss?'

'Yes. We can't keep Gill Quinn here much longer. Not in the state she's in. She needs medical attention, and in any case she's not telling us anything. But she can't go home, that's for sure. Not to a crime scene. Perhaps young Greg will take his mother home with him. That would probably be the best result.'

'Will you be wanting to interview him, boss?'

'At some stage, of course. Partly depends how his mother is by the time he gets here. And if we've got that doctor here by then . . .'

As if on cue PC Porter arrived with a woman Vogel did not recognize and who, rather to Vogel's surprise, the PC introduced as Dr Louise Lamey. How on earth had they got a doctor here that fast, wondered Vogel.

'Dr Lamey was already in the station,' Porter explained, almost as if he had read the DCI's mind. 'Custody were anxious about the condition of a drunk driver arrested in the early hours. He kept throwing up apparently, all over the—'

'Thank you Porter, I can do without the intimate details,' interrupted Vogel.

He turned to the doctor and told her how glad he was to see her, then escorted her into the interview room.

Gill Quinn had stopped sobbing into Saslow's shoulder, and the

DS had moved back to the safety of her chair on the other side of the table. Somebody had provided Gill with a box of paper hankies and she was blowing her nose loudly. She certainly looked calmer, but Vogel could see that her hands were shaking.

Dr Lamey pulled up a chair next to Gill, introduced herself and asked if it was all right to examine her. Gill made no objections.

Dr Lamey took Gill's temperature and blood pressure, listened to her heart, looked into her eyes, and asked her some basic questions about how she felt, which, again rather to Vogel's surprise, Gill Quinn answered, albeit in a monosyllabic fashion.

When the doctor had finished she moved to leave the room, gesturing for Vogel to follow her.

'Severe shock, as I'm sure you realize,' she began once the two of them were outside. 'And before you ask, no reason to doubt that it's anything but completely genuine. Her heart is racing, her skin is clammy, and her breathing is not quite as it should be. I'm going to prescribe a mild sedative. What she needs now is rest. A good long sleep. Are you keeping her in?'

Vogel shook his head. 'We don't intend to, no. We're nowhere near ready to charge her. We need to question her further, but at the moment we can't get anywhere with her.'

And I don't want her passing out on us, or worse, he thought, although he didn't say it. Vogel had never had a suspect die in custody or while being questioned, but he knew of it happening. It was something he had no wish to experience.

'Neither are you likely to get anywhere with her for the time being,' commented the doctor. 'Not until sleep has hopefully worked its magic. My advice to you is to send her home and give her at least twenty-four hours rest before you approach her again.'

If only, thought Vogel. But all he said was: 'Thank you, doctor.'

Perkins was not in sight. Vogel called him to check if Gill's son had arrived.

'Apparently he's just walked into the front office,' said Perkins. 'I'm on my way there. What do you want me to do with him?'

'Is there another interview room free?'

'I think so, yes, boss.'

'Good. Get it set up. I think I'll have a chat with young Mr Quinn straight away.'

Vogel delegated PC Porter, an officer approaching retirement who gave the impression that he'd seen it all before and nothing was going to faze him, to look after Gill. The DCI hoped that there would be no further outbursts from her, but reckoned there was probably no one better than Porter to play nanny.

He took Saslow with him to assist in the interview with Gregory, or Greg, Quinn.

Quinn was a handsome young man. Even Vogel noticed that. He was sitting at the table in the middle of the little room, but he stood when the two officers entered. He was exceptionally tall, probably six foot three or four, broad-shouldered, and with the naturally well-muscled look of a man who earned his living primarily by means of manual labour.

He had blonde hair which fell almost to his shoulders, perhaps unfashionably long in the present day and age, and a smattering of designer stubble, which, conversely, was fashionable. Tediously fashionable, Vogel often thought. And not always attractive. In his opinion Greg Quinn would look even more handsome without it.

The young man's features were even and chiselled. His eyes very blue and bright. They were also full of concern.

'Thank you for coming—' Vogel began.

Quinn interrupted him at once. His voice was not entirely level. 'I want to know what's going on,' he said, a sweep of one arm taking in what was clearly a formal interview room furnished with full video equipment.

He was well spoken, a legacy of that public-school education Vogel assumed, but with just a hint of Devon burr.

'I came here to get my mother,' Greg Quinn continued. 'Why've I been put in here? Am I a suspect or something, for God's sake? I just want to see my mother.'

'And so you shall, very soon,' said Vogel. 'But I do need to talk to you, Greg.'

Obliquely Vogel realized he had automatically addressed the young man by his first name without asking permission to do so. He really was youthist, he thought.

'We would have sought you out sooner or later, if you had not been kind enough to come in, talked to you at your home, first up, more than likely,' he continued. 'But as you are here, well I thought we would take the opportunity for an on-the-record chat. Quite a few points we rather hope you might be able to help us clear up. That's all.'

There was a brief silence before Quinn spoke again.

'Am I entitled to a solicitor?' he asked.

Vogel very deliberately raised both eyebrows. 'If you wish. Yes. Of course you are.'

'But I'm not a suspect?'

'You are merely helping us with our enquiries, Greg,' responded Vogel, deliberately dodging the question. In a murder investigation, everyone with even a tenuous connection with the deceased is a suspect, in the first instance at any rate. And family topped the list.

If Quinn realized that the issue had been avoided, he gave no sign of it.

'OK then, let's get on with it, shall we,' he said, as he lowered himself into his chair again.

'To begin with, Greg, may I say how sorry I am for your loss, and under such dreadful circumstances,' said Vogel. 'I don't expect this to take long.'

The young man merely nodded in response, but just a little of the tension seemed to leave him.

'I wondered if I could ask you to begin with, when you last saw your father?'

Greg looked mildly taken back. Almost as if he hadn't expected that question, even though to Vogel it was an obvious one in the case of a violent death.

'Uh, I'm not sure,' Greg Quinn muttered.

Vogel waited.

'Umm, about a month ago,' he continued after a short pause. 'Maybe a bit more.'

'And where did you see him?'

'Where? Um. Well, it was outside the yard. Where I work. I was having a smoke. He came by in his car, saw me, and stopped.'

'Right. So did he park? Get out of his car? Or did you get in?'

'What? With a fag in my hand? Are you kidding? He'd have gone mad. We just passed the time of day. That was it, really. Anyway the Northam bus came up behind him, and he had to pull away.'

Greg paused.

'Look. I want to see my mother. I'm worried sick about her.

She shouldn't be here. I mean, you can't keep her. Unless you've arrested her. Have you arrested her?'

'No, Greg. Your mother has not been arrested. She is helping us with our enquiries voluntarily. But actually, until we succeeded in contacting you, we were not in touch with anyone who might be able to take care of her, and we were unaware of anywhere else she could go. Your family home is a crime scene, as I'm sure you would expect. Also, we could not let her leave here until she had seen a doctor, which she now has.'

'A doctor? What's wrong. I-is she all right?'

Greg was a picture of filial concern.

'Your mother is in a state of extreme shock, Greg. The doctor has prescribed a mild sedative, and says that what she needs is rest—'

'I'll make sure she gets it,' interrupted Greg. 'She can stay at my place. For as long as she needs to. I'll sleep on the sofa.'

'That's good,' remarked Vogel. 'I'd appreciate it though if you would answer just a few more questions before you leave. It might save us bothering you later.'

Greg nodded his agreement.

'Good,' said Vogel again. 'So, could you please tell me when you last saw your mother?'

'Uh yes. It was a couple of days ago.'

'And where was that?'

'I met her after work. There's a café we go to. It's not far from her school. We go there quite often.'

'But you didn't see your father?'

'Uh, no.'

'So, presumably you didn't go back to the family home with your mother. Is that right?'

'That's right. I didn't go back. I don't . . . umm, you see . . .'

Greg Quinn looked as if he were about to say more. But he didn't.

He lived just a few miles from his parents' home. He had spent time with his mother only two days previously, and indicated that he saw her frequently. But not usually at the family home, it seemed. He had not seen his father for a month, and then only fleetingly. Vogel had noticed how even the tone of the young man's voice changed when he referred to each of his parents.

'Might I ask what sort of relationship you had with your father, Greg?' Vogel continued.

Greg Quinn took a moment or two reply. When he did so he shrugged his shoulders and held his hands out palm up.

'It's no secret,' he said. 'We didn't get on.'

'I see. Might I ask why?'

Quinn shrugged again.

'Oh you know, fathers and sons. To begin with, he couldn't stand it that I work as a builder, even though he started out on a market stall and doing odd jobs, for God's sake. He'd become a bit of a snob, I suppose. Thought it was beneath him. Him being this high-flying businessman, and all.'

Vogel thought there was more than a hint of sarcasm in Quinn's voice when he delivered his final few words. The DCI took note but made no comment.

'I see,' he continued. 'Did you argue about that?'

'No. Not any more. I moved out when I was seventeen, as soon as I could leave school and get a job. Since then I've avoided him. I've only ever gone to the house when I've known he wasn't there.'

'That sounds pretty extreme, Greg.'

'Not really. He didn't like me, and I didn't like him. That's all.'

'Perhaps you could tell me what sort of relationship your parents had? How did they get on? Were they happy?'

'I dunno. I didn't take much notice. They'd been married nearly twenty-four years. They must have got on OK, I suppose.'

'Are you absolutely sure you didn't see either of your parents yesterday?'

'Yes. Of course I'm sure.'

'And are you sure that you didn't go to your family home at any time yesterday, if only to see your mother?'

'Yes, I'm sure of that too. I didn't go near the place. Look, what is this? Whatever you say, you're treating me like a suspect. Do you really think I killed my father?'

'We just need you to help us with our enquiries, Greg. As I told you. And we are grateful to you for doing so.'

Greg Quinn stood up again, drawing himself up to his full height.

'Right,' he said. 'I presume I'm free to leave then, am I? And can I please take my mother with me.'

Vogel answered both questions in the affirmative.

'DC Perkins will take you back to the waiting area in the front office,' he said. 'And I'll have your mother brought to you.'

After Quinn had departed, escorted by Perkins, as Vogel had instructed, the DCI turned to Saslow.

'Well, what do you make of that, Dawn?' he asked. 'A father and son who apparently loathed each other.'

'I suppose it's another factor,' responded Dawn Saslow. 'But motive for murder? Greg moved out years ago. Has his own life presumably. Why would he kill his father now?'

'I don't know, Dawn, and I suppose it is unlikely,' Vogel agreed. 'But maybe he's lying, maybe he did go round to St Anne's Avenue yesterday, found his father at home, and they had some sort of row that got out of hand. Remember the evidence of that neighbour, Mavis something . . .?'

'Mavis Tanner,' Saslow supplied.

'Yes. She said she heard a row going on at about the time we believe Thomas Quinn was killed. She thought it was a man and a woman, but maybe that's partly because it's what she would have expected. Greg has quite a high-pitched voice, certainly for a big man. Perhaps Thomas said something that made him lose control. He picked up the nearest weapon, and years of anger and frustration just boiled over.'

'Possible, boss. Obviously. But you and I both know that Gill Quinn has to be the most likely suspect. No reason at all so far to believe this is anything other than a marital domestic. She's the one with maximum opportunity. We don't know about motive yet. But there'll be something, I expect. There usually is, within a marriage. Whether or not enough to kill for, well . . .'

Saslow was interrupted by the somewhat clumsy return of DC Perkins, who tripped over his own feet in his haste to enter the room.

'There's been a development, boss,' he began, his voice and manner both considerably more animated than previously. 'We've had a call from Helen Harris. Said she has important information regarding the Quinn case. Do you know who she is, boss?'

Vogel nodded. 'Yes, I do.'

He could feel a little shiver of interest running up and down his spine.

'So what did she have to tell us, Perkins?' he asked.

'She wouldn't say, boss, only that she wanted to speak to someone in authority.'

Vogel grunted. He would have expected little else.

In the short time since he had become permanently stationed in North Devon, Vogel had already had dealings with Helen Harris. She was well known amongst police as well as medical personnel in the area.

She ran the high profile and innovative Helen's House, a refuge and support centre for abused women – based on Sarah's House in Arizona, the groundbreaking leader in its field which provides legal advice, medical care, and sheltered accommodation for abused women; all under one roof and largely provided by professionals. Like Sarah's House, Helen's House worked closely with the authorities in the region, and even sent representatives to scenes of domestic abuse along with the police and other emergency services.

Vogel's previous encounter with Helen Harris had not been concerned with a live case, but rather at his first meeting of the regional police liaison committee which met periodically with social services, medical professionals, and others, to discuss what could be done to improve and develop procedure in what remained a vexed area of policing.

Such meetings might not immediately seem to fall within Vogel's remit, but the chief constable of the Devon and Cornwall force believed in prevention rather than cure, whenever possible. He expected MCT officers, and indeed representatives of almost all areas of policing, to make occasional appearances.

'He's got a point, Vogel,' Nobby Clarke had told him. 'After all, the vast majority of the major crimes of violence which we are called in to investigate are domestics of some kind.'

Vogel had instinctively taken a liking to Helen Harris, and quickly developed considerable respect for the work she seemed devoted to. She was bang up to date too, and had talked at length at that meeting about the effect of Covid, when couples and families had been forced to isolate and turn in on themselves for long periods of time, resulting in a sharp national increase in incidents of domestic violence.

'Well then, you'll have a good idea why she's called in, boss,' Perkins continued. 'It can only mean one thing, surely?'

Vogel was inclined to agree. If Helen Harris was in any way involved in this case, then the implications were pretty obvious. And if she had called in with information, then it would undoubtedly be important. She certainly wasn't a time waster. She wanted to speak to someone in authority. And Vogel wanted to speak to her.

'I'll talk to her myself,' he told Perkins.

'Right, boss. Shall I ask her if she can come in?'

Vogel shook his head.

'No. I'll go to her. I don't want to start by ordering her about, and I've never been to Helen's House. If there's any involvement there, I'd like to check the place out myself.'

He did know vaguely where the House was. In Bideford, in the area known as the top of the town.

'Tell her I'll be there within the hour,' he said. 'Saslow, with me. Perkins, speak to DI Peters. We should appoint a family liaison officer. Gill's husband has been murdered, and we do not yet know who the murderer is. We should remember that.'

Perkins looked slightly nonplussed. As well he might. Everything about the case so far, Gill Quinn's behaviour, the way in which she had reported her husband's death, and all the circumstantial evidence, indicated that the woman was guilty of his murder. And if Helen's House was involved in any way that surely added to the probability.

Vogel was not a man who was inclined to count his chickens. Nonetheless he could feel the pieces of the jigsaw beginning to fall into place in his head. And he strongly suspected that his imminent meeting with Helen Harris was going to be vital.

'OK, Perkins, get on with it,' he instructed. 'There's more than one reason for appointing a FLO, as you know. I'd like someone keeping a very close eye on both mother and son. Don't forget, Greg Quinn also seems to have a possible motive. Tell DI Peters I want both of them kept on our radar twenty-four-seven.'

'Got it, boss,' said Perkins, as he turned rather more smartly on his heels, and made his way out of the room without further incident.

TWELVE

It was around four thirty in the morning when Lilian arrived on the outskirts of the ancient West Country sea-port city. She stopped at a service station, put twenty pounds worth of petrol in the now extremely thirsty motor car, and bought herself coffee and sandwiches.

Maybe it was the adrenalin of doing something at last, but for the first time, not only since leaving hospital but actually since the night it had all happened, she felt genuinely hungry.

She was heading for the Westbury Park area of Bristol. Her married cousin, Laura Beggs, whom she had once been close to, lived there. The two women had grown out of touch, and Lilian no longer had a phone number for Laura. Neither, of course, did she have a phone – something she needed to rectify as soon as she managed to raise some funds. But many years ago she'd visited the house which she knew remained to be Laura's home because they did still send each other Christmas cards.

There was no one else she could think of who she could possibly turn to.

She skirted Bristol city centre using the inner ring road. At Clifton she turned off towards the famous old suspension bridge, parked by the visitors centre and walked along the bridge clutching her coffee and sandwiches. It was still far too early to go calling on anyone. Dawn was just beginning to break on what promised to be a beautiful day.

Lilian leaned against the safety fence on the city side of the bridge. Bristol lay before her, a still sleeping city. She could see the old docks, with their modern state-of-the-art residential developments, the huge lock gates and the floating harbour. She shifted her glance, looking downwards. The Avon, like a shiny black snake, wound its way along the gorge two hundred feet below. The Brunel designed triumph of nineteenth-century engineering upon which she stood was frequently used in suicide attempts. And anyone jumping from it was almost certain to succeed in their aim.

Lilian felt strangely grateful that the moment when, in such an opportune situation, she might well have taken her own life had passed.

She no longer wished to die. She was determined to live. But without Kurt. She just needed a place of refuge for a few weeks.

She'd had a career once, in magazine journalism, which she had ultimately found disappointing and had readily abandoned for Kurt. How glad she would be for the chance to return to it now. Apart from any other considerations she had no money. She was sure a husband wasn't allowed to just cut off his wife financially the way Kurt had done, and there must be a way of clearing funds. But how long would it take? Even if she could afford legal help.

She allowed herself to fantasize, just for a moment, that Kurt would be arrested, tried and imprisoned. It was the only real path of escape she could imagine.

Meanwhile she could do no more than take things by stages.

She fleetingly wondered just how pleased cousin Laura would be to see her, beaten up and bringing with her such awful problems, but Lilian did not think she would turn her away.

She glanced at her watch. It was still not yet six a.m., but she decided to find her way to Laura's house, in a tidy suburban cul-de-sac called Clarke Close, and wait there until an acceptable calling time. Laura and her husband had twin daughters, who Lilian reckoned would be nine or ten now and at school. So surely it would not be too long before the family would be up and about and preparing for the school run.

Just before eight a.m., which seemed like a respectable hour, she approached the front door of her cousin's house, a freshly painted semi with a neatly bordered front garden. The place seemed suspiciously quiet. There were no windows open and no vehicles in the driveway.

She rang the bell. Once, twice, three times. There was no reply. She walked around the gravelled path to the back of the house. She had not really expected to find the family breakfasting on the lawn, even though it was such a lovely morning, but it had been worth a try.

With a sinking heart she retraced her steps, back around the house and down the driveway towards her car. Stupidly perhaps, she'd just expected Laura, with her young family and working husband, to be at home.

Then it hit her. The previous day had been the last Monday in May. Of course. The Whitsun bank holiday and school half-term. It may have meant nothing to her, but the Beggs' family were quite probably taking a holiday. They could be away for the rest of the week.

She was glumly wondering what to do next when, just as she reached the pavement, he stepped out in front of her. At first she didn't realize what was happening. She tried to move to one side, apologizing, like you do when you almost bump into someone. If you're English anyway.

Then she realized the man must have been waiting for her, concealed by the high garden wall of her cousin's property. He was tall and well built. His hair and beard both very dark. The wrong colour for Kurt St John. His eyes were dark too. Also the wrong colour for Kurt St John.

All the same, it was him.

And Lilian had no idea why she was surprised.

She had known he was going to find her sooner or later, hadn't she? She'd known that he would come for her, wherever she was and whatever obstacles she and the forces of law had appeared to put in his way.

She just hadn't expected him to catch up with her this quickly, and he was supposed to be out of the country. Also she was sure she had shaken off William and the goons on that mad rush out of London, and that she had covered her tracks. She hadn't even left a paper trail. Indeed she hadn't been able to leave a paper trail as all her credit cards had been cancelled.

He stretched out a hand, placing it lightly on her left arm.

'Don't be afraid, my darling. I'm so sorry I hurt you so badly. That will never happen again.'

He smiled at her. The same smile she'd once found so utterly disarming. Now it just filled her with dread.

She tried to step back from him, shaking her head.

His fingers closed around her upper arm, their tips digging into the flesh. Her body remembered all the pain he had caused it. Remembered too that the more she resisted the worse it always was. That is what had happened the last time. The only time he had actually inflicted any damage other than superficial bruising and a twisted wrist or two.

She felt herself weaken. Felt her will leaving her. Felt her limbs begin to dissolve to jelly.

'How . . . how?'

She couldn't even get the words out. But he knew what she meant. She saw his glance shift briefly to the BMW and then back again to her. Of course. How could she have been so stupid? How could she have thought that he would take a chance on her getting away that easily. It was no accident that her car had been just waiting for her to drive it away from the one place even Kurt would not dare turn up at with the police looking for him, his own apartment. She had played right into his hands. He had put a tracker on her car. She should have realized that, bizarrely, she had probably been safer at Penbourne Villas than anywhere.

It was too late now.

'My darling Lilian,' he murmured softly. 'I just want to talk, that's all.'

She just wanted to run. Oh, she so wanted to run. However, she only had one fully functional leg. In any case she assumed he would have that option covered. She glanced around her. A black Range Rover, almost certainly the one which had stalked her in London, was parked at an angle at the end of the cul-de-sac, half blocking the road. She could see the shapes of two heads inside.

Kurt was still talking.

'I have a room in the best hotel in town. Won't you come there with me? We could have breakfast. Smoked salmon and scrambled eggs, your favourite. And maybe some champagne? Anything you want, you know how I like to spoil you . . .'

His voice droned on. He was smiling all the time. He began to stroke the side of her face with his free hand. The grip of his right hand on her upper arm did not loosen.

How had he dared to flout the law the way he had? He'd not only disguised himself, but, presumably, entered the country under a false passport. Or maybe, in spite of what the authorities believed, he had never left. She had been well enough aware of his obsession with her, his only weakness he always called it. How could she have underestimated it – and him – so? He regarded her as his property. Property he had come to reclaim.

'We need to spend some time together, just you and me, time to rebuild our marriage,' he continued, his tone soft and wheedling. 'I want you to let me show you how much I care—'

She interrupted him. Her voice sharp, louder than she had meant it to be.

'You bugged my car,' she yelled at him.

The smile faltered. Just for a second. He didn't bother to deny it. Well, there wouldn't have been any point, would there? He just continued as if she hadn't spoken. Only someone who knew him as well as she did would notice that the smile was now forced, and that his manner had grown that bit more assertive.

'The room is all ready for us, sweetheart. Why don't we go there now?'

It wasn't really a question and certainly not an invitation.

He placed a strong arm around her shoulders, and in one fluid movement began to usher her towards the Range Rover.

'My c-car. M-my bag . . .'

She stumbled over the words.

'The boys will look after that,' he said, reaching with his free arm to take the keys to the BMW from her.

She did not attempt to resist. She knew there was little point.

THIRTEEN

Helen's House was a rambling Edwardian semi, one of a number in a tree-lined street of similar properties. But there the similarities ended.

Whereas the others were immaculately cared for, clearly the homes of the more well-off amongst Bidefordians, Helen's House looked as if it could do with a coat of paint, at least two panes of glass, visible at the front of the house, were cracked, and its garden displayed none of the lavish and exquisitely cared-for horticulture of its neighbours.

Vogel knew that the refuge had been established almost twenty years previously, and he suspected that it may not have been a welcome addition to this part of town.

It disturbed him somewhat that in modern and allegedly enlightened times such a place remained necessary. And in a quiet country town like Bideford, too.

He was unsure whether the small, thin, bird-like woman with cropped dark hair who answered the door was a member of staff or a resident. She was not particularly welcoming. Nor did she appear at all surprised, or indeed much concerned, by a police visit. But then, Helen's House provided refuge from violence. Sometimes extreme violence. And that was in itself likely to not infrequently call for a police presence.

The two officers were immediately led to a small, cluttered first-floor office at the back of the house. Helen Harris was sitting before a computer in front of a narrow window which provided an unexpectedly spectacular slice of view over the roofs of Bideford and the River Torridge.

She stood up as the two officers entered. She recognized Vogel at once.

'Mr Vogel,' she said, by way of greeting.

She glanced enquiringly towards Saslow, whom the DCI introduced, before explaining that he was SIO of the Quinn investigation.

'I understand that you have information which you think might help us in our enquiries,' he remarked.

'Yes I do, although I'm not sure quite how helpful you will find it,' responded Helen Harris evenly, sitting down again, and gesturing for Vogel and Saslow to do the same.

Vogel wondered what she meant by that. But he did not speak, instead waiting for her to continue.

Helen Harris was a big woman, probably in her mid-fifties, taller than average and heavy. But she was not unattractive. Her face, maybe because of her excess weight, bore virtually no lines nor any other overt indication of the passing of the years. She wore wire-framed glasses, very slightly tinted, which seemed to add to, rather than detract from, the pleasantness of her features. Her long hair, a soft shade of brown streaked with pale grey gleamed in the shaft of morning sun shining through the narrow window, and hung in a single tress falling loosely over one shoulder. It suited her well. But more than anything the secret of Helen Harris' attractiveness was what Vogel's wife always called 'the light behind the eyes'.

Vogel had noticed it the first time he met her, and he was again struck by it.

It was only a few seconds before Helen spoke again. But it seemed longer to Vogel.

'First of all, I have to tell you that Gill Quinn is known to us here.'

'I see,' said Vogel, who was quietly confident that he did see.

'Yes, and I am sure you guessed that from the moment you heard I had called in, and you probably also guessed what it might indicate,' Helen continued.

'Indeed,' Vogel agreed. 'I assumed it was likely that there was at least some history of domestic violence in the Quinn household.'

'A reasonable assumption. You sat on a committee where we discussed the problems which still abound in dealing with violence in the home. And we learned long ago here at the House that it is only by operating under a strict code of confidentiality that we can be of any assistance at all to victims of domestic violence.'

'I completely understand that,' said Vogel, who did understand, but wondered exactly how Helen Harris was going to proceed from this point. If at all. But, of course, it was Helen who had contacted them.

'And so, Mr Vogel, before I take it upon myself to break that code, and I realize this might involve a certain breach of protocol for you, I wonder if you could clarify a couple of points for me,' she continued. 'I understand that Thomas Quinn was found dead at his home yesterday. Are you able to tell me at approximately what time he might have died?'

Vogel thought for a moment. This information would probably soon be publicly released as part of a call for possible witnesses. He saw no reason why he should not answer Helen Harris' question as best he could. And he suspected it would be in his interest and that of his investigation to cooperate with her as fully as possible.

'We think he died around mid-afternoon, probably between three and five,' he said.

'I see,' Helen responded. 'Also, I heard on Radio Devon that a woman had been taken to Barnstaple police station and was helping you with your enquiries. I assumed that would be Gill. The spouse of a murder victim is always the first suspect. Isn't that right?'

'Yes, on both counts,' said Vogel.

'So could I ask, have you arrested Gill Quinn? Do you have her in custody?'

'No, we have not arrested Gill, and we are not holding her in custody. But she is helping us with our enquiries. And I feel I should tell you that she is what we call a person of interest in this case.'

'As I thought,' muttered Helen.

There was another brief pause. And when she spoke again Helen Harris' tone of voice was loud, clear and unequivocal. Almost as if she was daring Vogel to challenge her.

'Therefore, I must tell you that Gill Quinn was here all day yesterday,' she said.

Vogel felt himself start to blink. He turned his head slightly to one side so that Helen Harris wouldn't notice.

'She arrived just after eight a.m., and stayed with us until early evening,' Helen continued. 'Somebody here was with her all the time. Either me, or another member of staff, or one of the other women. She did not leave the premises at any time.'

FOURTEEN

Kurt had booked a loft suite at the waterfront Hotel du Vin boutique hotel. It was lavishly appointed and designed, in the style of the exclusive hotel chain, to complement the original features of the Sugar House, the seventeenth-century Grade II listed warehouse from which it had been constructed. Lilian didn't notice any of that.

She wasn't aware of anything except Kurt's overwhelming presence. He was at his most charming. And she knew only too well how dangerous that could be.

He ordered the room service meal he had promised without asking her if she wanted it. And the champagne.

She toyed with the food. When he mildly chastised her she forced down a few mouthfuls. And she drank the champagne which he poured for her. She was used to doing his bidding.

His manner would have appeared to an outsider to be gentle, courteous and considerate. Did he really believe that he could win her over with his contrived charm, after what he had done to her? She thought that maybe he did. His ego was, of course, enormous.

After they had eaten, he stood up, put his arms around her, leaned over and kissed the top of her head.

'Don't worry, kitten, I just want to be with you, that's all.' He paused. 'In every way.'

Her heart missed a beat. But she had known he would get around to this sooner or later.

'I'll just go and have a shower,' he said, kissing her head again. 'Then maybe you'd like to have one too. I've had a bathrobe sent up for you.'

She looked down at the plate before her. It had always been like this. Kurt was a fastidious man when it came to personal hygiene. He had only rarely touched her without showering first. And he expected her to do the same.

The thought of sex with him repelled her. And, of course, there was the ever-present fear of what it invariably brought with it.

She heard the unmistakeable sounds of him using the lavatory then washing his hands, the buzz of his electric razor, the brushing of his teeth. Then after a moment or two the whir of the power shower.

She glanced towards the door. It appeared to have just a standard hotel room lock on it, designed to be opened from the inside without a key. Why had he left her like that? Was he testing her? Was his ego so enormous that he could even in his wildest imaginings think that she would ever again stay with him of her own free will? Maybe it was. Or maybe he just thought she would be too afraid to make a run for it, hampered by a broken ankle, and with him just yards away. In any case she knew all too well that he would soon find her again. And then, in one of his terrible rages, she dreaded to think what he might do to her.

She didn't care. She just had to try. She couldn't face the thought of sex with him, and of what it took for that to happen.

She ran to the door. In her haste she fumbled with the catch. Eventually she managed to shift it and was halfway out into the corridor when she felt a muscular arm around her pulling her back into the room. She hadn't heard him approach. His feet were bare and the room was thickly carpeted.

He held her quite gently, at arms' length, looking at her. His hair was its natural blonde again; he must have rinsed the brown colouring away in the shower. And his eyes were the all too familiar icy blue. Presumably he'd removed the tinted contact lenses he must have been wearing.

'You don't need to run from me, Lilian,' he murmured. 'Honestly, you don't, my sweet.'

He was naked and still wet from the shower. She glanced up and down his body. He remained in extremely good shape. Every inch of him masculine and hard. Except his dick, of course. That was as flaccid as it always had been. Except when he did what he had to do, with her anyway, in order to gain a decent erection.

He moved towards her. She stepped backwards, knocking against the little table by the door, rocking it, and slopping water from the big vase of flowers that stood on it.

She was desperate. She reached a hand behind her, groping. She closed her fingers around the neck of the vase, lifted, and swung with all her strength.

It struck him on the side of the head. Peonies, tall-stemmed lilies and ornamental fern flew all over the place. Water and pieces of smashed ceramic cascaded over her, the floor, and him. The vase disintegrated into many pieces. He staggered backwards. Blood gushed from a gash just above his ear.

Kurt kept staggering until he hit the wall. She could see the light in his eyes flickering and thought for one brief wonderful moment that she might have succeeded in knocking him unconscious. But Kurt St John was a fit and immensely strong man.

His knees had buckled, but within seconds he found his feet again. She remained quite still, frozen almost, in shock.

'What did you do that for?' he asked quite mildly.

She had no answer. He moved towards her. First he slapped her across one cheek with his right hand. Not too hard. Then with his left fist he punched her in the belly. Again not enough to do any real damage, just enough to wind her. She doubled up, wrapping her arms around her midriff, desperate to protect herself.

He moved closer. And she knew well enough what was about

to happen. It was all so familiar. His nakedness brought back every awful memory in sickening clarity. He had a fine erection now. He always did after he had hit her, or twisted her arm, or kicked her, or maybe pulled out a clump of her hair. Once he had hurt her, he turned into the rampant sexual animal which otherwise he could only dream of being.

He lurched at her. His smile more of a leer now. His eyes bright with lust. He pushed one hand hard between her legs, his thumb digging up into her, and began to rip at her clothes, tearing her shirt from one shoulder. His mouth sought a breast, and he bit her. Hard. She screamed and began to push and claw at him. He backed away enough for her to see the blood on his lips. Her blood. She watched his tongue seeking the salty liquid. His eyes closed for a split second, as if in a moment of ecstasy.

She screamed again, and somehow managed to escape his grasp. She ran into the sitting room. Without crutches, without the walking stick, yet feeling no pain in her plaster-cast ankle. Her fear was greater than any physical pain could ever be.

The remains of their meal and the champagne were on the table before her. And the cutlery they had used. She turned towards him. She fumbled with the cutlery behind her back, grasped a knife, clutched it with both hands and pointed it at him as threateningly as she could.

'Don't, Kurt. Just don't come any closer,' she said.

He paused, raising one eyebrow at the knife. She glanced down, realizing only then that she had managed to clutch just a small silver butter knife. It appeared to be such an ineffectual weapon. Kurt's leering smile grew even broader. His erection was so strong now that the tip of his penis pointed almost directly at the ceiling. He stroked it, lazily, with one hand, his gaze steady, intent oozing from every pore of him.

'Don't, Kurt, I will use this,' she warned.

'No, you won't.' he said. 'And what if you do?'

He was smiling again. The butter knife seemed to amuse him.

Then he came for her. Throwing his bulk at her. His penis jabbing into her sore belly. One hand around her throat, squeezing. Obliquely she wondered if this would be the time when he would finally kill her.

She was never sure whether she really stabbed him or if he

just impaled himself on the knife. And, in any case, she supposed later that she had not expected such an apology for a weapon to cause much damage.

But, somehow, the little silver butter knife pierced Kurt's flesh just below his heart and entered his body right up to its ornately decorated hilt.

Lilian let go of the knife at once and stepped back. No longer supported by her, Kurt dropped to the ground like a stone. He lay spreadeagled at her feet, his head to one side, legs and arms at impossible angles. She had little doubt that he was dead.

She backed away from his body, heart pumping, brain frozen. Then she experienced some kind of adrenalin burst. Or perhaps it was just blind panic. She took off. Running awkwardly, still without her stick, putting as much of her weight on her injured plaster-cast leg as the good one, holding her torn shirt around her with one arm, through the door, along the corridor, down the lift, past reception, out into the street below, and then on and on through the streets of Bristol with no idea at all of where she might be going.

The burst of adrenalin which had engulfed her in the hotel room did not last long. But she only stopped running when her left leg gave way. And only then did the pain from it hit her. She sank to the pavement, sobbing, overwhelmed by the enormity of what she had done. Passers-by glanced at her curiously, but nobody approached her. They probably thought she was a crazy woman. Her head was swimming. She put a hand to her face. She was burning-up. She struggled to gain some kind of control of herself, to gather her shattered senses.

Even if she could continue to run, she had nowhere to run to. That was the bitter truth.

She didn't even know where she was in this city of her childhood which had once been so familiar to her. It made no difference. There was only one thing left to do. She dragged herself to her feet, the throbbing in her left ankle now greater than it had ever been.

Across the road was a telephone box. She limped agonizingly over to it and dialled 999.

FIFTEEN

Vogel was still struggling to get his blinking under control. He was stunned. Of course, he had assumed that a call from Helen Harris meant there was at least some history of domestic violence in the Quinn household. He supposed he had been rather hoping that he might be provided with information which would build the evolving case against Gill Quinn, and possibly help bring his investigation to a swift and irrevocable conclusion. The last thing he had expected was what appeared to be a cast-iron alibi. And from such a reputable source.

'Are you absolutely sure of that, Miss Harris?' interjected Saslow.

Vogel rather wished she hadn't asked that question. Not of this woman. He turned to look at Helen Harris again. The line of her lips had tightened.

'I'm sorry, I don't believe I entirely understand the question,' Helen replied. 'Are you suggesting I might have made a mistake? That Gill Quinn wasn't here yesterday? That maybe I have the wrong day? Or even, perhaps, the wrong woman?'

'Uh, no, of course not, I mean . . .'

'Well then, what is the alternative? Do you think I have lied to you, detective sergeant? Do you think I am giving Gill a false alibi?'

'I don't . . . I mean . . . I'm not suggesting anything like that . . . we just need to confirm . . .'

Saslow was stumbling over her words. She sounded more than a little flustered. Which was unlike her. But it served her right, thought Vogel. She had spoken without thought. And Helen Harris had proceeded to make mincemeat of her.

He stepped in.

'I think DS Saslow merely wants to confirm that you could be absolutely sure that Gill did not leave the House at all during the course of yesterday,' he said. 'Is it not possible that she could have slipped out without anyone here realizing?'

'Slipped out to murder her husband, do you mean, Mr Vogel?' asked Helen.

Vogel noticed what was little more than a twitch, but might have been just the merest flicker of a smile, on either side of her mouth.

Vogel had instinctively liked the woman the first time he met her, and probably still did. He also had considerable respect for her. That didn't mean he was going to allow her to manipulate, or even to attempt to take charge of, his investigation. Vogel would never let anyone do that.

'Would you please answer my question?' he asked curtly.

The flickering smile, if it had really been there at all, evaporated.

'Of course, chief inspector,' she answered briskly. 'Absolutely no way at all. This is a busy house, full of people. There is only one way in and out. Nobody leaves or enters here without being noticed. In any case, if you really are suggesting that Gill returned home, with or without intent to harm her husband, she had no means of getting there. Not quickly, anyway. It's two bus rides away. And she didn't have any money on her. She left home in a big hurry yesterday morning, you see. So often the way.'

'But Miss Harris, Gill Quinn had a car,' commented Vogel. 'It's currently being checked by our forensic people. Why didn't she drive here?'

'Violence comes in many forms. With Thomas Quinn it primarily took the form of total control. Gill could only use her car when he allowed her to, mostly just to drive to and from work, and occasionally to go shopping. The rest of the time he kept the car keys from her.'

'Would it really have been out of the question for her to take buses home? What about a bus pass?'

'Completely out of the question in every way. I told you, she left home in a panic, without any credit cards, or anything of that kind, certainly not a bus pass even if she has one, which I doubt. I don't know this for certain, but I always assumed that Thomas kept possession of her money, and it's quite possible that she doesn't even have any credit cards in her own name. If she does, he would have controlled her use of them.'

'How did she get to you yesterday morning, then?'

'She walked, Mr Vogel.'

Vogel thought for a moment. St Anne's Avenue was nearly three miles from the centre of Bideford. The House was at the top of the town, almost a mile or so further up a steep hill.

'That's a fair walk, and not a particularly easy one,' he commented.

'Desperation, Mr Vogel.'

Vogel stared at her. He didn't like what he was hearing. He was by nature a kind man. Cruelty upset him. And it made him feel inadequate. He was a policeman. Perhaps a rather old-fashioned policeman. He supposed he had become one in order to do his bit to put the world to rights. It would always be his most abiding regret that he was so rarely able to do so.

'Oh yes, Mr Vogel,' Helen continued. 'Fear and desperation. Aspects of the human condition we are all too familiar with here. That is what we deal with on a daily basis here. A while back we had a woman turn up, with two little ones, who had fled her home down in Cornwall. She had nowhere else to go, and she'd heard of us and believed we would protect her. She had just enough money to buy train tickets to Barnstaple. Then she walked the rest of the way, with her baby strapped to her back, pushing her toddler in his buggy. That's more than twelve miles, Mr Vogel, and it took her nearly five hours.' She paused. 'I'm sorry, you don't want to hear all this.'

'Maybe I need to, Miss Harris,' said Vogel quietly. 'I certainly believe you have a lot more to tell me. You haven't said exactly why Gill came here yesterday morning, what actually caused her to flee her home and walk four miles to what she presumably considered to be safety?'

'Well, that's obvious, isn't it? Thomas attacked her. Not for the first time. The man specialized in all manner of tortures, Mr Vogel.'

'Gill was taken to hospital last night and kept in until early this morning,' said Vogel. 'She was thoroughly checked out. The medics found signs of old yellowing bruising around her ribs. But that was all. She said she received them when she had to do an emergency stop in her car.'

'And you accepted that, did you? Don't most motor cars have air bags which protect people riding in a front seat in such circumstances.'

'Gill drives a classic car. An MG. No air bags. Didn't you know that?'

'I have little interest in cars.'

'Well, in any case, the medics found no sign of any new injuries. What did Thomas Quinn allegedly do to her?'

'There's no allegedly about it, Mr Vogel,' said Helen caustically. 'Did anyone look behind her ears?'

'Behind her ears? I don't know. We certainly didn't at the station. And nobody mentioned anything at the hospital . . .'

Vogel was stunned. What was Helen Harris talking about? His imagination was beginning to take over. And the direction in which it was taking him was making him feel even more ill at ease.

'Medical professionals dealing with abuse should be aware of this kind of thing,' Harris continued. 'But I suppose that wasn't why Gill was hospitalized, was it?'

'No. It was because she appeared to be in deep shock that she was taken to the NDDH. Which, like all hospitals, is still suffering from the aftermath of the big Covid surge this last winter. It is possible that the physical examination was not as thorough as perhaps it should have been. That they just checked for obvious signs of injury.'

Helen Harris reached for her phone.

'I always take photographs,' she said. 'Women like Gill often go to considerable lengths to prevent their injuries being seen, by their friends and families as well as by strangers, and are most unlikely to tell a doctor, or a nurse, or a police officer, about what has happened to them unless they have absolutely no choice. Here they feel safe and shielded, partly because we pledge confidentiality. I would not be breaking that confidentiality except in the most extreme circumstances. And even then, and you may not approve of this, Mr Vogel, I quite probably would not do so if we weren't coincidentally able to provide Gill with an alibi.'

Helen tapped the screen of her phone a few times, then passed it to Vogel.

'These were taken yesterday, in case you're wondering,' she said. 'Soon after Gill arrived here.'

A series of photos appeared showing a woman, almost certainly Gill Quinn, although taken from behind, holding up her hair to reveal the backs of her ears. Behind each ear there were a number of old scars, and other small wounds in the process of healing. Also behind each ear there was one obviously new wound, raw and weeping. It seemed clear to Vogel that these were burns, old and new. And he was pretty sure they would have been inflicted by a lit cigarette.

The DCI was shocked. Silently he handed the phone to Saslow. The young DS made a small noise. It was a sharp intake of breath.

She too did not speak.

Vogel handed the phone back to Helen Harris.

'Systematic, calculated, and viciously cruel abuse, Mr Vogel,' she said, as she took the phone. 'That is what Gill Quinn has suffered at the hands of her husband for years. That is what we deal with here over and over again. Most people still have a very old-fashioned idea of domestic abuse. Like a husband coming home from the pub drunk and beating up his wife. The modern truth is far more sophisticated, and in my opinion often considerably worse than that. It's not entirely inflicted by men either. We had an elderly man here once who had endured years of abuse from his wife. He was frightened and emaciated. Every so often she would put a diuretic in his food. He barely dared to eat.

'Thomas Quinn was a sophisticated man. His physical attacks on his wife constituted merely the tip of the iceberg of his abuse.'

'That may be so, Miss Harris,' responded Vogel. 'But I've been more than twenty years a copper and I've never seen anything quite like this.'

He waved a hand at Helen Harris' phone.

'Indeed, Mr Vogel. And that is the whole point. You're not supposed to see it. The perpetrator makes sure of that. And the victims are all too often complicit in that. Some will even accept quite vicious injuries, like the burns Gill has suffered, in a place that is not readily visible, as long as their faces are not damaged.'

Vogel shook his head.

'I know that's true, but I must admit it does puzzle me a bit. There's so much more help available nowadays than there used to be, surely. People like you, and the police attitude to domestic abuse has changed dramatically over the years.'

'Probably, but not always to any great effect. Fewer than a quarter of reported incidents result in prosecution. The women, and occasionally the men, who come to us here are inclined not to have a great deal of confidence in the police or the UK's judicial system. In any case, the Quinns, way before yesterday's awful incident, were a perfect example of a couple living an abusive life, in which both victim and perpetrator were to some degree complicit. Gill has somehow managed to hold down a responsible job which gives her a certain standing in the community. She has a son she adores whom I understand also adores her, and whom she has always managed to see frequently, without her husband being present. She has always lived well and in a certain style. You've seen their home? More than comfortable, and beautifully situated. In addition to all his other dubious attributes, Thomas Quinn was an astute businessman, according to Gill, who was convinced, by the way, that she would finish up with very little if she tried to end their marriage.

'Also, like most who feel they are trapped in this sort of situation, Gill appeared to have convinced herself that Thomas wasn't all bad, and would always tell us that there were good times in between his violent outbursts. Albeit that she was always being controlled. So she kept that awful horrible part of her life a secret, and just put up with it. She used us as a refuge, which is at least partially what we are for, somewhere to escape to during the bad times.'

'When exactly did she start coming to you?'

'Last year, during the first lockdown, when the abuse she suffered reached a whole new level. A not uncommon scenario, as I'm sure you know, chief inspector, when people, particularly those in fragile and potentially violent relationships, were suddenly and unexpectedly trapped together with little or no outside influence to divert them from each other. It was after the first time Thomas had used a lit cigarette on her. She seemed as shocked as we were then. She told us that, although he had previously been violent on occasions, it was not severe – in her opinion – as long as she did exactly what he said. In everything. Which is that other kind of abuse I was talking about. Exerting total and quite stupefying control over another human being. Anyway, apparently Thomas was full of remorse for burning her, and promised that he would never ever do such a thing again. Having seen those pictures, Mr Vogel, you know just how well he kept that promise!'

Vogel knew. He also knew that those pictures would be indelibly printed on his memory. For ever. Like so much else he had seen during his career. But there were now a number of other questions crying out for answers. He made himself concentrate on that.

'You mentioned Gill's son, Greg,' he began. 'Whom she adores. Whom you believe adores her. Surely Gill couldn't have kept all this from him? Don't you think he must have been aware of what was happening to his mother? Didn't he ever try to help?'

Helen shrugged.

'People see what they want to see, Mr Vogel,' she said. 'And as for helping his mother, well, that was a hard thing to do. We can bear witness to that. Yesterday was just another example of that. Gill was more frightened and distraught than any of us had ever seen her. We really did hope that this time she would allow us to do something more constructive to help her. She was in a shocking state when she arrived. The burns to her ears were paining her dreadfully. She said she didn't think she could carry on. But as the day passed she changed her mind again. Told us she just wanted to wait until Thomas had calmed down, then go home.'

'That must have been very frustrating for you, Miss Harris,' commented Vogel.

'Yes,' Helen agreed. 'But it is also something we are all too familiar with.'

'It would appear that Thomas Quinn was guilty of criminal assault. You clearly have reservations about the help that is available from the authorities, but did you suggest to Gill that she might come to us and report his abuse, or at least take refuge with you more permanently?'

'We discussed all of that. We don't tell our women what to do. They have to reach the point where they want to take action, and feel confident in doing so. Yesterday we rather hoped Gill had reached that point. But she still went back to Thomas.'

'What did she do while she was here yesterday?' asked Vogel, changing tack slightly.

'Oh, the stuff that all our people do, cooed over the babies, helped get lunch, watched some TV, chatted about all sorts of things, rarely the things that really matter. It takes a while for any of our victims to be frank about their situation, and some never get to that stage. Gill was one of those, unfortunately.'

'Forgive me asking again, Miss Harris, but are you absolutely certain that she was here all day and never left the premises? Not even for a short time?'

'Absolutely sure.'

'All right. Can you confirm exactly when she left?'

'No I can't, not exactly. But I expect my partner, Sadie, can. She gave Gill a lift home. She'll be in the day room, I expect. If you don't mind waiting a moment I'll go and get her.'

Once she'd left the room Vogel turned to Saslow.

'Well, what do you think of that, Dawn?' he enquired. 'Seems like our leading suspect has a pretty strong alibi.'

'She also has a pretty strong motive, boss. Stronger than either you or I would have imagined, I reckon. Me anyway. I can't believe what that man did to her.'

'I agree, but it seems she may not have had the opportunity . . .' Vogel began.

He broke off as Helen Harris, and a second woman, returned.

'This is Sadie, Sadie Pearson, without whom I would be totally lost,' she announced.

Sadie turned out to be the birdlike woman who had answered the front door. This time she managed a brief smile. She had clear bright eyes which darted around the room almost as if they had a will of their own.

Vogel repeated his question concerning Gill Quinn's time of departure.

'Oh yes, I know to the minute,' Sadie Pearson responded immediately, and somewhat to Vogel's surprise.

'I keep my car radio permanently tuned to Radio Four,' she continued. 'Mostly, the only time I get to catch up on what's happening in the world outside of this place is when I'm driving. The six o'clock news was just beginning as Gill and I set off.'

'So what time did you get to Gill's home?' asked Vogel.

'Well, I turned the radio down because I had a passenger, but I kept it on. Habit, I suppose. And the news ended just as I dropped Gill off. It's only fifteen minutes on a Saturday, so it would have been pretty much dead on a quarter past six. Gill would have been home a few minutes later.'

Vogel was mildly puzzled.

'A few minutes later?' he queried. 'Didn't you drop her at her door?'

'Oh no. I dropped her just the other side of the playing fields at the back of St Anne's Avenue. She certainly wouldn't have wanted Thomas to see one of us with her . . .'

'Would he have known who you were?'

'I have no idea. Helen and I are quite well known locally. But in any case, Gill wouldn't have wanted Thomas to see her with almost anyone she had met without his knowledge, indeed his permission.'

Vogel nodded.

'However, you're assuming she was unaware that her husband was already dead,' he said.

'I certainly am,' Sadie Pearson affirmed. 'But she wouldn't have wanted any of her neighbours to see me, either. Just in case they recognized me. Don't forget, her dealings with all of us here was a big secret. As with so many of our people. Helen and I don't always agree with that, and certainly didn't in Gill's case. But that was how it was.'

Vogel turned to Helen again.

'You said she had come to you in a hurry, in a panic, without any money, or credit cards, or her phone—'

'Yes,' Helen interrupted. 'She told us Thomas had taken her phone again. He quite often did, especially if he was in a really bad mood, which was a not infrequent occurrence.'

'I see. But, I was wondering, did you know if she had her house keys with her?'

'No,' said Helen. 'I didn't think about it actually.'

'Neither did I,' agreed Sadie. 'But I kind of assumed she expected Thomas to be at home. It wasn't a working day for either of them. She kept saying she wanted to stay here long enough to be sure he had calmed down.'

'OK. What about Gill's state of mind? How was she when you dropped her off?'

'She was as all right as she could be,' said Sadie. 'Determined to go back to Thomas. In spite of everything. She was quite calm, Mr Vogel, if that's what you're asking.'

'Partly yes. Did the two of you talk at all on the journey, or at the end of it?'

'Not a lot. I told Gill to take care, and that we were always here for her. She could come to us any time. She said she knew that. But she had very little to say, really, which was pretty usual for her. Particularly when her initial panic had worn off. She got out of the car as soon as I pulled up and set off across the playing fields. She knew well enough that Helen and I thought it was high time she found a way of leaving Thomas. We were becoming more and more anxious about her safety. But, yet again, she wasn't prepared to take that final step. I just turned the car around and drove back.'

'You said she was calm. Was there anything about her behaviour which was in any way unusual or disturbing?'

'No there wasn't, chief inspector. And if you're asking if she looked like a woman who was planning to go home and stab her husband to death, no, she most definitely did not. Thomas Quinn was the abuser in that relationship, Mr Vogel, not his wife. Gill Quinn is the gentlest of souls. She would be quite incapable of killing anyone.'

Meanwhile Gill and her son were settling into Greg's home in Kipling Terrace, Westward Ho!, a row of converted Victorian properties which in their entirety had once been the boarding school attended by Rudyard Kipling, author of *The Jungle Book*.

Gill had liked it when her son had rented a flat there. After all she was a schoolteacher. Her first love had always been English literature. And almost all her younger pupils were still fans of *The Jungle Book*. Kipling was now an otherwise unfashionable writer, with views largely regarded as inappropriate in the modern world, but Gill personally thought he had merely been a man of his time and was a vastly underrated author.

None of this was on her mind that Sunday morning. She had grabbed her son and held him close when she'd been taken to him at Barnstaple police station. She loved him so much. He was always so kind to her, and she knew him to be much more sensitive than he sometimes at first appeared.

For many years now, Greg had been her greatest solace in life. There was perhaps one other source of potential consolation, but Gill had always been unable to cope with any sort of romantic attachment outside her marriage. For a start, she had rather suspected that Thomas would kill her if she strayed. But in fact it was Thomas who had now been killed.

She had taken a shower, hoping to wash away not only any remaining spots of Thomas' blood and the lurking taint of hospital and police station, but also the entire awful horror of the manner of his death.

It didn't work, of course. But Greg had stopped at a chemist on the way to Westward Ho! and picked up the sedatives the police doctor had prescribed for her. Gill hoped that they would bring her sleep and hopefully block out the persistent images of her dead husband which were filling her head.

She did need help. Her somewhat hysterical outburst at the police station had been genuine enough. She really hadn't known what she should say to the police, and had ended up feeling quite desperate. It was that which had turned her into a screaming, weeping wreck, as much as anything else. And she had certainly been in a state of some shock ever since it had all happened. But she had been pretty much aware of what was going on throughout. Apart perhaps from the time she'd been alone with the body of her husband after she had dialled 999. However, she had to admit, some of her unresponsiveness had been more a ploy to avoid answering unanswerable questions than anything else.

Greg had insisted she took over his bedroom. He had also lent her a T-shirt, which on her doubled as a rather baggy nightdress, and she felt clean and comfortable again. She hoped that rest would allow her to cope better, and had already climbed into Greg's bed when he knocked and entered, carrying a cup of tea and some biscuits.

'I thought you should try to eat and drink something, Mum,' he said.

She thanked him and said that she would indeed try.

'But I'm more interested in getting some sleep,' she continued. 'I'm about to take a couple of those pills.'

'Right,' said Greg.

He continued to stand by the bed staring at her. Saying nothing more. Gill was afraid he was about to burst into tears. They had barely spoken on the drive home or since their arrival at the flat. There was an unusual awkwardness between them. Gill supposed it was inevitable under the circumstances.

'Look, Greg, we need to talk,' she said suddenly. 'I know that, and you know that. Maybe not now. But certainly later, when perhaps we will both feel better.'

'Yes, I hope so,' said Greg, a little obliquely. 'And you will eat something, won't you?'

Gill obediently ate half a biscuit, took a sip of tea, then swallowed two of her prescribed pills, washed down with a swig of water.

'I'll see you later, then,' said Greg. 'Sleep well.'

She watched him leave the room, shutting the door quietly, then allowed herself to sink into the pillows, hoping and praying for oblivion, at least temporarily.

Greg made his way into the sitting room, which offered sweeping views of the Atlantic Ocean out to Lundy Island and beyond, and stretched out on the sofa. He was aware of nothing beyond his own growing sense of anxiety and apprehension.

He couldn't quite imagine how he and his mother were going to speak about anything. And he rather suspected it might be better for both of them if they didn't. But they would, of course. He supposed that they had to.

He couldn't be sorry that his father was dead. And he was pretty sure his mother wasn't sorry either. But he was deeply sorry about the mess Thomas' death had landed both him and his mother in.

From the moment he had received that call from the police telling him that his father had died in suspicious circumstances, and learned that Gill was at Barnstaple nick 'helping us with our enquiries', Greg had feared that she might be arrested. And then, once it became clear that he was also required to help with enquiries, and indeed was interviewed by that clever seeming DCI Vogel, he began to fear that he might be arrested instead. Or maybe as well as.

He couldn't see how the police could possibly have grounds to arrest either of them. Not yet anyway. But he had just learned the hard way how it feels to be formally interviewed in the pursuance of a murder investigation. And it didn't feel good.

Now, more than anything, all Greg wanted to do was ensure that his mother suffered no more pain. As ever, he just wanted to protect her. But he had yet to work out how to do that.

SIXTEEN

Lilian got through to the emergency services almost instantly.

'My husband is dead,' she told the operator. 'He attacked me. I . . . I've killed him.'

The woman's voice, steady and professionally calm, did not alter one iota. Lilian was asked for her name, where her husband could be found, and where she was.

'Are you hurt, Lilian? Do you have any injuries?'

Lilian heard herself reply in the negative. The throbbing in her ankle reminded her too late just how ridiculous her reply was.

The police came for her surprisingly quickly. She'd waited at the phone box as instructed. Indeed, she'd slumped to the floor as soon as she'd finished the 999 call. She remained in a crumpled heap, until a patrol car pulled up alongside.

Two officers stepped out of the car. The younger of the two, who looked barely out of his teens and had the acne to go with it, opened the door of the call box and looked down at her.

'Lilian St John?' he enquired.

Lilian nodded.

She struggled into a sitting position, still holding her torn shirt together with one hand. With the back of the other she dabbed ineffectually at the tears and the snot she knew must be all over her face, and glanced down at herself. For the first time she noticed that she was covered in blood.

The older officer reached out as if to help her stand up.

'You'd better come with us, love,' he said in a purposefully friendly tone of voice, his vowels distinctly Bristol. 'We'll take you back to the station. Get all this sorted out. Nothing to worry about.'

They drove her to Trinity Road police station where she was examined by a police doctor. Her clothes were removed from her and replaced with a white paper suit. Her fingerprints were taken, DNA extracted, and she was photographed. She had not been arrested, so she was asked for permission at every stage, which she gave at once. She didn't see how she could refuse. She felt as if she were in a kind of trance, and all of this must surely be happening to someone else. Her ankle continued to throb so badly, it was mostly impossible for her to think beyond the pain. The doctor muttered something about arranging an X-Ray.

Meanwhile Lilian was given paracetamol, escorted to an interview room and asked to wait. Occasional razor-sharp pains shot up and down her injured leg, but eventually it did become more comfortable. In any case, Lilian was a lapsed Catholic. She did guilt well. She thought that she deserved to suffer, after what she had done.

A tall thin constable, stoically silent and impassive, stood at the door. The time passed slowly. It felt as if she were alone in the little room, except for her poker-faced guard, for hours. She couldn't be sure, as she had no watch. She was brought food on a tray. But nobody spoke to her. At one point she asked to go to the toilet. A young woman constable was summoned to escort her. She waited right outside the cubicle.

Lilian felt like a criminal. She supposed she was a criminal. She had killed her husband. She wasn't afraid of the process of the law. Not yet. She knew that she had acted in self-defence and she just assumed, with the track record of her time in hospital and the attack that had led to it, and with a warrant already out for Kurt's arrest, that this would be accepted by the authorities.

She felt relief that she would never again be confronted by the man who had caused her so much pain, both physical and mental. But she already regretted that she had taken another human life.

Eventually two policemen, one in uniform and one wearing a dark grey suit and overly bright tie, arrived.

The suit, a small man with bloodshot eyes, introduced himself as Detective Sergeant McDermott and the uniformed officer as Constable Richardson. She recognized Richardson, overweight, his face more florid than was healthy, as the older of the two constables who had collected her from the phone box.

Richardson set the interview room's recording apparatus in

operation, and announced the names of those present, the date and the time as four fifteen p.m. It must have been around mid-morning when they'd brought her to the station, Lilian thought. She had indeed been waiting in the little interview room for several hours.

DS McDermott asked if she wished to have a lawyer present. She shook her head. No lawyer could alter what had happened, that was for sure. She had killed Kurt. She had to accept the consequences.

'Right, Mrs St John, what I would like you to do first is to tell me in your own words exactly what happened today between you and your husband,' began DS McDermott.

Lilian did her best to do so.

'I had to get away from him, that's why I came to Bristol,' she began. 'But he followed me. He put a tracker on my car. That's how he found me so quickly. He said he wanted to rebuild our marriage. He made me go to the hotel with him. I was so afraid. He has always been violent. He attacked me in the hotel room, and I panicked. I was desperate to escape again. That's when it happened . . . I didn't know what I was doing.'

Lilian was all too aware that she was not telling her story well, but was somehow incapable of doing any better.

DS McDermott smiled thinly. 'It's all right, Mrs St John,' he said, not unsympathetically. 'Obviously this is very difficult for you. But we do need a little more detail here. You say Mr St John attacked you. What did he do exactly?'

Lilian tried to explain the sequence of events at the hotel, how she had attempted to leave, and Kurt had stopped her, grabbing hold of her. She admitted that she had smashed the vase over his head, nearly knocking him out.

'But then he came at me, really came at me.'

'Let's be absolutely clear here,' McDermott responded. 'You appear to be admitting that it was actually you who was first violent to your husband earlier today. Is that so?'

'Uh, no. Well. I'm not sure. He grabbed my arm. Pulled me back into the room . . .'

'Right, so he grabbed your arm and pulled you back into the room. Then you smashed a heavy vase over his head with such force that he received a deep cut and was nearly rendered unconscious. That could be regarded as rather an extreme reaction, Mrs St John, don't you think?'

Lilian hoped she was imagining things but the policeman's voice seemed cooler, although his manner remained professional and unthreatening.

'You didn't know him, didn't know what he was capable of . . .'

Lilian realized she was making a mess of things. She felt the room beginning to swim.

'Are you all right, Mrs St John?'

Automatically Lilian nodded. She actually didn't think she'd ever felt less all right in her entire life.

'OK, so let's continue, shall we? You say that after you'd smashed a vase over his head, your husband "came at me, really came at me". Is that correct?'

'Yes. He hit me in the face, and in the stomach.'

'Again, we need to be very clear on this. You have been examined by our doctor who found no sign of any noticeable injury in your abdominal area. And your face is unmarked except for the shadow of some old bruising.'

McDermott looked down at what Lilian assumed to be the police doctor's report on the table before him.

'You know, Mrs St John,' McDermott continued almost gently, 'it could be regarded as understandable that your husband hit out at you in the circumstances you describe. After all by your own admission you had just very nearly rendered him unconscious—'

'It wasn't like that, I was so afraid of him,' Lilian interrupted. 'You don't understand . . .'

'And then you stabbed him,' DS McDermott continued. 'You have admitted that.'

'Yes. Well, he sort of lunged at me. The knife went into him, I didn't know quite how . . .'

'But you were holding the knife at the time, were you not?'

'Y . . . yes.'

'So, you had already nearly knocked your husband out. He hit you. You stabbed him just below the heart. Is that the correct sequence of events?'

'Yes, yes, and he bit my nipple,' Lilian blurted out, feeling herself blush, thinking at the same time how lame she sounded.

'He tore my shirt half off me and bit my nipple till it bled. Surely your doctor noticed that?'

McDermott shifted uncomfortably in his seat, as if the mention of a bitten nipple was far too much information. He glanced down again at the medical report.

'Yes, that is mentioned here. However this kind of injury is also consistent with rough sex, of course . . .'

Where did that come from? What could DS McDermott possibly know about Kurt's sexual preferences? Lilian simply stared at the policeman and said nothing more at all. Even facing the possibility of serious criminal charges, she could not bring herself to discuss the horrors of her sex life with Kurt.

Before she could dwell further on what had caused McDermott to make such a remark he had moved on.

'Did you intend to kill your husband, Mrs St John? Did you plan it?'

Lilian gasped. 'Of course not. I . . . uh, didn't know what I was doing.'

'Did you know what you were doing when you left your husband for dead and ran from the room?'

Lilian was aware of McDermott's line of questioning becoming harder. But then, she was also aware of how badly she was telling her story.

'I panicked. I told you. I was so afraid . . .'

'You keep saying that, Mrs St John. But frightened of what exactly? You were quite sure that your husband was dead, so he was no longer someone to be afraid of, was he?'

'I was confused. I just couldn't stay in that room with him. You must realize what he's done to me. Look at the state I'm in.' She gestured to her leg in its plaster cast. 'Contact the Charing Cross Hospital. And the Met. There's a warrant out for Kurt's arrest. They'll tell you what he did to me when I tried to leave him before. I ended up in hospital for nearly three weeks. He fractured my skull, for God's sake.'

McDermott and Richardson watched her impassively.

'Look, he abused me throughout our marriage . . .'

'Had you been hospitalized previously as a result of this abuse?' asked PC Richardson.

'No. Only the one time. He'd come back unexpectedly and found me packing a bag. That night he was punishing me. Usually . . .'

Lilian stopped abruptly. She just couldn't tell them how it had usually been. How it was Kurt's desperate need for sexual arousal which was the cause of his consistent abuse of her. She could not find the words. She never had been able to find the words.

'Usually what?' enquired PC Richardson.

Lilian shook her head and looked down at the table.

'Let's just concentrate on what happened in the hotel, shall we, Mrs St John,' said DS McDermott. 'You say you tried to escape from the hotel room because you were so frightened of Mr St John, and that you acted in self-defence. Is that the crux of it?'

'I suppose so, yes.' Lilian kept her eyes down.

She didn't want to look at the policemen. Why did she still feel more shame at the sheer humiliation of what passed for her sex life with Kurt than she did at having killed a man? It was bizarre.

'But wasn't Mr St John merely trying to rescue his marriage? You admit, don't you, that he told you that is what he wanted to do?'

'Well, yes. But it wasn't like that with Kurt. Everything he did was extreme. He was obsessed with me, you see . . .'

Her voice tailed off. McDermott and Richardson both looked as if they found that hard to believe.

'Mrs St John, you left your husband for dead,' McDermott persisted. 'You weren't just running away from the law, were you? It must have occurred to you that you could face a murder charge.'

Lilian shook her head. Bewildered, bemused.

'No. I didn't even think about that. Really I didn't. And I phoned the police. I confessed.'

'But hadn't you realized by then that you couldn't escape, that you'd left so much evidence behind, and indeed that you had nowhere to go?'

'No, it wasn't like that. I've told you the truth about what happened . . .'

DS McDermott leaned back in his chair and his voice was quieter when he spoke again.

'Well, Mrs St John, I have some news for you. You did not kill your husband. It was, however, a very close thing. Half an inch higher and that little knife you plunged into him would have entered his heart. As it was, you merely severely damaged an artery. The paramedics were able to revive him almost at once. I am told that if you had left it just a few minutes longer to call us they would not have been able to do so.'

Lilian was poleaxed. The first thing she felt was overwhelming relief that she was not a murderer. The second thing was a return of the dreadful all-encompassing fear which had been part of her life ever since her marriage. As long as Kurt St John was alive that fear would remain. He would never leave her alone. She would never get away from him.

Tears filled her eyes. The shock and the horror of it all overwhelmed her.

'No, no, no.'

She shouted out the words, rocking forward over the table, holding her head in both hands.

The two policemen just watched and waited until she slumped back into her chair exhausted.

'That's a very revealing reaction, isn't it?' remarked DS McDermott, his voice soft.

'What?'

'I tell you that your husband is still alive, and you scream "no no no". If you were me what would that indicate, Mrs St John?'

Lilian shook her head. It was all she had the strength for.

'It rather indicates that you're sorry he's alive, doesn't it?' DS McDermott continued. 'That you are sorry you didn't succeed in killing your husband, isn't that so?'

'No. I'm afraid, don't you understand, I'm afraid,' Lilian managed to blurt out. 'I've told you the truth. The absolute truth.'

'All right, Mrs St John.' McDermott stood up abruptly. 'Your husband has regained consciousness and we're hoping that he will soon have recovered enough to give us a full statement. So I'm going to suspend this interview until we have made further enquiries. I have no choice but to formally arrest you, at this stage on suspicion of causing grievous bodily harm, and I am afraid you will have to be held in a police cell overnight. You still have the right to make a telephone call if you wish.'

Lilian nodded numbly. She didn't know quite what she had expected to happen, but somehow, and probably extremely naively, she had not considered even the possibility of being locked in a police cell.

SEVENTEEN

'Where do we go from here, boss?' asked Saslow as the two officers left Helen's House.

'Well, we certainly should talk to Gill Quinn again as soon as possible, and her son,' Vogel replied. 'But we need her in a better state. So it's probably best to give her a bit more time to recover, and leave it until this afternoon. Meanwhile, let's head back to the incident room and liaise with the team.'

'Right, boss. Should we take a doctor with us when we do go to see Gill, do you think?'

'Yes, we definitely should. For all sorts of reasons. I want those ears of hers looked at for a start. If the pictures we've just seen are genuine, and I have little doubt that they are, we need a proper medical record of what has been done to her. I'd like to get hold of the same doctor who saw her this morning. What was her name again?'

'Lamey. Dr Louise Lamey.'

'Do we have a number for her?'

'I'll get it, boss.'

She did so using the car's hands-free, then Vogel called the doctor with his phone on speaker.

He heard Dr Lamey gasp when he described the burns which had been inflicted behind Gill Quinn's ears.

'You know, I have heard of this sort of thing,' said Dr Lamey. 'The most horrible abuse inflicted in such a way that its effects are not immediately noticeable. But I didn't think about that this morning. I didn't examine Mrs Quinn at all really for physical injuries. I do apologize, Mr Vogel . . .'

'You've no need to, doctor,' Vogel reassured. 'We called you in to deal with a woman in shock, and to attempt to calm her down. None of us had any reason to suspect at the time that she had been abused in that way, and she had been physically examined in hospital before being admitted for the night. They missed it there too. But they also were not looking for signs of abuse. Gill Quinn's only other visible injuries were some old bruises on her ribs which she explained away.'

Vogel asked if the doctor could accompany them to see Gill later that day. They agreed on three p.m.

As soon as the two officers arrived at the incident room at Bideford police station DI Peters hurried towards them.

'I was just going to call you, boss,' she began. 'We've had the headmaster of Elm Tree, Gill Quinn's school, on the phone. Wynne Williams, his name is. He'd just heard about Thomas' death. We had a team designated to contact him and arrange an interview, but they hadn't got to it yet. Sorry, boss. Anyway he was totally distraught. Almost hysterical. Kept demanding to know where Gill was, if we were holding her in custody. Even said he wanted to see her. Almost demanded again. It was a bit excessive, boss . . .'

'Well, a head and deputy head would work pretty closely together,' remarked Vogel, who had never been one to jump to conclusions without evidence to support them. 'And I'm sure everyone at her school, and indeed Thomas Quinn's place of work, will be pretty upset. Are you saying his reaction was more extreme than you would have expected from someone who was merely a work colleague, or rather her boss, I suppose? Is that it?'

'Yes. That is exactly it. And Williams' concern was almost entirely for Gill. Not the dead man. How can I put it, he spoke about her as if she was someone he was very close to. Very close indeed.'

'I see,' said Vogel. 'Well, we'd better check out just how close they are, then. Anything else?'

'Yes. Lake and Jamieson talked to Thomas Quinn's business partner late last night. There had already been mentions on local news, but Quinn hadn't been named. Patel was totally taken aback, apparently. Hadn't seen any news bulletins. This is their report.'

DI Peters began to read from her phone.

'"We arrived at Jason Patel's home at ten forty-four p.m. and informed him of Thomas Quinn's death. He expressed deep shock. He asked at once if we knew who was responsible for his death. We told him that our enquiries were proceeding and we needed him to tell us about his whereabouts that day. He said it wasn't his whereabouts we should be worried about. He answered our questions willingly enough, but he was clearly very uneasy. He said that he'd been at home all day yesterday watching cricket on TV. England versus Pakistan apparently. He's separated from his wife and lives alone, and claimed to have seen and spoken to nobody all day, except the boy who delivered a pizza at around six o'clock" . . .'

DI Peters paused.

'There's more routine stuff, and then this. "As we left Mr Patel asked if he could have police protection given that he was a close colleague of a man who had been violently murdered. We told him this would not be normal procedure at this stage, unless there was a specific reason for it. We asked if there was a specific reason. He muttered something about this not being a normal situation, which neither of us heard properly. When we asked him to repeat it, he said it didn't matter. He was probably worrying about nothing. We tried to push him without success. But both of us thought his reaction was a little curious, and that he might have information which he hadn't revealed."'

'Right Janet, well that's two men we need to get back to. Saslow and I have some time to kill before we go to see Gill Quinn again. Unless there's anything else we should look into here, then I think we'll take on Messrs Patel and Williams ourselves.'

Vogel paused, thinking.

'One last thing, have you appointed a FLO to the Quinns yet?'

'Yes boss, Morag Docherty. She's recently completed the course, and I thought as she'd already been involved in the case and spent time with Gill that she'd be a good choice.'

'Excellent. Is she with them yet?'

'Not quite, boss. I think I woke her up when I called, to tell the truth. But knowing Docherty, she'll soon be on her way.'

'Right, tell her to report to me directly,' Vogel instructed.

He and Saslow decided to visit Wynne Williams first.

The headmaster and his wife lived on the outskirts of the village of Abbotsham in a pretty detached cottage with rural views. There was a parking area set back off the lane outside, and the cottage itself was approached by a winding footpath. As the two officers reached the front door they could hear raised voices from inside, loud and clear enough for them to be able to decipher some of the rhetoric being heatedly exchanged.

They heard a woman's voice initially. High-pitched. Perhaps slightly hysterical.

'Why don't you admit it . . .?'

'I keep telling you. There's nothing to admit. I wish there was to tell the truth . . .'

'I've no doubt about that, you pathetic—'

'Look, she's in trouble,' the man interrupted, his voice very slightly quieter. 'I have to find her. I must go to her . . .'

'Oh, do what you bloody well like.'

'I bloody well intend to . . .'

'Yes. As bloody usual . . .'

There was some slamming of doors, and then silence.

Vogel and Saslow glanced at each other without speaking. Vogel rang the doorbell.

There was no response. He rang it again. Long and loud.

Eventually a woman of middle years, average height and weight, answered the door. She was wearing a dressing gown and slippers, and didn't look as if she had bothered that morning to even put a comb through her unruly brown hair. She also looked harassed, and when she spoke, although her voice was no longer raised, she still sounded irritable.

'Yes?' she queried.

'Mrs Williams?' enquired Vogel.

'Yes,' she said again.

Vogel introduced himself and Saslow.

'I need to have a word with your husband, Mrs Williams,' he said.

Mrs Williams sighed. 'No prizes for guessing what that's about,' she muttered.

Vogel thought her voice might be slightly slurred. Had she been drinking? If so, that was not necessarily untoward for lunch-time-ish on a Sunday. But it may have partially explained the level of her angry participation in the exchange he and Saslow had overheard.

'You'd better come in then.'

She led the two officers into the hall.

'Wynne, get yourself down here,' she shouted up the stairs. 'It's the police.'

An anxious looking man quickly appeared on the landing. His thinning grey hair was tousled and his eyes were red-rimmed. But at least he was fully clothed, in clean ironed jeans and a plaid shirt, and he looked considerably less dishevelled than his wife. However, he was clearly upset and uneasy.

He didn't give Vogel or Saslow time to speak, immediately asking, 'Have you come about Gillian? Is she all right? Where is she now? Is she still at the police station? I want to see her. Is she hurt? I want to help . . .'

'Mr Quinn, we are investigating the murder of Gillian Quinn's husband,' Vogel recited sternly. 'I am DCI David Vogel. DS Saslow and I are here to ask you some questions, and we are not able at this stage to give you information concerning Mrs Quinn, nor indeed anyone who might be helping us with our enquiries.'

Wynne Williams looked vaguely bewildered. 'I just want to help,' he repeated. There was the merest hint of Welsh lilt in his voice. His eyes were gentle and intelligent. He had a pleasant open face. He looked like a schoolteacher, and Vogel could easily believe that he was normally a good headmaster.

But none of this matched with the petulance of the angry outburst, presumably from him, which Vogel and Saslow had just overheard.

'Good, so perhaps we could sit down somewhere and talk properly?' Vogel suggested.

The other man nodded his head in a distracted manner, glancing uneasily at his wife who had so far remained silent, but had been looking on disapprovingly.

'Oh, for God's sake, get on with it, Wynne,' she snapped.

And she made no attempt to follow when Wynne led Vogel and Saslow into a comfortable, if rather old fashioned, kitchen at the back of the house. There were chintzy soft furnishings, and orange coloured pine units, reminiscent of the previous century, lined the walls. A large orange pine table stood in the middle of the room.

Williams gestured for the two officers to sit at the table. He seemed about to join them, before remembering the niceties of hospitality that would probably come naturally to him in less stressful circumstances.

'Would you like a cup of something?' he enquired.

Vogel immediately answered in the negative for both himself and Saslow. He had just had a cup of coffee at the incident room, and he wanted to press on as quickly as possible. A busy afternoon and evening lay ahead.

Williams sat, his body language more than a little awkward, rubbing his hands together nervously in front of him.

'I'd like to start by asking you your whereabouts yesterday afternoon,' Vogel began.

Williams looked alarmed. 'You want to know my whereabouts?' he queried. 'Me? I mean why? You don't think—'

'Just routine, sir,' Vogel interrupted.

'Oh yes, of course. OK. I was here, all day. We have a new curriculum for next term which needed sorting out. People think schoolteachers only work part-time. We actually work longer hours than almost anyone. And if you're the head, well, it never stops really—'

'I'm sure you're right, sir,' interrupted Vogel. 'Can anyone vouch for that?'

'Well, my wife, of course. Marjorie. She went shopping in the morning, Sainsbury's, I think, but she was here the rest of the day.'

'Thank you, sir. Now can you tell me how long you have known the Quinns?'

'I've known Gillian for about seven years,' responded Williams. 'Since she came to Elm Tree. She trained to be a teacher as a young woman but abandoned her career to bring up her son, only returning when she felt he was old enough to look after himself. Like quite a lot of women do. I was appointed headmaster a couple of years later, and a couple of years after that the position of deputy head became vacant, so I appointed Gill. She's a very good teacher, you know. Excellent. A good organizer too. And everybody loves her. The children. The other teachers. Everybody. It would be terrible if all this spoiled things for her, you know. Terrible. She could still have quite a career . . .'

Williams let the sentence tail off. Vogel wondered if he'd eventually started to listen to what he was saying. He studied the man wordlessly for a few moments.

'Mr Williams, Thomas Quinn has been murdered,' he said eventually. 'As you are well aware. And, as you would expect in such circumstances, his wife is helping us with our enquiries. She is one of a number of people doing so, yourself included, but, as the wife of the violently deceased, she is very much a person of interest to us. I do hope you understand that this is likely to overshadow all other considerations and anything else in her life until this investigation is completed.'

Williams looked suitable chastened. 'Yes. Of course. I didn't mean to suggest . . .'

'Mr Williams, you just spoke at length about Gill Quinn, but you have not yet mentioned the dead man at all. Surely you must have known him too, didn't you?'

'Not really, no. I hardly ever met him.'

'Gill, or Gillian, as you call her, was your deputy. I would have thought you would have crossed paths with him on a number of occasions over the years, at events at the school for example. Is that not the case?'

'Well, I met him obviously. But not often. He very rarely came with Gillian to anything at the school. He had his own work. I don't think he was interested in hers.'

'I see. Did you not socialize at all? You and your wife, maybe, with the two of them?'

'Socialize? With Thomas Quinn? No. Definitely not.'

Williams' voice changed slightly, becoming sharper, verging on the aggressive.

'Was there any particular reason for that?' asked Vogel conversationally.

Williams opened his mouth to answer, then shut it again. Vogel waited.

'Yes there bloody well was a reason,' Williams blurted out suddenly, as if no longer able to contain himself.

'I couldn't stand the man. He was a cruel manipulative bastard.

He made Gillian's life a total misery. He was a control freak. She had no freedom at all. And he hurt her too.'

'How do you know all this?' asked Vogel.

'It was obvious,' Williams replied. 'Well, I thought it was obvious. She tried to hide it from me. But she couldn't in the end, though she just told me that she and Thomas were having some problems which started after their boy had left home, and she was sure they would sort it out. Greg never got on with his father, apparently, and I don't blame him. And Gillian was clearly very unhappy in her marriage, whatever she said. Some days when she came to work you could see that she'd been crying. But it wasn't until last year that I found out he was actually violent towards her. It would have been just after the school reopened following the first lockdown, she stumbled coming through a door and I heard her cry out. She grasped her side as if she was in pain. She said it was nothing, that she twisted herself getting out of her car, but I just kept on at her. Eventually she admitted that Thomas had hit her, several times, and hurt her quite badly. I was horrified. I told her she should do something about it. That I would help her. She should see an expert, maybe report him to the police. We had become quite close by then, you see . . .'

The kitchen door suddenly burst open. In stormed Mrs Williams. Still wearing her grubby dressing gown and slippers. She was carrying a glass of what appeared to be red wine in her right hand. Vogel's first impression had been correct, then. She was drinking, all right. And clearly no longer had any intention of remaining silent.

'Close, close?' yelled Marjorie Williams, who was probably somewhat more drunk than she had been earlier. Her words were now quite definitely slurred.

'I should say close! Why don't you tell the truth, you snivelling coward. You were fucking the bitch. In your office I shouldn't be surprised. Up against the wall probably . . .'

Williams stood up and took a step towards his wife.

'Shut up,' he commanded.

His voice had become just as loud and angry as hers. 'Do not say another word. Or I shan't be responsible for my actions. Do you hear?'

Wynne Williams took another step towards his wife. His right arm was slightly raised and his fist clenched.

Vogel stood up too and, moving at speed for a tall man no longer in the first flush of youth, positioned himself between man and wife.

'That's enough,' he commanded.

Williams looked as if he was about to argue. But ultimately he sat down again, without saying anything more, either to his wife or to Vogel. He lowered his head into his hands.

'Typical,' yelled Marjorie Williams. 'Snivelling coward. Like I said. Pathetic snivelling coward.'

Vogel glanced towards Williams. He thought the man might be starting to cry, but couldn't see his face. Mrs Williams, meanwhile, was beginning to sway slightly on her feet. She did not speak either, instead taking a deep drink from her glass, dribbling just a little of the wine from one corner of her mouth.

Vogel was a non-drinker. Teetotal cops have always been a rare minority. They sometimes didn't get an easy ride in the police force either, particularly not in the Met where Vogel had spent most of his career, and a hard-drinking culture had prevailed, certainly during his time there. Vogel didn't care. Apart from one unfortunate episode in his youth, he had never drunk alcohol. He didn't like the taste of alcohol nor what it did to people. He particularly disliked seeing women drunk, although he knew better than ever to mention that. He supposed he wasn't meant to even think it any more, but he didn't much care about that either. Marjorie Williams was unpleasantly drunk. She might be a very nice and intelligent woman when she was sober, but, right now, Vogel considered her to be thoroughly monstrous. And he wanted nothing more to do with her in the state she was in.

'Mrs Williams, I need to continue to speak to your husband alone,' he said. 'We may well want to talk to you at some point, but for the time being I must ask you if you would be kind enough to leave the room.'

Vogel was being deliberately over courteous. He had always found that confrontation was the worst path along which to travel when dealing with drunkenness. Marjorie Williams leered at him. At least Vogel considered it to be a leer.

'Thish is my kitchen,' she said.

'Indeed it is,' commented Vogel, in his most reasonable manner.

Marjorie Williams stared at him through watery eyes, which may or may not have been focusing properly.

'Oh all right, whatever you want,' she said, after a moment or two. 'You're welcome to the useless fucker.'

Vogel watched as she turned round and made her way just a tad uncertainly out of the room.

Well, he thought, he and Saslow certainly had a fair idea of the state of the Williams marriage now. Indeed they had already learned quite a lot about Wynne Williams.

He turned his attention back to Wynne, who was still sitting with his head in his hands.

'So is your wife right, Mr Williams?' he asked. 'Have you been having a sexual relationship with Gillian Quinn?'

William looked up and leaned back in his chair. He wiped his eyes with the back of one hand. Vogel had been right. He had shed some tears, but mercifully seemed to have remained in reasonable control of himself.

'No,' he said. 'The woman's wrong. As usual. I've never had a sexual relationship with Gillian. I damned well wish I had, though.'

'What does that mean? Have you made advances which have been rebuffed?'

'You could say. More days than not, for some years, except when we were in lockdown and I couldn't get near her. But not the way you mean. It's never been about sex. I was in love with her. Head over heels. What am I saying? Was? I still am. I love her to bits. I would do anything for her. I begged her to leave Thomas. He didn't deserve her. I would have looked after her. Still would.'

'So you were prepared to leave your wife for her, were you?'

'No "were" about it. I'd leave Marjorie now like a shot, if Gillian would have me. I'd go anywhere with her. I'd leave everything else behind for her. The job. Everything. We could manage. I'll stand by her, you know. Whatever happens. Whatever you lot do to her.'

Wynne Williams' eyes shone with passion. There was nothing gentle about them now. Vogel was beginning to think it might just be possible that he would end up having a certain amount of sympathy for Marjorie Williams.

'When did you last see Gillian?' he asked.

'Friday,' Williams answered promptly. 'The day before Thomas was killed.'

'Was that at school, then?'

'Yes.' Williams paused. 'And afterwards. I may as well tell you, because I'm sure you'll find out. I persuaded Gill to come for a quick drink with me. There's a pub just off the Northam road that we use every so often to get away from it all. We call it "our place". Well, I do . . .'

Williams paused, smiling slightly, as if he were drifting away from what appeared to be the rather grim reality of his life.

'Please go on,' Vogel prompted.

'Yes. Our place. It was just somewhere to go. I had a bottle of lager and she had an orange juice. She barely drinks, Gillian. Unlike some.'

He spat the last two words out, paused again, then continued without prompting.

'Anyway, we'd only been there for five minutes or so when Thomas came barging in. He was hopping mad. He threw himself at me, and I think he might have knocked me down, if the landlord hadn't intervened. Then he just yelled at me to keep away from his wife, and more or less dragged Gillian out of the pub. I followed, but I didn't know what to do. I thought if I did anything it might make it worse for Gillian. Plus, Marjorie is right about one thing, I am a coward. Physically anyway. Thomas Quinn was a big strong man, and I already knew about his temper. As for me, well . . . I am as you see me.'

Williams was slightly shorter than average and narrow-shouldered. He had thin legs and arms, but the beginning of a belly. He did not look like a man capable of any sort of physical confrontation. However, Vogel reminded himself that you could never be sure about such things. After all, Wynne Williams had just squared up to his wife with fists clenched, and one arm raised.

'He half pushed Gillian into her car and ordered her to drive straight home or else,' Williams continued. 'He said he'd be right behind her. Then he got into his own car and took off out of the car park after her. But not before he'd shouted another threat at me.'

'What did he say?'

'That if he ever caught me near his wife again I'd be sorry.'

'What did you do then? Did you go back into the pub?'

'No. I went and sat in my car, tried to calm down. I was in a bit of a state. I did try to phone Gillian whilst she was still on her way home, though. I knew she wouldn't be able to speak once she was with him. But, well, he answered. I might have guessed. I didn't see it, but he must have taken her phone from her. Not for the first time, I don't think.'

Williams paused.

'What did Thomas say to you over the phone?' prompted Vogel.

'He said, "You don't fucking listen, Williams, do you." Then he carried on threatening me, telling me what he was going to do to me. It was awful. I just hung up in the end.'

'Did you try to contact Gill again?'

'No. How could I? Thomas had put the fear of God into me and, anyway, I knew he had her phone. I hoped she might try to contact me. But she didn't. Not surprising really. She lived in terror of him.'

'Mr Williams, Thomas Quinn was a successful businessman and a former town councillor. He's been described to me as a pillar of the community. What he may or may not have done to his wife in private would be one thing, but I'm surprised to hear that he behaved like that in public. Weren't you surprised by his behaviour?'

'No. I'd seen hints of his temper before, although nothing as bad as that.'

'But he could have been recognized. The landlord might have reported him. You might have reported him. At the very least that would not have gone down well locally, would it? A former councillor behaving like that. He could have been charged with causing an affray. The local press would then have picked it up. It might even have had a detrimental effect on his business, mightn't It?'

'I don't know. He was one of those who thought he was invincible. Certainly above the law. That's the impression Gillian gave me anyway. He did exactly what he liked, without any thought to the consequences. And I'm sure it didn't occur to him that I would have the nerve to stand up to him in any way at all. He was right, too.'

'So, did you see or hear from Thomas at all yesterday?' Vogel asked.

'No, I didn't. I told you. I was here all day, working. But I have to admit I made sure the doors were locked. I was half afraid he'd make good his threat and come round here. Or send some thug around. I wouldn't have put that beyond him. People like Thomas Quinn often have someone around to do their dirty work, don't they? To tell the truth, my imagination was running away with me, Mr Vogel.'

'What about your temper, Mr Williams?'

'My temper? What do you mean?'

'We saw you raise your fist to your wife, make as if you were about to hit her? Maybe you would have hit her if I hadn't intervened. Is that a regular occurrence?'

'No, no it's not. Sometimes she drives me to distraction, that's all. But I wouldn't have hit her. Really I wouldn't. I never hit her.'

'Not even when she drives you to distraction. Do you not sometimes hit her then? Mr Williams, do you ever attack your wife physically?'

Williams shook his head wearily.

'You've met her, you've met us both,' he replied. 'Do you honestly think I'd dare?'

As soon as Vogel and Saslow had gone, Wynne Williams tried again to call Gillian Quinn. He had been trying ever since he'd heard the news of Thomas' death. Her phone had seemed to be switched off throughout. Thomas couldn't be keeping it from her any more. That was for sure. But Wynne had no idea whether or not Gillian now had her phone with her. He was hoping that she had, and was merely unable to answer it while at the police station. If she was still at the police station. He didn't even know that. Of course the police may have taken possession of the phone. He just hoped not.

Yet again the phone switched to messages. Wynne was desperate to speak to his Gillian. He really believed he could help. And he was prepared to do anything, anything at all, to help. He always had been.

Just as he was wondering what to do next, Marjorie returned to the kitchen. Still drunk, still angry. But surprisingly lucid.

'You're a liar, as well as everything else, aren't you?' she remarked almost conversationally.

'I don't know what you mean,' Wynne muttered.

'Oh yes, you do. I overheard almost everything you said to those detectives. You just think I'm drunk. Not that drunk, I can tell you.'

Wynne did his best to hide how uneasy that made him feel.

'So what?' he enquired, displaying as much assertive disdain as he could muster.

'So, I know you lied. I know you weren't here all day yesterday, don't I? And you'd better keep on the right side of me, or I shall tell on you.'

With that Marjorie started to laugh. And she was still laughing as she turned and left the room, her gait a little uncertain, but at the same time purposeful.

Wynne cursed her under his breath. He also cursed himself. He should have been more careful. Perhaps he should just have told the truth from the start. After all, nothing was much worse than being caught out in a lie by the police. He was pretty sure that it was a criminal offence, perverting the course of justice, or something like that.

There had always been a chance that he might have been seen in the wrong place. That there might be a witness. Or that he might have been caught on CCTV. However, he had thought those were chances worth taking. But now Marjorie knew that he'd lied, and she gave every impression nowadays that she had come to hate his guts. It was quite likely that she would 'tell on him', sooner or later. The next time he upset her, or just the next time she got blind drunk – which was pretty certain to be sooner rather than later.

Wynne wondered if he should make a move first, contact the police again and confess what he had done. He thought it probably was his best option now, but, as ever, he wasn't sure he had the courage.

Meanwhile a large, metallic grey vehicle with tinted windows had just arrived in Northam. It's occupants followed their satnav to St Anne's Avenue.

There was, of course, still a substantial police presence at the crime scene there. Several police and CSI vehicles were parked outside number eleven, which was cordoned off, its boundaries watched over by two uniformed officers.

The vehicle motored slowly past without stopping.

Its occupants were alarmed. They had no idea what had happened, or what the police presence might signify. They pulled into the first lay-by they came to and Googled both the St Anne's Avenue address and the name Thomas Quinn. Immediately they learned that Quinn had been murdered.

This caused them considerable unease. They wondered whether it was an incident unconnected with their visit to the area, or if there was a link – or at least a link with the disquieting activities which had come to their notice and caused them enough concern to warrant their personal attention and their presence in North Devon.

They discussed what they should do next. There were three men in the vehicle. One of them was clearly in charge. He made the final decision. The driver started up again and headed towards Bideford.

EIGHTEEN

Lilian called Kate, her capable, almost always up-beat friend with whom she had trained as a journalist. There was nobody else. And actually, there was probably nobody better either. But Kate, of course, knew nothing of her sham of a marriage nor of the kind of monster her handsome husband had turned out to be. And Lilian was well aware of the leap of faith she would be demanding from her old friend in order for her to accept that she had acted in self-defence when she stabbed Kurt so seriously she'd thought she had killed him.

To Lilian's relief Kate answered the phone straight away and sounded her usual breezy self.

'Sweetheart, great to hear from you, are we finally going to have that lunch?'

Lilian didn't know how long she would be allowed to speak on the phone. She cut to the chase.

'Look, I-I'm in police custody. I've been arrested. I nearly killed Kurt. He's in hospital. I don't know how badly hurt he is . . .'

Lilian heard a startled gasp down the line.

'You what?' Kate's voice was no longer breezy.

Lilian poured out as much as she could of the whole awful story as quickly as possible. She told Kate of Kurt's consistent violence towards her, although not the cause of it, and how he had taken obsessive control of every aspect of her life.

When she had finished there was silence for what seemed like a very long time.

'So that's why we've seen so little of you since you married him?'

'Yes.'

'I'd just convinced myself you were too tied up in your glamorous new life . . .' Kate paused, as if a thought had suddenly struck her. 'The last time we were supposed to meet, lunch at Joe's just before Easter, why did you cancel that morning?'

'Well, uh, I had a black eye and a swollen lip. I didn't want you to see me like that. I'd have had to explain.'

'I knew something was wrong,' Kate said. 'And you were spinning a yarn, weren't you, when you said you'd been in a remote part of Africa and your phone didn't work . . . I'm kicking myself now. Oh my God. It all seemed like such a fairy tale. Kurt, the wedding . . .'

Her voice tailed off.

Yes, thought Lilian, the wedding had been a fairy tale. The local magistrate had officiated in a romantic ceremony at the St John family mansion high above Cape Town. She and Kurt had taken their vows standing on a gently sloping lawn on a perfect sunny day, the ocean in the distance providing a sparkling backdrop. Kurt had arranged everything, even her beautiful wedding dress. She hadn't had to think about a thing, and had been ecstatically happy, blissfully unaware that this would be a pattern for the future and one she would come to deeply regret.

Kurt's father, of English origin, had died some years earlier.

His brother William, and his Afrikaans mother Gilda both appeared to welcome Lilian with open arms.

'If only James were alive to see this day,' Gilda St John had told Lilian. 'He so wanted Kurt to find the personal happiness we enjoyed.'

Lilian had glowed.

There were over two hundred people at the wedding, almost all Kurt's family, his numerous uncles, aunts, cousins and second cousins, and various business associates. Lilian had had no family present. Her only friends there were Kate and her lawyer husband Charlie.

Lilian actually had very little family left, and there had been no one else she'd really wanted to invite, and certainly no one she thought would even consider travelling all the way to South Africa to witness her nuptials.

But that wasn't quite the point. Blinded by her love for this extraordinary man who wanted to spend the rest of his life with her, Lilian had failed to notice that Kurt hadn't even asked her if she would like to invite anyone to the wedding.

Even when she'd mentioned that she wanted to invite Kate and Charlie, he'd paused for so long before replying that she had fleetingly wondered if he were going to refuse. Or at least question her request. But he hadn't.

'Of course, my darling, she is your dearest friend, of course she should be there,' he'd said.

And Lilian had thought at the time that she must have imagined the hesitation, the possible hint of dissent.

Neither had Lilian noticed that Kurt hadn't even asked her if she wanted to marry in South Africa. He'd just told her how it would be.

'Lilian, Lilian, are you still there?'

Kate's voice was full of anxiety now.

'Yes, yes, I was just thinking . . .'

'Look, we'll come as soon as we can,' Kate said. 'Charlie's at some law society do tonight. We'll drive down first thing in the morning. I presume you don't have a lawyer?'

'N-no.'

'Well, you need Charlie then, don't you, ASAP?'

'B-but I can't afford to pay him.'

She explained how Kurt had cut off her finances.

'There's always legal aid,' responded Kate, sounding breezy again now that she was organizing things, which was what she had always been best at.

'Just don't say another word to anyone till Charlie and I are with you,' Kate commanded before ringing off.

As soon as she'd finished the call, Lilian was led to a cell by a woman officer. She felt sure she would remember for the rest of her life how she felt when the heavy steel door crashed shut behind her.

The tears she had so far managed to hold back suddenly overwhelmed her.

It was as if her heart were about to stop beating. She could not believe she had sunk to such a low. Her head ached. Her mouth was dry. The brief moment of optimism she had experienced while talking to Kate evaporated without a trace. She could hear screaming, followed by the voice of a man, presumably another prisoner, shouting, 'Shut the fuck up, will you.'

Only then did she realize that it was she who was screaming. She made herself stop.

She turned to face the door. It contained a viewing panel with a sliding shutter. The shutter was open. Lilian could see a pair of eyes watching. She struggled to control herself, leaning against the far wall of the cell for support.

After a few seconds the eyes disappeared, and the shutter closed with a sharp metallic clunk.

Then with almost unreal clarity came the rhythmic tapping of retreating footsteps, and Lilian was suddenly and irrationally quite sure that she would remain locked in this bare little concrete box for ever.

The cell was around eight foot by six, its grubby cream walls covered in old graffiti, half scrubbed out. A lone light bulb hung untidily from the ceiling. The only furniture was a thin plastic mattress laid on a narrow concrete platform. There was a single, folded blanket. No pillow.

In a recessed area off one corner there was a lavatory pan without a seat. The recessed area had no door, and the lavatory could be seen easily from the viewing panel in the door to the cell.

Prisoners, Lilian realized, forfeit the right straight away to even the most elementary privacy. Even before they are convicted.

She sat down on the concrete bed and wrapped the blanket around her. The cell seemed cold in spite of the warmth of the day outside, and the blanket too thin to help much. She pulled her knees up to her chest and wound her arms tightly around her legs.

A police cell is a very solitary and, to those who have never been in one before, shocking place. That first night at Trinity Road police station was probably the longest of Lilian's life. Longer, even, then any of the awful nights she had spent with her violent husband.

She could not sleep, so she had plenty of time to think, to reflect not only on the terrible mess she was in, but also the chain of events that had brought her to such a place. And the man, of course.

NINETEEN

Vogel's phone rang just as he and Saslow were leaving the Williams' home. It was Morag Docherty, the Quinns' newly appointed FLO, reporting directly to the DCI as instructed.

She was calling from outside Greg Quinn's flat.

'They won't let me in, boss,' she said. 'Or rather Greg won't. He didn't even come to the door. Just told me on the intercom to go away, that his mother was sleeping and they didn't need a police nanny.'

Vogel smiled wryly. This was not an unusual response and did not indicate anything in particular.

'That's all right, Docherty,' he responded. 'You head back to the nick. We can't force the Quinns to accept a FLO into their home. In any case, Saslow and I are about to pay them a visit.'

He checked his watch as he ended the call and turned to Saslow.

'So, let's go straight to Kipling Terrace,' he instructed. 'We'd better visit Jason Patel later. It's almost two thirty already. We're meeting Dr Lamey at Greg Quinn's at three, and also we have rather more to put to Mrs Quinn than expected.'

Once in the car he asked Saslow what she had made of Wynne Williams.

'He's a bit of a worm, isn't he, boss?' the DS responded. 'But worms are famous for turning.'

Vogel chuckled.

'They are indeed, Saslow,' he responded. 'However, the question is, even if he wanted to, would he ever dare to attack a man so much his superior physically, a man clearly capable of considerable aggression? Does he have it in him?'

'One thing this job has taught me, boss, is how you never can tell what people might be capable of under the right circumstances, or perhaps I should say, the wrong circumstances,' Saslow replied. 'Williams is obviously besotted with Gill Quinn. And we both know how many murders, sometimes brutal murders, are committed in the name of love. We even have a name for them, don't we? Crimes of passion. Love should play no part in the taking of a life. But it does.'

'Very philosophical, DS Saslow,' said Vogel.

Kipling Terrace took the form of a line of conjoined houses, each painted blue and white, and divided into flats, standing proud above the seaside village of Westward Ho!. It was tall, wide, and imposing. Vogel studied the terrace with interest as he and Saslow approached. He had been vaguely aware of it previously, of course, but never been there, not even looked at the terrace properly before. And his first thought was that young Greg had done well for himself. Not being local he was unaware that Kipling Terrace had a chequered past, and that both rentals and purchases there remained something of a bargain.

Vogel and Saslow were a few minutes early for their appointed meeting with Dr Lamey, but so was she. She had already parked in one of the visitors' spaces when the two officers arrived. She got out of her car to greet them, and they approached the apartment together. They had not notified Greg or his mother of their intended arrival. Vogel was confident of finding them both in. Not only had PC Docherty spoken on the intercom to Gregory Quinn less than half an hour previously, Gill Quinn was unlikely to have fully recovered from the state of extreme shock she had been in earlier. Vogel had seen Greg Quinn with his mother. He didn't think the young man would leave her alone.

Whether or not Greg would let them in without a tussle was another matter.

Greg answered the intercom quickly. 'Why don't you leave us alone?' he said. 'You know the state Mum's in. I thought she was sent home to rest. On doctor's orders.'

'That's correct, Greg,' said Vogel. 'However, there's been a development, and we cannot now wait any longer before seeing your mother again. I have Dr Lamey with me.'

'I don't care, you're not coming in,' Greg countered. 'I've just sent the other one away.'

Vogel knew the young man must be referring to Morag Docherty.

'Greg, it is entirely your choice whether or not you welcome a family liaison officer into your home,' he said. 'However, I am the senior officer in charge of a murder investigation, and if I wish to see you or your mother you have no choice. If you do not let us in I shall acquire a warrant and, if necessary, force entry.'

'Oh, for fuck's sake,' muttered Greg Quinn.

Almost immediately there was a buzzing noise, allowing Vogel, Saslow and Dr Lamey to enter the building.

Greg was standing at the open door of his first-floor flat by the time they had climbed the single flight of stairs. As they stepped on to the landing he half closed the door behind him.

'Mum's asleep,' he murmured sotto voce, adding accusatively, 'you did say you were going to let her rest, Mr Vogel. What is this new development?'

'I am afraid we have fresh evidence, primarily of a medical nature, which we really need to put to your mother as a matter of urgency,' he said. 'And with a doctor in attendance.'

Greg looked as if he might protest, but ultimately he led the way into his white-painted sitting room, simply furnished but high-ceilinged and spacious and, of course, offering spectacular views. He shut the door carefully, then spoke quietly again.

'I don't know exactly what you want with my mother now, but I can guess where you're heading, and I can tell you one thing,' he said. 'She didn't kill my father. There is no way she could do a thing like that. She couldn't do it, and she didn't do it.'

In view of the fact that Gill Quinn had just been supplied with what would appear to be an unimpeachable alibi, Vogel considered there was a fair chance the young man might be right. But he didn't intend to tell him that. Not yet. Meanwhile he wanted to see for himself the level of the abuse Gill had allegedly suffered at her husband's hands. And he wanted her examined again by a doctor before the signs of that apparently horrific abuse became any less visible.

'Greg, I really am sorry to intrude again so quickly,' he said. 'But I must ask you to rouse your mother and bring her to us. It could be imperative to our investigation, and it could also be very much in her interest.'

'All right,' said Greg resignedly. 'I'll get her. But I'm not happy. I'm worried about her. It won't take long, will it?'

Vogel shook his head. 'I hope not. And don't forget, Greg, Dr Lamey is here.'

Greg returned in a few minutes with his mother. Gill was wearing a dressing gown, presumably belonging to her son, which was far too big for her. She looked, unsurprisingly, to be still in considerable distress. In addition she had clearly just woken from a deep sleep. Dr Lamey's medication had obviously done the trick.

Vogel addressed her gently as her son led her to a chair. She seemed a little woozy. Also the effect of the medication, Vogel assumed.

'I'm sorry to bother you again so soon, Gill,' he said. 'But some further information has come our way and I do need to ask you some more questions as a matter of urgency. Firstly, was your husband ever abusive towards you, Gill?'

Gill Quinn's lower lip began to wobble. Vogel thought she might be about to cry, but she didn't.

'He, uh, he liked to be in control,' she said. 'That's all. He liked me do things his way . . .'

'He was a bully, a horrible bully,' interjected Greg, suddenly rising to his feet. 'He made her life a misery—'

'Please Greg,' interrupted Vogel. 'If you wish to remain whilst we talk to your mother then I must ask you not to interfere. I shall want to talk to you later.'

Greg sat down again without further protest.

'Gill, was your husband ever physically violent towards you?'

For what seemed to be an inordinately long time Gill did not respond. Vogel began to wonder whether she would reply at all, or whether there would merely be a repeat of the persistent silence she had inflicted on them earlier. Then she spoke. Falteringly, yet devastatingly. She stumbled over her words, but the message was clear enough.

'H-he didn't mean to be. He never meant it. I know that. It was nothing. R-really. I'm sure it h-happens in many marriages . . .'

Gill's voice drifted off.

'We've been told that he attacked you, on not infrequent occasions, and that he hurt you very badly sometimes. Is that not so?'

'N-not that badly.'

'Gill, we have also been told that you spent most of yesterday at Helen's House, which, of course, is a refuge for victims of domestic violence. Is that where you were yesterday afternoon, Gill?'

Greg looked for a split second as if he might interrupt again, but he didn't. Vogel noticed, though, that he was staring at his mother with what appeared to be a mixture of horror and amazement.

'It's confidential, everything that happens at Helen's House is confidential,' said Gill, almost as if she was reciting a mantra. 'Nobody there ever breaks a confidence. That's the rule.'

'We are conducting a murder inquiry, Gill. Your husband is dead, he has been murdered, and you are a person of interest. Helen Harris has informed us that you were at the House all day yesterday, and that could be vital evidence which she was absolutely right to present to us. It could also prove your innocence. If her evidence is correct you could not have killed your husband. I'm going to ask you again, were you at Helen's House yesterday?'

There was another pause before Gill answered.

'I, uh, y-yes, yes I was there.'

Gill's voice was a half whisper.

'Is it correct that you were there between the hours of approximately eight a.m. and six p.m.?'

'Y-yes,' stumbled Gill.

'Did you leave the House at all during those hours?'

'No.'

'Are you quite sure?'

'Yes.'

'Not even for a breath of fresh air?'

'No.'

'Gill, you must realize the impact this information has on your situation, and yet you chose not to impart it yourself. It changes everything. You have an alibi. Why did you not tell us that you were at Helen's House, Gill?'

'Because it's private, it's nobody else's business.'

'It's my business now, I'm afraid, Gill,' responded Vogel. 'And I need to ask you this: were you there because your husband had attacked you?'

'It was b-between us, it was nothing,' Gill replied almost inaudibly.

'Well Gill, as you can see I've brought Dr Lamey with me. I need her to examine you again.'

'No, no. I don't want that. I d-don't want to be examined. There's no reason to examine me, and you have no right. N-no right at all.'

'I think there is reason, Gill. And if you're not prepared to cooperate, then I shall have to arrange for you to be taken elsewhere. If necessary back to the hospital. And ultimately the station again. For another formal interview.'

Greg spoke again then, but more quietly, and addressing his mother. 'Mum, you should do as Mr Vogel asks,' he said. 'This is important. We don't want you going back to the police station, do we? And I want to know what's been going on too. Do it for me. Please Mum.'

Greg's voice when he was speaking to his mother was entirely different. Gentle. Full of concern and affection.

Gill shrugged. 'All right, if you must,' she said.

Dr Lamey took her temperature, checked Gill's pulse and her blood pressure, just as she had earlier in the day, and looked at her hands and wrists. Then she asked her to stand and pull up her tracksuit top, so that she could examine the fading bruising on her abdomen.

'I told them in the hospital,' began Gill. 'I had to do an emergency stop in the car, and the steering wheel . . .'

She stopped abruptly, perhaps aware that nobody in the room believed a word she was saying.

'Would you sit down again, please,' instructed Dr Lamey.

Gill did so.

'I would just like to check behind your ears, please,' said Dr Lamey, stepping forward.

Gill gasped. She held up both hands in front of her face, palms outwards.

'No. no, no,' she screamed. 'Don't you touch me. Don't you dare touch me. You have no right to touch me.'

Dr Lamey stepped back, perhaps involuntarily.

Greg ran to his mother's side, crouched down and put his arms around her, making soothing noises. Very gradually, the woman calmed down.

Vogel watched in silence. He reckoned anything he or Saslow said right then would only make matters worse. This was a moment when a police officer needed to do the most difficult thing of all. Take a watching brief and leave well alone.

'I want to know what's going on, Mum,' said Greg. 'I want to know what's been happening to you, why the doctor wants to look behind your ears. I'm going to take a look for myself, is that all right?'

Gill neither replied nor moved.

With great care, Greg brushed his mother's hair away from one ear and, pushing the upper part of the ear forwards, he leaned in slightly to look behind.

Gill winced.

'Oh my God,' cried Gregory. His voice was full of anguish now.

'Oh no, oh no. Mum, why didn't you tell me? I knew he was a bully. But this? Why didn't you tell me?'

'It was too much, just too much,' whispered Gill.

'Oh, my God,' said Greg again.

'I was ashamed, so ashamed,' Gill continued. 'I didn't want anyone to know. Not even you. Particularly not you, my darling . . .'

Vogel, Saslow and Dr Lamey were all facing mother and son. They could not see what Gregory was seeing. Dr Lamey was closest. She moved quickly forwards until she was standing behind Gill Quinn. Vogel saw her face change as she saw what Gregory had seen. No doubt the doctor was used to all manner of horrors. And like Vogel, she'd had a fair idea what to expect. None the less she appeared stunned and appalled.

'You have to see this, chief inspector,' she said.

Greg gestured to Vogel to come closer. His mother seemed compliant now. As if she had finally given in to the inevitable, Vogel thought.

He and Saslow moved alongside Dr Lamey. They had a clear view behind Gill Quinn's ear. The soft tissue there was covered with sores and scars, almost certainly burns administered by a lit cigarette, most in varying stages of healing, but one, red-raw and weeping, had obviously been inflicted very recently.

Vogel knew what to expect, of course, having already seen the photographs. But this was in the flesh. In more ways than one. And Vogel was shocked to the core. He had never seen anything quite like it, and he hoped he never would again.

'Gill, you have suffered quite terrible injuries,' said Vogel. 'Is your other ear like this?'

'Y-yes.'

Again she spoke in little more than a whisper.

'I'm just going to move your hair so that we can see behind your other ear,' said Dr Lamey. 'Is that all right?'

Gill remained sitting still, just nodding very slightly.

'I won't hurt you,' Dr Lamey assured her.

She reached out, and very carefully brushed Gill's hair away, pushing the upper part of the ear forward, as Greg had done with the first ear.

The flesh thus revealed was also horribly damaged, bearing a number of scars at varying stages and one very recent angry burn, almost certainly inflicted no earlier than the previous day, Vogel thought, the day Thomas Quinn was murdered.

'Gill, did your husband do that to you?' the DCI asked softly.

Gill did not respond at first. Again Vogel wondered whether or not she would answer at all.

'It's all right, Mum, I'm here,' said Greg. 'I'm always here. Beside you.'

Gill smiled weakly and clutched one of her son's hands in both of hers.

'Go on, tell Mr Vogel,' Greg continued. 'Dad did do it, didn't he?'

Gill began to weep. Big heaving sobs wracked her body.

'Yes,' she said, between her tears. 'He did it. Again and again and again. He burnt me. He hit me. He hurt me in ways so terrible I have never been able to tell anyone.'

'Why didn't you tell me, Mum, why on earth didn't you tell me?' asked Greg, distress and bewilderment clear in his voice.'

'You are my son, I didn't want you to be hurt, you are the last person in the world I would have told,' she said, suddenly quite articulate. 'And you would never have understood. How could you?'

TWENTY

Lilian had not given any proper thought to Kurt's reluctance to sleep with her before their marriage. He'd told her his respect and love for her was such that he wanted her to be his in every way before they had sex together, and that meant he wanted her to be his wife first. She had found it touching, unusual, refreshing, and more than a little romantic. His subsequent inability to have intercourse on their honeymoon she had, to begin with, dismissed as merely a nervous blip. There had been too much of a build-up to the big moment. Neither of them had been able to relax properly.

It was only after they returned to London, to Penbourne Villas, that he had succeeded in achieving complete intimacy with her. It was after he had hit her for the first time – but only a couple of light, if perhaps overly enthusiastic, slaps on her buttocks, nothing which concerned her unduly. She had simply been delighted that their marriage had finally been consummated, and that Kurt had been suddenly more than capable of full intercourse.

Nonetheless he'd apologized profusely afterwards, and hesitantly explained how much slapping her had turned him on. For which he apologized even more. She could not now believe how unconcerned she had been. There was just nothing about Kurt, so courteous, so apparently gentle, so obviously in love with her, to prepare her for the nightmare to come.

However, the slaps became more severe every time they had sex. Always he was apologetic afterwards, but always he seemed to go a little further than the last time.

The night when he finally punched her full in the face would be engraved upon her soul forever. Her head had rocked back on her shoulders, her nose began to bleed and her lip split open. The force was such that she was momentarily concussed. Even so she could not to fail to notice the sexual frenzy evoked in Kurt. His penis was rock hard and enormous when he lunged into her, and it hurt almost as much as the punch. There was no foreplay. His foreplay had been quite simply to cause her pain. She lay sobbing beneath him, and the greater her distress became, the more enhanced, it seemed, was his pleasure.

One half of Lilian still remained unable to accept that any of this could be happening to her. After all, hadn't she been the bright young thing of her year at school, sailing off to university to study literature, effortlessly entering the world of journalism?

But even that had not gone quite the way she had originally imagined, of course. She'd seen herself as a hard-hitting investigative journalist putting the world to rights. She'd ended up as the features editor of a monthly magazine called *Keyhole*, a showbiz glossy, a kind of downmarket *Hello*, with more smut and less airbrushing.

By the time she reached her early thirties Lilian had begun to harbour some serious regrets. She'd wondered if those other so important things in life, like a family, and having children, had passed her by.

Then she had met Kurt, at the *Keyhole*-sponsored wedding of a South-African-born supermodel, and when he had proposed marriage, only weeks later, she'd had no hesitation in accepting.

Lilian had found him irresistible. Not least because he seemed to want everything that she did. Neither of them had been married before. Kurt, at forty-three, was ten years older than her. They joked that they had saved themselves for each other. Only it wasn't entirely a joke.

In the beginning it wasn't Kurt who had pushed Lilian to walk so entirely away from her old life. It was she who'd expressed her willingness, even her eagerness, to give up her job and concentrate entirely on her forthcoming marriage and on having a family. She had no wish to be Ms Lilian Cook any more. She wanted to be Mrs Kurt St John. She wanted to take her man's name and to be taken into his world.

Lilian resigned at once from *Keyhole* and her editor agreed to waive her notice period. It was perhaps the greatest irony of her life that she had felt so wonderfully free when she'd settled into the first-class apartment of an aircraft bound for South Africa on her way to marry the handsome charmer at her side.

Even now she could remember clearly how happy and excited she'd been. In stark contrast, her present plight seemed like a terrible dream. It wasn't though. It was grim reality.

TWENTY-ONE

Dr Lamey left after completing her examination of Gill Quinn. She would be submitting a written report later. But she had already made her prognosis clear. The dreadful injuries Gill had suffered were burns, deliberately inflicted and almost certainly with a lit cigarette. No other conclusion was possible.

Gill had mercifully stopped sobbing. Saslow took Greg into the kitchen to make his mother a cup of tea, leaving Vogel alone with Gill. And Vogel took the opportunity to ask her about her relationship with Wynne Williams.

'He's my headmaster,' she responded quickly. 'That's all. Why are you asking me about him?'

Vogel ignored the question. 'Is he not something rather more to you than that?' he asked.

'No. Well, yes. He's a friend.'

'Just a friend?'

'Yes.'

'Your husband thought he was rather more than that, didn't he?'

'Thomas was always jealous. Usually of nothing. That's what led to . . . Well, all too often it led to him doing . . . uh, doing things to me . . .'

'We have spoken to Mr Williams today,' Vogel continued. 'He told us that he was in love with you. Indeed that he is still in love with you. He wanted you to go away with him, and he told you that. Isn't that the case?'

'I don't know. Well, y-yes, he did say things like that. I never thought he meant it. Like I said, I just thought of him as a friend. And my boss, of course.'

'Mr Williams also told us what happened in the pub on Friday evening. He called it "your special place", by the way, yours and his. He told us how your husband turned up in a fury and dragged you away. Very nearly literally.'

'Well yes, like I told you, Thomas was so jealous. He was very angry that night.'

'Mr Williams said you looked afraid.'

'Of course I was afraid. I knew what was in store for me.'

'Was it after that incident that he attacked you? That he inflicted those awful burns on you?'

'Yes. Almost as soon as we got home. H-he'd done it before, of course.'

'That much is quite clear. And this was a regular occurrence, was it not? We do have a doctor's opinion.'

'Yes, it was. But only relatively recently. His violent outbursts had got worse and worse over the last year. He couldn't cope with lockdown at all. His business was in trouble, too, although he wouldn't admit it.'

'I understood that your husband was a very successful businessman, and that he'd made a lot of money, particularly during lockdown, is that not so?'

'I think he did at first. But there was some big property deal that went wrong. He couldn't get planning permission or something. And I think he'd invested millions. Possibly money that he'd borrowed. He kept getting these phone calls, I don't know who from, but they seemed to scare him. He hated being stuck at home with me, of course, but I suspected it was his business troubles that sent him into such terrible rages. Thomas couldn't ever accept that he'd failed in anything. He didn't make mistakes. It was always somebody else's fault. But I was pretty sure things were going wrong even before Covid, whoever's fault it was.'

'Thomas also abused you in other ways, didn't he? By controlling you, bending you to his will.'

'I suppose so.'

'Why on earth didn't you leave him, Gill?'

Vogel wasn't sure he should have asked that, not even in an informal interview. He just couldn't help himself.

'Leave him?' Gill replied. 'Leave him for what? To go where? We married young. I was twenty and pregnant. Tommy, that was what he was always called in those days, was a year younger. I was at university in my home town, Plymouth, and I lived at home. Tommy was my first. He swept me off my feet. He was always a charmer when he wanted to be.'

'Not lately though, Gill, judging from those scars of yours.'

Gill smiled wryly. 'No, but it really was only since Covid that he turned into . . . well, he did become a monster. And I did think about leaving him. Several times. I also thought, when we all got back to normal after Covid, Thomas would get back to normal too. And I could cope with his normal. It wasn't all bad. I have some good memories too. You're like Greg. You could never understand.'

'You're probably right, Gill. I don't think I could ever understand. Funny thing is though, I can understand you wanting to kill him.'

Vogel had no doubt he shouldn't have said that. Again he hadn't been able to help himself.

'But you know I didn't, don't you? You know where I was at the time he died. You know I couldn't have done it.'

'So it would seem, Gill. I wonder, though, do you have any idea who might have killed your husband.'

'Me? No. Of course not. How could I?'

'Well, did Thomas have any enemies?'

'He would certainly have crossed a few people in business over the years, he was that sort, and I got the impression there were some pretty angry business associates out there at the moment. I told you, those phone calls. But I can't think that there would be anyone who would want to kill him.'

'What about Wynne Williams?'

'Wynne? Good God. You've met him. Wynne wouldn't hurt a fly.'

'He's besotted with you, Gill. It's amazing what people will do, the lengths to which they will go when they are in love. Mr Williams actually told us he would do anything for you . . .'

Greg, followed by Saslow, re-entered carrying a tray with four mugs on it and a bowl of sugar.

'What's this about Wynne Williams?' he asked.

'Mr Vogel thinks Wynne might have killed your father, and that I may have helped him do it, or perhaps that he did it just because he thought I wanted your father dead,' said Gill bluntly.

She was suddenly beginning to sound considerably more on the ball. Indeed quite sharp. Vogel could for the first time imagine her holding down a senior teaching and admin job. The miracle of sleep, he thought, not for the first time.

'What?' said Greg, looking and sounding perplexed. 'I mean, why?'

'Because, Greg, Mr Williams is in love with your mother,' said Vogel.

He too could be blunt, when he thought it might be to his advantage.

'And he was aware of your father's abusive behaviour towards her,' Vogel added.

'Mum?' Greg queried, sounding astonished. 'Are you having an affair with Mr Williams?'

'No, I'm not. Your father thought so though. Or at least, he said he did. Sometimes I thought that might be an excuse for . . .' She paused. 'For what he did to me.'

'So is that why Dad went for you on Friday night?'

'Yes. He caught us in the pub together.'

'You went out with him?'

'It wasn't "going out". Not like that. Not for me, anyway.'

'But you told him what Dad did to you. And you never told me.'

'I didn't tell him the half of it. Anyway, I've explained that. You're my son. I didn't want you to be affected by it all.'

'Well, I am now, aren't I? I'd have made you leave him, Mum, I'd have taken care of you. None of this would have happened if only you'd told me . . .'

Greg's voice tailed away. His eyes had filled with tears.

'I wanted to protect you from it,' said Gill.

'I wish you hadn't.'

Vogel stepped in then.

'Greg you lived at home until you were seventeen, with both your parents, you have continued to see your mother frequently, to spend as much time as possible with her. Did you really not know about your father's violence towards her?'

'No, I didn't. I swear. Upon my life. I knew he was controlling, and unkind. But I never imagined for a moment anything like I've seen today. I had no idea. If I had known, I'd have done something about it.'

Maybe he had done something about it, thought the DCI. He did not voice his thoughts though. He would save that for a formal interview. And, ideally, he would like to have at least some evidence first. Could it be possible, he wondered, that the young man really hadn't known about Thomas' physically abusive behaviour? Or was he acting?

'Yet you moved out of the family home when you were so young,' Vogel continued eventually. 'If you didn't know what your father was doing to your mother, why was that?'

'We didn't get on. I told you that before. And he tried to control me too. To make me do what he wanted, not what I wanted. I wasn't going to have it.'

'You had a privileged education, you could have gone on to university, taken up a profession, anything. Yet you gave it all up, left school with no qualifications, I understand, and walked away from both your mother and your father—'

'I didn't walk away from my mother, and I never would, she knows that,' interrupted Greg. 'And I did have a few GCSEs. But I wasn't an academic, that's for sure. I always liked working with my hands, making things. I'd already worked for Durrants in the school holidays. Mike Durrant took a shine to me, he offered to take me on as an apprentice. He fixed me up with digs too.'

'Greg's always been independent, and a hard worker,' said Gill, suddenly every inch the proud mother. 'He's done well for himself, too, I always knew he would.'

Vogel was just considering whether he should continue with this line of questioning, or whether he should save it for the inevitable formal interview, when his phone rang. It was DI Peters, calling from the incident room.

Vogel excused himself and stepped out into the hall.

'Boss, we've just had a report of a disturbance in Tide Reach, that new building on The Pill,' she began.

Momentarily Vogel wondered why she was telling him that, but he kept quiet. There was sure to be a very good reason. He had developed a considerable respect for Janet Peters.

'Thing is, boss, that's where Thomas Quinn's company have their offices,' the DI continued, immediately offering an explanation for her call, just as Vogel had expected. 'And the chap who called in heard what he thought could have been gunfire. Tide Reach is mostly made up of offices, so you'd expect them to be empty on a Sunday, but there are two apartments at the top of the building, and our caller lives in one of them. He's been told to stay put until we've checked the place out. The other apartment is unoccupied, apparently.'

Vogel experienced the familiar frisson of excitement he always felt when he suddenly learned something that might be of significant import in a case. This time it was accompanied by the merest tremor of fear. He'd been told there may have been gunfire. And Vogel didn't like guns.

'Has anyone tried to contact Thomas' business partner again?' he asked.

'Jason Patel? You and Saslow were on your way to see him, weren't you?'

'Yes. But we haven't got to him yet. We're at Greg Quinn's place. You could try him on the phone.'

'Will do, boss.'

'Are first responders on the way?'

'Yes, boss. Ambulance and armed response too, just in case. As there might be guns involved, we're taking no chances.'

Vogel had already learned enough about North Devon to have a reasonable grasp of logistics.

'We're fifteen minutes away,' he said. 'Will attend.'

TWENTY-TWO

Lilian lay for hours on the concrete bed unable to sleep, and in any case fearing that if she did her troubled head would be invaded by another nightmare. The blanket she'd wrapped herself in smelt strongly of disinfectant. After a bit she didn't notice.

She must have eventually fallen into a fitful, although mercifully nightmare-less, sleep. She was woken by the rattle of the lock to her cell as they bought her tea and a pre-packed breakfast at seven a.m.

Two hours or so later they came for her again and took her back to the same interview room where she had spent most of the previous day.

This time DS McDermott was sitting at the table waiting for her, a sheaf of papers stacked tidily before him.

'You may be interested to know that your husband's condition is improving rapidly and that he is expected to make a full recovery, Mrs St John,' the DS began.

Lilian nodded. She didn't trust herself to speak.

'As hoped for, we have been able to take a full statement from Mr St John and there are a number of points arising which require clarification from you.'

Lilian felt herself beginning to panic again.

'I've been told not to say any more until my solicitor gets here,' she said.

McDermott raised one eyebrow. 'That's your prerogative, of course, but I thought you were happy to answer any questions that might clear this matter up.'

'Well yes, but—'

'It's up to you, Mrs St John. I mean, perhaps you'd like to change your statement. Perhaps Mr St John didn't force you to go to the hotel with him?'

'Of course I don't want to change my statement. Of course he forced me.'

'How exactly? Was he violent towards you?'

'Well, not exactly, but I told you, I was already so afraid of him. With good reason. He even put a tracker on my car, for God's sake. Then he took my car keys from me and made me go with him, he had his thugs with him . . .'

Lilian was vaguely aware of McDermott and Constable Richardson exchanging a swift glance, as if they no longer believed a word she was saying.

'We found your car in the Hotel du Vin car park, where your husband told us it was, Mrs St John. The vehicle is currently being examined by our technicians. They have already completed an electronic scan and have discovered no tracking devices. The keys, by the way, were in the ignition when the car was collected.'

'But don't you see?'

One half of Lilian knew she should stop this interview right away, refuse to answer any more questions until Charlie arrived, just as Kate had instructed her. But the other half of her was desperate to put the record straight, in spite of being acutely aware of a subtle change in McDermott's attitude towards her, even though his manner remained polite and professional.

'He would have had his people do that,' she continued. 'Remove the tracker, put the keys back.'

'Your husband says you drove to the hotel and met him there of your own free will. That is what happened, isn't it?'

'What? No. Of course it isn't.'

'He says you hadn't responded to any of his phone calls after the previous incident, even though he made it clear that all he wanted to do was put things right between you. He did not go to the London apartment which was your marital home, because he believed that he was wanted by the Met. But his absolute priority was to see you. So he invited you to stay with him in a hotel, in Bristol, the city that had once been your home, a place he knew you loved. And you accepted the invitation.'

Lilian was staggered. Throughout their brief marriage she had frequently been taken aback by the gall of the man. But she hadn't expected Kurt to be able to twist the truth so plausibly under these circumstances, not when he was still recovering from being stabbed, anyway.

'If you were so afraid of him why did you go to a place where you knew you would be alone with him?'

'I didn't. Honestly I didn't. He damn near kidnapped me off the streets. That's what really happened. I told you before. You have to believe me. I was afraid he would hurt me badly again if I didn't do what he said.'

'And yet the only person who got badly hurt in all this, Mrs St John, was your husband, was it not?'

'I did spend nearly three weeks in hospital after the last time he attacked me.'

'I am really only concerned with the incident in hand, Mrs St John. But, since you brought it up, your husband tells a different story about that too.'

'What?'

'Were the injuries that landed you in hospital for so long really caused by your husband beating you up, Mrs St John?'

'Of course they were. What do you think, for God's sake? Do you think I broke my own ankle? Fractured my own skull?'

'Not exactly. But I think some of these injuries may, just may, have been caused by rough sex. Is that not the case?'

'Rough sex?' Lilian's head was pounding. 'Rough sex? A fractured skull, a broken ankle, and cracked ribs?'

'Rough sex that went wrong, Mrs St John. It is, I understand, a matter of record that your husband called for help the night you were injured, and you were found lying in the central courtyard of your apartment block, is it not?'

'I don't know, I was unconscious.'

Lilian shouted the words out. She was all too aware that she was beginning to fall apart. A night in a police cell followed by this kind of questioning was proving to be more than she could cope with.

'Yes. But your husband tells us you fell from the balcony of your apartment during a cocaine-fuelled sex session. Or to be more exact, you were so off your head that you threw yourself off the balcony. Isn't that right?'

'No, no. It is not right.'

'Well, you do admit that you had been taking cocaine, I presume?'

'Only because he made me. He made me.'

'I see.'

DS McDermott sounded as if he saw nothing at all.

'Look, please, will you at least speak to the police in London?' Lilian requested desperately. 'Detective Sergeant Mitchell, at West End Central. She'll tell you what happened. She was the one who got the warrant issued for Kurt's arrest.'

'Actually there is no warrant out for your husband's arrest, Mrs St John,' said DS McDermott. 'Although Mr St John was also under the impression that a warrant had been issued, which is why he went to the lengths he did of assuming a false identity in order to find a way to meet up with you and try to rebuild a marriage he valued enough to risk his freedom for. In fact Mr St John was merely wanted for questioning, which is an entirely different matter.'

Lilian slumped in her chair, feeling utterly defeated. Hadn't DS Mitchell told her there was a warrant out for Kurt's arrest? She had surely let Lilian believe that, either deliberately or accidentally. Or had she just said the Met was looking for Kurt, that he would be found? Lilian was no longer sure of anything. She did, however, realize glumly that it was probably she who had told Kurt that there was a warrant out for him.

'In any case, as I have told you, my interest is entirely in the current incident,' the detective sergeant continued. 'Your husband assures us that not only did you willingly agree to join him in his hotel, but that you gave every indication that you wanted to have sex with him, until you suddenly seemed to go off your head again and attacked him.'

'Off my head again? Oh my God! That's just crazy.'

'Is it, Mrs St John? Perhaps you're right. Isn't this just more crazy drug-fuelled behaviour from you?'

Lilian felt as if an icy finger was running up and down her spine.

'What do you mean, drug-fuelled?'

'Well, presumably you do admit that you had been taking drugs again.'

'Again?'

'Your husband says you have been a regular cocaine user throughout your marriage.'

'Cocaine. Oh no . . .'

'You deny that?' McDermott removed some sheets of paper from the pile before him on the table. 'This is a copy of the report from the Charing Cross Hospital where you were taken after the earlier incident. You tested positive for cocaine. Indeed, the results showed that you had ingested substantial amounts of cocaine within hours of your admission. Has there been a mistake?'

'Yes. I mean no.' Lilian didn't know what to say. 'Look, I only ever took drugs because Kurt made me. He, uh, he liked the effect they had on me. And I, well. The coke made it all more bearable. Just a little. But I wasn't a user. I wasn't. Not the way you mean . . . Only when . . . when he . . .'

Her voice tailed off.

DS McDermott continued to look down at the papers on the table.

'You recall that you were examined by a doctor here at Trinity Road only yesterday, Mrs St John? You may also recall that he took blood samples. These quite clearly show, once again, traces of cocaine in your system.'

'But, but, I haven't taken any coke. Not since before the hospital. I haven't taken anything.'

'So how do you explain the result of these tests?'

'I don't know. Kurt must have . . . We had breakfast. We drank champagne . . . He could have put some in the food. We had scrambled eggs. He could have mixed it in. That would be most likely. I'm pretty sure he's done that before. It's not supposed to be so effective . . . But . . . I did think I felt strange . . . I had this adrenalin rush. Everything seemed so clear. Only it wasn't clear. I wasn't thinking straight. That's why I ran . . .'

Lilian began to weep.

DS McDermott studied her dispassionately.

'Lilian Mary St John, I am charging you with the attempted murder of your husband Kurt Arnold Anthony St John,' he said.

TWENTY-THREE

Saslow swung off the main drag onto The Pill, an area of town close to the banks of the tidal River Torridge, just as a police patrol car arrived, all lights and sirens blazing. Two uniforms, one male, one female, emerged swiftly, looking suspiciously at Saslow's unmarked car as she pulled to a halt. Vogel quickly jumped out of the car holding up his warrant card for the uniforms to see. He and Saslow were not yet known throughout the local force.

'I'm SIO on the Quinn murder, and we think it possible there may be a connection as Thomas Quinn's offices are in this building,' he announced by way of explaining his presence.

'Right, sir,' said the male officer. 'We've been asked to wait for Armed Response before we do anything. The man who called in saying he'd heard shots, wasn't sure exactly where in the building they'd come from.'

Vogel nodded. He wasn't good at being patient. He wondered if he dared knock on a few doors. Just as he was deciding that wouldn't be a good idea because, if indeed gunshots had been fired, he could put others at risk as well as Saslow and himself, a second police vehicle roared up to the front of Tide Reach. It was a BMW X5, the high-powered four-wheel drive typically used by Armed Response. They'd been commendably fast. But then, the AR boys and girls were probably relishing the chance of some action. Vogel didn't think North Devon was an area of the UK that was exactly overrun with incidents involving firearms.

It took AR only minutes to find the source of the disturbance, in a first-floor office, and to check out the rest of the building. They reported 'man down', and called in the paramedics, who had also just arrived.

Vogel and Saslow could now enter the building. Vogel dispatched Saslow to the top to see if she could locate the resident who'd made the emergency call. Vogel headed for the first-floor office which was clearly the location of the incident. An AR officer standing outside instructed him to remain on the landing for the time being. The first thing he noticed was the name embossed on the door. Quinn-Patel Associates. Then, moving forward very slightly and peering through the doorway, Vogel saw the fallen man, lying on his back, spreadeagled on the floor. He appeared to have been shot. At least twice. His head was towards the door and his legs pointed into the room. Blood was seeping from a wound to his right shoulder and from a second wound, probably more dangerous, a little lower. Two paramedics were at his side applying CPR.

Were they too late? Was the man already dead? Vogel couldn't be sure. He certainly wasn't conscious. Had he been shot as he tried to enter the offices? Vogel couldn't be sure of that either.

The DCI took a careful look round. The room in which the fallen man lay was open-plan, very modern in design and containing several desks. It seemed to have been ransacked. One desk and a couple of chairs lay on their sides. Drawers had been pulled open, papers were scattered across the floor, a coffee machine had been knocked over, its glass broken, and sat in a murky pool of water and coffee grounds. One of a line of wooden panels on the far wall had been removed revealing a small internal steel safe. The safe remained intact, although Vogel noticed that there were scratches, and perhaps signs of attempted drilling on the metal framework, indicating that it may have been unsuccessfully tampered with.

He was still considering what that might mean, when a second paramedic team arrived, carrying a stretcher and more equipment, making it necessary for him to step to one side.

He knew he was in the way, and that in any case there wasn't much more he could do at the scene for the time being. Not even the crime scene investigators would be allowed in until the paramedics had done all they could to save the shot man's life. In any police operation the saving of life is the first priority.

Vogel took a last look at the man lying on the floor. He had never met Jason Patel, and could not even see his face properly because of the attentions of the medics, but he would bet his pension that the victim lying there was Patel.

Suddenly they stopped applying CRP. For a moment Vogel

wasn't sure if that was good news or bad. Then an oxygen mask was strapped on to the fallen man's face, over his nose and mouth. Vogel thought that must be a good sign. Nonetheless, he realized it might still be a while before the paramedics attempted to move their patient. He decided he really should get out of the way, and set off back to the staircase where he met Saslow on her way down from the top of the building.

'I've just been talking to our emergency caller, he's still in his flat, one of the two penthouses at the top, if you want a further chat,' she began. 'He doesn't really have much to add, though. He didn't see anything at all, and heard nothing except the bangs he suspected were gunshots, followed by some heavy footsteps, like somebody running down the stairs. One thing though, apparently he was in the military, he's done tours to Afghanistan and served in the Middle East. He says he knows the sound of gunfire when he hears it—'

'He certainly does,' interrupted Vogel. 'At least two shots have been fired. And in the offices of Quinn-Patel Associates. Plus we have a critically injured casualty. I should think it's still touch and go whether he will pull through or not.'

'Is it who I think it might be?' asked Saslow.

'I expect so,' said Vogel. 'Almost certainly one Jason Patel, I reckon. And if I'm right, what we need to find out now is whether or not the shooting of Jason Patel is connected with the fatal stabbing of his business partner.'

'Bit of a coincidence if it isn't, wouldn't you think, boss?' Saslow remarked. 'Don't reckon there are too many stabbings and shootings round here, are there? And we've had one of each in twenty-four hours.'

'It is possible this is merely a burglary gone wrong,' responded Vogel. 'It's a Sunday. The perpetrators wouldn't have expected there to be anybody in these offices.'

'No, but they came prepared, didn't they? Carrying firearms. Or, at least, one firearm.'

'Yes, they did.'

'And you don't like coincidences, do you, boss?'

'No, I most certainly don't, Saslow. If only because almost always when I find myself confronted with a coincidence, it turns out to be anything but.'

TWENTY-FOUR

Lilian was told she would be remanded in police custody. Kate and Charlie arrived just minutes after she had been charged.

As her legal representatives, albeit loosely speaking in the case of Kate, they were allowed to talk to her in the cell to which she had been returned.

'Why did you let them interview you before Charlie got here?' Kate asked, sounding somewhat exasperated.

Lilian tried to explain that she felt she had been more or less tricked into it.

'We'll deal with that later,' said Charlie. 'If the police haven't behaved correctly that may well help our defence.'

Charlie was as Lilian remembered him. Super confident. He was a tall handsome man with a mop of curly brown hair which Lilian had always thought to be rather wonderful. She was greatly relieved when he confirmed that he was willing to formally represent her. However, she felt she had little choice but to point out, as she already had to Kate, that she had no way of paying him.

'We'll sort that out later, too,' said Charlie. 'St John has no right to cut you off without a penny. We'll fight that in the civil courts if necessary. If not we can go for legal aid. Anyway, I don't see this case actually going for trial. Not with the injuries you've suffered at his hands. And, as well as beating you to a pulp, it seems St John fled to South Africa, then, having changed his appearance, came back into this country on a false passport. If there is any justice in this case, he's the one who should end up in the dock. We really ought to be able to get the charge against you dropped before there are any big legal fees.'

Lilian was more than a little cheered. Charlie was so sure of himself. And he was quite right, of course. She really was the victim, not Kurt.

'The first step is to get you out of here,' Charlie continued.

'As soon as you are formally charged, I feel sure we won't have a problem getting you bailed.'

'Thank you, Charlie,' said Lilian. 'I don't know what I'd do without you. And Kate.'

She meant it too.

'You won't have to do without us,' said Kate.

Then, ever practical and aware of the importance of appearances, she added: 'We'd better get you some clothes to wear too. God knows how long the police will hang on to your own stuff.'

Later that day Lilian was duly charged at Staple Hill magistrates court with the attempted murder of her husband Kurt St John. Wearing the neat navy-blue suit, and appropriate accessories, which Kate had deemed suitable for the occasion and acquired at a nearby Zara, she pleaded not guilty on the grounds of self-defence, as instructed by Charlie. And she was granted bail. As Charlie had predicted.

'Good job the bastard's not dead, you can almost never get bail for someone on a murder charge,' remarked Charlie conversationally.

Outside the court, Lilian thanked her friends profusely for coming to the rescue.

'What are you going to do now?' asked Kate. 'You can't go back to Penbourne Villas, that's for sure.'

'No, I can't, but I haven't really got that far yet. All I've been able to think about is getting out of that police cell,' answered Lilian. 'I suppose I could try to contact my cousin Laura again. I was outside her house when Kurt abducted me, after I'd fled London, but she wasn't there.'

'Look, you must come and stay with us,' said Kate quickly. 'Charlie and I have talked about it. You need to be somewhere safe until all this is sorted out. Anyway, we'd love to have you. It will be like old times.'

Lilian didn't think anything in her world would ever be like old times again. But she accepted Kate's invitation with immense gratitude.

Kate and Charlie lived in Islington, in a tall narrow house of which Lilian had many happy memories. She did feel safe there, at first, anyway, and was immensely grateful for the sanctuary her friends had provided.

However, her relief at being no longer held in custody was continually overshadowed by the enormity of what might lie ahead.

Her bedroom was at the front of the house, overlooking the main street. Lilian quickly fell into the habit of sitting in a chair by the window, trying to read, but more often just gazing out at the street, sometimes not looking at anything, sometimes people watching.

After a week or so she became aware of a black Range Rover driving slowly past. And she suddenly felt sure it was not the first time she had seen it. A few minutes later the same vehicle passed by again. She was also pretty sure she caught a glimpse of ginger hair. Of course, she couldn't be certain that it was the vehicle which had been used to stalk her in London, and had subsequently brought Kurt to Bristol, but, chillingly, it all fitted.

She told Kate, and was instantly aware that her friend thought she was overreacting.

'Look, this is Chelsea tractor territory, Lilian,' said Kate. 'SUVs of all makes are not exactly thin on the ground. You're in shock. Kurt wouldn't dare harass you now. Not with the trial about to happen.'

'You don't understand what he is capable of,' Lilian told her, and she tried to explain that it was absolutely in character for Kurt to be watching the house.

'He won't want me to go to jail,' she explained. 'I'm his property. That's how he sees it. He will still want me in his life. And he has always been prepared to go to any lengths to get whatever he wants. He'll be plotting something. I have no doubt of that.'

'We will help you get through this, whatever happens, you know that, don't you?' Kate assured her friend.

However, the truth was that Lilian did not believe she would ever get through it.

For a start, whatever happened with the police case against her, any financial settlement with Kurt was likely to take months. If not years. And whatever Kate and Charlie said, she realized that would soon cause her major problems.

Her rucksack containing the few belongings she had taken from Penbourne Villas – excepting the clothes she had been wearing when Kurt was stabbed, which were evidence – was finally returned to her. To her relief the Hockney was safely inside it. Lilian wondered if the police even realized what it was and its potential value. Certainly they hadn't mentioned it.

She just wished she could sell the little painting, but she had absolutely no idea how to go about it. She couldn't take it to a reputable gallery or dealer, or ask Kate or Charlie to do so for her. The provenance of the Hockney was clearly Kurt's, and the court case looming over her was a matter of public record. Nobody reputable in the art world would touch the painting.

She had assumed that her car, worth surely twenty or even thirty thousand pounds, would be released to her once the police finished examining it, and she had hoped to sell it. But when Charlie pursued the matter, he was told that the BMW had already been released to Mr St John. After all, Kurt was the registered owner.

Then came the biggest blow of all. Charlie's optimistic prediction turned out to be totally wrong.

'It seems the police and the CPS have no intention of dropping the attempted murder charge against you,' Charlie told her. 'I really didn't expect this. But don't worry. We will fight on, and we will win.'

Lilian was worried. Worried sick. From the beginning Charlie had not grasped the extent of Kurt's influence. Her husband was powerful, rich, charismatic and totally unscrupulous. He also had friends in high places. She felt that she did not stand a chance against him. After all, she had never stood a chance before.

Even the not insignificant matter of Kurt entering the country on a false passport had been held on file until after the conclusion of Lilian's case.

Lilian was going to trial. Her worst fears had been realized.

TWENTY-FIVE

Rather to everyone's surprise the man injured in the Tide Reach shooting regained consciousness within hours of his arrival at the North Devon District Hospital. It seemed that both bullet wounds had somewhat miraculously failed to penetrate any major organs.

Photo ID documents found in the wallet he was carrying in his jacket pocket had confirmed his identity. The man was, as Vogel had so strongly suspected, Thomas Quinn's thirty-seven-year-old business partner, Jason Patel.

As soon as they heard the news of his at least partial recovery, in spite of it being almost midnight, Vogel and Saslow set off for the NDDH. They had been told they could have just a few minutes with Patel, who was not considered to be out of danger, and remained in the intensive care unit.

DI Peters had earlier allocated a team to find out all they could about Patel and his background. It seemed his grandfather, Ali, had been a Ugandan refugee, expelled from his country of birth by the despot Idi Amin back in 1972. Unusually, the Patels had settled in North Devon. They were a hard-working family who integrated well into the local community. Ali, in the way that was to become something of a tradition amongst Asian immigrants, opened a small general store, selling everything from newspapers to hot bacon rolls. Ali's son Rohit, Jason's father, married an English girl, hence Jason's name. Rohit became an accountant, opening his own successful business in Bideford, which Jason, who also trained as an accountant, took over upon his father's unexpected death from an aneurism several years earlier. Also like his father, Jason married an English girl, from whom it was believed he was divorced.

When Jason had suddenly sold the family business three years previously and gone into partnership with Thomas Quinn, it had apparently been a big surprise to the local business community.

Not least because the seemingly solid accountant had entered a much less certain world.

In his hospital bed, Patel was propped into an almost sitting position with a nasal drip, tubes out of his arm, and all the usual paraphernalia of a specialist ICU, when Vogel and Saslow arrived at his bedside.

His eyes were closed when the two officers entered the room. But after Vogel spoke his name loudly a couple of times, Patel slowly opened them. It seemed to take him a few seconds to focus.

Vogel introduced himself and Saslow. Looking at Patel he did not think they were likely to glean a great deal yet. Nonetheless he began to ask questions, starting with an obvious one which would help him to judge the man's mental condition.

'Do you know where you are, Mr Patel?' he asked.

'Yes,' responded Jason Patel. 'I'm in hospital.'

'Do you know which hospital?'

'No . . .' Patel paused. 'Well, I'd guess the NDDH.'

'Do you know why you are here?'

'Yes. I've been shot.'

Patel's voice was weak, but he seemed lucid enough. So far.

'Do you know who shot you?'

Patel looked uneasy. Or perhaps just bewildered. He shook his head.

'Mr Patel, I'm going to ask you that question again, and this time I would be grateful if you could answer in words. Do you know who shot you?'

'N-no. I don't.'

'But last night, after you were told that Thomas Quinn had been killed, you asked for police protection. Who were you afraid of, Mr Patel?'

'I don't know. I w-was in shock. I couldn't believe Thomas was dead . . .'

'We believe there were armed men in your office when you arrived there today. Do you remember how many of them there were, and did you recognize any of them?'

'No. I d-don't . . . I don't know what happened. Only what I've been told . . .'

'Why's that, Mr Patel?'

'I don't remember anything. I don't remember anything before I woke up here.'

'Do you remember where you were when you were shot?'

'N-no. I remember leaving my house this afternoon. I think I was going to the office . . .'

'On a Sunday?'

'Is it Sunday? Well, y-yes. Sometimes . . . And because of Thomas. There were things to do . . .'

Patel slumped backwards, sinking more deeply into the pillows. His voice had become even weaker. His face was grey and sweaty looking. Vogel suspected the nurse standing by would not allow this interview to continue for long. In any case it was not getting them very far. Nonetheless he decided to continue until he was asked to stop.

'Mr Patel, have you any idea why anybody would want to shoot you?'

Patel shook his head again. He looked as if he might no longer have the strength to speak. Vogel did not press him. On cue the nurse stepped forward and placed a hand lightly on the DCI's arm.

'I think that will have to be enough for now, Mr Vogel,' she said.

'I understand,' said Vogel. 'When do you think we'd be able to try again?'

'Some time tomorrow, hopefully,' said the nurse. 'If all goes well.'

Jason Patel was clearly seriously hurt. But Vogel couldn't help wondering how much of his amnesia was genuine.

As they left the room, Vogel turned to discuss the matter with Saslow, but was interrupted before he'd begun by a woman who had been sitting on one of the row of green plastic chairs outside the ICU. As soon as she saw Saslow and Vogel step into the corridor she stood up and approached them. She looked red-eyed and upset.

'Are you the police?' she asked.

Vogel agreed that they were.

'Have you been to see Jason, Jason Patel?' she continued.

Vogel did not answer that, instead he asked his own question.

'Would you please tell me who you are, madam?' he said.

'I'm Jason's wife,' said the woman. 'Maureen Patel. Well, his ex-wife actually.'

'I see,' said Vogel, who then introduced himself and Saslow. He thought the woman looked rather more distraught than one might expect an ex-wife to be. It seemed that she read his mind.

'We were married for thirteen years,' she said. 'Together for almost fifteen. Jason is the father of my children. In the end I could not stay with him. I just couldn't take any more. But I suppose I will always love him. In a way.'

'May I ask when you last saw your ex-husband?'

'Yes. Last Sunday. He usually takes the kids on a Sunday. Or visits them, at any rate. He didn't turn up today. I was just angry, at first. They get so disappointed, you see. He's usually a good father. But lately . . .'

Her voice tailed off.

'Lately what, Mrs Patel?' queried Saslow.

'Lately he's been all over the place. Totally unreliable. It's been building up for a couple of years. Why we split up, actually.'

'What exactly has been building up?' persisted Vogel.

'Look. He's not been the man I married, since . . . well, since he got involved with that Thomas Quinn.'

Well, she's blunt, thought Vogel. And that suited him well. He liked a witness who got to the point.

'Mrs Patel, do you know that Thomas Quinn is dead, that he has been murdered?' he asked.

'Yes, I do.'

'When did you learn that?'

'On the news, a few hours ago. They named him on the BBC. I was sitting in the waiting room. I'd only just arrived. The TV was on. I couldn't believe my ears. That was the pair of them. Thomas killed yesterday, and my Jason shot this afternoon. I can't understand it. I've been here ever since. They let me see Jason for a few minutes earlier, but I couldn't get any sense out of him . . .'

That makes two of us, thought Vogel, who then reminded himself that he was dealing with a gravely injured man. He really shouldn't be so cynical. Cynicism was, after all, the copper's curse, in Vogel's opinion. All too often it clouded your judgement and prevented you from seeing what was right in front of your eyes.

'You indicated that you've been here for several hours, Mrs Patel?' Vogel continued. 'How did you know your ex-husband had been shot.'

'I didn't. Not at first. They just told me there'd been a serious incident, Jason was injured, and he'd been taken here.'

'Who's they, Mrs Patel?'

'I don't know exactly. Whoever answered Jason's phone when I called it this afternoon. A man. I assumed afterwards that it was a nurse or a paramedic. Or I suppose it could have been a policeman.'

If it was, Vogel considered, that policeman was going to get a rollicking for not reporting up the chain of command that he'd spoken to Patel's ex-wife. Either that or he'd filed a report which hadn't been properly passed on. Either way, somebody was in trouble, because the SIO had not been told. He had a feeling Maureen Patel was going to prove to be a very interesting witness. She would have been found in the end, of course, but it was only chance that he and Saslow had stumbled upon her so early in the investigation.

'Why did you call your husband?' he asked. 'Were you worried about him because he didn't turn up?'

'No. Not a bit. I told you, Jason's become unpredictable. Careless. It was because of the children, him letting them down, and not for the first time. They're teenagers now, or very nearly, twelve and thirteen. They don't admit it, either of them, but they get so upset. That's why I called Jason. To give him a roasting, I suppose, but also to see if I could make him come over, even if he was going to be hours late. I had the shock of my life when that fella answered and told me Jason had been hurt badly enough to be on his way to hospital, I can tell you.'

'Mrs Patel, you've indicated that your ex-husband's business partnership with Thomas Quinn played a part in the break-up of your marriage,' he continued. 'Why was that?'

'He changed. He was on edge all the time. He was hardly ever home. They used to go off clubbing, for God's sake. Or that's what Jason told me. And he'd come home with lipstick on his collar, that sort of thing. I never thought that was for real. I mean, it even sounds like something out of fiction. But he actually did come home with a lipstick smudge on his collar on more than one occasion. Although he always denied there was another woman. To begin with, I believed him. He'd always been a good husband before. And I'd always trusted him. But I didn't understand what was happening. It wasn't like Jason. Sometimes he behaved almost as if he were afraid of Thomas. If Thomas clicked his fingers, Jason jumped. That's how it was from the beginning. Once or twice I thought drugs might be involved. But Jason denied that too.'

'Did he offer any sort of explanation?' asked Saslow.

'He just said they had some big business deals going on, and he couldn't think about anything else. It was all going to be over soon, then we'd reap the reward. But that never happened, of course. Things just got worse and worse.'

'In what way?' queried Saslow.

'I said before. He wasn't the man I married. There was a new hardness about him. If I told him how unhappy I was, he'd just get up and go out. And I never knew where he went, or when he'd be back. And then he started staying out all night. Without a word of explanation. Even when I told him I couldn't stand it any more, that I wanted us to split up, that I no longer wanted to share my life with him, he just shrugged his shoulders and walked out the door. The kids could see what was happening, of course. Can't they always? More than you, half the time. And they were getting affected by it all. Bad marks at school. Bad behaviour. Particularly our Jennifer, the thirteen-year-old. Girls grow up quicker than boys, don't they? You can't believe there's only a year between them sometimes. Paul is still a little boy. Jennifer's fast becoming a young woman. But she's always been a proper Daddy's girl. I could see it was breaking her heart.

'One night we were watching telly and *Invasion of the Body Snatchers* came on. Paul said, "Do you think that's what's happened to Daddy, Mum? Has he been invaded by an alien?" We all had a laugh. And goodness knows we needed it. It was funny after all. But Paul had only been half joking. I really think it seemed to him like an alien had taken over his father and come to live with us.'

'When did you split up, and was there an incident which brought things to a head?' asked Vogel.

'About eighteen months ago. There was nothing special. Just more of the same, really. Finally, one day I told Jason he had to go. I wanted him out. He didn't argue. Barely said anything. Just went upstairs and came back down ten minutes later with a bag. The sort of bag you'd take on a week's holiday, not something you'd even start to pack your belongings in if you were leaving home. Then he left. And he barely said goodbye. We got divorced as soon as possible after. He cooperated with everything.'

'Where did he go?'

'I found out that he'd gone straight to this flash new apartment overlooking the estuary, just outside Instow. It almost seemed as if he had it there waiting.'

'So presumably he and Thomas Quinn were successful in their business venture, if he could afford an apartment like that as well as running the family home?' Vogel continued. 'Or were you doing that, Mrs Patel?'

'No, I didn't work. Not at all when Jason and I were together. He never wanted me to. He wasn't a chauvinist. We both thought bringing up children was a full-time job. And I never needed to work. Or I didn't think I did. But I always suspected that it was because of money that he set up the partnership with Thomas. Not that he ever consulted me about that either. And that wasn't like him.'

'Does he pay you maintenance for the children?'

'Yes. Although come to think of it I noticed a couple of days ago that this month's payment was overdue. I was going to ask him about it. He gave me the house too, by the way. Just signed it over. Didn't bring in a solicitor or anything to argue the toss.'

'Did that surprise you?'

'Not really. That was more like the old Jason. Kind, and generous to a fault. There was a mortgage on it though, much bigger than I thought, but he's carried on paying the instalments.'

'Clearly you still care about him., Mrs Patel.'

'Always. For the kids' sake, if nothing else. But I have been driven to distraction. And now this . . . well! You know, it's strange, but it seems almost inevitable that something horrendous was going to happen. And I tell you this, if Jason survives, and it looks like he's going to, you lot needn't worry about interviewing the truth out of him. I'm going to get the full story from him, if I have to stick a hot poker in his wounds.'

Vogel winced. Mrs Patel had used a very graphic turn of phrase.

Vogel didn't like the picture her words conjured up. Extreme violence, even in the abstract, always disturbed him. Vogel wasn't sure whether that was a good or bad thing for a police officer with almost twenty-five years' service behind him. He did know it was unusual.

'He will tell me the truth now,' continued Mrs Patel, in much the same vein. 'He darned well will. Or he'll end up wishing he had died in that shooting.'

TWENTY-SIX

The next few weeks were not easy for Lilian. But at least there were no further signs that she might be being watched. No more sightings of that black Range Rover. And Charlie's continued cheery optimism about the outcome of her trial was reassuring.

One Sunday, in a bid to take their minds off all that lay ahead, Kate arranged a lunch party, inviting people from both her own and Lilian's pasts. For Lilian it was a bittersweet experience. She found herself enjoying the occasion more than she had enjoyed anything in a very long time. But she was also reminded even more of the old days, of how her life had once been, and how cruelly different it had become.

Then, long before anybody wanted the gathering to end, Kate confessed that they'd run out of wine. She normally had it delivered. She must have forgotten to reorder.

Lilian, free at last of the plaster cast on her left ankle and able to walk quite well again, offered at once to be the one who would pop to the off-licence a couple of streets away. Kate and Charlie both expressed doubts. Lilian insisted. This small gesture of independence suddenly seemed very important to her. It was a salient moment, the first time she'd been out of Kate and Charlie's home alone since her arrival there following her arrest.

She was slightly mellow. And the lunch had cheered her considerably, as Kate had hoped.

She bought four bottles of the cheapest available claret, using almost all of the small amount of cash she had left, divided them between two plastic carrier bags, and began the journey back to Kate's house.

Suddenly Kurt stepped out in front of her.

At first she thought she must be mistaken. It couldn't be him, could it? He wouldn't dare, would he? She'd half expected his brother, or at least his goons, at first anyway. But not him. Not like this. Standing there, his usual cool, confident, handsome self.

She found the very sight of him chilling. All the same, she did not cry out. But she involuntarily dropped the two carrier bags she was carrying, containing the wine. The bottles exploded as they hit the pavement. There was red wine, glass and plastic everywhere.

She tried to run away. This was déjà vu. Kurt merely blocked her way. He didn't even try to grab her. He just stood in front of her, his bulk making it impossible for her to escape.

'Relax, I'm not going to touch you,' he said. 'I just want to talk.'

Relax? Was he mad? Lilian didn't want to know the answer to that question.

'Which is what you told me the last time,' she said, trying desperately to at least sound calm.

'I know. I'm sorry about that.'

'You've lied to the police. You've had me accused of attempted murder. You know I was just trying to defend myself. You know that.'

Kurt told her he hadn't wanted her to be charged, hadn't wanted to make the statement he had to the police.

'I was forced into a corner, because I was still wanted for questioning for assaulting you,' he said. 'But look at the risks I took to see you again, to make it right with you. I even flew back into the country on a false passport. When the police came to interview me in Bristol I'd only just regained consciousness. My brain wasn't working properly. I was afraid I might go to jail. I had to come up with a story—'

'Well, you did that all right,' Lilian interrupted. 'And, thanks to your story, I'm now facing prison.'

'I didn't intend for that to happen,' he said. 'I want you with me. For the rest of my life. Like before. In spite of what you did to me.'

'What I did to you?' Lilian could no longer keep up any pretence of calmness. She screamed the words out. A young couple walking by glanced towards her, then looked away and hurried by. This was London, after all.

'I was afraid you were going to kill me,' Lilian continued. 'I've been afraid you were going to kill me for a long time now.'

'Can't we start afresh?'

'Are you really crazy?'

'I'll find a way of getting the charges dropped. You know I could do that. I'll get the best criminal lawyers in the land working on it. I'll change my story. I'll come up with something that will allow us both to be free. We can start a new life together. Go to South Africa maybe. Cape Town if you like. Buy a beautiful new house if you don't want to move into the family place. Have a fresh start in the sun by the sea. I just want to take care of you. Come away with me, Lilian. Please. Be my wife again.'

Kurt spoke in a torrent of words. He sounded, and looked, so loving and sincere. But only if you didn't know him.

Somehow Lilian found the strength to side-step him. This time he made no attempt to impede her. She ran. As best she could with her still weak left leg.

'Never! Never!' she shouted back over her shoulder. 'I'd rather be dead!'

'Maybe,' he called after her.

The ice she remembered so well was back in his voice. There was no longer a hint of loving sincerity about him.

'But would you rather rot in prison?' he shouted. 'That's the choice, Lilian. Be my wife again, or go to prison. And I will make sure you never get out.'

TWENTY-SEVEN

Vogel contacted the NDDH first thing in the morning to check on Jason Patel's condition, and when he could be interviewed again.

He was told by the senior nursing officer in charge of IC that

Patel was 'comfortable', and that he was due to be examined again by the doctors later that morning.

'In view of last night's setback, Mr Vogel, we would much prefer you to wait until after that before visiting Mr Patel again,' said the nursing officer.

Vogel agreed. He didn't feel he had any choice. In any case there was little point in reinterviewing Patel until he was in a considerably stronger state than he had been the first time.

Saslow picked up Vogel at his Airbnb at seven thirty a.m. The incident room at Bideford police station was to be their first stop. It was an unseasonably wet and windy Monday. Vogel always thought bad weather was appropriate for a Monday. Although, as a police officer the days of the week had never had much influence on his working hours. Particularly during a murder investigation.

'How did you sleep, boss?' Saslow asked, by way of greeting.

'Not good,' replied Vogel. 'I've been going over this case in my head all night. Or what there is of it . . .'

'Me too, boss. Bit of a puzzle, isn't it.'

'Certainly is, Saslow. What looked at first like a straightforward domestic, an all too familiar family tragedy, is taking us off in all manner of directions.'

The two officers had just arrived at the Bideford incident room, and were exchanging notes with DI Peters, when the team who were still door-stepping the areas around St Anne's Avenue called in. They had just caught up with a neighbour of the Quinns who had been out on Saturday night, and away visiting her daughter all the previous day.

She had provided information which caused Vogel to decide that a second formal interview with Gregory Quinn should be delayed no longer.

'Send a pair of uniforms to bring him in straight away,' Vogel told Peters. 'Make sure they take Morag Docherty with them too. Somebody has to babysit Gill now. And tell them this time we're not asking, we're telling. I don't want Quinn arrested yet, but if he doesn't cooperate then that's what they must do.'

Greg Quinn did cooperate. Albeit with some reluctance. But once again he had not requested legal representation. And he was already sitting in the interview room DI Peters had set up at Bideford nick when Vogel and Saslow entered an hour or so later.

As soon as they walked in he stood up.

'I hope you've got a very good reason for having me brought here, Mr Vogel,' he said. 'My mother needs me. She's still in shock. I should be with her.'

'You're here because I have more questions for you, Greg,' Vogel began. 'Important questions that cannot be avoided. Some of them I shall be asking for the second or even the third time. And I want you to think very carefully indeed before you answer. Because I must warn you that lying to a police officer is a criminal offence. You could be charged with perverting the course of justice.'

Greg sat down with a bump. Hs face had acquired a high colour. He didn't say anything.

'So, Greg, when did you last see your father?' asked the DCI.

Greg answered without hesitation.

'I told you. About a month ago. And then only for a brief time.'

'Are you sure of that?'

'Yes. Of course I am.'

'All right. When did you last visit your family home?'

'I told you that, too. Three weeks or so ago, when I knew Dad was at work.'

'Are quite sure you didn't go there on Saturday?'

'Yes.'

'Absolutely sure?'

'Yes. Of course, I'm sure. What is this?'

'Greg, we have a witness who saw your van parked at the family home on Saturday afternoon.'

'What? No. You can't have. Nobody could have seen . . .'

Greg Quinn stopped abruptly.

'Nobody could have seen what, Greg?'

'Nothing. I mean, they've got it wrong. They can't have seen it.'

'Do you mean that nobody could have seen your van where it was parked, or rather, that you thought nobody could see it.'

'No. I didn't mean that. Not at all. I mean, that it wasn't there. Whoever told you it was has made a mistake.'

'Do you think your parents' immediate neighbours would recognize your van?'

'Maybe. I mean, I'm not sure. I told you. I hardly ever go there.'

'But we understand that you have done work for at least one of the neighbours. Mrs Jane Harvey. Is that not so?'

'Uh yes. I have.'

'Quite a big job, wasn't it? Weren't you one of the team that built a kitchen extension for her?'

'Well, yes. It was a couple of years ago though.'

'How long were you working at Mrs Harvey's house?'

'I'm not sure. Five or six weeks maybe.'

'Do you still drive the same van?'

'Yes. Well, most of the time.'

'And it's a van supplied by your employer, I understand, bright orange with the company name and logo on the side in black and purple. It's very distinctive, isn't it?'

'Well yes, I suppose so . . .'

'Indeed. So, do you not think that if Mrs Harvey saw that van, she would have recognized it and known that it was yours?'

'My boss drives a van that's the same.'

'Does he? We will have to ask him, then, if he was parked outside your parent's house on Saturday. But I think it's unlikely that he was, don't you?'

'I wouldn't know . . .'

Gregory Quinn paused. He seemed to be thinking hard.

'Look. I almost always park at the back,' he said eventually. 'There's a parking area and two garages which are completely walled in. It's a high wall. If I was parked there yesterday, and I'm telling you I wasn't, nobody would have been able to see my van anyway. Not Mrs Harvey, or any of the neighbours. They almost certainly wouldn't even see anybody driving into our place either, because my parents' house is tucked away at the top of the back lane.'

'Do you like dogs, Greg?' asked Vogel abruptly.

'What?'

Greg Quinn looked completely wrong-footed. Which, of course, had been Vogel's intention.

'You don't have a dog, do you?' Vogel continued, without waiting for Greg Quinn to reply to his first question.

Quinn shook his head, seeming totally bewildered now.

'Did you perhaps have one when you were growing up?'

Quinn shook his head again.

'Mrs Harvey has a dog, a small black poodle. Pretty little thing, I believe. Presumably you know that, don't you?'

'Y-yes,' stumbled Quinn. 'But what's that got to do with anything, for God's sake?'

'Barnaby, his name is. He's one of those dogs that's ball crazy. Mrs Harvey often throws balls for him in her garden. She uses one of those plastic ball-throw things dogs love that make the ball go further. Occasionally they go a bit too far. Yesterday afternoon Mrs Harvey accidentally threw one a lot higher and further than she meant to, and it flew over the wall which surrounds your family's parking area. She'd done it before, though not very often. So she went out of her back door and walked around. There's a little driveway, isn't there, with double gates across, which leads to your parking area? They were standing open, which I understand is usual. So she went in to pick up Barnaby's ball. She has told us there were three vehicles parked there. Your mother's old MG. Your father's Lexus, and your van . . .'

'She's made a mistake. I just said. I wasn't there.'

'Do you expect us to believe that, Greg?'

'I don't care what you believe. It's the truth. Anyway, it's just her word against mine. It doesn't prove anything, does it?'

Vogel was very afraid that Greg Quinn might be right about that, and was considering which way to best continue the interview when his phone, laid on the table beside him, flashed. It was Perkins. And Perkins knew his senior officer was in the process of interviewing Greg Quinn. Vogel answered the call, partly because under those circumstances Perkins wouldn't be calling unless it was urgent and almost certainly relevant to the current interview, and partly to give himself time to contemplate his next move.

The call lasted just a couple of minutes, during which Saslow halted the video recording. Vogel barely spoke, and maintained eye contact with Greg Quinn throughout – until the younger man could stand it no longer and looked away.

After ending the call Vogel remained silent for a few seconds more before instructing Saslow to restart the video, and addressing Greg again.

'CSI have finally found your mother's phone, Greg,' he remarked casually.

He thought Quinn flinched, but wasn't entirely sure. It may just have been an involuntary nervous twitch.

'There are a number of voice messages on it which appear to be from you, recorded on Saturday, the first just after eleven a.m., and several texts. But then you know that, don't you?'

Quinn shrugged.

'It seems you had arranged to meet your mother at the local Morrisons supermarket, is that so?'

'Uh yes.'

'Why didn't you tell us about this yesterday?'

'Well, in the end we didn't meet, so I didn't think it was important.'

'Is this something you and your mother do regularly?'

'Most Saturdays, yes. We do our shopping at the same time, then go to the café.'

'I see. But on this occasion your mother didn't turn up, isn't that right? So did you not think that might be significant on the day your father was murdered?'

'I, uh, I didn't really think about that.'

'I see. Was it not unusual then?'

'Well, yes. It was quite unusual. Although . . .'

Again Greg Quinn didn't finish the sentence he had begun.

'Although what?'

Greg sighed. 'All right. You know about my father now. What a bastard he was. He'd always been a control freak. And he had Mum right under his thumb. She was completely dominated by him. If he decided for some reason that he didn't want her to go shopping, or whatever it might be, then he'd make sure she didn't. And that was that. She couldn't do anything about it, and I was always under strict instructions not to interfere.'

'I see. So you weren't surprised when she didn't turn up on Saturday morning?'

'No. Not that surprised. A bit worried about her. I always worry about Mum. And what Dad might be doing. I didn't know he was actually hurting her though, not physically. I told you that yesterday, Mr Vogel. And I swear it's the truth. If I had known, I would have done something about it, whatever Mum said.'

'Are you sure you didn't do something about it?'

'Of course I'm sure. What are you accusing me of? I never touched my father. I didn't go anywhere near him.'

'Greg, an officer has listened to the messages on your mother's phone and read her texts. At two forty-five p.m. you texted saying you'd had enough. That you were going around to the St Anne's Avenue house. Isn't that right?'

The young man shrugged.

'Greg, I need you to answer the question,' continued Vogel.

'I might have done.'

'There's no might about it, Greg,' said Vogel. 'I've just told you. We have your mother's phone. And I think I've now been forwarded the appropriate messages.'

The DCI consulted his own phone and began to read. '"I know what's happening. He's keeping you in the house again. It's time you stopped that bastard ruining your life, and if you won't I will. I'm coming straight round. I'm on my way." That is one of the messages you sent, the last one, in fact. Perhaps you would like to save us all a lot of trouble and confirm that you sent this text?'

'Look, OK, yes, that's what I said,' admitted Greg. 'It doesn't mean I actually went round though. It doesn't mean anything.'

'Perhaps not. It's circumstantial evidence, of course. But coupled with your van being spotted by a witness, I think it's reasonable to conclude that you were at your parents' house on Saturday afternoon, is that not the case?'

Quinn shrugged again.

'Greg, for your own sake you really should cooperate. There is more, of course. We have established that you phoned and texted your mother several times from just after eleven a.m.—'

'I told you, I was worried,' Quinn interrupted.

'But after the two forty-five p.m. text, when you told your mother you were going around to the family house, you did not call or text her at all. Not once. And we couldn't raise you until seven o'clock yesterday morning. It seems to me that something happened to stop you trying to call your mum. Perhaps to stop you worrying about her? Is that not so?'

'Look, Mum texted me, from a borrowed phone. That's what stopped me calling or messaging her again. She said she was with a friend from school, that she'd finally managed to get out of the house, and she'd be staying away from home until Dad had had time to cool down. She said not to call her phone again because he'd taken it from her. That wasn't particularly unusual either. She said she'd call me when she could. And I wasn't to worry.'

'I see. Could I see your phone please, Greg.'

Quinn handed it over with a marked lack of enthusiasm.

Vogel scrolled down the list of messages, noticing the several Greg had sent to his mother during the course of the morning and early afternoon.

There was just one incoming message from an unnamed mobile number which indeed appeared to be from Gill, and its content was almost exactly as Greg had just recounted.

Vogel held up the phone towards Greg and pointed at it.

'So this is the message from your mother, on a borrowed phone, yes?'

Greg agreed that it was.

'Do you recognize the number?'

'No.'

'So you don't know who your mother was with?'

'No.'

Vogel made a quick note of the number.

'OK, Greg,' he continued. 'This text was not sent until four forty-seven p.m. You'd been calling and texting your mother repeatedly . . .' Vogel glanced at the phone again. 'About every half hour until two forty-five p.m. But then you let more than two hours pass without trying to contact her. And, after she texted you from her friend's phone, you then made no attempt to contact her again, perhaps to try to speak to her, even though you have already described how worried you were about her. Why was that?'

'I didn't want to make matters worse.'

'But we couldn't get in touch with you all night. Your phone seemed to be switched off. It wasn't just that you weren't picking up to an unknown number, or to us. Surely if you were so worried about your mother you would make sure you were able to answer her if she called again?'

'Look, I was fed up and upset. I drove to my mate's in Torrington, and we went out drinking. We got stuck in. I was bladdered. That's why I stayed over with him. I didn't even know my phone was switched off.'

'Greg, our medical experts tell us that your father died between approximately three and five p.m. on Saturday. This fits in rather well with the visit you told your mother you were about to make. Wouldn't you agree, Greg?'

'I'm not agreeing with anything.'

'I'm going to say this once more, Greg. I really would advise you to cooperate with us. We are building quite a case against you.'

This time Greg Quinn said nothing at all.

'All right,' said Vogel eventually. 'I'm going to suspend this interview, and you are free to go, Greg. But we shall be continuing to investigate you. And I must warn you that we are likely to be in touch again very soon, and that we are now treating you as a person of interest in this inquiry.'

'What does that mean?'

'It means what it says. You are of interest to us in the pursuance of this inquiry.'

'Right. But I can leave now, yes?'

'Yes.'

'I'll get back to my mother, then, if that's all right by you, Mr Vogel,' said Greg. 'I'm still more worried about her well-being than anything else. Only, that wouldn't concern you, would it?'

'Good morning, Greg,' said Vogel.

The uniform on sentry duty escorted Greg from the room. As soon as he had gone Vogel turned to Saslow.

'Get Perkins after him, Dawn, and arrange back up with DI Peters,' he said. 'I want to know that young man's every movement.'

Vogel immediately dialled the number he had copied from Gregory Quinn's phone. It appeared to be out of service. He then checked the phone number he had jotted down against a number saved to his own phone. They didn't match. Saslow returned just as he finished doing so.

'I thought the number Gill texted Greg from would probably turn out to be Helen Harris',' Vogel remarked. 'That would further back up her alibi, too. But it isn't. And there's no response at all from it at the moment.'

'Well, the phone could belong to someone else at the House, couldn't it, boss?' offered Saslow. 'Another staff member, or one of the other people sheltering there. And it could be a burner that's run out of juice.'

'Yes, it could be all of those things. But clearly it was in service yesterday, and if Gill used a phone unconnected with someone at the House, that offers up all sorts of other possibilities. For a start it indicates that she may not have been there all day, after all. I think we should pay another visit to Helen's House.'

'I agree, boss. I mean, if Gill Quinn didn't have that cast-iron alibi she would still be our principal suspect, wouldn't she?'

'Yes, probably. The attack on Thomas Quinn's partner presents all sorts of intriguing possibilities and, at the very least, it looks like Greg has been lying to us. But yes, without that alibi Gill would still be first in the frame, particularly now we know about the terrible abuse she has suffered at Thomas' hands. It's certainly an alibi we need to be absolutely sure of.'

'The evidence is stacking up against Greg, though, isn't it? And he makes no secret of how much he loathed his father.'

'Indeed. Although, from what we've learned today, Saslow, I don't blame him.'

'I thought you might arrest him, boss.'

'Yeah. I considered it. But Quinn is quite right. Everything is circumstantial. And we certainly haven't got enough to charge him. I'm actually hoping he may further incriminate himself. Assuming he's guilty, of course.'

'If you'd arrested him, though, we could search his home and his van.'

'Yes. And taking a watching brief is always risky. But as long as we make sure he isn't busily disposing of any evidence, I think it's a risk worth taking. Meanwhile let's see what Helen Harris has to say . . .'

TWENTY-EIGHT

Lilian was almost hysterical when she arrived back at Kate and Charlie's house. Shaking uncontrollably, she blurted out what had happened.

Charlie called the police at once. The lunch party ended abruptly. Two officers arrived to take statements. They introduced themselves as PCs Birch and McKeach, and treated Lilian with considerable sensitivity. It was in sharp contrast to the way she had been dealt with by the police in Bristol.

Everyone seemed sympathetic. Lilian, although deeply shocked and scared out of her wits again was, if not reassured, at least calmed and encouraged.

Charlie told her that he believed that Kurt had really shot himself in the foot.

'When your case comes to court his evidence and character will be irrevocably tainted by what he's done,' said Charlie. 'I'd go as far as to say that there's now just a chance again that the case won't even come to court.'

The police arranged for the house to be kept under surveillance throughout the night.

Ultimately Lilian went to bed feeling, under the circumstances, better than she would have thought possible. And she slept surprisingly well. Early the following afternoon the same two police officers returned. They had tracked Kurt down.

'It appears that Mr St John has a solid alibi for the time you say you were confronted by him, Mrs St John,' said PC McKeach.

He sounded weary, certainly no longer at all sympathetic. Indeed the attitude of both police officers had changed, in much the same way that the attitude of the police in Bristol had changed after they'd interviewed plausible Kurt.

'Do you think I made it up, for God's sake?' asked Lilian. 'Kurt gets people to lie for him. That's what he does.'

'Not these people, love,' interjected PC Birch, in that vaguely patronizing way that men in positions of any sort of authority were inclined, as a matter of routine in the 1990s, to adopt towards women. 'Mr St John was having lunch with a government minister and the South African High Commissioner at the time. At South Africa House.'

'On a Sunday?' queried Lilian. 'All afternoon? Do they confirm he was there all afternoon? And South Africa House is in Trafalgar Square. Less than half an hour away from here on a Sunday. It was the first time I'd been out of the house on my own. His goons could have tipped Kurt off. I know the house has been watched—'

'Even if Mr St John was not at lunch all afternoon, and did

leave earlier or break away for a while, he could not have got here from Trafalgar Square in time to interrupt your trip to the off-licence,' Birch interrupted. 'It's only five minutes' walk from this house, and you wouldn't have been in the store for more than a few minutes at the most, would you?'

'That's assuming he was lunching at South Africa House,' countered Lilian.

PC Birch shrugged. 'We have highly reputable witnesses, whom we believe would in any case have no reason to lie, pledging that he was at South Africa House,' he continued. 'Wasting police time is an offence, you know. You should be careful, Mrs St John. You have been charged with a very serious crime, and you are on bail. That bail could be rescinded at any time. You could end up behind bars before your trial even begins, if you don't watch it.'

After the police officers left, a bewildered looking Charlie turned to Lilian, and asked her earnestly: 'What is going on, Lilian? Are you sure you were accosted by Kurt yesterday?'

'Of course I'm sure,' Lilian replied. 'It happened, Charlie. Kurt was there. Waiting for me. I'm not likely to make a mistake about that, am I? I don't care what sort of alibi he's supposed to have. Nobody understands how powerful he is. He has holds over powerful people. Important people.'

'Yes, of course,' said Charlie.

However, Lilian feared he was not convinced.

All the same, he did not stop fighting Lilian's corner. First of all ensuring that she wasn't returned to custody following the unfortunate outcome of her brush with Kurt.

But he warned her, 'One more incident like this and there will be nothing I can do, Lilian. You do understand that, don't you?'

Lilian confirmed that she understood only too well. She could see that Kate was beginning to doubt her too, although her old friend was trying hard not to show it.

Lilian was distraught. History seemed to be repeating itself. She wondered what other tricks Kurt might have up his sleeve.

How could she or anyone else fight this man?

TWENTY-NINE

Helen Harris was in the front garden of Helen's House when Vogel and Saslow arrived.

She was accompanied by two other women, who were on their knees attempting to weed the unkempt and overgrown flower beds which lined the path leading from the pavement to the house.

Helen was mowing the lawn with a Flymo machine. Or to be more exact, fighting the Flymo, which seemed to have a mind of its own.

None of the three looked happy in their work. Helen perhaps least of all.

She stopped when she caught sight of Vogel, switched off the mower, and approached him and Saslow at once. She stumbled slightly over the edging to the grass and cursed under her breath. Vogel suspected she might welcome the interruption. Almost any interruption.

'Dratted machine,' she began, as if reading Vogel's mind. 'I fear I'm not cut out to be a gardener. City girl through and though. Have to have a blitz on this every so often, though. We do try to keep the neighbours happy.'

'Always a good plan,' said Vogel.

'Indeed, so what can I do for you today?' she asked, as she pulled off her heavy-duty gardening gloves.

Vogel noticed her hands then. They were smooth-skinned and long-fingered, and her nails were perfectly manicured. He thought that Helen was undoubtedly telling the truth. She was certainly not cut out to be a gardener. Her hands were trembling slightly too. From the effort, he thought. She did not look like a woman who much enjoyed any sort of exercise or physical work.

'Which city?' he asked obliquely.

'Sorry? Oh. Several over the years. I was brought up in Manchester. Sometimes I'm not sure how I ended up here, but at least Bideford has roads and pavements.'

She shot a look of distinct distaste around her, at the straggly lawn and the flower beds unworthy of the name, then took a step sideways so that she could sit on the low wall which separated Helen's House from the property next door.

'I'm quite out of breath,' she remarked. 'I suppose a garden is all right if you have either the time and inclination or the money for it, but the countryside generally is not for me.'

Vogel allowed himself a small appreciative smile. He was not a lover of the countryside either. He was content enough being driven across the moors and around the winding lanes of Devon, but he had no wish to tramp through them. He disliked wellington boots and had never quite got around to acquiring the suitable attire to deal with the persistent rain of the south-west peninsular.

'How did you end up here, anyway?' he asked.

'Oh, it's a long story. But the précised version is very familiar in these parts. I was brought here on holiday when I was a child. I just fell in love with the place. The countryside is one thing, being by the sea is completely another, don't you agree, Mr Vogel?'

Vogel thought this woman must be quite an astute judge of character. As she probably had to be in her line of work. She certainly seemed to have assessed him fairly quickly. Superficially at any rate.

'I do agree,' he affirmed. 'I had never really spent time by the sea before I first came here on a case a couple of years ago. I found it . . .' He paused, searching for the right word. 'Compelling. I think that's it.'

'Yes, it is compelling. And, many years later, when I was looking for a change, for a purpose, fate brought me back here. This house was on the market. I noticed the for sale sign. I could see the house was big enough, and it turned out to be cheap enough, for me to start a venture that had been close to my heart for some time. I'd come into a little money. Unexpectedly. I always think such windfalls should be put to good use, something special that would not have been possible without the unexpected funds. I suspect that might be what you think too, isn't it, Mr Vogel?'

Vogel was about to answer that he most certainly did think that, when he caught Saslow's eye. The DS was staring at him in some amazement. It was not like Vogel to be easily diverted when he was on a case. Particularly not when the case was a murder inquiry. He was genuinely fascinated by Helen Harris and her project. It wasn't just that, though. Sometimes he found it best with certain people who were part of an investigation to create an illusion of friendship. What he really wanted to find out today from Helen Harris was just how far she would go to protect those staying at, or regularly visiting, Helen's House. He suspected it would be a very long way indeed. Whether or not she would go so far as to provide a false alibi he had yet to discover. And he was about to take a big step towards doing so.

'I think you have created something very special here, Miss Harris,' he replied. 'As I am sure do the many people you have helped through this venture. Which, of course, would include Gill Quinn, would it not?'

Helen Harris shot him what Vogel's mother would have called an old-fashioned look.

'I certainly hope we have helped Gill,' she said. 'Although she is going to need a great deal more help now, I have no doubt of that.'

Vogel thought that was certainly true, whether or not Gill Quinn had played an active part in her husband's death.

He reached into his pocket and removed the piece of paper upon which he had scribbled the number of the phone Gill Quinn had used to text her son the previous day.

'Do you recognize this number, Miss Harris?' he asked.

'Helen, please,' said Helen Harris, as she took the piece of paper from him.

They had sat on a committee together. In some ways they were colleagues. All the same, Vogel did not suggest that she called him David. Apart from anything else he thought that might finish Saslow off.

Helen studied the number thoughtfully for a moment or two, and still looked thoughtful when she spoke again.

'I don't think so,' she said. 'Indeed I'm pretty sure I don't recognize it. But I'm not great with numbers. May I ask why you are asking me about it?'

'Because this is the number of the mobile which Gill Quinn used to contact her son on Saturday, when she did not have her own phone.'

'I see,' said Helen.

'Could it be the number of your partner's phone, or another member of staff here?'

'It's definitely not Sadie's phone. And being a Saturday, we didn't have any other members of staff in. None of our specialist workers, therapists or legal advisors are here over the weekend. Except in an emergency. And, as you may have guessed, finances are very tight at the House. We can't even afford a professional gardener.'

She waved a hand, taking in with a sweep the two women weeding the flower beds and her incalcitrant lawn mower.

'My windfall is long gone, and we rely primarily on charitable donations and a small local authority grant. We do everything we can ourselves, including, of course, our own cooking and cleaning. Gill could have borrowed one of the other women's phone. You'd have to check with them. But can't you just call the phone?'

'We've done that. It's a pay-as-you-go, and there's no response. The phone seems dead.'

'Ah. Probably run out of juice.'

'More than likely,' Vogel agreed. 'I'd like DS Saslow to check with the other women here straight away. I hope you have no objections to that?'

'Of course not,' responded Helen. 'That's Mary and Celia over there. You could start with them. We have two other residents at the moment. They'll be inside somewhere. Feel free to seek them out.'

Vogel watched as Saslow duly approached Mary and Celia. Then he turned back to Helen.

'You do recognize the significance of this number, don't you?' he asked.

'Yes. Of course I do. Gill must presumably have been with whoever owns the phone with this number. And if it isn't someone who was here at the House, then that indicates that she was probably somewhere else for at least part of the day. Is that what you are thinking, Mr Vogel?'

'Yes, it is.'

'And are you therefore suggesting that I may have given Gill a false alibi? Is that why you have come to see me again?'

'Possibly. Although not necessarily deliberately . . .'

'Well, thank you for that, at least,' responded Helen Harris with a wry smile.

Vogel did not smile back.

'On the other hand, I am sure you would always do everything you can to protect and assist any victim of domestic violence,' he said.

'Yes, I would. Though not to the extent of perverting the course of justice, I can assure you. We encourage our victims to work within the law to escape from the clutches of their abusers. That is what we are for. We do not encourage anyone to take the law into their own hands.'

'I'm going to be blunt, Helen, if, and I say if, you suspected that Gill Quinn had murdered her viciously abusive husband, wouldn't you feel that his death was a kind of justice?'

'I feel all sorts of things, Mr Vogel, that I wouldn't dream of acting upon. In any case I do not suspect Gill of murdering her husband, if for no other reason than that she had no opportunity to do so. She was here, I assure you, Mr Vogel, all day.'

Vogel was still contemplating where he would like to take this conversation next, when Saslow reappeared. The DCI glanced towards her enquiringly.

'I've drawn a blank, boss,' she began. 'That phone doesn't belong to any of the women here today, or, as Miss Harris told us, to—'

Vogel interrupted, again addressing, not Saslow, but Helen.

'Curious then, don't you think, Helen?' he enquired.

Saslow spoke again before Helen Harris had chance to reply.

'There was another woman here on Saturday though, according to Sadie, Maggie Challis.'

'Ah, yes, of course,' Helen spoke quickly. 'Maggie. She's another one like Gill. A regular, if not necessarily frequent visitor. She uses us as somewhere to retreat to when things get bad at home. As a refuge. Which is exactly what we are. Like Gill she comes for as little as an hour or two, and rarely stays overnight. Women like them always say the same thing. He'll have calmed down by the time they get home. He doesn't mean it. And so on. Gill has been coming for well over a year now, and Maggie for even longer. I still find it rather extraordinary, but it really isn't unusual. It is quite likely that they would have met before yesterday, and that Gill might have borrowed her phone.'

Vogel turned to Saslow. 'Do we know if the phone number is Maggie's?' he asked.

'Sadie checked. It's not the number listed here for her. That's for another burner which also isn't responding right now.'

'A lot of the women have at least one burner, so that they have a phone their abuser doesn't know about,' offered Helen Harris. 'But that carries its own risks. Sometimes the abuser finds the phone, and sometimes the women just throw it away because they fear they're in danger of being found out. Then, eventually, they may acquire another one.'

'Did Sadie say when Maggie was here, and for how long?' Vogel asked Saslow.

'She said she came in the afternoon, and stayed about three hours. I've got her address, boss. She lives in Torrington.'

'Good,' said Vogel. 'Give DI Peters a call, will you? I want a team sent round.'

Vogel turned back to Helen Harris again. 'Did you see Maggie Challis, did you speak to her?' he asked.

'Uh, no. I didn't.'

'And why was that?'

'I had a pressing amount of paperwork to do. Weekends are often the only time I have for that. I spent quite a lot of the day in my office.'

'Helen, did you even know Maggie Challis was here?'

Helen Harris hesitated for just a split second. 'No, I didn't,' she said.

Vogel held out his hands in front of him, palms up.

'So if one woman could be present in this house for three hours on Saturday afternoon without you knowing, why couldn't another be absent from the house for three hours without you knowing? I am beginning to think, Helen, that the alibi you have given Gill Quinn may be somewhat flawed.'

Helen frowned. When she spoke again her voice was slightly louder and firmer than previously. 'I did not give Gill Quinn an alibi. Not personally. Not for the entire day. You are quite wrong, Mr Vogel, to suggest that I did. I said that either I, or Sadie, or one of, or indeed perhaps all of, the other women who were here on Saturday, could, between us, vouch for Gill having been present here all day. Without leaving the premises. That is an entirely different premise. We provide a one-hundred-per-cent group alibi. I stand by that absolutely. And I take exception to your insinuation that I might in some way be dissembling.'

Vogel found himself blinking rapidly behind his spectacles. He so wished he did not do that when he felt embarrassed or ill at ease. He turned his head slightly in the hope that Helen Harris wouldn't notice. But he hoped in vain.

'Do you have something in your eye?' she asked casually.

Vogel thought it might be the very first time anyone had actually drawn attention to his mild affliction. Or certainly anyone he was interviewing, albeit informally.

'I think you know that I do not,' he replied equally casually. 'And I am sorry if I offended you,' he continued. 'However, you must see that unless we can prove that the phone number belongs to Maggie Challis, or unless you recall another visitor you had overlooked . . .'

He paused, studying Helen carefully, and was gratified to see that she appeared to have coloured slightly, and might no longer be quite so sure of herself. 'Unless either of those eventualities are realized,' he continued, 'then it would seem Gill must have left these premises in order to borrow a phone from someone and call her son . . .'

'Unless the burner belongs to Gill herself,' suggested Helen, who was clearly not entirely wrong-footed.

Vogel hadn't actually considered that. In any case he didn't think it likely. It didn't fit.

'Her son claimed he didn't recognize the number, and I believe he was telling the truth,' said the DCI. 'If Gill had a secret phone it would seem unlikely that she would have kept it a secret from Greg. It is also probable that the burner would still have been on her person, or certainly somewhere in her home, when we encountered Gill after her 999 call. We have found no such phone.'

'Perhaps you should look harder, Mr Vogel. Alternatively, you could ask Gill whose phone she used. Or indeed if it was her own phone. Have you thought of that?'

The same wry little smile flickered around Helen Harris' lips. Vogel could clearly detect a note of sarcasm in her voice. She was perfectly sure of herself again, and the DCI was no longer entirely sure that he liked the woman as much as he'd thought he did. She was sharp as a needle, a characteristic he always appreciated. And clearly a great friend and ally to those who came to her for help, which was admirable. But perhaps she was a tad too acerbic. Certainly in her dealings with a senior police officer.

He had deliberately not yet sought out Gill Quinn to ask her whose phone she had used to call her son, because, when he asked questions like that he preferred, whenever possible, to already know the answer. Which was classic interviewing technique. However he had no intention of sharing any of that with Helen Harris.

Instead, without responding at all to her final remark, he bid her farewell and took his leave.

THIRTY

Lilian stood trial at Bristol Crown Court.

It felt as if the odds were stacked against her from the start. She continued to fear that Charlie was no longer a hundred per cent behind her. He had not been quite the same with her since the incident with Kurt in Islington. In turn, she was beginning to realize, neither was she any longer sure that this kind and decent man was quite clever enough. His judgement had so far been way off almost throughout. It was possible Kate may not have done her that big a favour in persuading Charlie to take up her case, she reflected disloyally. And her legal aid barrister was, it soon became clear, not a patch on the prosecuting barrister, who put the case against Lilian swiftly and succinctly.

According to the prosecution Lilian was a calculated and violent woman who, under the influence of drugs and alcohol, had attempted to kill her devoted husband. And she had acted without provocation.

Kurt was called to the witness box straight away. Cool, handsome and collected, he was at his most charming. He managed not only to look sorrowful and virtuous, but even vulnerable. In spite of herself Lilian could not help being impressed by his performance. It also seemed almost inevitable to her that she was about to be destroyed by it.

Kurt expressed fluently his great regret over everything that had happened. Even the way he talked was attractive. He spoke beautiful English, with just the merest hint of a South African accent.

His barrister began by asking him about the earlier incident at Penbourne Villas.

Looking embarrassed, his body language awkward, Kurt told how rough sex and drugs led to the wife he so loved throwing herself from the balcony of their home and being seriously injured.

'I just wish I could turn the clock back,' he said. 'I certainly wish I'd never agreed to her demands, never agreed to get drugs for her. But she begged me to.'

Kurt went on to explain how he had fled the UK – after what he called 'the accident' – because he didn't think anyone would believe his version of events.

'I panicked,' he says. 'And when I heard the police were looking for me, I panicked even more. But I soon realized I couldn't live without Lilian. So I disguised my appearance and acquired another passport in order to re-enter the country, find Lilian, and see if I could persuade her to try again.

'I knew the risks, and I realize I have behaved stupidly, and that in using a false passport I have committed a serious offence with which I could be charged at any time. But I was prepared to do whatever it took to save my marriage. I was desperate. Really desperate.'

'Have you ever deliberately hurt your wife, Mr St John, in any way?' asked the prosecution barrister.

'Absolutely not,' said Kurt, his eyes blazing with sincerity. 'The only injuries she ever suffered, until she fell from the balcony, were the result of the bizarre sexual demands she insisted on making of me. I hated it. But I love her so much. She is still the only woman in the world for me.'

He lowered his voice almost to a whisper. Lilian couldn't swear to it, but she was pretty sure his eyes had filled with tears.

'I would still have Lilian back in spite of what she has done to me, however many times she stabbed me, it makes no difference,' he said. 'If she goes to jail I will wait for her. I will never walk away from her.'

Those words were quite chilling to Lilian. But she was all too aware of the jury melting.

As he spoke, Kurt turned in the witness box, so that he was directly facing Lilian, staring at her. And there was nothing remotely melting to her about the look in his pale blue eyes. It was pure menace. The jury did not see it. Neither could they possibly have understood what he really meant by his last remark. She understood. He had merely confirmed what she had come to believe a long time ago, since way before he finally put her in hospital, pretty much since she had married him. She now knew absolutely for sure, that Kurt St John would never let her go. He would never leave her alone for as long as they were both alive. Not under any circumstances.

Lilian didn't know which was the most frightening prospect, being found guilty of attempted murder or the certainty of Kurt's continuing presence in her life.

Fleetingly she wondered if she wouldn't be better off in jail. At least she would be safe. Kurt surely wouldn't be able to get to her there. Not directly, anyway. In any case a prison sentence seemed increasingly to be the most likely outcome.

Her barrister cross-examined, of course. But it seemed to Lilian that he missed many of the most salient points. Amongst other things, he failed to ask Kurt how it was that, by his own admission, he could with such apparent ease obtain illegal drugs, and acquire a false passport. Lilian tried to point this out, but was told that there was a reason for everything Charlie and her barrister did, that they were taking a particular route, and hers would take them into territory that was too dangerous. Or words to that effect. She did not have the strength to argue.

She also had little doubt that the woman judge's manner indicated that she had quickly become weighted against Lilian. Even in matters of court procedure and any technicalities which arose, it seemed to Lilian that she consistently favoured the prosecution.

From the moment the defence case began, Lilian felt that it was highly unlikely that Mrs Justice Hadley would consider that there was any evidence at all that could be presented which would come even close to justifying Lilian attacking her husband with a knife.

As the proceedings progressed, Lilian became so disheartened that she feared she was falling apart. She couldn't stop trembling. And it was only with great difficulty that she held back her tears.

Minutes before she was due to take the stand her barrister called for an adjournment. He and Charlie then asked her if she felt capable of giving evidence.

Lilian knew there was only one answer to that question. Yes, of course she was able to give evidence. Had she not been waiting for months for the chance to tell the world what a monster Kurt St John was?

But she didn't say any of that.

Instead she merely said: 'I don't know. I just don't know anything any more.'

Ultimately Charlie and the barrister suggested that they should attempt a plea bargain.

'I think it's our only hope now,' Charlie told her. 'The signs are clear. Both the judge and the jury seem to have turned against you. Kurt was just so convincing. And we can't deny that you stabbed him. All the rest of it is pretty much your word against his, and there really doesn't seem to be much chance of persuading this court that Kurt is lying.'

Lilian agreed with all of that. Kurt had been as convincing and plausible as he always was. The judge and jury certainly seemed set against her. It wasn't fair. But nothing was fair in her life. And she had no idea how to fight it.

With great reluctance she agreed to a plea bargain. And it was ultimately accepted by both sides that the charge of attempted murder would be dropped in return for Lilian pleading guilty to a charge of grievous bodily harm.

The judge sentenced her to five years imprisonment, the maximum allowed.

In her summing up Mrs Justice Hadley justified this by referring to Lilian as 'wilful' and accused her of having 'planned this outrage against her husband coolly and calculatedly'. She also described her as 'being of murderous intent'.

Lilian was desolate. As she had feared, she was on her way to prison. And for a substantial period of time.

Kurt had won again.

THIRTY-ONE

As soon as he and Saslow left Helen's House, Vogel called DI Peters to check on Greg Quinn's whereabouts.

'It seems he went straight to work after we let him go,' she said.

That presumably meant Gill Quinn was alone with Morag Docherty. He called Docherty at once and asked her to try to find out from Gill whose phone she had used to text her son.

'If she says she can't remember, don't let it go,' he instructed. 'It's time to start putting some pressure on her.'

Vogel and Saslow then headed for the NDDH. It seemed more important than ever that they talk again to Jason Patel.

'I know he's recovering from serious injury, but we've left this long enough now,' said Vogel, as Saslow turned off the Northam road onto the New Bridge.

'It does seem that Gill's alibi probably still stands, certainly if that phone she used to text her son belongs to this Maggie Challis. Although we are still waiting to confirm that. So Greg looks the most likely suspect now. Or he would if his father's partner hadn't been shot, and their business premises ransacked, within twenty-four hours of Thomas' murder.'

'That could still be a robbery gone wrong, boss.'

'It could, yes. Though what would burglars expect to find of value in the offices of a North Devon export and import firm, for God's sake? It's not the sort of outfit which would carry vast amounts of cash stashed in its safe, is it? Yet the perps attempted to break into it. That's been confirmed. And they came tooled up too. That's heavy.'

'Maybe it was known in certain circles that Q-P Associates were cheating the tax man, and they did stash cash in their safe,' responded Saslow.

'Possibly, I suppose, but I would find it easier to accept that it might be a random burglary that went wrong, if it wasn't for what has happened to the two partners in this firm within such a short period of time. They've both been violently attacked. One is dead, and the other is critically injured. That's one big coincidence—'

'Yes, and you don't believe in coincidences, do you, boss?' interrupted Saslow.

Vogel chuckled. 'Is there a copper who does?' he asked.

Nobody at the hospital attempted to stop Vogel and Saslow from interviewing Jason Patel again. Which was all for the best, because Vogel was beginning to feel somewhat frustrated, and was in no mood for any sort of obstruction, however valid the reason for it might be.

Patel was still in ICU, a number of tubes remained attached to his body and various pieces of serious looking medical equipment, but he was sitting up in bed sipping a glass of water when Vogel and Saslow arrived at his bedside. All in all, he looked considerably better than he had the previous day.

Not for the first time, Vogel reflected on the human race's astonishing capacity for recovery. Certainly in these days of advanced medicine.

He was not sure if Patel would remember them from the previous visit, so he began to introduce himself and Saslow for the second time.

'I know who you are,' interrupted Patel. 'I haven't been shot in the head. Yet.'

His voice was weak and shaky, but his words were clear. And if it wasn't for the look in his eyes and the beads of sweat on his forehead, Vogel might have thought he was being sarcastic.

But Patel was afraid. Very afraid. Vogel had seen fear many times in his life. He recognized it at once. Jason Patel could be afraid of his own physical condition, of course. He could be sweating because he was in pain, or had a fever. Vogel didn't believe that, though.

'What do you mean by "yet"?' the DCI asked.

'I don't know, I don't know anything except I've been shot,' Patel replied, a distinct note of desperation in his voice. 'Twice. I've been shot twice. My God. How do I know they won't come and finish me off? Anyone can walk in here. I want police protection. I should have it. I demand police protection?'

'I can see that you are afraid, Mr Patel,' Vogel began. 'But I need you to tell me why, and why you think you need police protection, before I can take any steps to arrange that. At the moment all we have to go on is that your office was broken into and ransacked. It looks like a burglary, and the burglars wouldn't have expected you to be in there on a Sunday. They panicked and shot you. That's the obvious assumption. Unless, of course, you have something else to tell us. Do you, Mr Patel?'

'Look. I don't know anything. Just that there are men wandering around with guns.'

'To start with, we need you to tell us exactly what happened yesterday, when you were shot,' Vogel continued. 'Can you remember that, now?'

'I suppose so. A bit. I remember arriving at the office. I was about to unlock the door, but it opened as I touched it. So I just pushed it and walked in. Stupid really. After that, I still don't remember much. I think I must have been shot pretty much straight away. Everything since is a blank. Until I woke up in hospital.'

'Did you see anyone before you were shot?'

'Well yes, I suppose I did. Men in masks. Surgical masks. And baseball hats. I couldn't see their faces. I guess I interrupted them. I may have told them to get out. I'm not sure.'

'Do you know how many men there were?'

'Two. I s-saw two. I suppose there could have been more. But I definitely saw two. Look, I need police protection. Really I do. I think they're after me.'

'But again, why? Why would these men be after you, Mr Patel?'

'I don't know, do I?'

'I think you do, Mr Patel. Your partner was also violently attacked over the weekend, and he died. You don't think that was coincidence, do you?'

'I don't know,' said Patel again.

Vogel stood up. 'In that case, I can't help you,' he said. 'C'mon Saslow, let's go.'

He turned towards the door, with Saslow following.

'No,' Patel called out, his voice high-pitched and even more desperate. 'Don't go. Please. I'll tell you what I can. But you have to protect me. These are people who live outside the law.

I'm terrified of them. I have no idea how to deal with this sort of thing. I never realized . . .'

He paused, his breath coming in short sharp gasps.

Vogel and Saslow turned back and sat down again by his bedside.

'It's all right, Mr Patel, we can help you, if you will just be honest with us,' said Vogel. 'Who are these people, and what is your connection with them?'

'It was Quinn, he got me into it, I didn't realize what he was like, you see,' Patel began. 'He's a manipulative bastard. He came to me for my accounting skills. And he offered me the world. I knew he sailed close to the wind, and I should have guessed it was all too good to be true. Maybe the truth is that I did know that, but I didn't have a clue what he was really into, or what he was going to expect me to do for him. Honestly I didn't. Not to begin with, that's for sure. Anyway, I was desperate. I was in big financial trouble, you see.'

'Why was that, Mr Patel?' asked Saslow. 'We know that you inherited a thriving business, which had a very good reputation locally. What went wrong? It was way before Covid that you joined up with Thomas Quinn, wasn't it?'

Patel nodded. 'Yes,' he said. 'It was all my own fault. I never wanted to be an accountant. I always thought it was the most boring job in the world. My father pressurized me into it, and when he died, way before his time, I found myself running the show, and I hated it. I looked for excitement. That's my excuse anyway. I started to gamble. It became an obsession almost at once. I spent everything I could get my hands on. I ended up mortgaging not only my business premises, but also my house. To the hilt. When Thomas approached me I was about to go bankrupt.'

'Did your family know?' asked Saslow.

Patel shook his head. 'How could I tell my wife that we were about to lose our home? I mean, what about our kids?'

He paused, his breathing laboured. 'I saw Thomas as a way out. It was as simple as that. He lent me enough money to at least buy myself breathing space. I didn't ask too many questions. Like where that money had come from.'

'He lent you money?' Saslow queried. 'So presumably you were having to pay it back, weren't you?'

'Not exactly. I was supposed to be working off the debt. It was my job to juggle everything, move money around, at least on paper, keep all our balls up in the air. I never liked accounting, but I'm actually rather good at it, you see. I can work magic with numbers. Nobody can do it for ever, though. That's always the problem. I couldn't do it for myself for goodness sake. I've ended up with nothing. I don't even have a lease on the flat Thomas let me live in, and I don't know who really owns it, except it's some sort of scam, for sure.'

'What sort of scam? What exactly was it that Thomas Quinn was involved in?' asked Vogel.

'I never knew the whole of it, I just did what I was told. I kidded myself I was such a small part of everything, that I would be all right.'

'Yes, but a small part of what?' Vogel asked.

'Thomas' business dealings. Property was the front, mostly. They were . . . uh, very varied.'

'Indeed. Were they also a little illegal, perhaps, Mr Patel?'

'No. Uh. Well, perhaps. We were moving money around day and night all over the world. I guessed it was probably what is known as money laundering, but I never asked, and I was never told. I maybe turned a blind eye. But I had nothing to do with that side of things. Honestly I didn't. Or at least not until everything started to go wrong. We were both being threatened, you see. I realized then that I'd got myself into an even bigger mess than I was in before . . .'

'Who exactly was threatening you?' asked Vogel.

'Thomas called them his "international business associates".' Patel managed a strangled mirthless laugh. 'International business associates?' he asked rhetorically. 'They're thugs. Nothing but thugs. And crooks.'

'Yes, but who are they?'

'Who are they? They operate under many different names, and form companies which both appear and disappear at speed. They don't exactly give you a business card. Not one which means anything, anyway. I've always tried to have nothing to do with them.'

'Well, presumably if you've been Thomas Quinn's business partner for nearly three years you must have had dealings with them, email and phone surely, even if you didn't meet them. Isn't that so?'

'I told you, they're not local. I've no idea where they're based even. I don't think it's in this country. And no human contact. Not even phone calls. Not with me anyway. Everything was electronic. Email. And portals. WhatsApp. Sometimes texts. That was all.'

'And yet you seem to believe that they came all the way to Bideford to break into your offices and do you harm. C'mon, Mr Patel. You must have some idea who they are and where they are from, do you not?'

'All I know for certain is that they do what the hell they like. They're ruthless, ruthless . . .'

Patel's voice had risen again, his breathing even more troubled. Suddenly he stopped trying to speak, let out a cry of anguish and slumped back on the pillow. His eyes rolled back in his head.

'Shit,' said Vogel. 'Saslow, get a nurse. Fast.'

One of the machines by Jason Patel's bed began to bleep furiously. He looked as if he had lost consciousness. Had he also stopped breathing? Vogel wasn't sure.

Saslow didn't need to fetch anyone. Two nurses, a man and a woman, arrived almost at once. Vogel realized Patel must be linked to an alarm system which had alerted the nursing station of what Vogel feared might be a potentially cataclysmic change in the man's heart function.

He and Saslow were immediately asked to leave. Within seconds, it seemed, a Resus unit had arrived. For a moment or two Saslow and Vogel watched from the doorway as the team sprang into operation, each individual clearly knowing exactly what he or she had to do and yet all working smoothly together. Then a nurse, hurrying past, told them in no uncertain terms to get out of the way.

The two officers retreated to the row of orange chairs positioned just outside ICU where they had encountered Patel's ex-wife the previous day. Perhaps mercifully under the circumstances, thought Vogel, she was not there today.

The sounds of emergency resuscitation continued to resonate from inside the ward. Then suddenly, there was silence.

Vogel looked at Saslow. Saslow looked at Vogel. They sat

quietly for another minute or two. Then they approached the entrance to the unit. The same nurse who had earlier moved them on was just inside the double doors.

She approached them at once.

'I'm afraid we've lost him,' she said, without prevarication.

The strain showed in her face. Vogel felt for her. In all his many years in the force, and his many confrontations with death in all manner of situations, Vogel had never known a health professional, any first responder or emergency worker, or indeed a police officer, who did not suffer enormous shock and distress when losing a soul they had fought to save.

More often than not, certainly now as a senior officer, Vogel found himself standing by, watching others on the front line. He too never failed to be deeply moved. It was the human condition, he considered. And the passing of Jason Patel was no exception.

'What happened, nurse?' he asked. 'I thought Mr Patel was recovering.'

The nurse shrugged almost imperceptibly.

As she began to speak again she brushed away a strand of hair which had fallen across her face. Vogel noticed that her fingers were trembling.

'A heart attack of some sort,' she said. 'His heart just stopped. It's not unusual in cases of extreme trauma like this. A patient seems to be recovering but their body cannot ultimately cope with the shock it's received. That's why we keep trauma patients in ICU. Resus did their best. But in the case of Mr Patel, we just couldn't save him.'

It was pretty much as Vogel had suspected. He hoped he and Saslow had played no part in the instigation of the attack.

'I'm sorry, nurse,' said Vogel.

The nurse stared at him levelly for a few seconds. 'Yes,' she said eventually. 'I believe you are. Even though I probably wouldn't have let you in if I'd seen you arrive. Now, if you'll excuse me, I have to contact Mr Patel's next of kin.'

Vogel watched her walking away, glad that was one death call he wasn't going to have to make.

His first thoughts had been simply sadness at the man's quite unnecessary passing. Then he experienced just a fleeting concern that he may have inadvertently played a part in it. But Jason Patel had been shot. Twice. That's why he died. And no doubt that heart attack could have happened at any time.

It was only as he and Saslow were leaving the hospital that he allowed himself to consider the full significance of Patel's death. He and the team would now be investigating two murders. And Jason Patel would never finish telling his story, a story which, Vogel felt, could eventually have gone a long way towards solving the mystery of the two attacks, one leading to Patel's own death and one to the death of his business partner. Now any information that he might have imparted might never be fully learned.

Saslow, who Vogel invariably considered to be far tougher than him, had already got there.

'Christ, where does this leave us now, boss,' she asked, her facial expression showing very little other than professional irritation. 'When Patel started blabbing I reckoned we were really going to get somewhere. Now we're left with two murders and bugger all else.'

'That's a very accurate assessment of exactly what Mr Patel's death means to us,' remarked Vogel mildly.

'Sorry, boss,' muttered Saslow.

'Don't be,' said Vogel. 'It's a good job one of us is focusing on nothing but the job in hand. And you're so right about us having bugger all else. Every time we get a new lead it seems to be ripped away from us.'

He called Detective Superintendent Clarke to tell her about Patel's death. She said she would send additional back-up from Exeter.

'Two murders in Bideford and Northam, within twenty-four hours,' she muttered. 'For God's sake, Vogel, what's going on?'

The truth was that Vogel didn't know. But he was determined to find out. And fast.

'Right, Saslow,' he said. 'Let's head back to Bideford nick and call a team meeting. We need to put together a broader picture of these murders and find out how they fit together. If indeed they do at all.'

'Yes, boss,' said Saslow.

THIRTY-TWO

Lilian was taken to Eastwood Park prison in Gloucestershire, the nearest women's prison to Bristol.

Charlie suggested at once that they should appeal against the severity of her sentence. But Lilian could tell his heart wasn't in it.

She couldn't even offer to pay him generously in order to keep him on her side. Up against Kurt's legal team, Charlie's attempts, through the civil courts, to achieve any kind of financial settlement from Kurt had been blocked at every stage. The legal aid package she was ultimately granted – not without considerable difficulty as on paper she remained a rich woman – had already failed to come close to rewarding him for the many hours he had devoted to her case.

In addition to that, there was the little matter of Charlie not being the brightest kooky in the court. It had become tragically clear that his skills did not match his levels of confidence. She hadn't realized that until too late, and in case had had neither the funds nor the energy to do anything about it. But she was no longer optimistic about Charlie succeeding in any of his expressed aims.

Meanwhile, Lilian had to deal with the grim day-to-day realities of prison life. Inmates in all prisons invariably need to establish their place in the pecking order. It became instantly and abundantly clear that Lilian's place was right at the very bottom. She knew she needed to stand up to the bullies in order to survive, but she had neither the strength nor the know-how to do that.

She quickly descended into a state of total misery.

There was, however, one bright side to it all. She heard no word from Kurt for several weeks, and had almost come to believe, or certainly to hope, that he may finally have tired of her. After all he had found himself on the run from the police, then ended up in hospital, because of her. She knew that was how he would see it, anyway. He would consider it to be all Lilian's fault.

Then, on her birthday, a card from Kurt arrived through the prison postal system, expressing, as usual, undying love and devotion. Also on her birthday, rather less officially and far more disturbingly, another prisoner brought Lilian what she described as 'a little gift from your old man'.

It was an envelope containing a sachet of cocaine. There was a brief note inside: 'I'll be waiting for you, darling, with as much of this as you will ever want.'

Lilian was devastated. Not only was she suffering the misery and humiliation of a substantial jail sentence, but she was not even free from Kurt's attentions within the walls of her prison.

She immediately flushed the cocaine down the toilet. Afterwards she rather wished she hadn't. Coke had in the past lessened the pain for her, which was, of course, why she'd allowed herself to be persuaded to take it. Particularly when faced with the prospect of violent sex with Kurt.

A couple of days later, Kate visited for the first time. She seemed ill at ease. She told Lilian she had some news. She was pregnant. Lilian was genuinely delighted for her. She was well aware that Kate and Charlie had wanted a child ever since their marriage eight years earlier. Repeated fertility treatments had failed. They had more or less given up.

The pregnancy was unexpected, and a wonderful surprise, said Kate.

'The only thing is,' she said. 'Well, we're going to need all the money we can get now we are having a child. We still have a hefty bill from the fertility clinic to pay. And the house needs serious attention. The damp problem is getting worse. So I'm afraid Charlie won't be able to continue handling your case, Kate. He can only take properly paid work now. He doesn't have any choice.'

She also explained to Lilian that her own work as a freelance journalist had very nearly dried up since the closure of *Today* newspaper, which had been by far her primary employer.

'And I'm likely to be doing even less work after the baby is born,' she said. 'We're really sorry, Lilian.'

Even though she had doubts about Charlie's capabilities, Lilian found herself saddened and disappointed. After all, Charlie and Kate were the only real friends she had, and they had stood by her, and supported her in every way, even giving her a roof over her head. Now they were going to have the baby they had so longed for, and she was locked up in prison. She just hoped they would not drift out of her life entirely.

Nonetheless, she told Kate it was fine, that she totally understood. And she did too, in spite of her own increasing sense of desolation.

One thought occurred to her.

'There's the Hockney,' she said. 'You and Charlie could sell it. Then I could pay him properly.'

'Lilian, how can we?' Kate asked. 'Kurt is the legal owner. Charlie's a lawyer. We can't go around flogging what is in effect a stolen painting. To be honest, we don't even like having the thing in the house.'

Lilian knew that Kate was right. She shouldn't have made the suggestion. But she did think it ironic, considering all that Kurt St John had taken from her, that she could now be seen as a thief on top of everything else.

'You will keep it for me, though, won't you?' she pleaded. 'Please. It's all I have.'

Kate said that they would keep the painting for her, of course they would, even though Lilian could see that she really wasn't happy about it.

'And Charlie is going to do his absolute best to make sure you get a really good legal aid solicitor,' Kate assured her as she took her leave.

Lilian wondered fleetingly if such a creature existed. In any case, several weeks passed and she heard nothing from Charlie. But Lilian found that she didn't care. She had become convinced that going to appeal was pointless. And she made no effort herself to find a legal aid solicitor. The truth was that even the unlikely event of having her sentence either quashed or reduced interested her very little. After all she would still be imprisoned on the outside. Kurt was out there somewhere waiting for her. He had made that quite clear.

The final straw came in the form of a major *News of the World* exclusive.

'"She nearly killed him, but Kurt St John still loves his wife and wants her back. 'I will always want her back,' he says".'

The story, which also predictably made much of Lilian's alleged sexual preferences, was presented as the heart-warming lament of a devoted husband. But Lilian was chilled to the core. She could not eat, she could not sleep.

Her surprisingly sympathetic cellmate arranged an appointment with the medical officer who prescribed a mild sedative, to be administered nightly by prison staff.

Lilian had sunk to the depths of despair. She did not believe she could be helped. She did not want to be helped. She hid the tiny pills under her tongue, only pretending to swallow, instead collecting the drugs which, having made the most minute incision, she concealed inside her mattress.

She had no idea how many of them she would need to kill herself. The only thing she knew for certain was just how much she wanted to die.

THIRTY-THREE

Vogel and Saslow were silent as they drove away from the hospital heading for Westward Ho!, to once again try to interview Gill Quinn. For quite a while all Vogel could think about was the sheer horror of watching another human being die.

He was pretty sure Saslow felt much the same as him. It was just that she dealt with that sort of thing better. Indeed, Vogel suspected that most police officers dealt with it better than he did.

As it turned out the DCI didn't have long to dwell on the death of Jason Patel, nor even its significance.

DI Peters called with news of yet more evidence against Gregory Quinn. Vogel considered the significance of the additional information for a moment or two. Then he turned to Saslow.

'Change of plan, Dawn,' he said. 'I reckon the time has come to arrest young Quinn. The Patel shooting could still be a red herring as far as our first murder is concerned. At the very least we need the chance to eliminate Greg from our enquiries.'

'Should we get backup?' asked Saslow.

Vogel agreed that they should. He didn't think Greg Quinn would resist arrest. But he was a big strong chap, and it could be somewhat embarrassing if he did. In addition, the presence of a couple of uniforms when making an arrest always added gravitas, Vogel reckoned. Not to mention a little extra intimidation.

Perkins, and the surveillance team detailed to keep watch on Quinn, had reported that he was one of several Durrants employees working on a house the company was renovating in the East-the-Water district of Bideford.

Vogel and Saslow turned off the old Barnstaple road into the narrow lane leading to the riverside property just as a patrol car, with its blue lights flashing and siren wailing, approached from the opposite direction.

As soon as the two vehicles pulled to a halt, Gregory Quinn, wearing work clothes including steel-capped boots and a hard hat, emerged from the house and walked towards them. He took off the hard hat and stood just back from the pavement, waiting. He was a picture of resigned dejection, not even remotely resembling the rather full-of-himself young man Vogel had first encountered. And he rather looked as if he had been expecting them.

Whether or not this was a further indication of guilt had yet to be learned, but Vogel considered that it might be.

'You didn't need an escort, Mr Vogel,' said Quinn quietly.

Vogel ignored that. 'Gregory Malcolm Quinn, I am arresting you on suspicion of the murder of your father, Thomas Albert Quinn,' he said.

Then he recited the standard UK police caution.

'You do not have to say anything. But it may harm your defence if you do not mention when questioned something which you later rely on in court. Anything you do say may be given in evidence.'

Quinn held out both his hands before him, as if expecting to be handcuffed.

'I don't think we need cuffs, do we, Greg?' Vogel enquired quietly.

Quinn shook his head. 'No, you don't,' he said. 'But you are making a big mistake, Mr Vogel, I can tell you that. I didn't kill my father. I couldn't do a thing like that.'

Vogel knew it was still possible that the young man was telling the truth. But the evidence was now beginning to stack against him.

He instructed the uniforms to take Quinn back to Barnstaple and put him through the custody procedure. He and Saslow followed in Saslow's car. On the way he called Morag Docherty to tell her about Greg's arrest.

'We'll be sending a team round now to search his flat, of course,' he said. 'You'll need to keep Gill out of the way as much as possible. And we will want to talk to her again later, but first I have a question for you to ask her as soon as you can. Certainly before the search team arrive, when you would be more or less forced to tell her about Greg's arrest. It would be good to get in before she knows. I'm going to text you the number of the phone she used to text her son on the afternoon of Thomas' murder. I want you to ask her who the phone belonged to.'

'OK, boss, I'll do it straight away.'

'If she plays true to form, she won't be very forthcoming. But just keep on asking. We think it belongs to one Maggie Challis, only don't tell her that. Just stick at it, and stick with her. Right?'

'Right, boss,' said Docherty.

Whilst Vogel and Saslow were waiting for Gregory Quinn to be processed, a series of clips from the CCTV footage filmed in the vicinity of the Bideford office block where Jason Patel had been shot were patched through to them by DI Peters. A specialist team had been hard at work, as directed by Vogel, and had extracted material that was without doubt highly relevant. Two men wearing dark clothing and baseball hats, tinted glasses, and standard surgical face masks, had been caught on camera entering Tide Reach at three thirty-one p.m. the previous day. At four ten p.m. there was footage of Jason Patel arriving. And there was footage of the two men leaving, in rather more of a hurry, at four fifteen p.m.

'These are our killers, all right,' said Vogel at once. 'They have to be. Look at the timings. But we've not got a hope in hell of anyone recognizing them from this stuff, that's for sure. You can't see their faces at all.'

'Covid's done evil bastards like this a bit of a favour, hasn't it, boss?' remarked Saslow. 'In the current climate masked men can wander around towns like Bideford without attracting any attention at all.'

'I'm afraid that's so . . .' Vogel began, then he paused as another section of footage from a different camera played out.

This showed a large metallic grey vehicle with tinted windows parked in The Pill car park. It was a Range Rover. After a few seconds the driver's door opened and a bulky figure, also wearing dark clothes, baseball hat and mask, stepped out. He leaned against the vehicle, then reached into his pocket for something, and removed his mask, bowing his head as he did so.

'My God,' said Vogel. 'This has to be those guys' driver. And he's trying to light a cigarette. The cool bastard.'

'Hang on, something's startled him,' said Saslow. 'Look, he's turned his back on us and he's getting right back in the car. I reckon he heard gunfire, boss.'

'So do I, Saslow,' said Vogel.

The officers watched for a few minutes more, then the two men they had seen entering and leaving Tide Reach appeared running towards the vehicle. They climbed in, and the Range Rover was driven swiftly, but not at excessive speed, towards the car park exit.

Vogel immediately replayed the footage of the man leaning against the vehicle.

'There's not a clear shot, his head is bowed throughout the few seconds when he's not wearing a mask, but I think we've got a glimpse of his face, don't you, Saslow?'

'Yes, boss, I do. But it's pretty grainy stuff, isn't it? Looks like the camera from which this footage was taken was quite a long way away. It's a fairly distant shot. We can zoom in, of course, but then it will be even grainier. I think the number plate might be decipherable, though. Shall I get DI Peters to put out a trace, boss?'

'I reckon she's already onto that, Saslow. And I'll bet my mortgage the plates are false, too. But I think it's worth releasing that footage of the driver to the media. I know there's not much to go on, but there might be just enough for somebody to recognize him.'

Gregory Quinn was already installed in the designated interview room when Vogel and Saslow arrived. This time he had asked for a legal presence and a duty solicitor had been appointed and was also present.

The young man and his solicitor, Philip Stubbs, a local man Vogel had previously encountered on more than one occasion, were sitting together on one side of the central table. Vogel and Saslow positioned themselves opposite them. A uniformed officer stood by the door.

Saslow recited for the record the names of all present and the time of the start of the interview.

Vogel came straight to the point.

'Greg, I understand you are the owner of a highly powered inflatable boat and trailer which you keep in a garage just up the road from your flat,' he began without prevarication. 'Is that so?'

'U-uh yes,' responded Gregory, only a little hesitantly. 'I go sea fishing.'

'Did you take that boat out to sea on Saturday evening, the day your father was killed?'

This time Gregory Quinn's hesitation was distinctly noticeable. 'Y-yes, I did, b-but only for a quick spin,' he responded eventually.

'Yet when we previously asked you to tell us your whereabouts on that day, you did not mention that you had taken your boat out, nor indeed that you owned such a boat.'

Quinn shrugged. He might well have been making a huge effort, Vogel suspected, but when he spoke again he sounded rather more like his usual self, or at least what appeared to Vogel to be his usual self: confident, almost cocky.

'Well, why would I? I didn't think any of that was important.'

'You merely told us that you had gone drinking with a mate in Torrington and stayed at his place all night. Why?'

'Why did I tell you that, or why did I stay at my mate's place?'

Quinn was definitely back to being cocky now. Well, two can play at the same game, thought Vogel.

'Why both?' he countered deadpan.

'Because that's what I did. Because it was the truth.'

'Didn't you think there was a fair chance somebody would have seen you in that distinctive van of yours, taking your boat down to the beach, and launching it off the slipway?'

'I didn't think about that at all. Why would I? I hadn't done anything wrong. There's no law against taking your own boat out, is there? Or should I have asked police permission first?'

Vogel chose to ignore that. He had no intention of allowing himself to seem even remotely provoked.

'We do have a witness who watched you launch your inflatable,' the DCI continued. 'He said you loaded a rucksack into it. He noticed that particularly because you were carrying it as if it was heavy. He thought that a bit odd. Why would you be carrying a heavy bag on a fishing trip? He also noticed that you didn't appear to have any fishing equipment with you—'

'Yeah well, I'll bet my wages I know who your witness is,' interrupted Greg. 'That nosey arsehole who thinks he's in charge of bloody Westward Ho!, but actually he's just a car park attendant by the slipway. I keep most of my fishing stuff in the bow locker. He knows fuck all, that one. In any case, I told you, I just went out for a quick spin. I didn't go fishing.'

'What about the heavy bag?' asked Saslow. 'What were you taking out to sea, Greg? Was it something you planned to drop overboard? Something you didn't want found, weighed down so that it would sink? Was that what you were carrying?'

'I didn't have a rucksack with me. I wasn't carrying anything. Your witness talks a lot of bollocks. Anyone will tell you that. He doesn't like me. And he always wants to be the centre of attention.'

'Does he? Whoever killed your father, Greg, would have been covered in blood. Their clothes would have been soaked. They'd need to get rid of them if they were to have any chance of getting away with what they had done. And we have yet to identify the murder weapon. Is that what you had in that rucksack, Greg? The knife which you used to kill your father, and bloodstained clothes?'

'No. I told you. There was no rucksack. No damned knife either. Nor bloodstained clothes.'

'We will of course be conducting a forensic search of your flat, your van, and your boat, Greg.'

'Do what you like. I didn't kill my father. I couldn't kill anyone. I just couldn't.'

'Not even in the heat of the moment? I'm not saying you planned to kill him. Indeed, it seems unlikely your father's killer had any sort of plan. I think you went around to your family house looking for your mother, that you had some sort of row with your father, the neighbours heard raised voices, and you just lashed out.'

'No. That's rubbish. Total bloody rubbish. I wasn't even there. I haven't been to the house for weeks.'

Vogel studied the young man in silence for a moment. Sometimes in a case like this he would have a definite opinion on whether or not an interviewee was telling the truth. With this particular subject he remained unsure. Although he did believe the neighbour who said she had seen Greg's van parked at the family house. After all she had no reason to lie. He decided to push the point.

'Are you absolutely sure of that, Greg?'

'Yes, I am,' said the young man.

'I don't think I believe you,' Vogel remarked mildly. 'As you know, we have a witness who told us that she saw your van parked at the house on Saturday afternoon. Why would she lie?'

'I don't know. Another attention-seeker probably.'

Vogel and Saslow continued their interview for a further ten minutes or so, without making any significant progress, until they were interrupted by DC Perkins.

'Can I have a word, boss?' he asked. 'Something you should see.'

Vogel was aware of Gregory Quinn's eyes boring into his head as he stepped out of the interview room. He was with Perkins for just a few minutes, during which Saslow sat with Quinn in silence.

When Vogel returned he was carrying an iPad. He put it down on the table in such a position that all four involved in the interview, himself, Saslow, Quinn and Quinn's solicitor, could see the screen.

Then he ran the video he had just been shown. It comprised aerial images of the immediate area around the Quinn house. The initial shots had been taken from high over the estuary. The camera had then panned in, following a network of roads towards St Anne's Avenue, and finally homing in on the avenue itself, offering close-ups of most of the houses including number eleven. One shot clearly showed Gregory Quinn's distinctive orange van, with its purple logo and markings, parked in the parking area by the garages at the rear of the house. An area that could not be seen from any vantage point other than from directly above.

A numerical display in the bottom right-hand corner of the screen gave the date and time when each shot had been filmed. The date was the previous Saturday, the day of Thomas Quinn's murder. The time was three thirty-one p.m. Quinn looked confused and anxious. As well he might, thought Vogel.

'What the fuck's this?' he asked.

'This is some footage of your parents' house shot on the day of your father's murder by a professional cameraman using a drone. The cameraman was gathering background material for a new TV drama being filmed around Northam and Appledore. One of our chaps noticed the filming going on and made some enquiries just in case they had anything that might help us. You could say he struck gold, Greg. Turned out this cameraman had been carrying out a kind of blanket drone coverage of the area, as he didn't know exactly what the director would require. It is now undeniable that your van was parked at the back of the house on the day in question. In addition to its distinctive colour and markings, the registration number is quite legible.'

Vogel zoomed in.

'Also, there is a figure walking away from the van. We can now see that the person walking away from the van and entering your family house through the back door is you. And the date and time is shown on the screen.'

Quinn said nothing more, instead glancing anxiously at his solicitor, who did not intervene.

'Greg, you really can no longer deny that you were at your parents' house on Saturday afternoon, and this film places you there within the exact time frame during which we believe your father was killed,' Vogel continued. 'Do you understand me?'

'All right, yes, I was there,' Quinn suddenly blurted out. 'But I didn't kill my father. Honestly I didn't.'

These moments of breakthrough on a major case always took Vogel's breath away. He had to make a real effort to continue with his line of questioning without revealing his excitement.

'All right, Greg, we'll move on to that later,' he said. 'For the moment I just need you to formally confirm for the record that you were at your parents' house on the date and at the time indicated by this film.'

He tapped the side of the iPad.

'I just said I was there. He was alive when I arrived though. I m-mean he w-was alive when I left. But there's no film of my leaving, is there? Well, if there had been you'd have seen there was no blood on me. There c-couldn't be. Because he wasn't bleeding when I left. I m-mean, he hadn't been stabbed. I hadn't stabbed him . . . I m-mean, I didn't stab him . . .'

Quinn was stumbling over his words and beginning to gabble.

'Would you please tell me if you and your father quarrelled on Saturday afternoon?' Vogel interrupted.

'Well yes, I suppose so. I mean, we never got on. We always q-quarrelled. I only went to the house to try and find Mum. When I realized she wasn't there I left. I didn't attack my father. I didn't touch him, w-why would I? What would I gain? It's only my mother I worry about . . .'

Again Quinn was gabbling. Vogel let him do so until he paused for breath, before speaking again. 'Now that we have formally ascertained that you were at the scene of the crime at the relevant time, I would like you please to go through exactly what happened from the moment you arrived until you left.'

Greg looked as if he were about to respond. Then his lawyer stepped in.

'Chief inspector, I am advising my client to say nothing more unless or until you formally charge him, and I have had time to discuss this matter with him fully,' said Philip Stubbs suddenly.

Vogel wasn't best pleased. Greg Quinn had begun to talk. The DCI had thought they might be getting somewhere at last. On the other hand, he didn't blame Stubbs for interjecting. If Vogel had been a lawyer representing Quinn he would have done exactly the same. He decided to have one last try.

'I thought you might like to get this sorted out now, Greg,' persisted Vogel. 'It could help you a lot if you told us honestly everything that happened between you and your father on Saturday afternoon.'

Greg glanced towards Philip Stubbs who said nothing more, merely shaking his head just very slightly.

'C'mon Greg. This is your chance to get it all over with,' encouraged Vogel.

'No,' said Greg after another few seconds silence. 'I'm going to do as Mr Stubbs says. I'm not saying anything more.'

Morag Docherty had walked out into the hallway of Greg Quinn's flat to take Vogel's call.

When she re-entered the sitting room where she had left Gill Quinn watching TV, or at least staring at the set, Gill was standing right behind the door, holding the house phone in one hand.

'What's going on?' she asked at once.

Morag suspected that Gill had been listening to her conversation with the DCI.

'Nothing's going on,' Morag lied.

'I've been trying to get Greg on the phone ever since you went outside to take that call,' Gill continued. 'He's not picking up.'

'Does he always pick up when you call him?' asked Morag, avoiding Gill's question as best she could. 'Even when he's at work?'

'Pretty much, yes.'

'Well, perhaps he just can't at the moment,' said Morag, truthfully enough. There seemed little doubt that Gill and her son were very close, the PC reflected, and she wondered what relevance that might prove to have as the investigation into Thomas Quinn's murder progressed.

'Maybe.' Gill looked thoughtful. 'So what is it you want to ask me then?'

That question from Gill confirmed, of course, that Docherty had been correct in guessing that she had been eavesdropping on her conversation with Vogel. The PC didn't think that her side of the conversation would have given much away, but clearly it had aroused a suspicion in Gill Quinn that something was happening which affected not only her but also her son.

Morag had suspected for quite a while that Gill's state of shock wasn't really as extreme as the impression she'd attempted to impart. Now the PC was becoming pretty sure of that. Or, at least, that Gill had recovered considerably more than she was letting on.

'I need to ask you whose phone you used when you sent Greg a text message on Saturday afternoon?' Docherty queried.

'Do you indeed?' countered Gill. 'Well, I'm not answering any of your questions until you answer mine. Something's going on with my son. Where is he? That's what I want to know for a start.'

Docherty wondered whether she could risk lying again. But she was an experienced officer. She knew well enough that lies usually landed coppers in hot water. Her earlier fib had been oblique and almost certainly explicable. Another would be far too dangerous. But she made one more attempt to first get the other woman to tell her whose phone she had used.

However Gill Quinn was intransigent.

'You'll get nothing from me until you tell me where my son is,' she insisted, shaking her head ferociously.

'I'm not at liberty to say,' said Docherty. 'But if you would just cooperate with me . . .'

'Well that's a giveaway, isn't it?' Gill snapped. 'Greg's been arrested, hasn't he?'

The search team was on its way. Docherty would in any case then have to tell Gill where her son was, in order to explain their presence and that no search warrant was required. She certainly suspected, in the light of her new sharp demeanour, that Gill would ask for one.

'Yes, you're quite right,' agreed the PC, a tad reluctantly. 'Greg has been arrested and is currently being interviewed at Barnstaple police station.'

'As I thought,' retorted Gill sharply. 'And I will answer your question now. I actually don't know whose phone I used.'

Not that again, thought Morag. Vogel had warned her of this, nonetheless it was annoying.

'Look Gill,' said Morag, putting on her most conciliatory voice. 'If you want to help yourself and also help Greg, I really suggest that you cooperate . . .'

'It isn't a question of not cooperating,' the other woman interrupted. 'I am cooperating. I have told you I don't know whose phone I used, and that's the truth.'

'Would you mind explaining that.'

'Certainly, dear.'

My goodness, thought Docherty, Gill Quinn had made some recovery. What was with the 'dear', all of a sudden? She sounded condescending. And even, perhaps, a tad superior. Docherty feared she hadn't handled this well. She waited in silence for Gill to continue.

'I don't know whose phone I used because it belonged to somebody I met in the street,' said Gill Quinn. 'I needed some fresh air. I left Helen's House just to go for a walk around the town and look at the shops. Anything to try to clear my head. When I started to think straight again, I remembered that I'd arranged to meet Greg at Morrisons that morning. I knew he'd be worried sick about me, so I approached a stranger, a woman I'd never seen in my life before as far as I'm aware, and asked her if I could borrow her phone to send my son a text. I told her I'd inadvertently left my own phone at home. That was true, of course, except that it wasn't inadvertent.'

Gill chuckled, in a bitter sort of way.

Docherty thought about the CCTV in wide use throughout Bideford town centre.

'Where were you when you used this woman's phone?' she asked.

'I have absolutely no idea,' Gill replied quickly. 'I have very little idea where I was all afternoon, as a matter of fact, or what I was doing.'

'But you're quite sure now that you left Helen's House, are you?'

'Oh yes, for at least a couple of hours. Probably more. Maybe three hours or so.'

'Do you know what time you left the House?'

'Well, I didn't take any real notice of the time. But let's see . . . We'd had lunch. A while before, I think. I expect I left about two. Something like that.'

'And when you said you walked around the town, do I assume you meant Bideford?'

'Yes, I think so.'

'But how did you get to Bideford. I understand you didn't have your car. You had no money. You didn't have your wallet.'

'I suppose I walked.'

'It's a fair walk.'

'I'm a good walker. But maybe I didn't go to Bideford. Maybe I just walked around Northam, or into Appledore. I really don't know. You saw the state I was in on Saturday.'

Morag had seen, all right. And, perhaps unfairly, she was beginning to wonder if even then at least some of Gill Quinn's state of shock had been an act.

'That was after your husband had been killed, and we'd just found you covered in blood sitting with his dead body,' she pointed out.

'Yes. I was pretty shaken before that, though. You know what he did to me.'

'All right, but why did you go back to the House?' asked Docherty.

'I don't understand, why wouldn't I?'

'Well, you reported your husband's death at six-forty-something. If you stayed out for three hours or so you couldn't have been back at the House for long before you left again to go home. It doesn't make much sense, does it?'

'I hadn't made up my mind what to do when I returned to the House. My head was all over the place.'

'Then what made you decide that you wanted to go home, after all?'

'Who knows? I always did go back in the end. The alternative was to admit that I was a victim. And I've never been able to admit that, you see. Even though I was, of course.'

Docherty was further surprised by Gill's lucidity, and more than ever convinced that the other woman now knew exactly what she was doing and saying.

'Gill, you must realize that what you have just told me suggests that Helen Harris, Sadie, and the other women residents at the House, have all lied to the police, in order to give you an alibi.'

'Oh no, dear, Helen and Sadie would never lie. Not to anyone, and certainly not to the police. I'm sure they were just mistaken. As for the other women, I expect they just didn't realize I'd gone out. It's not a prison there, you know.'

'I realize that, Gill,' said Docherty. 'But I would like to ask you if you realize that you have just totally destroyed your own alibi?'

'Oh yes, I do realize that,' agreed Gill.

'And the timescale you have given me means that you almost certainly would have had time, even on foot, to return to your home in St Anne's Avenue, kill the man who had abused you for so long, and then return to Helen's House, albeit apparently without anyone there realizing you had left. Do you agree that is so?'

'Oh yes, dear,' Gill Quinn agreed. 'I had motive and opportunity. Isn't that what you say in the police force? But I didn't kill Thomas, of course. Neither, I can assure you, did my son. And you won't be able to prove that either of us did.'

THIRTY-FOUR

Ultimately Lilian's cellmate, Kelly, discovered Lilian's cache of pills, and in so doing probably saved her life. She confronted Lilian at once.

Lilian explained that she had nothing to live for.

'It isn't prison that I can't cope with,' she said. 'That will end sooner or later. It's knowing I will never be free. In or out of prison. Kurt will always be there, you see. He will never leave me alone.'

Kelly was a lifer. Lilian never knew what offence she had committed. It was an unwritten rule in prison that you didn't ask. And, in any case, Lilian suspected she would rather not know. Although she felt she was in no position to judge. And, of course, Kelly insisted she was innocent. But it quickly became apparent that not only was Kelly a force to be reckoned with within the walls of Eastwood, which made life much easier for Lilian when it became known that she was her mate, but also that she had moved in ominous circles before her conviction. Kelly also frequently implied that she had retained connections on the outside with powerful figures in the world of organized crime. It was almost as if she were boasting. All the same, she continued to demonstrate unexpected kindness, and did her best to convince Lilian that she would have a future after her release. If the authorities were prepared to help the likes of James Bulger's killers start up a new life with a new name, surely they could be persuaded to help her.

'And if you do ever need any help sorting out that bastard

husband of yours after you get out, then you just let me know,' said Kelly.

Meanwhile Kelly encouraged Lilian to find ways of dealing with imprisonment. She helped her acquire a plum job in the library and encouraged her to visit the gym and get fit. Kelly was one of those who believed strongly that physical fitness also made you feel better and stronger mentally.

Lilian became inordinately fond of Kelly, an attractive twenty-something whose perky positivity remained as yet undimmed by her confinement. Lilian had heard of sexual and romantic relationships developing between women prisoners whatever their normal sexual preferences, but she feared those feelings were dead in her for ever whether with a man or a woman.

It was the prison governor who, to Lilian's astonishment, provided what was probably the most potentially important assistance. She told Lilian that she had been looking into her case, and put her in touch with barrister Jean Carr, a leading silk in civil liberties and a committed fighter on behalf of women who had been victims of violence.

'You can never second guess these things, but I do believe you may have grounds for appeal,' the governor told Lilian. 'And you could have no one better on your side than Jean.'

Jean did indeed prove to be dedicated, energetic and clever. Best of all she was willing to take on Lilian's case.

Suddenly Lilian didn't feel quite so alone. She had three strong women in her corner, all rather impressive in very different ways.

Jean successfully applied for leave to appeal. At the same time she began to quietly let it be known in the small world of the British legal system, that she had heard a rumour doing the rounds concerning an illicit relationship between the widowed Mrs Justice Hadley and the married barrister who led the prosecution against Lilian. It could of course be just a rumour, murmured Jean into the nervous ears of various legal bigwigs, some of who already suspected that it was actually far more than a rumour. Of course, Jean wouldn't dream of suggesting improper behaviour which may have prejudiced a fair trial for her client, but . . .

Lilian did not learn of any of this until much later. At the time she had been quite unaware of the carefully orchestrated behind-the-scenes activity which preceded her appearance before the

Court of Appeal at the Royal Courts of Justice on The Strand in London. And, in view of her succession of distressing experiences when dealing with the forces of law and order, the ruling ultimately delivered by this mighty court came as a big surprise.

The justices did not overturn the verdict reached by the jury at Bristol High Court, which would have been highly unusual, but they slashed Lilian's prison sentence on the grounds of undue severity, and strongly criticized the way her trial had been conducted. There were mitigating factors, the justices decreed, not least the apparent misconception of events on the part of the high court judge. The appeal court ruled that the level of Lilian's fear of her husband had not been taken into consideration, and also that there was no evidence of any premeditation, which should have been made clear to the jury and taken into account by the judge. The police investigation was also criticized.

Lilian's sentence was reduced from five years to fifteen months. This meant that with remission she had only two months left to serve.

Jean Carr was pleased with the result although, as a woman who clearly liked to win, she admitted she had wished for even more.

'If we really had justice in this country the verdict would have been overturned, unlikely though that always is,' she grumbled. 'I had hoped at least that the justices would reduce the sentence by enough so that you didn't have to spend another day in jail.'

Lilian was non-committal. On the one hand she was pleased and relieved that her time in prison was now nearly over. However, on the other hand, she still had a criminal conviction against her name. And Lilian continued to believe that she was in any case facing a life sentence, whether she was in or out of jail, a sentence she felt no one could ever help her with.

She was therefore not at all surprised when a card arrived from Kurt congratulating her on her successful appeal. She had been expecting something of the kind.

'I just can't wait to see you again,' he had written. 'I am still waiting for you. I will always wait for you.'

THIRTY-FIVE

Vogel had switched off his phone during the Greg Quinn interview and asked not to be disturbed for anything. After all, he had arrested the young man on suspicion of murder, and that had to take precedence over anything else, if only for an hour or two.

When he switched on again he saw that he had a missed call from Morag Docherty. He returned the call at once.

'Hang on while I step outside, boss,' said Docherty.

In view of Gill having without any reasonable doubt listened in to her last conversation with the SIO, Docherty was taking no chances this time. She stepped out on to the communal landing, pulling the door to the flat to behind her before speaking again.

'She says she doesn't know the person whose phone she used, and she claims she was away from Helen's House for most of the afternoon, boss,' the PC began.

She then related more or less exactly what Gill Quinn had told her. And she confessed that she had, probably crucially, been more or less trapped into revealing that Gill's son had been arrested before asking her about the phone call.

'That's all right, Docherty,' said Vogel. 'Do I take it that Gill is now recovering rather well from her state of shock?'

'Too right, boss. She's become a bit of a can of worms actually. And I'm wondering just how genuine her behaviour has been all along. I mean, she's not a stupid woman that's for sure. And probably a heck of a lot sharper than we've given her credit for.'

'And yet she has effectively destroyed her own alibi, or tried to. Do you agree, Docherty?'

'Yes, boss.'

'So, do you believe her account of her whereabouts on Saturday afternoon?'

'Not a word of it, boss,' said Docherty.

* * *

Whilst Docherty had been reporting to Vogel, Gill Quinn took the opportunity to phone Helen Harris.

'Oh Gill, how are you?' asked Helen at once, her voice full of concern. 'I didn't know how to get hold of you. I didn't know where you were. Are you with Greg?'

'Not exactly. I'm at his flat. Greg has been arrested.'

'Oh my God. What for?'

'What do you think for?' snapped Gill.

Almost immediately she added: 'I'm sorry. I don't know what I'm saying half the time. He's been arrested on suspicion of murdering his father. He didn't do it, of course.'

'Uh, no. Of course not. I'm sure he didn't.'

Helen sounded definite enough. But Gill suspected that she probably wasn't at all sure. Why would she be? But she was glad that Helen had not directly challenged her.

'The thing is, I should be the prime suspect,' Gill continued.

'I see,' said Helen Harris.

'I don't think you do,' said Gill. 'If I have a cast-iron alibi, then it focuses police attention almost entirely on Greg. It shouldn't, but it does. I don't want that. I want to create a smokescreen.'

'And you want me to be your smokescreen?'

'Part of it, yes.'

'Well, presumably the police wouldn't have arrested Greg without evidence. Do you know what evidence they have?'

'No. Nobody has told me anything.'

'Has he been charged, do you know?'

'I don't know that either.'

'Well look, he may have been arrested on suspicion of an offence, but that does not necessarily mean he will be charged. That will depend on whether or not the Crown Prosecution Service consider there's enough evidence to charge him. And if they don't, the police can't keep him in custody indefinitely. Greg could well be released very soon—'

'I'm not prepared to take that chance,' Gill interrupted. 'I need you to do as I've asked, Helen.'

'OK, let me get this straight. What exactly are you asking me to do? Do you want me to lie to the police? Is that it? Because I'm not sure I'm prepared to do that.'

'No, of course not. Just tell them the truth. Tell them you can't be sure whether or not I was in the House all afternoon. Tell them you were shut away in your office. You were, weren't you?'

'Part of the time, yes. But you know that, because you were there. As were at least five other women, including Sadie.'

'I was only there part of the time too. And I've told the police that.'

'Look Gill, I can understand that you want to save your son, but . . .'

'There is no but,' said Gill. 'I'm going to save my son. I'm going to make the police accept that he is innocent.'

'Well, let's say he isn't innocent, just for a moment. Then there would be no doubting his motive, would there? He wanted to protect his mother from a truly monstrous man. You mustn't forget that, Gill. Thomas was a monster and, to be honest, whoever killed him could be regarded as having been totally justified. Certainly if his killer was a family member.'

'And do you think a court could be persuaded to see it that way, Helen?'

'Who knows, but Greg was abused too—'

'No,' Gill interrupted. 'Greg wasn't abused. Well, not really.'

'What does that mean?'

'His father never lifted a hand to him.'

'There are other kinds of abuse, Gill. As you know only too well.'

'Look Helen, all I am asking is that you tell the police you couldn't be certain that I was in the House all afternoon. Surely that isn't too much to ask?'

'I am on your side, Gill, probably more than you will ever realize,' said Helen noncommittedly.

And with that she ended the call.

Helen was disturbed. She was an assertive woman, confident and sure of herself. Her work was her passion. And she rarely had any doubts about what to do in the pursuance of her abiding aim. Which was to protect and nurture the victims of abuse.

She had thought she had known what was best for Gill Quinn. She still thought she knew what was best for her. But Greg's arrest was a new and perhaps unexpected factor. However it was one that she supposed she should have expected.

After all, if Gill had an indisputable alibi, then it was pretty obvious who the police would focus their attention on next. They would undoubtedly consider Thomas' murder to be a domestic. In such a situation that was statistically almost always the case. So if they were unable to prove the wife was guilty, then a son who loathed his father, and had left home at seventeen in order to escape from his father, would immediately be first in the frame.

Helen didn't know what to do any more. She was just considering her options when her phone rang. The caller was DI Vogel.

He came straight to the point. 'Gill Quinn tells us that she was not at Helen's House all day on Saturday when her husband was killed,' he began. 'I need to ask you again about the alibi you have given her.'

'I see,' said Helen. Not for the first time in her life she was beginning to feel trapped by circumstances beyond her control.

'So are you sure that Gill was at the House all day and did not leave at all, if only for an hour or two. This is a very serious matter. Are you quite sure, Helen?'

'I understand that you have now arrested Greg Quinn on suspicion of his father's murder, isn't that so?' enquired Helen.

There was an almost imperceptible pause.

'Will you please answer my question,' said Vogel sternly.

'Mr Vogel, Gill is a doting mother, she has a loving relationship with her son, which is more than she ever had with her monster of a husband,' responded Helen. 'Wouldn't you think she would go to any lengths, say or do almost anything, to protect her son?'

'Miss Harris, please, I just need you to confirm the alibi you have given Gill.'

Helen sighed. She could not afford to get on the wrong side of the law. She had close relationships with the police and all of those dealing with violent crime in North Devon, including legal and medical professionals. And, if she wanted Helen's House to effectively continue in its work, she needed to avoid putting those relationships at risk.

'All right, Mr Vogel, I will once again confirm that Gill Quinn was with us here at Helen's House on Saturday,' she said, trying not to sound too reluctant.

'All day, Miss Harris?' queried Vogel.

Gill's words came back to Helen. Could she be absolutely sure that Gill hadn't left the House during that fateful afternoon? She thought of Gill as a friend, as she did all the women who came to her for help. But she did not wish to mislead the police. Not at this stage. In any case, she was beginning to form a plan. Another way in which she could help Gill Quinn and her son.

'Look,' Helen responded. 'It is, I suppose, remotely possible that Gill could have left the House on Saturday at some stage without my knowledge, or the knowledge of anyone else who was here, although highly unlikely. But it is really quite impossible to see how she could have been away from here for long enough to get herself to St Anne's Avenue, between Northam and Appledore, kill her husband, and then get back here without anyone noticing she had gone.'

'Thank you, Miss Harris,' said Vogel, a tad wearily. 'Could I ask you, by the way, how you knew we had arrested Greg Quinn? We've not released a public statement yet.'

'No. Gill told me.'

'Did she indeed? And did she also ask you to withdraw her alibi, by any chance?'

'Not exactly. Just to say I could have been mistaken.'

'So, and this really is the last time, is there any chance at all that you could have been mistaken?'

'No, Mr Vogel, there is not.'

As soon as the call ended, Helen began to execute her alternative plan to help both Gill and her son.

She made two further phone calls. The first was to the senior custody sergeant at Barnstaple police station. The second was to Philip Stubbs, the legal aid solicitor who was representing Greg Quinn.

THIRTY-SIX

The day of Lilian's release came around fast. Faster than she actually wanted. She may have expected to hear from Kurt. Nonetheless she was chilled by his message.

With Kelly's encouragement, she asked Jean Carr to push for her to be granted lifelong anonymity. Jean was not optimistic. She pointed out that whilst there were a number of people in the UK living under new identities through the witness protection scheme, there were only six criminals throughout the country who had been given lifelong anonymity, in each case because the crimes they had committed were so notorious.

Lilian was relieved that she did not fit into that category, but disappointed to be reminded that she remained, in law, a convicted criminal. She was even more disappointed that the persistently positive Jean Carr held so little hope.

Predictably enough Jean proved to be quite right, and Lilian's cellmate quite wrong. Neither the police nor the courts would even consider providing her with a new identity.

Jean continued the legal battle to force Kurt to provide Lilian with funds. But the process, complicated by Lilian's conviction for committing grievous bodily harm against her husband, threatened to be endless and had yet to produce a penny.

She would have found herself released with nothing more than a discharge grant with which to attempt to restart her life, had it not been for Kelly, who arranged for one of her dubious associates to collect the Hockney from Kate and Charlie and sell it. Lilian ultimately received only a fraction of its real value, of course, but she hoped it might be enough for her to start a new life.

She called Kate, now the mother of a little girl, and explained that she was going to do her best to go to ground, and she had no idea when she would be able to call again. Lilian actually thought it was quite possible she would never feel able to call Kate again. But she didn't say that.

Kate sounded both taken aback and saddened. She was warm, concerned and slightly apologetic.

'One of Charlie's police contacts has told him they now believe the South African High Commissioner and the government minister who claimed to be having lunch with Kurt when you said he'd confronted you, here in Islington, may both be on his payroll,' she said. 'I guess we shouldn't have doubted you. But it does still seem a little far-fetched.'

'Not to me it doesn't,' muttered Lilian.

With the help of various prison charities Lilian was able to acquire a shorthold tenancy on a studio flat in Reading, which seemed like a suitably anonymous sort of place in which to hide. And Lilian had no doubt that was what she needed to do. Jean arranged for her name to be changed by deed poll. It wasn't the same as being given a new identity, but, hopefully, it would help. She had her red-blonde hair cut very short and dyed an unattractive mousey brown. She hoped it would not only radically change her appearance but also help make her inconspicuous, somebody no one would bother to look at twice. She also took to covering her distinctive freckles with high quality concealer and foundation. All she wanted was to disappear into the background wherever she was.

The studio flat was far from the kind of accommodation she had been used to. Just a posh name for a bedsit, in Lilian's opinion, and this one was not even a posh bedsit. She had also acquired a job, stacking shelves in a supermarket, again a far cry from what she had once been used to. But none of this bothered her at all. She desired only to be left alone. And she was grateful for any kind of peace in her life. Although she was a long way from finding any real peace, and indeed doubted that she ever would.

At first she just could not believe that Kurt would fail to find her again. And quickly. She wasn't really living. Just waiting. But eventually she did allow herself to relax a little, to risk a casual friendship with one or two workmates, and even to build the beginnings of something resembling a social life, going to the cinema or the pub occasionally.

Then, just as she was beginning to dare to wonder if maybe Kurt had walked away from her after all, perhaps even found someone else, or even that he had lost his touch, and couldn't find her – he turned up.

It was late afternoon on a Sunday. She had been to the cinema with a workmate who had come back to her second-floor flat for a coffee, and only left a minute or two before. Lilian's guard was down. It had been almost a year since her release from jail. A year that had passed without incident, and without any sign of Kurt or his people. The communal front door downstairs was permanently locked and operated by an intercom system. When the doorbell to the studio rang, Lilian just assumed her workmate had returned for some reason. She opened the door at once, without even attempting to check who was outside. Kurt was standing there, smiling a huge smile. He immediately lunged forward through the doorway, unceremoniously pushing her to one side.

Fearfully she backed into the room. He kicked the door shut behind him, dropped his coat and briefcase carelessly onto the floor, and moved closer to her, until his face was just inches from her face. He was clutching the biggest bouquet of flowers she'd ever seen. With cool indifference he tossed it onto the bed then grabbed hold of Lilian by the shoulders. His fingers dug into her flesh.

'You can have it the easy way or the hard way, Lilian,' he remarked conversationally. 'Why don't you make it the easy way?'

Lilian had always known better than to try to resist Kurt, and he was well aware of that. This time, it seemed, he was not even going to bother to pretend to court her. He just wanted sex straight away. He slapped her, once, twice, maybe three times, across the face. His usual foreplay. Then he forced her down on the bed, ripping and tearing at her clothes and his own. She lay quite still, in order that he would hurt her as little as possible. She even began to try to give the impression that she was enjoying their sex session. She scratched his chest with her fingernails. He scratched her back, only rather more viciously. On her arms, her breasts, and her belly. His fingernails were perfectly manicured, and kept slightly longer than most men's, just as they had always been. She so wanted to make it stop. But he kept on going. And he kept on hitting and scratching her. Then, somehow, perhaps he was climaxing, she neither knew nor cared, she managed to wriggle from under him.

It had all gone too far again. Much too far. Just like at the hotel in Bristol. Lilian was bleeding from her nose and mouth. She could only open one eye. She ran for the door. Half-naked. Terrified. She just wanted to get away from him. But, as before, he had no intention of letting her leave. He came for her again. There was a struggle. A violent struggle. Like the last time. But different.

This time there was a gun. A small lethal handgun. And suddenly, in the middle of what turned into an ill-matched wrestling match, Lilian had the gun in her hand. She fired it, barely aware of what she was doing. It was point blank range. The gun's barrel was almost touching his flesh. The room exploded in a flash of fire and a blaze of light. And so did Kurt St John's chest.

He dropped like a felled animal onto his back on the floor. There was a hole in the middle of his body. Blood, tissue, and bits of bone spewed everywhere, including all over Lilian. This time there was no doubt about it. This time she had killed him.

Kurt St John was dead.

THIRTY-SEVEN

Vogel was thoughtful as he ended the call to Helen Harris. He wondered if Helen was playing him. Certainly he felt she was holding back, that she at the very least knew something he did not.

He and Saslow were together in his office. Both with laptops.

'What background do we have on Helen Harris?' he asked.

'I'm not sure, boss,' said Saslow. 'I mean, she set up her house here around nineteen years ago, and is held in pretty high standing locally, as you're aware. Not much beyond that, I don't think.'

Vogel had already checked all the obvious computer sources. He knew that Helen had no criminal record, that both she and Helen's House, which operated as a registered charity, were solvent, if barely so, that there was no mortgage on the House, nor did Helen have a mortgage on any other property, nor indeed own a property other than the House, that she was not a director of any company, that she appeared to have no professional qualifications, and that her dealings with the police and officialdom generally had always been conducted in an exemplary manner.

Vogel was good with computers. He had, in the past, been accused by colleagues, and even his wife, of preferring them to people. Often he could extract online information which others had failed to discover. But not in the case of Helen Harris.

The House had its own website which described its philosophy and detailed exactly what it could offer victims of domestic abuse. That too gave very little personal information on its founder and owner-proprietor, beyond saying that Helen had previously worked as a social worker specializing in cases of domestic abuse, and been deeply moved by the plight of abuse victims. She had ultimately come to feel limited by the confines of her position and, inspired by Sarah's House in Arizona, had decided to create a unique independent support service.

Basically the website chronicled almost everything about the project, and next to nothing about the woman who had founded it, thought Vogel. He suddenly had the desire to delve deeper into the life of Helen Harris. Much deeper . . .

'Who might be able tell us more?' he asked.

'DI Peters, boss,' replied Saslow at once. 'She was born and bred around here, what in these parts they call a "proper Bideford maid", boss. And she was stationed in the town as a young PC. If anyone can help, it'll be her.'

Vogel called Peters in.

'Oh yes, Helen had just opened the House when I joined the force here as a probationary,' the DI began, in answer to the DCI's query. 'It was all a bit controversial at first, and I'm not sure the neighbours are mad about it even now, but Helen quickly became quite a respected figure in the town. She was go-to for us. She lightened our load, you see. No copper likes domestics, boss, do they? Suddenly there was someone to call on who would help sort it.'

'Was she known locally when she arrived?'

'I don't think so.'

'On the Helen's House website, there's a reference to her having previously been a social worker. Do you know where she worked?'

'Bristol, I believe, boss.'

'Right. I couldn't find a record of any professional qualifications. She'd have had to have something to work in any area of social services, wouldn't she?'

'I believe so, boss.'

'And surely there should be some employment history listed somewhere. Let's do some more digging, please Janet. Get on to social services in Bristol. I want to build a past for our Helen. I'd like to know exactly what I'm dealing with. I think there may be a lot more to her than meets the eye. I know it's after office hours, but there must be somebody on duty. Just tell them it's a murder investigation.'

DI Peters returned to Vogel's office less than an hour later. She had managed to get Bristol social services on the case and had just heard back from them.

'They say they have no record at all of any Helen Harris being employed by them in any capacity,' Peters reported.

'Can they be certain?' asked Vogel. 'Maybe she slipped through the net. It's possible she was employed before computer records. Do they still keep paper files from previous to that?'

'Apparently they started computerizing their data, including employment records, in the early 2000s,' said Peters. 'And they plumbed in most of the paper files going back over a decade. But it is possible that Helen could have slipped through the net, I suppose. It's also possible that she worked in social services somewhere else. I certainly can't be absolutely sure that it was supposed to be Bristol.'

Nonetheless, Vogel called his old number two at the Avon and Somerset, DI Margot Hartley, who had served as his deputy SIO on a number of major cases during his time there, and still worked for MIT in Bristol.

He gave her a quick rundown of his so far unsuccessful quest to build a background on Helen Harris, and why.

'We've drawn a complete blank with Bristol social services,' he told her. 'But you're the one with the local knowledge.'

'From what you've told me she would have been working here twenty years or more ago, it might be a big ask, and being out of hours doesn't help. But I'll give it my best shot, David,' Hartley responded.

Vogel knew from his previous experience with her that DI Hartley's 'best shot' was about as good as it got. She was fast too. So he was optimistic when she called back a couple of hours later.

'I've tried all the usual sources,' she said. 'I'm still looking, of course, but thought you'd want to know, I've found nothing so far. I've checked medical and education records, even looked for old parking tickets. I've double checked with social services too. Officially and unofficially. I have a contact who used to run human resources for the entire social services network in Bristol. Ted Martin. Has a brain like a Rolodex. You can virtually hear it clicking. And he's never heard of Helen Harris. I can't swear to it, David, but in my opinion, if Ted hasn't heard of her, then she didn't ever work as a social worker in Bristol.'

Vogel was now like a hound following a scent. He was aware that he might be veering off onto a tangent that could well prove to be irrelevant. After all, not only did it seem highly unlikely that Helen Harris was ever going to be a plausible suspect in this case, but he also very much doubted that her credibility as an alibi was in any serious doubt. And he was beginning to feel increasingly confident that they already had Thomas Quinn's murderer locked up a cell at Barnstaple nick. Even though Gill Quinn, the victim's wife and mother of the arrested man, had just done her utmost to destroy her own alibi for the crime. Vogel was, however, becoming more and more convinced that there was a mystery surrounding Helen Harris. And it was a mystery he was determined to solve.

He'd had an idea. DVLA and Passport Office records could be routinely accessed through the PNC, the police national computer. Vogel initiated a search of both. He found that Helen Harris held a valid UK passport which had been first issued in 2000. There was no record of her having held a passport before that. She also held a valid UK driving licence which had been first issued in 2000. And there was no record of her having held a driving licence before that.

Vogel was not surprised. He was starting to arrive at a conclusion which he was confident would cause him nothing but trouble. All the same, he now felt he had no choice other than to proceed.

He was just about to make a third call, to the head of MIT, Detective Superintendent Nobby Clarke, when Peters returned.

'We've heard from Forensics, they've got DNA from a fingerprint taken from Thomas Quinn's shirt,' she began excitedly. 'It's an exact match to Gregory Quinn. I think we've got him, boss.'

'Well, well,' said Vogel.

Recovering fingerprints from fabric, and subsequently

extracting DNA, was a relatively new procedure first developed by forensic scientists in Scotland ten years or so previously. It was not always a successful process, and still depended to a considerable extent on the type of fabric. All he remembered of Thomas Quinn's shirt, from the crime scene, was that it had appeared to have once been a particularly pale shade of blue. Or maybe it had just looked that way in contrast to the abundance of blood splattered all over it.

'Was the shirt made of cotton, by any chance?' he asked.

'It certainly was, boss,' answered Peters.

'How convenient,' murmured Vogel, who knew that cotton was the best fabric for the recovery of fingerprints, and the finer the cotton the better.

'Get on to Custody at Barnstaple nick,' he told DI Peters. 'Tell them Saslow and I are on our way. I want to interview young Quinn again straight away. And almost certainly I shall be charging him. We'd better get his solicitor there.'

They were just crossing the new bridge over the Torridge when Peters called.

'It seems Philip Stubbs is already with Quinn in his cell,' she said.

'Good, that should speed things up,' said Vogel.

'Yes boss, but there's something else, Helen Harris is also there. With Stubbs and Quinn in the cell.'

'What?' Vogel cried. 'How the hell did that happen? We've arrested Gregory Quinn on suspicion of murder. He has free access to his solicitor and can confer with him in private, but not members of the general public, for God's sake.'

'It seems Barnstaple Custody don't regard Helen Harris as general public, boss.'

'I don't believe it,' snapped Vogel. 'Tell them to get that bloody woman out of it, smartish.'

'I've already done that,' said Peters. 'In view of our investigations earlier I had an idea you'd feel this way.'

'Too right,' said Vogel. 'What on earth are they playing at? Don't they realize nobody is above suspicion in a murder investigation? What they've done is totally against procedure.'

'Almost everyone in Bideford and Barnstaple nick has worked

closely with Helen Harris for years, boss,' said Peters, by way of an attempt at an explanation. 'They think of her as one of us.'

'One of us?' queried Vogel irritably. 'And yet nobody knows a damned thing about the woman. Rest assured, I'm going to change that. Smartish.'

THIRTY-EIGHT

Kurt was taken to the morgue. Lilian was taken to hospital. She was not only bruised, battered and covered in scratches, but also she had been badly cut on her shoulders and arms.

She had explained to the police who came to interview her that her husband had tracked her down even though she had relocated, changed her name, and kept the lowest of low profiles.

'Just as I always feared he would, he came to find me,' she told them. 'I tried so hard to hide away, but he found me. He pushed his way into the flat and forced himself on me. He started to hit me straight away. He slapped me a couple of times then punched me in the face. Hard. You can see what he did to me.'

She gestured towards her damaged face. 'This is what he has always done to me,' she continued. 'The only way he can achieve an erection, with me anyway, is to cause pain. And it works. It always works. Rather spectacularly. The rest of the time he is totally flaccid.'

Two police officers were by her bedside. A young male PC and an older female CID officer who had introduced herself as Detective Sergeant Brenda Smythe.

The PC was blushing, a common enough reaction amongst so many, Lilian had found, when she attempted to describe Kurt's sexual preferences.

'You can use the past tense,' commented DS Smythe. 'Your husband is definitely dead.'

Lilian thought that approach was a little ambivalent. She wasn't sure whether DS Smythe sympathized with her or not. But she could not be anything other than relieved to hear that Kurt really was dead. Even though she already feared the consequences of that. She had known he was dead. This time. Of course she had known. But she could hardly believe it.

DS Smythe asked first about the stab wounds Lilian had suffered. Which, although little more than flesh wounds, were serious enough to require a number of stitches.

'We found what we think is the weapon he used, at the scene,' the DS said. 'A silver butter knife. A strange choice.'

Lilian shook her head. 'Not so strange,' she said.

And she did her best to explain about the incident at Bristol when she, in desperation, had stabbed him with a butter knife.

'He told me he intended to do to me what I did to him. Kurt is – was – a very strong man. Usually I just submitted to him, because it would end up worse for me if I didn't.'

'But not this time,' commented DS Smythe. 'It was your husband it ended up worse for. He died.'

Lilian could only nod her head in agreement. She remained silent.

'Could you please tell me exactly what happened which led to you shooting Mr St John?' the DS continued.

Lilian did her best to do so. She explained how all she had ever wanted to do was to escape. How she'd managed to get off the bed and away from him, she had no idea how, and run for the door, but he'd come after her, and grabbed her.

'Then suddenly he pulled a gun on me, a handgun, I was terrified,' she continued.

'But wasn't Mr St John naked?' asked DS Smythe. 'He was certainly naked when we found him.'

'Y-yes he was,' affirmed Lilian. 'And if you're asking me where he got the gun from, well I didn't think about it at the time, I was so terrified, but I realized we were standing where he'd dropped his jacket when he forced his way into my flat. I think it must have been in his pocket.'

'Did your husband often carry a gun?'

'Perhaps not often, but I had seen him with firearms before, he would have certainly known how to get hold of one.'

'What did he actually do with the gun?'

'He threatened me with it, of course. Why else would he have brought a gun with him? He told me that if I didn't stop trying to get away he would shoot me. In the heart, he said. He pointed the gun straight at me and he told me that I was never going to escape him, that I shouldn't try. Then he said that if he couldn't have me, he was going to make damned sure nobody else did.'

'But you have mentioned what a big strong man he was, how on earth did you manage to get the gun away from him?'

'I'm not quite sure. I remember thinking that if I tried to get out of the door again, if I tried to run, he really would shoot me. As he had said. So I just stood there and begged and pleaded with him. We were standing close together. I'm not sure, but I think at one point the barrel of the gun was sticking into me. I think I tried to push it away, I must have tried to grab it, I suppose. Instinctively. I really don't remember.

'Then the gun went off. At very close quarters. It fired. I realized it was in my hand. That I must have pulled the trigger. But I have no real recollection of that. All I really remember is a bang and a flash, and watching him sink to the floor. He just collapsed, with this massive gaping hole in his chest. It was the most awful thing I have ever seen. And all I know is that I have killed a man. Killed my husband. And I doubt I will ever come to terms with that. But I had no choice, DS Smythe. It was him or me. He was going to kill me. And if I hadn't, by some extraordinary freak, got hold of that gun and fired it first, he would have done. I have no doubt about that. He would have killed me.'

Lilian called Jean Carr as soon as the two officers left the ward. They had given little away, and she had no idea really what they had made of her and her extraordinary story.

She did know she was going to need extensive professional help if she was going to avoid being locked up again, and this time for a great deal longer.

The barrister was positive from the start.

'You killed in self-defence,' she said at once. 'Absolutely no doubt about it. For God's sake, the man pulled a gun on you. He came to you carrying a firearm with presumably that intention. That's premeditation. Then he threatened to shoot you in the heart. You had no choice but to do whatever you could to defend yourself. Don't worry. This time you're going to walk free. Just leave it to me.'

Lilian was encouraged. But she had been down this road before, and on that last occasion Kurt had only been injured. She just hoped Jean Carr would prove to be right.

But, whatever happened next, whatever might be in store for her at the hands of the forces of law and order, one thing was certain. Kurt St John was gone from her life for ever.

THIRTY-NINE

Once she learned that Vogel was on his way, there had been no need to tell Helen Harris to leave. She did so at once.

Her mission, such as it was, had been at least partially accomplished. Philip Stubbs had stepped out of Greg's cell as she had requested, allowing her just a few minutes alone with the young man.

Helen did not intend for either Greg or his mother to stand trial for Thomas Quinn's death. Vogel had been quite right about one thing, Helen did not think that Thomas Quinn had deserved to continue living. And she did not believe that anyone should suffer for having caused his death. Particularly not his son or his wife.

She now had a clear picture of the evidence against Greg, and her extensive knowledge of the law led her to believe that the young man would not be charged without a substantive further development.

But she also thought it possible that Greg might confess to the crime merely in order to protect his mother. Certainly his mother had been prepared to put herself in the frame in order to protect Greg. So she considered it vital that she had the chance to assure him that the alibi she and the other women at Helen's House had given his mother stood, and that all he should worry about was himself.

'And you are innocent,' she had told him. 'Just remember that, whatever happens. Don't give them anything. And if things change, if they do charge you, make sure that lawyer of yours calls me at once. There are things I can do that he can't. I want you to remember that. Whatever happens, remember that.'

It was the truth, too. Helen had the knowledge and the will to turn Vogel's investigation upside down. The only question was, she mused, as she drove back to Bideford, did she have the courage?

Upon arriving at Barnstaple nick just after nine thirty p.m., Vogel stopped by at Custody where he rounded angrily on the officers on duty.

'What on earth were you thinking?' he queried in bewilderment.

'We're used to having her around, I suppose,' said the duty sergeant. 'We think of her as a welfare worker, I mean that's what she is, really, isn't it?'

'Actually, sergeant, I don't know what the hell Helen Harris is,' Vogel replied angrily. 'And neither do you. Which is, of course, my point.'

Meanwhile, Greg, accompanied by Philip Stubbs, was already sitting in an interview room waiting for Vogel and Saslow to arrive.

Greg had been overwhelmed by Helen Harris' visit. He had never met her before. He'd heard of her, of course, albeit only vaguely. It was pretty much impossible to live in the Bideford area and not have heard of Helen Harris. He had actually suspected for years that his father had been more than just an unpleasant control freak towards his mother, and that he had also physically abused her – even though she had always denied it when he had challenged her. But he'd no idea that his mother had become involved with Helen's House. And it was absolutely true that he'd also had no idea of the extent of Thomas Quinn's abuse. He had been shocked to the core by the wounds that his father had inflicted upon his mother. Burning another human being with a cigarette end wasn't domestic abuse in Greg's opinion. It went beyond his conception of what that might mean. It was torture. And he was glad his father was dead. He would never mourn him. Like Helen, he believed absolutely that Thomas deserved to die.

However, he had no wish to go to prison for his father's murder. And Helen's somewhat bizarre visit had brought with it the hope that he could avoid even being charged with that. And also that neither would his mother face a murder charge. Before Helen's visit he had been quite convinced that at least one of them was going to end up in court.

So, as he prepared, yet again, to face DCI Vogel, Greg was feeling a little better about his situation than during the previous interview. And considerably more optimistic. Neither had his solicitor turned out to be quite the muppet he had thought at first. Philip Stubbs seemed to know his stuff, had so far stepped in smartly when needed, and had bent the rules without too much prevarication so that Helen Harris could not only visit Greg in his cell, but also spend time alone with him.

Philip had also explained to Greg something he already half knew from watching TV detective dramas. Except in exceptional circumstances, and Philip doubted there was anything exceptional about this case, Greg could only be kept in custody for thirty-six hours without being charged. Philip had also explained that he did not consider the evidence presented so far by DCI Vogel would persuade the Crown Prosecution Service that there were grounds to proceed.

'Almost totally circumstantial,' said Philip.

Greg had half known that too.

'Just don't put your foot in it and you'll be right as ninepence,' Philip had said, unknowingly echoing at least the tone of Helen's advice.

Philip was inclined to talk in clichés. Occasionally, not very often, Greg recalled something from his posh education. This was one of those occasions. Greg remembered his old English teacher telling him that clichés had become clichés because they were usually the truth. He sincerely hoped that would prove to be so.

Certainly Greg had no intention of putting his foot in it. Philip had also said that if he played his cards right he reckoned Greg could be home in time to make his mum a bedtime cuppa.

He stood up as Vogel and Saslow entered. An unconscious gesture of respect that was another legacy of his public-school education. He even dared to smile at them. Just a little.

Within seconds his cautious optimism had been shattered.

'We have DNA evidence that you were with your father at the crime scene after his death,' Vogel began bluntly. 'It would therefore be highly advisable for you to change your earlier statement. Your father was not alive when you left the family home on Saturday, was he, Greg?'

Greg was stunned.

'Y-yes, yes, of course he was alive, I-I told you,' he stumbled. 'You can't have any evidence. You can't. You're just trying to trick me, aren't you?'

'No Greg, I'm not trying to trick you,' said Vogel quietly.

He then told the young man about the fingerprints that had been lifted from the fabric of Thomas Quinn's shirt and the DNA extracted from them which was an exact match to Greg's DNA.

Greg was shocked. He hadn't expected this. He hadn't even known such a thing was possible.

'W-we're talking about my father, I could have touched him at any time while I was there, and left fingerprints on his clothes,' he blurted out. 'While he was alive, I mean.'

'Indeed, but we can prove that your prints were left after, or perhaps during, your father's killing.'

'W-what?' stumbled Greg. 'You can't, I mean h-how on earth . . .?'

'The DNA we extracted contains relatively substantial traces of your father's blood. Enough for us to reasonably deduce that the fingerprints from which that DNA was obtained were left on your father's body after his death. So, do you understand what that means, Greg?'

Greg felt absolutely shattered. He understood only too well. This was quite devastating evidence. He glanced at Philip Stubbs, desperately seeking assistance. The solicitor stepped in at once.

'Don't answer that,' he instructed Greg, before addressing Vogel.

'I am advising my client to answer no more questions at this stage,' he said.

'Right,' said the DCI. 'You should know that I shall be approaching the CPS with a view to charging your client later tonight.'

Vogel turned to Greg. 'Are you absolutely sure that you have nothing else to say?' he asked mildly. 'You could make things worse for yourself, you know.'

Greg had no idea what he could say. He merely shook his head. He didn't know how things could be worse. It felt as if his world was about to end. He wanted his mother. He needed to talk to his mother. Desperately. Although he wasn't entirely sure what he could say to her, either.

FORTY

It really did look now as if the Quinn case was about to reach its obvious conclusion. But Vogel was far from satisfied. There had been a second murder which he still could not believe was totally unrelated to the first. After all, it was Thomas Quinn's business partner who had been shot. Also, he had a mystery woman on his patch, already connected, albeit at a certain distance, with Thomas' murder. And that continued to bug him.

It was rare to find people living their lives in the UK who did not have a documented history by the time they reached adulthood. Building an entire new identity, without even the hint of a past, was not easily done. Even in the age of the internet, let alone more than twenty years previously. Indeed, it was pretty nigh impossible without assistance at the highest level.

Vogel really needed to call Nobby Clarke. He and Nobby went back a long way and he had always admired and respected her. That had sadly changed the last time he worked with her, due to a situation which Vogel continued to believe had seriously compromised them both and, ultimately, he had taken the decision to move permanently to North Devon in spite of Clarke rather than because of her. As a result the easy banter of their old relationship had been lost, and they were inclined to speak only when professionally necessary. This was definitely one of those occasions. He had developed a theory about Helen Harris, and he was eager to check it out. Also, he needed to give Clarke a further progress report.

He called her mobile and she picked up almost at once. They

both dispensed with any niceties, Vogel swiftly and concisely gave her an update on the progress of his investigations. Basically the Patel murder inquiry was ongoing, and the Quinn case had almost certainly been resolved.

'I would therefore like to charge Gregory Quinn tonight with the murder of his father,' he concluded.

To his relief, but only as he had expected, Clarke immediately agreed that he should do that. 'And I'll leave you to liaise with the CPS, you're the one running the show,' she added. 'But I don't see any problems there, do you?'

Vogel conferred that he did not, and hoped that would prove to be so. But you could never be totally sure with the prosecution service, in his experience. He then explained his dilemma concerning Helen Harris.

'I think I know what you're getting at here, Vogel,' responded the superintendent. 'But you'd better spell it out.'

'Yes, ma'am,' said Vogel.

Once upon a time she would have rounded on him for calling her 'Ma'am'. Detective Superintendent Clarke was not much given to formality. She actually preferred to be called Nobby, but she would put up with 'boss'. At a push. Nowadays however, her relationship with Vogel was different, and she invariably made no comment whatever he addressed her as.

'Well, I think Helen Harris might be on witness protection,' Vogel continued. 'It's just about the only thing that makes any sense. It's as if she wasn't born until 2000. Nobody can recreate themselves to that degree without help at the highest level. We both know that.'

'Possibly,' said Clarke. 'So what do you want me do about it?'

Vogel was aware that she knew perfectly well what he wanted her to do about it. He played it straight.

'I'd very much like you to find out if I'm right, boss,' he replied evenly.

'I'll see what I can do,' said Clarke.

She ended the call without any further prevarication. Sometimes Vogel so missed the way things used to be between them. But he had accepted that they would never be able to get those days back.

And, anyway, he had no time for pondering the past. He had

work to do. He needed to present his case to the CPS. He wanted Greg Quinn charged as soon as humanly possible.

Helen Harris was in her office with the door shut. That in itself was unusual. She didn't feel particularly well. Her eyes were sore. Her hands were trembling. She had just knocked half the contents of her coffee mug over the newspaper spread out on her desk.

And it was that newspaper, the *Daily Mail*, which was causing her so much concern that she believed it to be affecting her physically.

Helen rarely read newspapers, certainly not the *Mail*, and had only just seen the paper, that day's edition, even though it was past ten o'clock in the evening. Sadie had handed her a copy when she had returned from her visit to Barnstaple police station, and suggested she should take a look

Sadie hadn't appeared overly disturbed. Why should she have been?

'They've made you famous,' she'd remarked lightly.

Helen was deeply disturbed.

The *Mail* had done one of its major investigations into what it had dubbed 'Murder by the Seaside'. A snappy front-page blurb led into a spread and a further page inside the paper.

It was the spread that initially alarmed Helen. The *Mail* had published a row of mug shots of people involved in the police inquiry into the deaths of Thomas Quinn and Jason Patel, which stretched across two pages. Vogel was there as the senior investigating officer, also Saslow, the two victims of course, and Gill and Greg Quinn. The *Mail* had clearly done its homework. Wynne Williams also featured, as did a summary of his possible affair with Gill. And Patel's ex-wife Maureen, along with some perhaps ill-judged comments about her husband and his business partner Thomas' possible links with organized crime.

However it was the final picture in the line-up which had stunned her. The *Mail* had somehow acquired a close-up photograph of her, which looked as if it had been snatched just outside the House. Nonetheless it was pin-sharp. And if the photographer's intention had been to present her as some sort of deranged half-wit then he had done an excellent job. Her hair was all over the place, her mouth appeared to be hanging open, and there was a distinctly wild look in her eye. Neither was she wearing any make-up, which meant that the freckles on her face, which she had habitually masked with concealer and foundation for so long, were starkly evident. Helen couldn't believe she had been so careless, particularly when she'd known there were press photographers about. But, upon further studying the picture, she realized that it had been taken early the previous morning when she had stepped into the back alley to put out some rubbish. And she'd had no idea that there was any particular press interest in her. She certainly hadn't noticed the presence of any journalists in the vicinity of Helen's House – not even the photographer who'd so successfully snapped her. Helen had missed a call from a *Daily Mail* reporter who'd left a message saying that she wished to speak to her about issues concerning domestic violence following the death of Thomas Quinn, but nothing about that message had indicated that they were aware of her personal involvement in the case. Which presumably had been the caller's intention. She'd ignored it for no other reason than that, under the circumstances, she hadn't wished to further draw attention to herself.

However, the *Mail* spread drew attention to her, all right. The elongated caption accompanying the snatched photograph not only commented on the work of Helen's House and its probable relevance to the case, but also, with careful ambiguity, referred to Helen herself having offered Gill Quinn an alibi which the police were currently examining.

Helen was aghast. She wondered where on earth the paper had got its information from. They were good at what they did, there was no doubt about that. And they were taking full advantage of nobody having yet been charged for either murder, which meant they were, so far, free of the constraints of the laws of sub judice. All the same, she hadn't expected anything like this.

She turned over to the final page, which focused on the shooting of Jason Patel. And that brought another shock. Possibly an even bigger one. A still taken from the CCTV footage which Vogel had authorized to be released to the press filled almost a quarter of the page. A one-line caption read: 'Do you know this man?'

Helen felt a shiver run up and down her spine. She made herself study the picture with care. She couldn't see the man clearly, his features were blurred and partially concealed by the peak of his cap, which was pulled well down. Nonetheless, there was something so familiar about him, his build, and the bullish set of his shoulders. There was a similarity, too, in the way he was leaning, both legs thrust out straight in front of him, against the vehicle – which also seemed familiar, but it couldn't really be the same one, of course. Not after so long. However, a Range Rover with tinted windows had always been his motorcar of choice.

The more she stared, the more she came to believe it was him. Back again. And not only was his photograph in the same newspaper in which hers had been printed, on the very next page, but also his image had been captured here in Bideford. Only a mile or so away from the place that was so much more than her home, it was also her refuge, hers and that of so many other women.

But how could it be? And what on earth could he possibly be doing here? Nothing in North Devon had ever alarmed her, or given her cause for concern, from the moment she had settled in Bideford. Until now. She felt she would have known if he or any of the family or their associates had been operating in the area. Yet would she have done? How on earth would she have known? Particularly if he had been unable to be here in person until now.

She wracked her brains, trying to think back to anything that could have forged a link. Suddenly deep in the past something came to her. Something she should have perhaps remembered before. But it had held no significance to her. Not then. And not since. Until now.

All the same, perhaps her mind was playing tricks on her.

She looked again at the picture. At the stocky broad-shouldered man leaning on a big dark-coloured motor car. This could not be him. It really wasn't possible. She knew where he was. She knew where he had been for the last twenty years. And she had allowed herself to think she was protected from him for ever. Or, at the very least, that he would never again become a danger to her without her being forewarned.

She had a phone number for use in situations like this. An emergency number. She didn't keep it in her mobile. It was scribbled on a Post-it note stuck to the underside of the top of her desk, on a folded piece of paper tucked into the drawer of the built-in unit by the side of her bed, and on another piece of paper stowed in the glove compartment of her car.

She leaned to one side and peeled off the Post-it from beneath her desktop. She wondered if the number written on it would even still work. She had never had cause to use it. Not since the very beginning. And nobody had called her, either. After all, that would have defeated the object.

Very deliberately she punched in the number, carefully checking each digit. Rather to her surprise, a male voice answered after just two rings.

Back at Barnstaple, Vogel had been given the go ahead by the CPS to charge Gregory Quinn.

He did so in the company of Saslow, a custody sergeant, and Quinn's solicitor, Philip Stubbs. A charge sheet had already been prepared detailing the crime Quinn was accused of.

The young man would be held in police custody until his first court hearing at Barnstaple magistrates court, which would probably be the following day. In view of the seriousness of his offence and as is virtually de rigueur in the case of murder, he would then almost certainly be held in custody until his crown court trial.

Quinn looked totally devastated, although not particularly surprised. After all, Vogel had already warned him of his intentions, and he assumed that Stubbs would have also attempted to prepare Greg for the inevitable.

He protested his innocence several times, in spite of his solicitor repeatedly advising him to stay silent.

But even as he was being led back to the cells he called out over his shoulder, 'I didn't do it, Mr Vogel, I couldn't do it, you have to believe me,' he cried, his voice full of anguish.

Unfortunately Vogel didn't believe him. The DCI had not considered Greg Quinn to be the most likely of suspects at the beginning. He had seemed a decent enough young man, with no apparent motive strong enough to have led him to want to kill his father. After all, if not getting on with your father was sufficient motive for murder, then there would be an awful lot of dead dads around, Vogel reckoned. Neither had it seemed, at first, that Greg would have had the opportunity.

However, all that had changed. Quinn could now be placed irrefutably at the scene of the crime within precisely the designated time frame. The forensic case against him was also irrefutable and utterly damning. And the more Vogel had learned about the violent and abusive behaviour of Thomas Quinn, the stronger Greg's possible motive for killing his father had become.

It was to be hoped, and indeed expected, that a court would take Thomas Quinn's behaviour into mitigation when dealing with Greg. But the young man must stand trial. And Vogel no longer had any doubts about his guilt. Vogel was a copper who believed in evidence. An overwhelming weight of evidence was now stacked against Gregory Quinn.

The DCI was quite sure that the right man had been arrested and charged.

However, his thoughts turned to Gregory's mother, a woman who had suffered enough already. He was sure she was not sorry to have lost the husband who had treated her so cruelly, but now she looked likely to also lose the son she adored. For a very long time.

He called Docherty, who was still babysitting Gill, and asked her to break the news, as gently as possible.

'Then call me back,' he instructed. 'I want to know how she reacts. I have a feeling she won't be surprised.'

Docherty called back only ten minutes later to report that Gill had appeared to barely react at all.

'You were right, boss, she certainly didn't seem to be surprised,' said the PC. 'She said she wanted time to herself, time to think, and she was going to bed. She's in the bedroom now, do you want to speak to her.'

'No, let her rest. I'm hoping this indicates that she will accept the inevitable. Look after her, though, she's had it rough, that one, and her life is now likely to get rough again.'

'I'll do my best, boss,' said Docherty.

It was now almost midnight. The day had already been a long one. He sent Saslow home, telling her he would make his own way back to his digs. But Vogel's day hadn't quite finished yet. He needed to touch base with DI Peters, who he knew was still at work at the Bideford incident room, and he had yet to hear back from Nobby Clarke concerning his suspicions about Helen Harris.

He was just wondering whether or not to give her a nudge, when the detective superintendent called on his mobile.

'You're quite right, Vogel,' she began. 'Helen Harris is on witness protection, and has been for more than twenty years, as you suspected. She gave evidence in a case involving a gang of powerful and highly dangerous international criminals. Her testimony was entirely in camera, but of course the criminals knew exactly who she was. And she knew that they knew. It was therefore decided to agree to her request to be given a new identity.'

'So who is she, then?' asked Vogel, although he didn't really expect an answer. He didn't get one either.

'You know I can't tell you that,' replied Nobby, almost wearily.

'I know the protocol, well enough, ma'am,' said Vogel. 'But in view of the Patel murder, and the manner of it, it's quite clear that we are dealing with a dangerous criminal element here. We have armed men running amok in a quiet Devon town where stuff like this does not happen. It's my job to make sure it doesn't happen again. And there has to be a connection somewhere, between Patel's shooting, Thomas Quinn's stabbing, and the history of the woman I know only as Helen Harris. I don't believe in coincidences, ma'am, and I know you don't. They have to be linked. Can't you tell me something?'

'No, Vogel. I can't. I'm afraid—'

'Just give me a clue,' Vogel interrupted, his voice rising. 'Set me in the right direction, I'll do the rest.'

He distinctly heard Clarke sighing down the telephone. He didn't care.

'I hope we're not getting a repeat of that Instow case,' he continued tetchily. 'I don't take kindly to being kept in the dark.'

'Vogel, this isn't about being kept in the dark,' said Clarke, beginning to sound angry herself now. 'This is witness protection. The whole premise of which relies on nobody, but nobody, outside those directly responsible, being aware of a witness's new identity. Not even you, Vogel. In any case, I can't tell you because I don't know myself—'

'What, they haven't even told you, boss?' cut in Vogel, forgetting in the heat of the moment that, as a matter of principle, he now only called her 'ma'am'.

'No, Vogel, they haven't told me. I'm just another regional copper to these guys.'

Vogel didn't think that was very likely. He did, however, think she was telling him the truth. All the same, he continued to persist.

'But there is a protocol, is there not, for revealing the identity of a protected witness under certain circumstances, there must be—'

'I suppose so Vogel,' Clarke interrupted. 'But I've no idea at all what those circumstances might be.'

'What if that person were suspected of a serious crime?' asked Vogel bluntly. 'Surely their identity would then be revealed to the SIO of any police investigation.'

'You'd think so,' Clarke replied. 'But I wouldn't hold your breath if I were you.'

Helen Harris had been thoroughly shaken by the outcome of her phone call. It appeared that there had been a development of which she had not been informed. That there had been an unfortunate oversight.

To the person she had been talking to, an anonymous representative of some anonymous administrative unit, that oversight doubtless meant very little. To Helen it could mean the world. Or, rather more accurately, the end of the world. Her world, at any rate.

She was still pondering what she should do next when Philip Stubbs called to tell her that, following the acquisition of damning new forensic evidence. Gregory Quinn had been charged with the murder of his father.

For just a moment, she couldn't think of a single thing to say.

'Helen?' queried Stubbs. 'Can you hear me? Are you there? Helen?'

'Uh, yes, uh yes,' said Helen, trying desperately to pull herself together. 'I'm so very sorry to hear that, Philip. Nobody deserves to go down for that monstrous man.'

'No. They don't. I'm still hoping we may be able to avoid that, after all, there's such overwhelming mitigation. But the odds are probably against it. This is murder, after all.'

'Do I take it then that Gregory is going to plead guilty?'

'No, we won't plead guilty to murder. Certainly not at his first hearing. There's a mandatory life sentence, with a stated minimum term, for murder, as I'm sure you know, which is unavoidable however sympathetic a court might be. Greg has to plead not guilty. And he does continue to proclaim his innocence, by the way. However, the evidence against him is substantial, and I just can't see him winning. The best thing we can hope for is a plea bargain. If we could get the charge reduced to manslaughter, it really is possible that Greg might escape jail altogether, or at least serve a very short term. Domestic violence is high profile right now. And everybody hates men like Thomas Quinn.'

'Yes, but surely there isn't much chance of you getting the charge reduced, is there? As I understand it, a certain criteria has to be adhered to for murder to be commuted to manslaughter. Diminished responsibility, self-defence, abnormality of mind. That sort of thing. And Thomas Quinn was stabbed eleven times. That's pretty excessive. I can't believe you're very optimistic, are you, Philip?'

'Well, it won't be easy. We'll need a damned good barrister on board. But there's also loss of control. All we can do is try, Helen.'

'Yes, I suppose it is . . .' Helen responded quietly as she ended the call.

Philip Stubbs was a decent man and a pretty good solicitor. But he still operated within the restraints of legal aid, without anything like the size of team and level of backup enjoyed by the top private solicitors. And goodness knows what sort of barrister Greg would end up with if he had to rely on legal aid. It was possible that Gill would inherit some family money which she could pitch in to finance her son's defence, but, in view of what she had already heard about Thomas' financial troubles, Helen didn't think there would be much. Gregory Quinn was in deep, deep trouble.

Helen had even more to think about now. Her life's work had, in the final analysis, been devoted to creating a world where this sort of situation would never arise. Whichever way you looked at it, the ultimate plight of Greg and his mother had resulted from domestic abuse. Yet they, both of them in Helen's opinion, were the victims. And it made her angry. Very angry indeed.

Her head was aching and her eyes still hurt. Helen reached for a couple of pills from a bottle she kept in the top drawer of her desk.

She had to do something. She would do something. She checked her watch. It was nearly midnight. Whatever she decided would have to wait until the morning now. Not least because it would be better if she slept on it. And she needed a clear head in order to formulate a plan. Whatever she did next was going to have far-reaching repercussions. Not only for her, but for a number of others.

Ultimately it was gone two a.m. before Vogel climbed into bed at his Airbnb. He was woken by PC Phil Lake, who was on earlies, at five thirty-one. It felt as if he had only just got to sleep.

'It's Gill Quinn, boss,' the young man began excitedly. 'She's in the front office. She says she wants to confess to the murder of her husband.'

'Say that again,' muttered Vogel drowsily.

Lake did.

'Oh, for God's sake,' said Vogel.

He dressed, completed the most arbitrary of ablutions, and walked to Barnstaple police station. He had decided to give Saslow the opportunity for a little more sleep. After all, he didn't think he was going to need her assistance. Or that of anybody else.

Gill was still in the front office. Phil Lake and the duty sergeant gave the impression that they really didn't know what to do with her.

However this was an investigation into a murder, and Vogel had no choice but to follow the correct procedure, whatever his private thoughts on the matter.

He told Gill he would be with her in a moment, then took Phil Lake to one side.

'Where's Docherty?' he asked.

'I was about to say, boss,' responded Lake. 'She just called in. Apparently she fell asleep on the couch in Greg Quinn's sitting room. When she woke up she stuck her head into the bedroom to check on Gill and discovered that she was gone. Must have snuck out, Docherty said. She's on her way in, and she says to tell you she's very sorry, boss.'

'For God's sake,' said Vogel again. 'I don't expect my officers to do entirely without sleep. I'm glad Gill hasn't gone missing, though. Right Lake, you're with me. We need to set up a formal chat straight away. I presume there's an interview room free at this ungodly hour?'

Lake agreed that there was, and led the way, with Vogel escorting Gill Quinn in silence, apart from reminding her that she had the right to have a solicitor present if she wished. She declined. Like most coppers Vogel usually welcomed that. On this occasion he would have preferred his interviewee to have legal advice, in the hope that this might help her reconsider her position before too much time was wasted.

'So, how can I help you this morning, Gill?' he began noncommittedly, once the preliminaries had been completed.

'I've already said, several times,' responded Gill a tad impatiently. 'I want to confess to Thomas' murder. I did it. It was me.'

'I see. And yet you appear to have a watertight alibi, provided by the staff and residents of Helen's House, covering the period of time when your husband was killed, do you not?'

'I told that PC Docherty, they were mistaken. They didn't realize I went out, left the House. For more than three hours in the afternoon. I had plenty of time to go back to my place and . . . and stab Thomas to death.'

'Right. Perhaps you would like to explain why you have decided to tell us this now, Gill?'

'You know why. You've charged my Greg with his father's murder.'

'Indeed. You've come forward to protect him, to try to stop him standing trial, haven't you?'

'Yes, I have. But that doesn't mean I didn't do it. I did kill Thomas. And I think Greg is trying to protect me.'

'Gill, Greg isn't admitting that he murdered his father,' said Vogel, as gently as possible. 'In fact I understand he will be pleading not guilty at his first hearing later today. We have charged him because we have built what we feel is an irrefutable case against him. We have gathered a dossier of quite damning evidence, including substantive forensic data.'

'Yes, well. He's a clever boy, my Greg. Cleverer than you might think. He's probably arranged it all. I'm telling you. I killed Thomas. I thought he was going to attack me again. I picked up the nearest knife and stabbed him over and over, until I was sure he was dead. You found me by his body. I was covered in his blood. I'd have thought it was obvious.'

'OK, let's say I believe you, Gill. Can you tell me what you did with the knife that you used? We have yet to find the murder weapon.'

'I uh, I put it in the dishwasher and switched it on, in order to destroy any forensic evidence. Your murder weapon was in the dishwasher. Squeaky clean. Maybe still is.'

Vogel made a mental note not to underestimate Gill Quinn. She was a very different woman now to the one in a state of deep shock who he had first encountered. Or certainly, she seemed to be. He wondered if she'd come up with that one on her own, or if perhaps she'd seen it in a TV drama or maybe read of a similar instance in a newspaper report of another real-life crime.

'We found your son's DNA on your husband's body, containing traces of Thomas' blood, which is definitively incriminating,' the DCI continued.

'I should think you found plenty of mine too,' Gill Quinn persisted. 'If there was any of Greg's DNA on Thomas, then he must have gone to the house after I killed the bastard. But he's not told you any of that because he guessed straight away that I'd killed Thomas. I mean who else could it be, for God's sake? And he wanted to protect me.'

'Gill, we know you were at the House in the early evening on Saturday, and that you were given a lift home to St Anne's Avenue. Do you expect me to believe that you went back there covered in blood, as you were, and nobody noticed?'

'No, of course not. I took the bloodstained clothes off.'

'And then you put them back on when you returned home?'

'Y-yes. Umm, well. Well, there was just something that made me think Greg may have been to our place. I can't explain. And then, when I saw again what I'd done. When I saw Thomas lying there. Well . . . I was so shocked I didn't know what I was doing . . .'

The woman was beginning to gabble. Vogel continued to question her for a while longer, and the answers she gave continued to be confusing, to say the least. He was confident that

Gill was lying through her teeth, however he could not entirely dismiss her story. But neither did he consider it necessary to detain Gill Quinn.

'How did you get here from Westward Ho! this morning?' he asked suddenly.

'I called a taxi,' she replied.

'But I thought you didn't have any money?'

'That was two days ago. My son is a builder. There's always plenty of cash lying around at his place.'

Vogel reckoned that was sure to be the truth.

'Right,' he said. 'I think PC Docherty should be here by now. I'll get her to run you back to Kipling Terrace. Unless, of course, there's anywhere else you'd like to be taken to?'

'You mean you're letting me go?'

'Yes.'

'But I've just told you I killed my husband. Why aren't you arresting me? You should be arresting me. Don't you believe me?'

'I don't feel I have sufficient grounds to arrest you, but I haven't said I don't believe you, and our enquiries will continue,' Vogel explained patiently.

Docherty had arrived, and duly came to the interview room to collect Gill, who continued to express her desire to be arrested, but allowed herself to be escorted from the building and into Docherty's car without too much trouble.

Vogel was as confident as he possibly could be that his judgement was correct, and that Gill Quinn's confession was false. But Gill was clearly a much trickier customer than he had originally thought her to be. And maybe her son was too. Perhaps she was executing some complex kind of double bluff? Perhaps mother and son were in on this together? Perhaps their joint plan was to lay a series of false trails and create a smokescreen in order to blindside Vogel's investigation?

And if that was so, Vogel's job was to ensure that they did not succeed.

He was just considering his next move when he was informed that Wayne Williams had arrived at the front office and was desperate to see him. That he wanted to amend his statement.

First Gill, now Williams. Vogel wondered what on earth this

might mean. Again he asked Perkins to arrange an interview room. Williams looked even more anxious than he had the previous day.

'I'm afraid I haven't told you the truth,' he blurted out as soon as Perkins had completed the preliminaries. 'I've been worrying ever since yesterday. I'm a law-abiding man, really I am, chief inspector, I didn't mean to do anything wrong, I've been getting myself in such a state. I was afraid I might have been seen, and there's CCTV all over the place, isn't there, and if you found out I didn't know what might happen . . .'

'All right, Mr Williams, just calm down, and tell me the truth now,' said Vogel, in his most reassuring voice.

'Right yes. Well, the thing is, I wasn't at home all day on Saturday. I went out. In the afternoon. I drove round to Gill's house. I was so worried about her. I really had thought she would find a way to call me after Friday night. Eventually I couldn't stand it any longer. But when I got there, well, I told you I was a coward, didn't I? I got as far as the front door, I was about to ring the bell, but I didn't have the courage. I was afraid Thomas might answer. And I just couldn't face it. So I got back in the car and drove home. I didn't tell you because I thought it would look bad for me, but now I realize I've been really stupid—'

'What time was this?' interrupted Vogel.

'Well, I'm not sure exactly, well gone four, maybe half past.'

Vogel felt himself stiffen. It would seem that Wayne Williams had been at the Quinn house during exactly the time frame in which Thomas had been killed.

'Did you see or hear anything which gave you any cause for concern whilst you were at the house? he asked.

'No, nothing,' replied Williams. 'Everything was quiet. I couldn't even tell whether anyone was in or not.'

The DCI questioned Williams further for a few minutes, particularly concerning the timing of his visit to St Anne's Avenue, and the possibility of his having witnessed something of relevance without realizing it. He then asked Williams if he was prepared to be fingerprinted and undergo a DNA test, to which the headmaster agreed readily enough.

Vogel thanked him and told him he would then be free to go.

'Does that mean you believe me?' asked Williams, who looked

both palpably relieved and somewhat surprised. Vogel wondered what he had been expecting.

'You should know that late last night a man was charged with the murder of Thomas Quinn,' he responded obliquely. 'However, we may well want to talk to you again, Mr Williams. Lying to the police is a very serious matter, as I am sure you are aware.'

As he watched Perkins lead Wayne Williams from the interview room, Vogel couldn't entirely suppress a certain sense of unease. The case against Gregory Quinn was overwhelming. The DCI remained as sure as was ever possible that the right man had been charged. And he really couldn't believe that Williams would have the guts to murder anyone. But as he had told Saslow after they'd interviewed the man on Sunday, you never can tell.

Helen Harris had been allowed even less rest than Vogel. Indeed virtually none at all. Her head was all over the place. And she had only just managed to drift into a fitful sleep when the house phone woke her at two forty a.m.

Groggily she lifted the receiver.

'Hello Lilian,' said a voice she had hoped never to hear again.

'Who is this?' she demanded. But, of course, she really didn't need to ask.

'It's William,' said the voice. 'Your dear brother-in law. You know that though, don't you, Lilian?'

She attempted to dissimilate.

'I don't know who you are, and I don't know any Lilian,' she said.

There was a humourless laugh at the other end of the phone.

'I'm sure you've seen the papers,' William continued. 'Both our pictures, almost next to each other, but yours by far the most bold and clear. You look very different though. Older, of course, and your face is plumper. You must have put on a lot of weight, and your hair is not at all how I remember it. I might not have recognized you, if it hadn't been for your freckles. I'm surprised you don't cover them up with something. They're such a giveaway, so distinctive. But I suppose you've grown complacent, after all this time—'

'What do you want?' she interrupted, trying not to let her desperate anguish sound in her voice. 'What the bloody hell do you want?'

'I wanted to let you know that I'd found you. Of course, I was always going to find you sooner or later. You must have known I could never let you get away with what you did. You killed my brother, Lilian, and then you dared to get me put away. You should have been told I was out. So you must have known you were living on borrowed time. But, thanks to Tommy, you've been offered to me on a plate . . .'

Tommy. For a few seconds Helen stopped listening to William. The name registered with her suddenly, in spite of the awful shock of hearing William's voice. Tommy must be Thomas Quinn. And it was Thomas who had maintained a link with the St John family that Helen had completely forgotten about, Thomas who had brought William and his henchmen, even more monstrous men than Thomas himself, to this little town which had for so long been a haven to Helen.

'Unfortunately, due to circumstances beyond my control,' she heard William continue with another mirthless laugh, 'I have to lie low for a bit. But I will come to you, have no doubt about that, and I will make you suffer—'

'You may not get the chance,' interrupted Helen with a bravado she did not feel. 'The police are looking for you, and they're going to find you. You and your thugs are wanted for murder. Did you come here intending to kill?'

'No, just to give Tommy a wake-up call. Frighten him a little. And the other one, of course. But it was too late for Tommy, although we didn't know that until we arrived in Bideford. All too many of our, uh, business interests had fallen a little by the wayside whilst I was, umm, unable to take care of them. I decided to take a bit of a tour around the UK before going back home to South Africa, to remind certain people of who they were dealing with. Nobody was supposed to get shot though. That was just a bit of youthful overenthusiasm. Worth it of course, Helen, just to find you. What a bonus.'

Unlike Kurt, William spoke with a strong South African accent. Helen determined not to show just how threatening she found everything about him.

'You don't scare me any more,' she lied. 'You're going to be back behind bars way before you can to get to hurt me,' she continued, attempting a bravado she definitely did not feel.

'The police don't even know who they're looking for, and nobody would recognize me from that grainy old picture, not even you,' said William. 'You can barely see my face—'

'You're wrong, I did recognize you,' Helen interrupted.

'It makes no difference. I won't be in the country long enough to get arrested . . .'

'Really? I thought you said you were lying low?'

'Don't get cute with me, Lilian, or you won't even live to regret it.'

With that William ended the call.

Helen had been half expecting something like this from the moment she had learned that the man she had been instrumental in sending to jail twenty-one years earlier really had been released. Nonetheless his phone call had chilled her to the bone. Her whole body seemed to be shaking. She took two of the pills she kept by her bedside. Now she had to make decisions fast. The first one was easy. Whatever she did, she would sleep no more that night. So she dragged herself out of bed, dressed, and made her way to her office.

She spent the next three hours or so assimilating the events of the last few days and going over and over in her head what she would do next. Finally, she spent some time reorganizing her affairs, and ensuring, to the best of her ability, the future of Helen's House, regardless of the actions she was about to take. She also wrote two letters, one to her solicitor, and one to Gregory Quinn.

There had already been more than one enormous sea change in her life. Another, probably greater than all, now beckoned.

At six o'clock she moved to the kitchen, removed some unbaked croissants from the freezer and put them in the oven, and prepared juice and coffee. Then she woke Sadie.

'I'm sorry, but I need to talk to you,' she said. 'And it has to be now. There's some breakfast waiting.'

In spite of the hour, Sadie did not demur. It was as if she knew, thought Helen, that this might be the last breakfast they would ever share.

FORTY-ONE

Vogel called Peters to arrange a team meeting at the Bideford incident room for later that morning, and had just finished briefing her about Gill Quinn's confession, Wayne Williams' admission of deliberate falsehood and, in confidence at this stage, what he had learned from Nobby Clarke of Helen Harris' past, when Saslow arrived at Barnstaple nick a few minutes after eight a.m.

'C'mon, Dawn, let's head for Bideford and stop at the café on the Instow road,' he said. 'I'll fill you in over breakfast.'

Saslow looked mildly surprised. As well she might. Vogel was not given to planning meal breaks during a major investigation.

With obvious enthusiasm she ordered a full English – no doubt chosen because she had no idea when she would have the opportunity to eat again – but was only halfway through it when Vogel's phone rang.

The DCI, a vegetarian but not a vegan, had nearly finished his scrambled eggs, mushrooms and hash browns. He took a final mouthful as he answered the call. It was DI Peters.

'We've got Helen Harris here, boss,' Peters began. 'She just arrived. Claims she has something very important to tell us, but she'll only speak to you.'

Vogel was on his feet at once.

'Take her along to the interview room, and tell her I'm on my way,' he said as he ended the call.

He was already heading for the door as he spoke to Saslow. 'C'mon,' he said. 'We have a rather extraordinary visitor.'

Saslow had experienced Vogel's tendency to abandon meals before. She clearly had a survival plan. She swiftly picked up her last sausage and rasher of bacon along with the remaining two slices of toast in her paper napkin, leaving only her second fried egg and some baked beans behind. She also remembered to pay, dropping a ten-pound note and a handful of change on the table.

'C'mon, Saslow,' yelled Vogel from the doorway.

He just couldn't wait. He knew this meeting was going to be highly significant.

But he most certainly wasn't prepared for the revelation which greeted him when he and Saslow walked into the interview room to join Helen Harris, who had duly been escorted there by Peters and was already sitting at the table in the middle of the room, with her back to the door. She stood up and spoke before either of the two officers had time to say anything.

'I would like to confess to the murder of Thomas Quinn,' she announced at once.

Vogel was amazed. He glanced at Saslow. Her jaw had quite literally dropped. He suspected his may also have done.

'Well, why not?' he enquired rhetorically, after a brief silence. 'Everybody else is today.'

Helen looked bewildered. 'What do you mean?' she asked.

'You should know that we've already had Gill Quinn in at dawn confessing to the murder of her husband,' Vogel replied.

'Oh c'mon, surely you don't believe that?' asked Helen. 'She's just trying to protect her son. You know she couldn't have killed Thomas.'

'Do I?' asked Vogel, as he moved behind the table and lowered himself into a chair. 'I'm beginning to wonder exactly what I do and don't know about this case. Would you please sit down, Helen. I think we have rather a lot to talk about, don't you?'

Helen lowered her head slightly in acquiescence. She obediently sat opposite Vogel, and Saslow sat next to the DCI.

Vogel offered Helen the opportunity for legal representation, which she refused, and Saslow started the video and recited the names of those present.

'I'd like to begin by asking you to repeat what you told us concerning the murder of Thomas Quinn before we had formally begun this interview and commenced the video recording,' began Vogel.

Without a moment's hesitation Helen repeated her confession.

'I also know who killed Jason Patel,' she added.

'Do you indeed?' asked Vogel, again rhetorically. He glanced at Saslow once more. Her eyes were riveted on Helen Harris. It was already clear that this meeting was going to reach far beyond anything he had even considered.

'All right,' he said. 'Now, before we go any further, I think you'd better tell me who you are, don't you?'

Helen raised both eyebrows.

'You know who I am,' she said.

'I know who you've been for the last twenty-one years,' said Vogel bluntly. 'I also know that you are on witness protection. But I have no idea who you were before you were supplied with a new identity. And I would very much like to know, as I suspect it will have a substantial bearing on the investigations I am heading.'

'Ah,' said Helen. 'I'm sorry, I wasn't expecting this.'

Suddenly she looked unsure of herself. Vogel knew that he had probably overstepped his authority. He thought he'd better cover himself.

'You should be aware, however, that I have no right to try to make you tell me your original identity,' he said. 'And that those who arranged for you to be able to start a new life have chosen not to share that information with me, as is normal in these situations except in the most exceptional circumstances.'

'Would confessing to one murder and being prepared to give evidence on another count as exceptional circumstances, do you think?' asked Helen, very nearly echoing the question Vogel had asked Nobby Clarke the previous day.

'Well, it might—' Vogel began, wondering where this was going to take things exactly.

'Don't worry, chief inspector,' she interrupted. 'I came here this morning prepared to tell you everything I know, and everything about my past and my involvement in both murders, albeit only very tenuously in one of them, that might assist you in getting to the truth and bringing your investigations to a successful conclusion. I just don't know quite where to start, that's all.'

'You could start at the beginning,' interjected Saslow.

Helen looked at her thoughtfully. Then she half smiled. 'Yes, I suppose I could,' she said. 'I am afraid it's a very long story though.'

'Please,' said Saslow. 'Take your time. We're not going anywhere, are we, boss?'

Vogel shook his head. He noticed not for the first time that Helen's hands were trembling, and watched as she clasped them together on her lap, took a deep breath, and began.

'Twenty years ago I was Lilian St John. I was born Lilian Cook. When I was thirty-two I met, fell in love with, and married a rich handsome South African called Kurt St John, with whom I believed I was going to live the dream. But that dream quickly turned into an unimaginable nightmare . . .'

Vogel and Saslow listened in silent enthralment as the woman they knew as Helen Harris told an extraordinary tale, of a dream wedding, the abusive horrors that began on her honeymoon, the final terrible beating that led to her fleeing the London flat she had shared with her husband. How he had caught up with her and she had stabbed him with an unlikely weapon, a butter knife, in desperate self-defence, yet had been imprisoned for causing grievous bodily harm. How he had continued to stalk her even inside prison, and how, when she had her sentence slashed on appeal she had even changed her name by deed poll and cut herself off from everyone she knew in a desperate bid to finally escape him.

'He caught up with me in the end, of course; it took him a year, but he found me as I knew he would,' she said. 'And that was when I killed him.'

Saslow looked totally shocked. But Vogel had started to recall the case. It hadn't got enormous publicity at first, except the more salacious aspects in the more salacious newspapers, because of the tendency at the time not to pay any great attention to crimes that were regarded as domestics. But there were certain aspects of it which had attracted considerable interest and led to further police enquiries and an Old Bailey trial not directly connected with Lilian St John's actions.

'I know who you are now, and I remember what you did,' he said. 'Yes, you killed your husband, you shot him with his own gun, but you didn't even go to trial. You suffered terrible abuse at Kurt St John's hands, not for the first time, and it was accepted that you acted in self-defence. Isn't that so?'

'Yes, that is so,' she replied. 'I had a very good lawyer, though. Jean Carr, do you remember her?'

'I do. She was a famous human rights barrister, retired now, I think, and she certainly was good. But, anyway, your case was considered cut and dried, Hel – uh – Lil . . .' Vogel paused. 'I'm sorry, I'm not quite sure what to call you . . .'

'Call me Helen,' she said. 'Always Helen. I never want to go back to being Lilian St John. And yes, you're right, the case was considered cut and dried. By everyone. Kurt had hurt me quite badly again, and the police even found his bloodstained fingerprints on the little butter knife which I told them he must have brought with him, in order to do to me what I had done to him previously. It was just the sort of twisted thinking he specialized in, actually. Most importantly they were able to trace the gun to Kurt via his brother, William St John. It was a Vector Z-88, the type of pistol used by South African police and security services. Also by thugs like William, who was head of what the St John family call "security". And I guess still is, hence his visit to Bideford at the weekend.'

Helen paused. She reached into her pocket, pulled out the pages she had extracted from the previous day's *Daily Mail*, and pointed at the picture Vogel had released to the media.

'This is William St John, of the notorious South African St John family. They run a network of international businesses, some way beyond the law, and others designed only to camouflage their more lucrative activities. They are, in reality, no better than gangsters, and they are quite ruthless. Particularly if they think they've been crossed. I believed, as I was assured did the police at the highest level, that the family and their activities were effectively destroyed in the UK more than twenty years ago. It would seem not, and that William was responsible for Jason Patel's death. The gunmen who pulled the trigger were doubtless on his payroll.'

'You'll need to explain that,' responded Vogel at once. 'How can you be so sure? And how do you know for certain this is William St John? It's not the best of pictures.'

'I do know,' Helen replied firmly. 'I was almost sure it was him just from the picture, but then he called me. Last night. And threatened me. It was just like the old days really. He'd recognized me from my picture, as I did him, even though we were both twenty years older. I'm several stone heavier too, unfortunately; my hair is totally different, and I wear glasses instead of contact lenses. But I still have my freckles, and they were always distinctive.'

She touched her face with one hand, perhaps involuntarily. Vogel could see no freckles.

'Ever since I stopped being Lilian, I have hidden my freckles with concealer and foundation,' she continued. 'The *Mail* photographer caught me without my make-up. A rare event.'

She pointed at the newspaper pages again.

'So you see, there is no doubt that is William St John. And he has made it quite clear that he will not rest until he has achieved revenge for his brother's death, and also for what I did to him. Or what he perceives I did to him.'

'What did you do to him?'

'I was instrumental in him facing a series of charges for his involvement in organized crime, drug running on a massive scale, international fraud, theft, money laundering, and one count of murder. Another exercise in frightening suspect associates that went too far, apparently. I gave evidence against him. I was never named in public, of course, but William knew who I was.'

Of course, thought Vogel, that was what Nobby Clarke had said. The witness gave evidence in camera, but the accused had known full well who they were. That was why Helen had been given witness protection.

'There was a bit of a stroke of luck all round, the night Kurt died,' Helen continued. 'He had brought a briefcase with him, which was found to contain a whole load of incriminating information, mostly pointing at William, "the muscle" as the family have always called him, but some indicating that Kurt was not entirely Mr Clean.

'The police interviewed me about it, and it turned out that, by default, I knew rather more of the nature of "the family business" than I had realized. Certainly my knowledge, which I had considered so limited, filled in a lot of gaps, and led to William being convicted on almost every charge. The judge sentenced him concurrently on several counts and William was given thirty years. The St Johns were outraged, and the story went round that the woman judge was the granddaughter of the man who gave the Great Train Robbers enormous sentences. It wasn't true, of course.'

Vogel had a vague memory of that, and told Helen so.

'He hasn't served anything like it, obviously,' Helen explained. 'Out six months ago, on parole. Only nobody remembered to tell me. You should initiate a search for William and his cohorts straight away, chief inspector. I have reason to believe they intend to flee the country.'

Vogel thought for a moment. He saw no harm in doing just that. He asked Saslow to text DI Peters accordingly. Then he turned back to Helen.

'You've indicated that the St Johns were in business in some way with Thomas Quinn and Jason Patel here in North Devon. That seems like something of a coincidence, particularly if it led to William and his minders coming to the town where you have lived your secret life for so many years on the very weekend that Thomas Quinn was killed. Unless you think they were responsible for that too?'

'No, the last bit must have been a coincidence, but not the rest of it,' responded Helen. 'I remember telling you before that I had fallen in love with North Devon when I came here as a child. I suggested to Kurt that we came here, during what was really a rather wonderful courtship, or seemed to be, before the nightmare began. We stayed at the Saunton Sands Hotel across the estuary. When William phoned me last night he referred to Thomas Quinn as Tommy – which brought back a vague memory from all those years ago. Kurt went to play golf and returned enthusing about Tommy, a young man, I think he was little more than a boy, whom he had met by chance. Kurt said Tommy was just the chap to expand the family business into North Devon.'

'Was that normal behaviour on the part of your future husband?'

'Oh yes. Kurt was always looking for the main chance. And for what he called "the talent". Bright, hard-working people – usually young, he liked to get them young – who were eager for success. And, of course, they had to be thoroughly unscrupulous and prepared to do almost anything as long as the price was right. Although I didn't realize that at the time. Anyway it all made sense after William's call. Thomas Quinn was Tommy, and that was the link with the St Johns.'

'So, are we to assume that this business arrangement has been going on for more than twenty years, without incident, until this weekend?'

'There is always something suspect about even the most innocent looking business activity, if the St John family is involved, so I would very much doubt that,' said Helen. 'The big difference is that William is at large again. And he wouldn't tolerate anything even slightly amiss in any of the family outposts. Indeed he would take it as a personal insult.'

'All right, well thank you for that,' said Vogel. 'We will look into it. Meanwhile, I don't think you'd finished telling me about the night Kurt died, had you?'

'No, I hadn't. The most important part of my story. And the most dreadful.'

She paused yet again. Vogel wondered how anything could be more dreadful than what he had already heard.

'Go on,' he encouraged.

It was still several seconds before Helen spoke again. She looked as if she might be struggling to find the right words.

'The thing is, I planned it,' she blurted out suddenly.

Vogel was momentarily puzzled. 'Planned what?' he asked.

'I planned Kurt's death. I planned exactly how I would kill him. Down to the last detail.'

Vogel looked at Saslow. Saslow looked at Vogel. Neither of them dared speak.

'I was ready and waiting for him when he came for me, even though I had prayed every day that he never would,' Helen continued. 'Everything was organized. My weapons, the gun and the little butter knife, were concealed underneath the table by the door. Waiting, as I was, just in case. I wanted Kurt to think I was running, trying to get away. And I wanted it to look that way to the police too.

'I had the gun behind my back, ready, when he came at me, and I shot him at point-blank range in the chest. I didn't hesitate, Mr Vogel.

'When I was sure that he was dead, I set about framing him. I put the gun in his hand so that it would have his fingerprints on it as well as mine. Then I stabbed myself with that little butter knife. It might have been little, but it hurt like hell. I had to do it though, Mr Vogel. Everything had to be extreme, to justify and explain my shooting Kurt.

'I wiped my own prints off the butter knife, but not my blood, of course, and smudged Kurt's prints all over it. The DNA, the blood pattern, the prints, all matched my story. A neighbour reported hearing my screams. That was a bonus. I wasn't even aware that I had screamed.

'I didn't want to kill him. Really I didn't. I just never wanted to set eyes on Kurt St John again. Even though I had planned every detail, it was a plan I hoped never to execute. But, was I glad he was dead? Oh yes, Mr Vogel, so very very glad.'

Quite abruptly, Helen stopped speaking.

Vogel had been quite mesmerized. And he suspected it was the same for Saslow. He had to struggle to think like a policeman again. Could it really be true?

'That's quite a story,' he said eventually. 'There are parts I don't totally understand though. The gun, as you said, was traced to Kurt—'

'I was imprisoned for fifteen months, I had all the right contacts,' Helen interrupted. 'Prison gives you that. You come into contact with people who know how to get a gun if you want one. And people who are more than willing to teach you the tricks of their nefarious trades. You can learn how to cover your tracks. You can learn how to lay a false trail, how to frame someone else. And, if you're desperate enough, you can even learn how to kill and get away with it . . .'

Again she paused. Again Vogel glanced at Saslow, and Saslow glanced at Vogel. Again neither of them dared speak.

'I didn't want it to come to that, chief inspector,' Helen continued eventually. 'I did everything I could for it not to happen. I changed my name, I went to live in a crap bedsit in a place where I knew nobody and nobody knew me. I did everything I could to hide from Kurt. I was prepared to exist like that for the rest of my life. And it would have been just an existence. I didn't go after Kurt, Mr Vogel. And I so hoped he wouldn't come after me again. But when he did, I had no choice.

'It was still self-defence, in my opinion, chief inspector, but I don't think a court would have seen it that way, do you?'

'No, I don't,' Vogel agreed. 'It would have been regarded as premeditated.'

'I never thought I'd have the guts, you know, not if it came to it,' Helen continued, almost as if Vogel hadn't spoken. 'But ultimately I did it without batting an eyelid. I killed my husband. I blew a hole in his chest. And I planned it down to the last detail. That's something I've had to live with for more than twenty years.'

'Yes, Kurt St John died a very long time ago,' commented Vogel. 'So why are you telling us this now?'

'One reason is that I'm a lapsed Catholic, I've been waiting a long time for this confessional.'

Helen laughed, almost as if she were telling a joke, before turning deadly serious again.

'Another is that I can no longer be hurt. Not really. Not by William, although he doesn't know that. And not by the forces of law. I have multiple sclerosis. It was diagnosed not long after I killed Kurt. At the time my Catholic guilt told me that it was just retribution. Mine is relapse-remitting MS, the commonest sort, and most of the time I have been able to live more or less a normal life. There have been bad episodes over the years, of course. And it's largely because of the MS that I became so overweight, which I've always hated. But it's only recently that I've had to accept I am approaching end-stage MS. My attacks have become more frequent and I am often in considerable pain.'

'I'm sorry to hear that, Helen,' murmured Vogel.

With the benefit of hindsight, however, he was not entirely surprised. He had, after all, noticed her trembling hands before, and the way she'd stumbled and then needed to sit after she'd attempted to mow the lawn. But at the time he had thought nothing of any of that, and totally misinterpreted what now seemed to be quite clear indications of a potentially serious health issue.

'Yes, but it means I am unlikely to ever stand trial, not for anything,' Helen replied, with another small laugh.

'However, the most important reason is that I want you to know what I'm capable of,' she continued. 'I know how to kill. I know how to commit a murder. I've done it before. I also killed Thomas Quinn, I don't want there to be any doubt about that, and I don't want the wrong person to be convicted of his murder.'

'Well maybe,' responded Vogel. 'But killing a man who has caused you such terrible suffering and repeatedly put you in fear of your life is one thing, killing somebody you don't even know on behalf of a third party is something entirely different.'

'Yes it is, isn't it?' remarked Helen conversationally.

She looked thoughtful and paused yet again.

'The thing is, I've done that before too,' she said.

Vogel could hardly believe his ears. 'What do you mean?' he asked, although surely the meaning had been clear enough.

'I want to tell you something, Chief Inspector Vogel and Sergeant Saslow, something monumentally catastrophic that people who have never been directly involved rarely even consider. I doubt either of you really know about domestic abuse. Not really. I don't think you're married, are you, sergeant? Or not to a man anyway. And I doubt you've ever had a close relationship with a man, have you?'

Saslow shook her head. She couldn't trust herself to speak. She felt her cheeks begin to colour. Saslow liked to keep her private life exactly that. She never talked about her sexuality at work.

'As for you, Mr Vogel, I doubt you're an abusive husband somehow. And attending a few select committee meetings on the subject tells you nothing. Absolutely nothing. I am sure you know the basic facts, two women a week in this country are killed by men. Yet there are government strategy initiatives looking into homelessness and knife crime, and all manner of other crucial issues, but not into domestic violence – despite the fact that almost two million women and 800,000 men suffered domestic abuse during 2019, the last fully recorded year. And those, of course, are only the cases that were reported to the authorities. Data is limited since the pandemic, but we know the situation has become much much worse. During the first lockdown the National Domestic Abuse Helpline reported a sixty-five per cent increase in calls. For me every statistic is a stab to the heart. But there is something else, perhaps the greatest horror of all, for which there are, as far as I am aware, no recorded figures, no substantiated data.

'I am talking about the darkest place there is, which I inhabited all those years ago, and which Gillian Quinn was in and would have stayed in always until and unless released by Thomas' death. Whatever nonsense Gillian told you and her son, she stayed with her monster of a husband for one reason and one reason only. She was afraid to leave him. Thomas told her that if he left her he would kill her. She could not leave him. That is why she stayed with him.

'I killed Kurt for more or less the same reason. I knew that he would never let me go. That I would never be free of him. That wherever I fled he would find me. And yes, I knew that sooner or later he would kill me.

'I killed Thomas Quinn for Gill, because as long as he was alive there could be no escape for her. And don't tell me I should have asked for police help. Please. Only three point two per cent of reported cases of abuse against women currently result in prosecution. And domestic violence convictions have shrunk by twenty-three per cent in the past decade. I always thought things would get better, which is why I started Helen's House, to do my bit to help. With, ironically enough, the relatively small amount of money my lawyer managed to extract from Kurt's estate. But actually things have got worse.

'So in recent years, I have occasionally taken the law into my own hands. Two years ago I killed the husband of Rebecca Jane Conway in Bude, Cornwall, for the same reason. He had some lovely habits. He used to make Becky strip naked and stand in the back yard for hours on end. If she attempted to move, or indeed could simply no longer stand and fell, he would beat her with a cane. She was the woman I told you about who, with a baby and a toddler, walked nearly ten miles get to us. Unfortunately her husband came for her. And she was too afraid ever to try to escape again.

'So I took action. Not for the first time. Over the last seven years, in addition to Thomas Quinn, I have killed three monstrous men. Mark Conway, and two others who came to my notice. Marshall Morgan in Cardiff, who whenever his wife upset him, which was extremely easily done, locked her in a windowless outside shed, often overnight, usually without food and water. And Jerome Finch in Birmingham. He liked to make his wife crawl around the house on her hands and knees scrubbing the floor with a toothbrush, and would kick her in the face if she missed a bit.

'I killed these men because it was the only way to stop them. And because they didn't deserve to live. And I have to tell you, Mr Vogel, I would do it all over again.'

FORTY-TWO

Vogel suspended the interview almost immediately. He asked Helen if she would remain in the interview room and left a uniform in charge of her.

He and Saslow were both stunned. But they had work to do.

He instructed Saslow to check out the cases of the three men Helen Harris claimed to have killed, in addition to Thomas Quinn and her husband Kurt St John.

The DS set to with gusto. It quickly became apparent that there were similarities between the three later murders. In each case the wife had been the prime suspect from the beginning, not least because of the history of abuse which became evident. But all three women seemed to have solid alibis, and no other definitive evidence revealed itself. In each instance the investigating officers had continued to believe that, in spite of the alibis, the wife was guilty, but had been unable to prove it. And in each instance the case had been held on file. Which presumably had been Helen Harris' intention. Assuming she really had committed the crimes in question.

Saslow then studied the MO, the modus operandi, of the three murders, each of which were different, but similar in that they all occurred in the home of the victim when no one else was present in the house. Mark Conway was hit over the head from behind with a heavy object, probably, from the imprint left on his skull, a hammer. Marshall Morgan was stabbed in the heart with a heavy pointed implement which had entered at an angle suggesting that it might have been an ice pick. Jerome Finch's throat had been cut, sliced from ear to ear with a large sharp knife, quite likely a kitchen knife not dissimilar to the one which had been used to kill Thomas Quinn. In each case, no murder weapon was ever found.

But clearly nobody in any of the police forces involved had looked outside their own investigation. The murder of Mark Conway would have been investigated by their own Devon and

Cornwall Police, but had not attracted the attention of the current investigation, and neither she nor Vogel, both new to the D and C, had any previous knowledge of the Conway murder.

Saslow was disappointed that she and Vogel hadn't picked up on it, but unsurprised that a broader view had not been taken on any of these murders. After all, they would all have been regarded as domestics. Albeit of the most serious kind. Nobody would have suspected any sort of serial killer.

Saslow then attempted to establish a specific link between the previous murders and Helen Harris. One such link was already known, and would be simple to check. Mark Conway's wife had sought refuge at Helen's House and had stayed there on at least one occasion.

Saslow called Sadie Pearson and asked her to check the House records on the other two. The DS had already learned that careful records were kept of all who turned to Helen's House for help and were retained for years for future reference. Helen, in particular, liked to keep in touch, whenever she could safely do so, with any victims of domestic violence known to the House.

Sadie did not seem surprised to hear from her, leading Saslow to suspect that the other woman knew a lot more about her partner's alleged activities than she was, at this stage anyway, letting on.

Sadie quickly confirmed that the wives of both Jerome Finch and Marshall Morgan had also sought refuge at the House, but had ultimately been coerced into returning to their abusive husbands.

Everything seemed to back up Helen's story. And what possible motive could she have for lying, particularly in the case of the murders of Conway, Morgan, and Finch? Her account of the killing of her husband, and the way in which she had so meticulously planned it, surely also had to be true. Therefore, Helen had indeed revealed herself to be more than capable of premeditated murder. There was therefore little reason to doubt that she had done the same thing again, and in cold blood killed Thomas Quinn, knowing that she herself could give his abused wife an alibi. Which was something of a double whammy.

Saslow now had few doubts. Helen Harris was a serial killer. Of a very particular kind.

She was a victim turned vigilante.

* * *

Meanwhile Vogel, who still didn't know quite what to make of it all, called both his deputy SIO, Janet Peters, and his immediate superior Detective Superintendent Nobby Clarke, to keep them abreast of the latest extraordinary development.

Then he called Gill Quinn.

'Are you going to tell me that you have dropped the charge against my son and are coming to arrest me?' she asked immediately.

Vogel wasn't sure whether or not she was being serious. So he ignored the remark, instead asking Gill about her and Thomas' early life. Some of the logistics Helen had chronicled, particularly concerning the start of the relationship between Thomas Quinn and the St Johns, didn't seem to quite add up. But Gill was quickly able to confirm that Thomas had spent his summers working in North Devon from his mid-teens and was even willing to elaborate somewhat.

'He had a mate in North Devon whose father ran a golf club and had a stake in a caravan park,' Gill related. 'Thomas always said that was where our future lay. As soon as I got pregnant he insisted that we got married, but he agreed that I should stay living with my parents in Plymouth until I'd finished my teacher training, because he knew how much it meant to me. He was like that in those days. Once I'd qualified he whisked me off to Bideford. I thought it was very romantic at the time. Little did I know . . .'

It all fitted.

Vogel was just finishing the call to Gill when Saslow arrived at his office ready to give a full report of her enquiries.

When she had done so Vogel immediately homed in on a factor that she had not even considered.

'Did you notice how the murder of Thomas Quinn is the odd one out?' he asked.

Saslow admitted that she hadn't.

'Well, the other murders were all quite clinical,' Vogel explained. 'Which suggests to me that they were indeed premeditated. Each involved in effect one blow, albeit with two different sorts of sharp instrument and one blunt instrument, in the case of Conway, Morgan and Finch, and one shot from a gun in the case of Helen's own husband. But Thomas Quinn was killed in a wild frenzy. He was stabbed eleven times.'

'I suppose so, boss,' responded Saslow. 'Maybe Helen was

more personally involved with the Quinn case, though. And maybe she didn't plan it in the same way, but just seized the opportunity on the spur of the moment when Gill turned up at the House yet again. I mean Helen couldn't have known that was going to happen, could she?'

Vogel agreed that she couldn't have done. He remained puzzled. It was time to give Helen Harris a serious grilling.

As soon as the two officers returned to the interview room, Vogel began what he hoped would prove to be an incisive line of questioning.

He pointed out that Helen had claimed, when giving Gill Quinn her alibi, that it would have been impossible for Gill to have left the House without being noticed.

'In which case, how could you have left without being noticed?' he asked.

'Impossible for Gill, not me,' countered Helen. 'Have you heard of a flying freehold, Mr Vogel?'

Vogel, a Londoner, confessed that he had not. Helen explained that these had once been common in Devon, and it was partly because the property which became Helen's House had a flying freehold that she'd been able to afford to buy it. She'd had cash. Such properties were usually unmortgageable.

'We have a basement which runs beneath the house next door, with a door leading out onto an alleyway at the back,' Helen explained. 'Only Sadie and I have access to it. I have found it extremely useful over the years, I can assure you.'

'How much does Sadie know of your activities?'

'Absolutely nothing. Well, not until early this morning, anyway.'

'But she is your partner, Helen,' Vogel persisted.

'Oh how fearfully modern of you, chief inspector, not to mention simplistic,' Helen responded acerbically. 'I am not in a relationship with Sadie. She is my business partner. She only moved into the House following the death of her husband – who was one of the good guys, by the way – thus releasing some funds which she invested in the House, about which she is every bit as passionate as I am. I've therefore already today arranged for Helen's House to be transferred entirely to Sadie, in the hope that she can continue its work regardless of what happens to me. But you are quite wrong to assume that because I had been so badly abused by a man I would automatically change my sexual preference.'

Vogel found he was beginning to blink rapidly, but for once, and to his immense relief, he managed to control it.

'However, I was more or less rendered incapable of having any sort of relationship ever again,' Helen continued rather more softly. 'And therefore denied the opportunity of the family life I had always desired.'

Vogel feared that they were drifting away from what he felt should be the main focus of this interview.

'The frenzied stabbing of Thomas Quinn would have left his murderer covered in blood,' he continued. 'What did you do with your bloodstained clothing, and weren't you afraid of it being noticed when you left the crime scene?'

'I wore a long raincoat, overshoes, and gloves,' Helen replied. 'Just like on the other occasions. As I left the scene I removed them and put them in a bin liner I had brought along for the purpose, along with the knife I used to kill Thomas, which weighed it down nicely when I threw the lot into the river from the new bridge.'

Very neat, thought Vogel.

'Helen, you have multiple sclerosis, very nearly end-stage, you told us. You are not a small woman, but how on earth did you manage to overpower a man like Thomas Quinn? Indeed any of these men.'

'I did not attempt to overpower Thomas, nor indeed any of them. I used the element of surprise. Thomas was totally taken aback by my arrival. He made no attempt to stop me entering his house, and I struck the first blow before he even knew what was happening.'

'Why did you stab him so many times?'

'I lost my temper, chief inspector. I knew that, whatever happened, this would be the last one. I was not going to have the strength to do it again. So I vented all I could of my remaining rage on Thomas.'

Vogel continued to question Helen insistently. He queried the logistics of some of the murders. She said that she drove through the night. He asked how she knew when the wives of Conway,

Morgan and Finch were going to be away from their homes, and able to supply a convenient alibi for themselves.

She explained that she kept in touch with these women, providing help and support from a distance whenever possible, and she made it her business to know when they were taking their children to school or nursery, visiting relatives, or working. At least two of them had part-time jobs.

'Life goes on, Mr Vogel,' she said. 'Even within a framework of senseless abuse. It goes on, cloaked in pain and misery, until the abusers are stopped. And, sometimes, only death will stop them. That is why I have done what I have done.'

Vogel, Saslow and the team continued with extensive enquiries throughout the day and into the night, further exploring each of the murders Helen Harris had confessed to. And they interviewed her several times more.

Vogel also attended a series of meetings with the CPS, and with Nobby Clarke, head of MIT and the chief constable of Devon and Cornwall, both of whom drove over from Exeter.

Helen's story never wavered. She had a quiet certainty about her. Eventually even Vogel had to be convinced that she was telling the truth.

Early on Wednesday morning it was decided to charge her with everything that she had confessed to: the murders of Kurt St John, Marshall Morgan, Jerome Finch, Mark Conway and Thomas Quinn.

Under the circumstances Gregory Quinn was released from custody at once, and all charges against him were dropped.

Vogel had never known anything like it. A press conference was called for later that day. The media went into a feeding frenzy. And who could blame them, thought Vogel.

Helen Harris remained cool and calm throughout. Vogel still thought she was a remarkable woman and maintained a sneaking admiration for her. She was, however, a serial killer. And he was a policeman. So he thought it best not to mention it.

Gregory's Quinn's van was returned to him upon his release. He drove along The Quay past the old bridge, turned off by the Kingsley Statue, and parked on the riverbank.

He wasn't ready to go home yet. He needed to compose himself before he faced his mother.

He found a bench overlooking the Torridge and sat there taking in deep breaths of salty fresh air. The tide was high and the water glistened in the morning sun. Greg thought this might be the most beautiful day he had ever experienced.

He hadn't expected to be free again for a very long time.

He reached into his pocket for the letter Helen Harris had written to him. She had dropped it off to Philip Stubbs the previous morning and asked him to pass it on to Greg. Philip had done so, unopened, even though Greg suspected he shouldn't have.

Greg reread the letter. For the umpteenth time. He almost knew it by heart.

> My dear boy,
>
> You may know by now of the statement I am about to give the police concerning the murder of your father, and several other abusive men. For many reasons, I am quite unafraid of the consequences of this. And I want you to know that it is my sincerest wish that you live a long and happy life as a free man, and that you and your mother are able to move on from the horrors that have been inflicted upon you. Look after her for me, won't you?
>
> With love, Helen.
>
> PS. When you have read this letter you should destroy it.

Greg could hardly believe what had happened. He had been living a nightmare since Saturday afternoon, when he had gone to the family home and found his father alone there, slightly drunk, and very belligerent.

They had rowed, as usual, mostly about the way Thomas treated Gill. Thomas called Greg 'a mother's boy' and mocked him for being so close to Gill. Then, Thomas went further than ever before. Too far. He called Gill a whore, and suggested that Greg was in a sexual relationship with his mother. And he did so in such a foul and disgusting manner that Greg couldn't bear to even think about the language Thomas had used.

It was then that he had taken a knife, from the kitchen knife rack, and stabbed his father over and over again. It had indeed been a frenzied attack. Once he'd started he had not been able to stop. And he would always remember the look of total surprise in Thomas Quinn's eyes.

Very slowly, Greg stood up and walked to the river's edge. He tore the letter into small pieces and threw them into the water.

'Thank you, Helen,' he whispered. 'You will never be forgotten.'